Flirting with Trouble

LOVE IN BLOOM COLLECTION

New York Times Bestselling Author

MELISSA FOSTER

Wells Silver has held a special place in my heart since I first met him in The Steeles at Silver Island series, and I am thrilled to finally give him his happily ever after. I knew he needed a special heroine who would love him for all his charm, wit, and flirtatiousness. When I met Victoria "Victory" Braden, I had no doubt she was his perfect match. I just had to convince them of the same. As a widow, Victory thought she'd found her first and last love in her late husband, and she's definitely not looking for a replacement when Wells walks into her life with scorching chemistry, great banter, and understanding of her big, complicated family. But that's the great thing about love. It finds us when we least expect it. In each other they find everything they never knew they wanted or needed. I hope you enjoy their story and getting to know their families as much as I did.

If you're new to my books, while interconnected, all Love in Bloom stories are written to stand alone, with no cliffhangers or unresolved issues, so dive right in and enjoy the funny, steamy, emotional ride.

Be sure to check out my online bookstore for preorders, early releases, discounted bundles in all formats (ebooks, audiobooks, and print books), and exclusive special editions. Purchasing direct is easy, and if you join my VIP mailing list, you'll also enjoy extra discounts. Ebooks can be sent to the e-reader of your choice, and audiobooks can be listened to on the free and easy-to-use BookFunnel app. Shop my store: shop.melissafoster.com

Sign up for my newsletter so you never miss a release or sale.
www.melissafoster.com/newsletter

SILVER ISLAND
Wildlife Refuge
Rock Harbor
Fisherman's Wharf
Seaport
Seaport Primary
Brighton Park
Rock Bottom Bar & Grill
Trista's
Happy End
Silver Island Airport
Rock Harbor Primary
Lover's Cove
Top of the Island Winery
The Bistro
Silver Monument
Silver Island Community College
Silver House
Majestic Park
Brighton Bluffs
The Sweet Barista
Scoops
Silver Island High
Silver Harbor
Sunset Beach
Silver Haven Primary
Marina
Fortune's Landing
Silver Haven
Fortune's Cove
Chaffee
Bellamy Island
Cuddlefish Cove

Chapter One

Wells

"I know I'm looking for a needle in a haystack, but the right vibe is everything. Rock Bottom is the hottest bar and grill on Silver Island, and I don't want to settle for anything less for my flagship restaurant here," I say to Kent Pyle, the real estate agent who has spent the last few hours showing me properties in New York City.

"I appreciate that. Finding the right location is a process. I think you'll like the properties we have lined up for tomorrow. I'll see you in the morning."

We shake hands, and as Kent heads out to a waiting car, I step onto the busy sidewalk feeling like I'm stepping into a cattle chute. The hustle and bustle of the Big Apple, with its bright lights and skyscrapers, is a far cry from the quaint island towns where I grew up off the coast of Cape Cod. Tourist season on Silver Island is chaotic, but it's nothing like this, and the heat here is oppressive. If I were back home, I'd be heading to the beach right now with my surfboard to catch some waves. In lieu of that, I'll take a cold drink, a few laughs, and maybe a willing woman to take the edge off.

It's been too long since I scratched that particular itch.

My cell rings, and my older brother Fitz's name flashes on the screen. I can barely hear myself think past the traffic noise and the din of the fast-moving crowd as I put the phone to my ear. "Hey, Fitz. What's up?"

"How'd it go? See anything promising?"

"No. They were all run-of-the-mill."

"What did you expect? It's the Big Apple. The goal is to squeeze as many people as possible into cracker-box-size rooms and charge astronomical prices."

No shit. I want the challenge of making a restaurant stand out among hundreds of others, and money is not a problem. Our ancestors discovered Silver Island, and our family owns the largest resort there, the Silver House, which Fitz runs with our parents. We have family money. Boatloads of it. But while Fitz followed in our parents' footsteps, my three other siblings and I have blazed our own paths and have barely touched our trust funds to do so.

"You've got to pay to play, and if I can make it here, I can make it anywhere," I say, stepping around a couple as I cross the street.

"If anyone can do it, you can. Fair warning, Mom met with Charmaine this afternoon."

Charmaine Luxe is a real estate agent on the island. As much as my mother supports all of us following our dreams, I know she'd rather I open another restaurant on the island. I think she's afraid I'll move away for good, though I haven't made that decision yet. I love my family and my life on the island, but lately I can't shake the feeling that there's something more out there for me. My restaurant is doing phenomenally well, and I hired an excellent manager who has spent the last year proving to be efficient and capable. With Meghan Young at the helm, I finally feel comfortable spending more time off-site and expanding my business.

"Thanks for the warning. You should come out here with me sometime. I think you'd like the city." Fitz rarely leaves the island. None of us do. That's part of my problem. I'm not just feeling stifled professionally. I'm also feeling it personally. I'm not into long-term relationships, but the island is close-knit, and gossip spreads faster than weeds. Hooking up with tourists isn't as thrilling as it was when I was in my twenties, and I'm well past wanting to be the talk of the town.

"No thanks," Fitz says. "City life isn't for me. Where're you heading now?"

"Hopefully into a bar. Maybe I'll find a hot city girl who wants to have a good time."

Fitz laughs. "Good luck with that."

"I don't need luck." I slow my pace to glance through the window of a bar and stop in my tracks, my attention locking on Victoria—*Victory*—Braden, the wild-haired brunette beauty I met over the holidays on the island, when my friend Sutton Steele got engaged to Victory's brother Flynn.

"Hey!" a guy complains as he bumps into my shoulder.

"Sorry." I step aside, my gaze still trained on Victory, who is sitting at the bar staring into her drink.

"What'd you do, Wells?" Fitz asks with amusement.

I all but forgot I was on the phone. "I just found exactly what I'm looking for."

"A place for the restaurant?"

"No. Victory Braden sitting alone at a bar, like a gift waiting to be opened."

"Dude, she's blown you off every time you've hit on her,

and don't you have a meeting with her brother Seth tomorrow?"

Seth Braden lives in the city and owns a major retail conglomerate as well as several restaurants and nightclubs. We got to talking at Sutton and Flynn's wedding, and when I told him I was looking to open a restaurant here, he said he'd be happy to let me pick his brain about the differences between operating a business in a small town versus a big city.

"Yes, I do, but *that* is business, and *she* is pleasure. I'll catch up with you when I get back." I pocket my phone and head into the bar.

Met with the pulse of music and the din of the happy-hour crowd, I make a beeline to Victory, remembering the way the air had sizzled between us when I saw her a few weeks ago at Sutton and Flynn's wedding. She pretended the attraction was one-sided, but the lust in her eyes betrayed her words. I haven't been able to stop thinking about her since. She's a rarity, as elegant as she is brilliant, and as the president of Blank Space Entertainment, she has a reputation for being a ruthless businesswoman. The kind that mesmerizes you with her striking blue eyes and radiant smile as she cuts you to pieces.

I fucking love that.

"This must be my lucky day," I say as I sit on the stool beside her.

She turns with a serious expression, but those plump lips I've thought about far too many times curve into a taunting grin. Her hair is styled sleeker than it was on the island, bringing out streaks of gold in the tamer waves. "Wells. What brings you into the city? Have you worked your way through all the island girls? Meeting your latest *swipe* date?"

Damn, I love her snark. "I don't play the swipe game."

"No?" She arches a perfectly manicured brow. "Did they

add a one-click bulk-match option on those dating apps?"

I laugh. "Can I buy you a drink, or"—I drag my gaze down her body, admiring the way her sleeveless designer dress hugs her curves, exposing just enough thigh to whet my appetite; she is stunning—"are you waiting on a date?"

"My dates just left, so I'll happily take another whiskey, thank you."

Whiskey? That's hot. I flag down the bartender. "*Dates?* As in more than one?" A slow grin tugs at my lips as *that* imagery takes hold. "No wonder they call you Victory."

She gives me the look she gave me on the island. The one that says she's enjoying our banter but trying to act annoyed. "In your fantasies, maybe."

"Maybe my ass. That image has already taken root and moved to the top of my fantasy list. Like I said, it's my lucky day." That earns a soft laugh and a shake of her head as the bartender arrives to take our order.

Victory taps her fingernail against her glass, watching me talk with the bartender as he fills our orders. There's no missing the spark of interest in her eyes. For me, *not* the bartender.

When the bartender walks away, Victory cocks her head and says, "Why are you *really* in the city?"

I can't resist fucking with her. "I felt your energy calling me across the ocean, so I caught the first ferry out. I booked a hotel room around the corner, and here I am. At your service."

She deadpans.

"What can I say? A woman like you leaves an indelible mark."

"Because I turned you down for a night of hot sex at my brother's wedding?"

"Yes. It was a first, and it stung." I put my hand over my

heart. "Like it or not, we're now connected forever."

She smiles. "Wells Silver, you are too much."

"I hear that a lot. Is *that* why you turned me down?" I lean in, palming her hip as I swivel her stool so she's facing me, and lower my voice seductively. "Don't be nervous, gorgeous. We can take it slow. *Ease* into it until we find our rhythm." Her eyes flame, spurring me on. "I guarantee I'll hit the spot so many times, you'll forget your own name."

Our gazes hold, her eyes darkening. I'm tempted to lean in and show her what she's missing.

She smirks. "Why do guys overestimate their skills in the bedroom? Is it a size thing? Are you lacking in that department?"

I scoff. "Hardly. You must be dating the wrong guys."

Her smirk falters, and she sits back, sipping her whiskey. "It's okay if you don't want to tell me why you're really in the city."

I have a feeling I hit a nerve, but I let it go for now. "I don't mind telling you. I'm here looking for property to open another restaurant."

Her eyes light up. "You own a restaurant?"

"Are you messing with me, or did I really pass right under your radar?" Shit. Is it possible I'm reading her wrong? I can't be that far off my game.

"Not *under* it. I mean, I'd have to be blind not to notice your movie-star good looks." She motions toward my face. "With that thick dark hair, sexy scruff, and chiseled jaw, you look like you could be one of the actors we rep."

I grin. "I knew you were into me."

"Don't get ahead of yourself, Mr. Silver. I might've found you attractive when we met, but then you opened your mouth and rang the player bell, and nothing else computed."

Why do I find her challenges so sexy? "Damn. I don't usually have to say shit like this, but I'm kind of a big deal on the island."

A playful glint shimmers in her eyes. "Because you were born with a Silver spoon in your mouth?"

"No." I've worked hard to shake that assumption. "Because I'm a great guy, and it doesn't hurt that I own Rock Bottom Bar and Grill."

"That *is* impressive, and I liked that place. It was the *in* spot." She takes another drink.

"Now we're getting somewhere. What did you like?" I nudge her with my knee. "The owner?"

"The *food*."

"Well, that's something. To the food." I lift my glass, and she joins me in a toast. "A'right, beautiful, you got the truth out of me. Now it's my turn. Your friends left after you had dinner, and you stuck around hoping I'd come by, right?"

Her eyes dance with amusement. "More like, to drown my sorrows."

"Your sorrows? Those words should never come out of your gorgeous mouth. Did you lose a big business deal?"

"Ha! You clearly don't know me. I *never* lose business deals, big or small." She runs her finger around the rim of her glass, her expression turning contemplative. Those pretty eyes flick to mine. "Today is the anniversary of the day I met my late husband, Harvey."

My chest constricts. "Oh, shit. Sorry, Vic." I knew she was a widow and had lost her husband a while back. "That's got to be rough."

"It is what it is."

I lift my glass. "To Harvey. He must've been a hell of a guy to have won your heart."

"He was." She taps her glass to mine, smiling again. "To Harvey."

We drink, and then I ask, "Do you want to talk about him?"

"Thanks, but *no*," she says emphatically. "He's been gone for several years, and I've had enough alcohol that I'm not overthinking it. I'd like to keep it that way."

"Okay, Harvey is off the table." I sweep my arm between us like I'm pushing Harvey away and go for a smile, waggling my brows. "How about me? Am I on the table?"

An almost-silent laugh tumbles out, and she takes another drink. "You do make me laugh."

"That means I have a shot. Who's my competition? The friends you had dinner with?"

"No, but you have dated one of them," she taunts.

"At least I know they're female."

"I had dinner with Leni and Shea. They plied me with alcohol and upbeat conversation, as good friends should."

Leni was Sutton's sister. She worked for their cousin Shea Steele at her PR firm. Shea didn't grow up on the island with us, but Leni and I dated in high school, and it didn't end well. We remained friends, despite Leni carrying a chip on her shoulder toward me, which I fully deserved. We finally talked about what had happened a year and a half ago and smoothed things over, but I'm curious about what she's told Victory.

"Leni, huh? Did she sing my praises?"

"I wouldn't go that far, but she thinks you're a good guy. Even if you're a shameless flirt who will probably never settle down."

Thank you, Leni. "She knows me well and she loves me. You will, too, one day." I lift my chin. "You can't resist this face forever."

"It's a wonder I've lasted this long."

"It is a little shocking, but hey, it's the thrill of the chase, right?"

"The chase," she says longingly, and gazes absently over my shoulder as if she's watching a scene play out. She picks up her glass and swirls it, watching the alcohol slosh over the ice. "I was the one who chased Harvey."

"He's a lucky man. I like a woman who goes after what she wants. To the thrill of the chase."

We toast, and then her attention returns to her glass as she sets it on the bar and wraps both hands around it, her fingers tapping to the beat of the music. "I haven't been chased in so long, I can't even remember what it feels like," she confesses.

"Come on. You're joking, right? A smart, attractive woman like you must have guys lining up to take you out. You can level with me," I say coaxingly. "Are you swiping the right way on the apps? Do you need a tutorial?"

She winces, and when her eyes find mine, they're daring and slightly cautious. That hint of vulnerability in this fierce lioness is the sexiest thing I've ever seen. "Actually, I haven't gone there yet."

"I don't blame you. Dating apps have their purpose, but they pretty much suck. You probably don't need those apps anyway. You must meet plenty of guys in your line of work."

"I do. I meant I haven't dated since I lost Harvey."

My thoughts stumble. "At all?"

"Other than my standing solo date at our favorite restaurant every Friday night?" She shakes her head. "I married the love of my life. I'm not looking for a replacement."

"Who said anything about getting married? We're talking about dating, going out, and having fun with a guy. You said it's been several years. Did you mean like *two*?"

"No." She leans forward and whispers, "It's been five."

"Five *years*?"

"Don't say it like that." She smacks my chest, laughing.

I catch her wrist, noticing a small pink butterfly just below her palm. "Sorry, but this is a tragedy. Don't you miss human touch?" I place her hand on my cheek and slowly move it along my jaw and across my chin. When her fingertips graze my lips, she breathes harder. "Touching a man?" I run her fingers down my neck and over my pecs. "Feeling a strong body against yours?" I press a kiss to the back of her hand. "Warm lips on your skin?" Lust shimmers in her eyes. I lean in and brush my scruff along her cheek, speaking low, into her ear. "The scratch of a man's scruff on your thighs?"

As I sit back, she drags her teeth over her bottom lip, but as if she's caught herself tempted by me, she tugs her hand free and reaches for her glass. "I need more alcohol for this conversation." Downing her drink, she waves the bartender over.

So fucking sexy.

An hour later, we're swapping funny stories about dating and being hit on, and she's still trying to explain why she hasn't dated. "From what I've seen, dating is overly complicated now. What happened to getting to know each other over a game of Scrabble and some sushi? Or a movie and pizza? My life is busy and complicated enough. Just thinking about dating is a lot. Maybe it's different for men. Have you watched any of those *Dateline* shows? You can't even invite someone you've just met over to your place because they might be a serial killer."

"That's what you're worried about? Then you might want to keep this zipped so nobody swipes your wallet and figures out where you live." I reach over and zip the small purse that's dangling from thin straps draped across her body.

"I thought it was zipped. Thanks. But I'm serious, and it's not just serial killers. I can't imagine trying to find someone who's not intimidated by my success or into me *because* of it. I bet there are plenty of gold diggers out there who want *your* silver spoon in their mouth."

I smirk. "You said it, not me."

Her eyes widen as understanding dawns on her, and she laughs. Her laughter is contagious, and that smile is fucking with my head the way it did at the wedding and at my family's annual holiday dance at the resort after Sutton and Flynn got engaged.

Victory is so unguarded tonight, I wonder if it's because we're not surrounded by her family. I feel like I'm seeing a side of her she rarely unveils. Or maybe she reveals it often and just hadn't around me. All I know is, it's intoxicating, and I want to see more of it.

"I guess that's one way to get to your fortune," she says, and picks up her glass. "To gold diggers." We toast. "All right, Silver, give me your best gold-digger story."

"My *best*? I don't usually spend enough time with women for them to get their claws into me, but there was one who my brothers and sisters will never let me forget. She was a tourist on the island for the weekend, and she was older than me."

"How much older?"

"Seriously?"

"Yes, I need a visual. How old? What color hair?" She motions with her fingers for me to give her more.

"She was blond, curvy, and probably eight or ten years older than me. I don't know. I was twenty-three and had just taken over the restaurant. I thought I was hot shit."

"Wait, wait, wait." She waves her hand. "You *thought* you were hot shit? Are you telling me there was a time when the great Wells Silver was not arrogantly confident?"

She's a fucking trip. "Hell no. I was trying to be humble."

"Nice try, but that's *not* your strong suit." Her eyes glitter with the tease. "Okay, go on. You're a hot-shit twenty-three-year-old restaurateur, and in comes this gorgeous woman, one of a long line of them, I assume, who wanted to sleep with you."

"You're good. That's accurate," I say arrogantly. "Her name was Kelly, and we hooked up once."

"Did you enjoy it?" she asks.

"What kind of question is that? Who doesn't like sex?"

She rolls her eyes. "Have you honestly never had bad sex?"

"I'm driving the train, so *no*, I haven't."

"You're so arrogant. You've never been with a woman who just lay there?"

It's time to show her who she's dealing with. I thread my fingers into the ends of her long hair, tugging her closer. "I'm going to let you in on a little secret, sugarplum. I could make a dead woman squirm."

She laughs, like I've made the funniest joke ever.

"Don't laugh."

"That wasn't a very humble thing to say."

"I was just being honest."

"Okay, *magic dick*," she says sarcastically.

"Maybe you've forgotten that there are many other ways to pleasure a woman besides fucking her."

"Yes, I'm aware," she says a little sharply.

"Are you?" I tug her closer. So close I can smell the whiskey on her breath. "I could make you beg for my cock using nothing more than a single finger."

Her mouth opens like she's going to say something, but she doesn't say a word, and her brow furrows. "No way."

"*One* finger." I let that sink in. "Or the tip of my tongue." I slide my tongue over my bottom lip, and her gaze tracks it. "My teeth are lethal, and don't get me started on my—"

She puts her hand on my chest, her cheeks flushing as she pushes back, but only a few inches. "You're an excellent storyteller. That's more action than I've gotten in years." She fans her face. "How about we go back to the tourist story?"

I was so caught up in her, I forgot I was in the middle of telling a story. I clear my throat, trying to shake the lust from my brain.

There's no chance of that happening.

"Right. The tourist," I say, forcing my brain into submission. "We hooked up, and the next day she told everyone who would listen that she was my girlfriend. I found her in the kitchen of my restaurant giving orders to the chef."

Victory leans forward again. "No way."

"It's true. My brothers call her Kitchen Kelly. Some women are off their rockers."

"Guys are no better," she insists.

"Guys can be assholes, but are you saying guys have done worse to you than what she did? Because that was pretty bold."

"You be the judge," she says casually. "You know my company is fairly large."

"How large? I need a visual," I tease, earning another smile.

"Between the New York, LA, and London offices, we've got about sixteen hundred employees."

"Now, *that's* impressive." We've been having so much fun, I lost track of the fact that she runs an entertainment empire. No wonder she wasn't wowed by my owning a single restaurant. "So what happened? Did an employee try to climb you instead of the corporate ladder?"

"It wasn't an employee. I'm too busy running the company to meet all the talent we sign, but I try to support them when I can. We'd just taken on a new fighter, and I went with the agent who signed him to see one of his big fights. After the fight was over, the agent stepped out to take a call, and I went to introduce myself to her client." She tucks her hair behind her ear. "He was schmoozing the crowd, and when he saw me, his whole face changed."

"How? Like, damn, you're hot? Or like, oh shit, there's the boss?"

"Like a lion on the prowl who had just found his prey."

"Seriously? Not that I blame him, but that's ballsy."

"It gets better. He swaggers over to me and says, 'Hey, baby. I noticed you when I was in the ring. You looked good holding up those numbers.' I was like…*numbers?* And then it dawned on me that he thought I was a ring girl!"

I bark out a laugh. "The perils of being beautiful. I bet you look great in booty shorts."

"I *do*, thank you very much. I work hard for this ass."

"And I appreciate that hard work." We finish our drinks, and I push to my feet. "Come on. Let's give that ass a workout."

"*Wells.*" The surprise in her eyes wars with the desire brimming in them.

I take her hand, pulling her up to her feet in front of me. "It's no secret I want to get my hands on you, but I meant, let's hit the dance floor." I slide my arm around her waist. "I'm not an animal. I've got better lines than that to get you into my bed."

Victory

Yes, you do, and I'm enjoying them far too much.

Wells keeps me close as we weave through the crowd. He's striking in a short-sleeve fitted gray shirt and jeans, and I don't miss the women checking him out. Little do they know it's his wicked sense of humor, dirty mouth, and unnerving confidence that make him dangerously seductive. I've been hit on many times, and a few men have crossed the line and needed to be set straight. But never have I encouraged it or wanted to take it further.

Until now.

Something about Wells and his delivery makes it feel less skeevy, which makes no sense, given that he's a self-confessed player. He's also several years younger than me, and some of his lines border on cheesy, all of which should have me rolling my eyes and coming up with an excuse to leave, but I'm having fun. I can't remember the last time I've been turned on by nothing more than words, and *God* is Wells good with words. His slick-tongue promises are still taunting me. I've missed the edgy high of anticipation that's been humming through me for most of the evening.

He claims a spot on the dance floor and sets those piercing dark eyes on me as we move to the beat. I love to dance, but it's been a long time since I've danced with a man. Harvey was a good slow dancer, and I loved being in his arms, but he wasn't great at dancing to a faster beat. Wells moves like the music is part of him, and it's as powerful and seductive as his penetrating gaze as we fall into sync on the crowded dance floor.

All around us, people are lost in each other, bumping and grinding, giving the night a dark, erotic feel. I miss that, too, and I chase the feeling—the escape—as we dance to one song after another, bodies brushing, hips swaying, and eyes taunting. As Zendaya's "Repeat" blares through the speakers, Wells's hot hands skim down my waist, his eyes drilling into me like he wants to play *me* on repeat.

His attention is addicting. I give myself over to the beat and to the desire mounting inside me, dancing more provocatively. He flashes a devilish grin, matching my moves, his hands roaming over my hips and up my sides, bringing a rush of desire. As Gracie Abrams sings about burning for him and wanting to be closer, every graze of our bodies makes me want that, too.

I can't stop thinking about how good it felt to touch his face, neck, and chest. My fingers itch to do it again. I throw caution to the wind, letting them travel over the hard planes of his pecs and down his abs, dancing like I did with men in my early twenties, loving the way his eyes flame and his muscles flex beneath my fingers.

His eyes flicker with a wickedness that tells me he's a man who knows how to fulfill his dirty claims. He draws me against him, pressing one hand on my lower back. I feel every hard inch of him and oh, how I've missed *this*, too. He dips his face beside mine, speaking low and gruff. "Like what you feel?" He nips at my neck, and my entire body prickles with desire.

Yes is on the tip of my tongue, but I keep it to myself.

"Maybe."

"It's okay to admit you like it," he coaxes. "I like your hands on me." He holds me tighter. "I bet I'd fucking love your mouth on me."

Not as much as I'd enjoy yours on me.

The thought is so brazen, it should slow me down, but it has the opposite effect, emboldening me.

"You're an incredibly sexy woman, and you deserve to have some fun."

I haven't felt sexy in forever, but in his arms, with his body moving tantalizingly against me, I not only feel sexy, but I'm greedy for more. He brushes his scruff along my cheek, and my body floods with desire.

"A beautiful woman like you should never go years without being pleasured." He slicks his tongue along the shell of my ear, sending shivers of heat down my neck and chest. "You deserve to be touched and teased."

I cling to him, craving his affirmations, as he slides his hand lower, palming my ass, and he nips at my earlobe. I gasp a sharp inhalation at the shock of pain and pleasure it causes.

"You deserve to be cherished," he says huskily, and sucks my earlobe into his mouth, grinding his hips slower, more purposefully, setting off fireworks beneath my skin. "You should be kissed and licked and thoroughly *fucked.*"

The breath rushes from my lungs.

He pushes one hand beneath my hair, grasping the nape of my neck and angling my face up. The look in his eyes is primal, mirroring the visceral need inside me. I'm used to being in control, but I'm so lost in the heat between us, I have to fight to regain a shred of it.

"And you're just the man to do it?" I challenge.

"We both know I am." His thumb strokes the edge of my jaw. "Tell me you don't want me to kiss you."

My body is on fire, anticipation clawing at me. For the first time in years, I shut off my brain and lead with lust. "Why would I lie?"

A feral look flashes in his eyes, and his mouth descends mercilessly over mine in a kiss so passionate and all-consuming, my head spins. His tongue sweeps and delves, possessing and caressing in a mesmerizing rhythm, stoking a long-buried passion I almost forgot existed. I push up on my toes, taking more, and he growls, "*Fuck*," against my lips. My body screams, *Yes please*, as he reclaims my mouth, intensifying his efforts to a mind-numbing level. He kisses me deeper, more sensually, giving and taking in waves of lethal seduction and electrifying roughness, igniting me like an inferno. My sex throbs. My chest burns. How could I have forgotten what it was like to be kissed like I was the very air someone needed to breathe? How the right kiss could steal my breath and fill me with want and need so hot and sharp, it's inescapable?

Every swipe of our tongues, every press of our bodies, sends desperation pulsing through me. When our lips part, our eyes reconnect like a brewing storm, and "Want to get out of here?" tumbles out.

"More than you know."

Chapter Two

Victory

The warm summer air sobers me up just enough to make me epically nervous as we walk into Wells's hotel suite. He reaches for my purse and must see something in my eyes, because the smile that appears is softer and more compassionate than the wicked one he sported when we left the bar.

"Having second thoughts?" he asks gently.

"No. It's just been a long time since I've gotten naked with a stranger, and I ended up marrying the last one."

"Well, we're in no danger of wedding bells, sweet thing." He takes my purse and places it on the table. "We're just two people enjoying each other for a night."

Being on the same page helps ease my nerves a little. "This stays between us, right? I don't want you telling anyone who will listen that I'm your girlfriend and find you in my office tomorrow giving orders to my assistant."

"I assure you that will not happen. Come here, sexy." Taking my hand, he draws me closer. "Let me remind you why you want to be here."

His warm hands frame my face, and he brushes his lips

lightly over mine, whispering, "You deserve to feel good." He kisses me soft and sweet, so different from our smoldering kisses in the bar, and it's doing the trick, easing my nerves. "There's no pressure." He lowers his lips to mine in a slow, sensual kiss that goes on so long, I feel like I'm floating.

The man could give a master class in seduction. When he says, "We can stop at any time," I don't hesitate to say *"Don't stop,"* and pull his mouth back to mine. He takes that green light and runs with it, pushing a hand into my hair, his other arm circling my waist, holding me tight as he deepens the kiss. He gives and takes, then takes even more. Desire courses through me, so thick and hot, there's no room for nerves. I grasp at his shoulders, kissing him harder, but his fingers tighten in my hair, and he reclaims control, refusing to give in to my demand.

He holds me exactly where he wants me, keeping me from taking more as he continues his expert seduction. I was twenty-six to Harvey's forty-two when we met, and I was drawn to everything about him, from the way he commanded boardrooms to the kindness and attention he gave to his employees and clients, and the way he adored me. He took charge in the bedroom but in a gentler way. Wells is dirtier, and I *like* it. He taunts me with tantalizing kisses that go from sweet and sensual to rough and unforgiving and back again in an endless cycle that has me straining against his grip, moaning, grinding, whimpering for more.

He grins arrogantly into our kisses, but he doesn't break our connection. He *intensifies* it with a blistering kiss as he unzips the back of my dress. My nerves try to rise to the surface, but I want him—I want *this*—too much. I reach between us, unbuttoning his shirt, trembling a little from sheer desire. He takes over, those dark eyes holding me captive as he strips off his shirt and drops it to the floor.

My breath catches at the sight of his beautifully sculpted tan body and the slight dusting of chest hair, so different from Harvey's thick salt-and-peppered barrel chest. That should probably give me pause, but it only further arouses me. I'm excited for this new adventure. "You were right. It's been *way* too long since I've touched a man." I reach for the button on his slacks.

He catches my hand and moves it to his chest. "You've given me the honor of reminding you that you're a beautiful, sexual woman and not just the queen of an empire. I don't take that honor lightly, and I won't rush through it."

He kisses my neck as he slides my dress off my shoulders. It falls to my feet, leaving me in my lace bra, matching thong, and heels. My nerves prickle, but they don't stand a chance against the needy ache inside me. His gaze rakes devouringly down my body, causing a rush of butterflies, goose bumps, *and* flames.

"You are stunning." He presses a kiss to my shoulder, murmuring, "I cannot wait to get my mouth on you."

A shiver of anticipation races down my spine.

His fingers trail lightly over my nipples. "These beautiful tits need some attention." He lowers his mouth to mine in a soul-searing kiss that reaches deep inside me, drawing out a moan. Leaving me breathless, he steps behind me and caresses my ass. "This gorgeous ass needs attention, too." His touch turns to rough, greedy gropes, and my entire body pleads for more as he dips his face beside mine and says, "I can't wait to see you on all fours, taking my cock from behind."

It's been so long, "*Yes,*" slips out before I can stop it.

"There she is, that beautiful, sensual being you've kept

chained down. You want to feel my cock driving into you, don't you, sweet thing?" he asks arrogantly, and that makes me even hotter. "You want to come on my cock?"

I don't even try to hold back. "God yes." I'm here for sex, and I'm going to take everything he's willing to give.

"I bet your thong is drenched for me, isn't it?" He gathers my hair over one shoulder and gives it a tug, gritting out, "*Isn't it?*"

"Yes—" He's going to take me to the edge before he even touches me.

"That's my girl," he says as he takes off my bra.

It's such an intimate endearment, it gives me pause, but before I can overthink it, he grabs my hair again, tugging my head to the side, sending scintillating stings like hot needles down my body, and practically growls in my ear, "I like you wet and needy." He seals his mouth over my neck, kissing, licking, and sucking, driving me out of my freaking mind.

"*Wells*," I plead.

"That's it, baby. Let me hear you beg." He palms my breasts and rolls my nipples between his fingers and thumb, sending shocks of pleasure burning through me.

"*God*," I pant out, and try to turn around, but he holds me in place.

"You're a powerful woman, used to being in control." He kisses my neck. "Tonight, you relinquish that control to me." He nips at that tender skin, and I gasp in surprise. "Do you want that, sweet thing?"

"You're going to make me crazy."

His laugh is low and sinful. "I'm going to make you come so many times, you won't have the energy for crazy."

"You'd better be able to fulfill that promise, boy toy."

He gropes one breast and grabs my jaw with his other hand, turning my face to the side. His eyes bore into me. "Boy toy, huh?" His tone is amused, but he takes me in a brutal kiss that electrifies me and squeezes my nipple, sending a bolt of lightning between my legs. I cry out into the kiss, and my hips buck forward. He does it again, and the pleasure is so intense, my knees buckle. He holds me up and growls against my lips, "Is that the way a *boy* kisses, sugarplum?"

I'm so racked with pleasure, it's all I can do to breathe.

"That's what I thought." He releases my jaw, and his hand slides down my stomach, stopping just above my thong.

"*Touch* me," I demand, shocking myself and clearly amusing Wells.

"I'm not sure if I want to just yet." He drags his fingers along the edge of my thong. "Maybe I should make you beg a little more."

He has me wound so tight, I'm ready to snap. "Don't you *dare*."

"I like the idea of you on your knees for me."

Another moan slips out. *Holy crap.* What is he doing to me?

"You like that, too, don't you?" His hand flattens on my stomach, holding my back flush against his bare chest. His skin is hot and enticing. "What a sight you'll be," he says gruffly. "Naked and on your knees, your pussy dripping for my cock."

I close my eyes, breathing harder.

"My hands tangled in your hair. Those sexy blue eyes trained on me as I fuck your mouth."

"*Wells*" rushes out, as drenched with need as I am.

"*Fuck*, sweet thing. I love hearing you say my name like that." He pushes his hand into my thong, and I gasp as his finger slides over my clit and through my wetness. "*Mm.* I bet you taste sweeter than honey." He withdraws his hand. "Give me your mouth."

Like metal to magnet, I turn my head, ready and willing to do anything he wants.

"Good girl." He paints my lips with my arousal and drags his tongue over them. "So fucking sweet." He crushes his mouth to mine and pushes his hand back into my thong, zeroing in on my clit with lethal precision, and only *one* finger.

Holy hell. He wasn't kidding.

I can barely think as he tangles his free hand in my hair, holding *tight*, sending an erotic mix of pain and pleasure whirling and billowing inside me. It spreads through my chest and down my limbs to the very tips of my fingers and toes. His kisses are fierce and possessive. I hold on to his arms to keep my knees from buckling again as he takes me higher, working me into a writhing frenzy of need and want. Sinful noises spill from my lungs, earning a growl that arouses me even more. My entire body pulses with the need to come. He must feel it, too, because his finger works faster, and he says, "Time to come, gorgeous one."

He yanks my head back and sinks his teeth into my neck, sending a hailstorm of sensation raining down on me. "*Wells—*" flies from my lips, and the world spins away.

"That's it. Say my name," he grits out as pleasure ravages me. "You're so fucking sexy."

I try to catch my breath, but he pushes his fingers inside me and uses his thumb on those oversensitive nerves, catapulting me right back up to the peak of another mind-blowing orgasm that goes on and on. When I finally start coming down from the high, foggy-brained and breathless, I wobble on my heels. I forgot I still had them on.

Wells steadies me. "I've got you." He turns me in his arms, and I blink several times, trying to bring his handsome face into focus. "There you are," he says, low and seductive, as if he's been looking for me his whole life.

"If you can do that with one finger," I say breathily, "I can't wait to see what you can do with the rest of yourself."

"By the time I'm done with you, you won't be able to look at another man without comparing them to me."

He lifts me into his arms, and I laugh in surprise as he carries me into the bedroom. I have *never* been carried into a bedroom. Not even on my wedding night. I might think he's trying to be romantic, if not for the facts. Neither of us has any interest in romance, and he is the king of seduction, with skills I'm sure he's honed on too many women to count.

"A magic finger, a wicked mouth, and you're chivalrous, too?" I tease. "What other superpowers do you possess?"

He lowers me to sit on the edge of the bed and kneels in front of me. As he takes off my heels, he says, "You're about to find out just how wicked my mouth can be."

My body clenches in anticipation as he hooks his fingers into the sides of my thong, but now that I have my wits about me, I feel more like myself and put my hands over his, stopping him. "They don't come off unless you're getting naked, too."

"You want to see the goods, huh?"

"I've got to make sure all of this isn't going to end in disappointment." I have no doubt about the heat he's packing, but this is *my* night. My coming-out party. As much as I've enjoyed relinquishing control, I'm not about to give it all up in the bedroom.

He cocks a grin and plants his hands on the mattress on either side of me, leaning in so close, I have to lean back. "If this ends with disappointment, it'll only be because you'll wish you hadn't limited us to one night together."

"We both know that's not going to happen," I say as he pushes upright.

His eyes never leave mine as he toes off his shoes. He takes his wallet out of his back pocket, tosses it on the nightstand, and strips down to his boxer briefs. My gaze slides south to the thick outline of his formidable cock as he steps toward me.

"Excuse me, but those need to come off." I motion to his boxer briefs.

His eyes narrow, and he leans over me again. This time he brushes his lips over mine, and his tongue follows. Reveling in the heat thrumming between us, I close my eyes as our mouths touch, but he doesn't kiss me. The bastard hovers there, his lips barely grazing mine, teasing me with his wicked tongue. Dipping it deep to explore, withdrawing, then sliding it over mine and dipping in again, making me want more so badly, I lean up to claim his mouth. But he lifts just out of reach, and his hands move over mine, pinning them to the mattress. I open my eyes and find him watching me with a mix of amusement and passion.

"My underwear stays on until you come on my mouth. Got it, sweet thing?"

I narrow my eyes. "If I say no?"

"You won't. You want my mouth on you." He leans forward, taking me down on my back and drawing my arms over my head, holding them there. "You want to come more than you want control, and you know I can deliver." His big body presses down on me, and he gently grinds his rigid cock between my legs. The exquisite friction makes it hard to think. He angles his hips, hitting the place I need it most so perfectly,

"*Ah*" falls from my lips.

A slow grin stretches across his face. "What'll it be, sugarplum? My mouth making you lose your mind, or are we done for the night?"

I pant out, "I'm not your sugarplum."

"You are tonight."

He grinds harder, and damn it, heat spreads through me like wildfire. "*Fine*. Your mouth. Just hurry up."

"We've already established that hurrying is not on tonight's agenda."

He takes his sweet time, kissing and tasting his way down my neck and across my breastbone. He kisses the swell of my breast, all the way up to one throbbing nipple, and lingers there, teasing the taut peak with the tip of his tongue. "I told you these gorgeous tits need attention." He lowers his mouth over my nipple and sucks, alighting sparks beneath my skin.

I bow off the mattress, making greedy noises as he lavishes my breasts with attention, using his teeth, tongue, and hands until I'm dizzy with desire, writhing beneath him.

"I'm going to taste every inch of you, so every time you see me, you'll think of my mouth pleasuring you."

"Keep dreaming, boy toy." I close my eyes, telling myself he's wrong as he moves down my body, making me shudder and moan. But his mouth is hot, his tongue and teeth tantalizing, and those strong hands are everywhere at once, groping, skimming, tweaking, *claiming*, and I know I'll hear his deep voice taunting me in my sleep.

He hooks his fingers in my thong and strips it off. His mouth trails below my belly button to the apex of my thighs, and he presses a kiss there. "Look at this drenched pussy, aching for me." He slicks his tongue along it, and I moan at the pleasure slicing through me. "Lean up on your elbows, sexy girl. I want those beautiful eyes on me when I make you come."

Boy did I pick the right man for this.

"You're so needy," I tease, pushing up as he asked.

"Fuck yeah, I am." That wicked grin is back, and the predatory look in his eyes as he guides my legs over his shoulders sends my heart into a wild flurry. "I've wanted to taste you and feel your pussy wrapped around my cock as you scream my name since the moment I met you."

"You're a player. You probably want that with every woman you meet."

"Not *every* woman," he says all too charmingly.

His eyes never leave mine as he teases my most sensitive nerves with his tongue. My hips jolt off the mattress, and a gloating grin appears. He puts a hand just above my pubic bone, holding me down, massaging me there as he teases and taunts me with his mouth. He fucks me with his tongue, licking and lapping and driving me out of my mind. "You taste too fucking good. I could eat you all night."

Thrills rush through me as he devours, savors, and teases, making me writhe and moan, so consumed with pleasure I can hardly think. He brings his other hand into play, pushing his fingers inside me, and then his mouth is on my clit again. His appreciative growls and guttural noises make me as wild as his touch. I claw at the mattress, rocking against his hands and mouth, but my eyes never leave his, because there's no bigger aphrodisiac than the pleasure gleaming back at me. I have a fleeting thought that this is a world away from what I had with Harvey, but I force it down deep, unwilling to give up this pleasure-drenched night.

Pressure mounts inside me, prickling like fire and ice. He

works me faster, crooking his fingers inside me, stroking that hidden spot that makes the edges of my vision blur. He takes my clit between his teeth, does something magical with his tongue, and I detonate. "*Wells—*" flies from my lips, and I gasp for air as my body clenches and bucks.

He continues fucking me with his fingers, flicking my clit with his tongue. When he slows his efforts, drawing long, needy sounds from my lungs, he withdraws his fingers and laps up my come. Watching him takes me right back up to the edge, and then *he* sends me over it. I spiral into ecstasy, crying out, squeezing his head between my thighs as excruciating pleasure unravels me.

When I finally sink to the mattress, breathless, my body jerking with aftershocks, he licks me again. I inhale sharp breaths with every slick of his tongue. "*Too much*," I pant out. "I'm too sensitive."

He kisses my inner thigh, then crawls up my body, taking me in another toe-curling kiss before gazing down at me and saying, "Too sensitive to fuck, sweet girl?"

The way he says it is cute, not crass, and it makes me smile. "Never."

With a quick peck, he gets off the bed like a kid anxious to open his birthday present. I lie there trying to recover, watching him strip off his boxer briefs to unveil that promising cock, and a wave of arousal washes over me anew. He retrieves a condom from his wallet and sheathes his length.

As he climbs onto the bed, reaching for me, I go up on my knees, playfully batting his hand away. "You've had enough control, boy toy. Lay your handsome ass down, and let me ride that cock."

Chapter Three

Wells

Jesus Fucking Christ. This incredible woman is going to be the death of me.

I saw the sadness in Victory's eyes when she talked about her late husband warring with the lust radiating toward me. That twisted me up inside, and I almost backed off, but something about her refused to let me. Now I can only imagine the magnitude of what she's feeling after all these years, and I want to help her bridge the gap between her past and her future. I want to give her whatever she needs, even if for only one night, to help her feel as confident, desirable, and empowered as she is outside the bedroom.

She plants a hand on her hip, her gorgeous eyes narrowing in warning, that pink butterfly on her wrist teasing me like a secret I want her to unveil. "Don't even think about telling me no."

"You're not going to hear any complaints out of me. There's nothing sexier than a woman who takes what she wants." I lower my back to the mattress, happy to let her fuck me to her heart's content, and reach for her. "Climb on, cowgirl."

That earns a sexy smile as she straddles me. "Eyes on me, boy toy."

"I look forward to seeing you take my cock, but I'll be damned if I'll let you call me *boy* while we fuck." I grab the base of my cock, aligning it with her entrance with one hand, and grab her hip with the other.

Her eyes narrow. "Oh, I think you will." She holds my gaze, hovering over my cock, and palms her breast, fondling it as she slides her other hand between her legs, teasing herself. Her face contorts with pleasure. "*Ah. I'm so wet.*" She rolls her nipple between her finger and thumb, moaning.

She's so fucking sexy, my dick jerks, and I grit out a curse.

"What's it going to be? Boy toy, or should I get dressed and go?"

I realize she's playing off what I said to her earlier. "You sassy little minx. You can call me your boy toy tonight, but I'm going to fuck you so thoroughly, you'll never make that mistake again."

"This is a onetime thing, so you don't have to worry about that."

I grit my teeth, wondering why that bothers me, but I don't have time to overthink it as she lowers herself, taking every inch of my cock. She's so tight, I clench my teeth at the raw pleasure burning through me, and grit out, "*Fuck*," as she pants out, "*Holy cow.*"

"Did you spend the last five years doing Kegels?"

She laughs, and her pussy tightens around me. The pleasure is excruciating. "Jesus, Vic. You're like a goddamn vise." That makes her laugh even harder, her inner muscles clamping around me. "You keep laughing, and this'll be over before we get started." I grab her hips as more melodic laughter rings out, and her hands land on my chest, her hair curtaining her face. "We've got to move, sweet thing." I thrust up, and she gasps. *Fuck.* I freeze. "Did I hurt you?"

She shakes her head, her hair trailing over my chest, her smile lighting me up inside. "I'm just not used to having half a baseball bat inside me."

"Get over here." I pull her mouth to mine, and we kiss through our laughter. I move slowly, giving her body time to adjust. She feels so fucking good, but this isn't about me. "Feel good, baby?"

"*Mm-hm.* So good." She sits up, grinding against me.

I let her set the pace, and what a stunning sight she is as she gathers speed, riding me faster, grinding harder, her gorgeous tits and hair bouncing in the best fucking show on earth. "That's it, baby. Ride my cock like you own it." Those are not words I've *ever* uttered before, but hell if they don't feel right. I tease her clit with one hand, grabbing her hip with the other, helping her move faster, trying to outrun that feeling.

"*Ohgod,*" she pants out, arching against my hand. "Feels so good."

"I need those tits."

"*Yes—*"

I sit up, sweeping an arm around her, and take her nipple into my mouth. My teeth graze over it, and she cries out. Those fucking sounds are killing me. I do it again to earn another, and she doesn't disappoint. I can't get enough of her—her body, her humor, this whole damn night—and one word plays in my mind like a mantra. *More. More. More.*

I grab her ass with both hands, taking control of our speed as I devour her other breast.

"Don't stop...*ohgod...Wells...*"

The desperation in my name tugs at something deep inside me. What is it about this woman that's fucking with my head? She moans and writhes, her hair falling over our shoulders, her fingernails cutting into my flesh. It hurts so good, I thrust harder. It doesn't take long before she shatters, her pussy pulsing around my cock as she cries out my name. *Music to my fucking ears.*

We ride that wave, and as she comes down from the peak, I lavish her other breast with attention, rougher than before, sending her crashing into another climax. When those baby blues hit me, I get the strange urge to sweep her beneath me and gaze into those hauntingly sexy eyes while I come.

I don't *ever* do that, and the fact that I want to twists me up even more. When she comes down from the high, I lift her off me, gritting out, "On your hands and knees, sweet cheeks." She's like a fucking dream, doing as I ask. "Look at you, so trusting, with your gorgeous ass in the air."

"Shut up and fuck me before I change my mind."

Like I said, a fucking dream come true. I grab her waist with both hands and drive into her. *"Yes—"* flies from her lungs, and she pushes her hips back, taking me impossibly deeper.

As I pound into her, I grab a fistful of her hair, tugging her head back, testing her limits, eliciting greedy pleas and more sinful sounds. The urge to claim her, to rip off this condom and come on her ass, slams into me. I haven't wanted to claim a woman since I was a teenager. I ran from the urge then, and I try to chase it away now.

"Squeeze your legs together," I demand, and she does. Pleasure consumes me. My cock aches for release. I reach around her, touching her where I know it'll set her off like a fucking bomb. Her pussy clamps tight, and she screams my name so loud, it echoes off the walls, severing my restraint. Pleasure slams into me, and I roar out her name. A string of curses follows as we thrust and grind, riding the explosive torrent of our passion.

Our bodies jerk and thrust, and I stay with her until the last aftershock rumbles through us. I realize I'm still holding her hair and release it, hoping I didn't hurt her. Her head falls between her shoulders, and she goes down onto her elbows. *Jesus.* I've never gotten so lost in a woman. I press a kiss to her spine. "Was I too rough?"

She shakes her head and sinks to the mattress.

I lie beside her, gathering her in my arms. "I didn't mean to pull your hair so hard."

"It's okay. I liked it." Snuggling against me, she whispers, "I miss this."

"I thought you might. You're a passionate woman. Sex is good for your body and your brain."

She tilts her face up with a sweet smile, in stark contrast to the snarky, sexual animal she was a minute ago. "I missed that, too, but I was talking about lying in someone's arms. I forgot how much I like cuddling."

I hold her tighter and kiss her forehead. I've never been a cuddler, but hell if I'm not loving this.

"There should be a business where you can rent a man for cuddling." She puts her hand on my chest and tilts her face up. "I bet there are professional cuddlers. They have everything else in this city."

"You don't want some random guy in your bed. I'll be your cuddler anytime you want."

"That's sweet of you, but you've more than fulfilled my boy-toy needs, and I truly appreciate it."

"I'll give you *boy toy*." I nip at her lower lip, and she laughs. I lift her hand and kiss that tiny pink butterfly. "Cute tattoo. Does it have a special meaning?"

"No. I just like butterflies," she says a little wistfully, and lowers her hand.

I get the feeling there's more to that story, which only makes her more intriguing. "I'll be right back." I head into the bathroom to get rid of the condom.

When I return, she's in the living room getting dressed. She turns her back to me as she puts on her dress. This fucking stings. I pull on my boxer briefs and jeans and head over to her. She's reaching for her zipper.

"I'll get that." I zip up her dress. "You in a hurry?"

"No, I just…" She turns with an apologetic expression. "This was fun, but I need to go."

"I'll get you a car or walk you home. How far is your place?"

"It's not far, but I've got it. Thanks." Averting her eyes, she reaches for her bag and pulls out her phone, focusing on it. "There's a car right around the corner."

"I'll walk you down." She's still not looking at me, so I put my arms around her, drawing her eyes to mine. "What's going on, Vic? Are you embarrassed?"

"*No,*" she says emphatically. "We had fun, and now the night's over. I thought we were on the same page about this."

"We are," I say, wishing we weren't, which I don't fully understand, so I take a step back. "I'm just making sure you're good."

"I'm totally fine, but I need to use your bathroom before I go."

As she hurries into the bathroom, I put on my shirt and shoes, wondering why it bothers me that she's taking off so fast.

It shouldn't. We were good together, and it was fun, but I knew she was using me. This was a big step for her after so many years of grieving her husband. She's got to have a lot of emotional shit going on in her head. I guess it makes sense that she wants to get out of here, but I can't shake the feeling that there's more to us than what went on tonight. Our connection feels too real to be a one-off.

"There's no need to walk me down," she says when she comes back into the living room, heading for the door. "Thanks for a great night, boy toy."

"Victory," I say sternly. *I'm not a fucking boy toy.* "I'm walking you down to the car."

Victory

My emotions are reeling. I feel like I can't breathe as we head downstairs, and I know Wells feels it, because his hand is on my lower back as we hit the busy sidewalk, and he keeps looking at me like he's going to say something, but he doesn't. I feel like an ass rushing off and dismissing him the way I did. It's not like he did anything wrong. He did exactly what he agreed to do, and he did it surprisingly well. I'm the one who's messed up. When I was lying in his arms afterward, without the constant distraction of his hands and mouth and other talented body parts driving me wild, I couldn't stop thinking about Harvey.

I still can't.

Thankfully, the car is waiting out front. "Thanks again," I say awkwardly, needing to get out of here before I break down.

"Do me a favor and text me when you get home, so I know you got there safely."

"I don't have your number, but I'll be fine."

He pulls out his phone. "Give me yours and I'll text you. Then you'll have it."

I rattle it off, and he thumbs out a text. My phone chimes in my purse.

He leans down and kisses my cheek. "You're an incredible woman, Victory. I appreciate the trust you put in me tonight."

I don't know what I was expecting, but it wasn't *that*. I manage a smile, and he opens the car door for me. "Thanks again," I say too cheerily, as if the guilt isn't eating me alive, and slide into the back seat. After he closes the door, he stands there, his arms crossed, watching us drive away from the curb.

I look down at the butterfly tattoo on my wrist, guilt and sadness swamping me.

Shit. Shitshitshit. What have I done? I squeeze my eyes shut against tears, but I see flashes of Harvey, and on the heels of seeing him, comes Wells. The guilt is too consuming, and tears break free. I clench my teeth, telling myself to get a grip. This is *not* who I am. I am always in control.

Except when I'm not.

Guilt stacks up inside me. I stare out the window, trying to stop the tears, but my thoughts circle back to dancing and kissing Wells and how much I enjoyed everything we did, which makes me feel even guiltier. I hate feeling out of control. I need to talk to someone who will give me tough love and help me get my head on straight.

Leni, Shea, or Sutton would give me the harsh talk I need, but I can't tell them about Wells. They're too tangled up with the Silvers, and as much as I love my brother Clay's wife,

Pepper, they just got married six months ago, and they're still in the honeymoon stage. They're so happy, I don't want to dump this crap on her. This is one of the rare times I wish my circle of friends weren't so small. I've never had many close girlfriends. Growing up in newly developing countries with my wildlife biologist and photographer parents until I was in high school, marrying young, and running a multibillion-dollar business for the last several years doesn't leave me with much in common with many women my age.

Without any sisters to lean on, I count myself lucky to have four wonderful younger brothers. They've all helped me through rough times, but Seth has always been my confidant. He's the closest to my age, the most levelheaded, and he never judges me. Seth and I have always needed a level of structure our younger rambunctious brothers, Clay, Flynn, and Noah, didn't. That's probably why Seth and I became comrades in arms, talking out issues and taking solace in order and our studies.

Seth never gets too caught up in emotions, which is exactly what I need right now. It's after midnight, but he's a night owl, and he knows how tough today is for me. We had breakfast together this morning, like we do every year on the anniversary of the day I met Harvey.

I reach into my purse for my phone and find a napkin from the bar. I have no idea how that got there. I remember Wells zipping my purse, but why would he put it in there? I fish my phone out, and my pulse quickens at the sight of Wells's text. It hadn't fully registered that he sent one.

Wells: *Hit me up the next time you're down for some fun.*

Hit me up? What was I thinking? I read it again, and it screams of our age difference, driving that guilt deeper into my chest. Not that I know how old Wells is, but my guess is around thirty. The car stops, and I look up from my phone. We're at a stoplight, and the driver is watching me in the rearview mirror. He averts his eyes, and Wells's voice whispers through my mind. *The perils of being beautiful.*

Ugh. The heck with good genetics. I'll take a new brain, please. At least for tonight.

I call Seth, and he answers on the first ring. "Hey, Vic. Everything okay?"

As usual, his calm, deep voice is reassuring. I imagine him putting down whatever book he's reading and pushing his black-framed glasses to the bridge of his nose as he sits back in his leather recliner. "*No*," I whisper-hiss. "I just cheated on Harvey."

Seth doesn't immediately respond. As a business magnate and named *Forbes*'s Most Eligible Bachelor twice, he didn't get where he is by speaking before he thinks. I'm sure his dark brows are furrowed and he's rubbing his jaw, weighing his answer. "Vic, you can't cheat on a man who's not here."

I roll my eyes. "You know what I mean. I'm such an idiot."

"You're *not*, which means one of two things. You're either drunk and overthinking, or you've finally let yourself move on. Neither is bad as long as you're in a safe place."

"I'm not drunk."

"Okay. Then a guy caught your fancy? Good for you. Did you enjoy it?"

"*Yes*. It was fun and exciting, and…different. But then I was lying there in his arms and…" Tears well in my eyes.

"He wasn't Harvey," he says empathetically.

"Exactly. I feel *so* guilty." The driver pulls over in front of my building. "Hold on a sec. I have to get out of the car."

I thank the driver, and Ivan, the silver-haired doorman who has worked in my building for at least the ten years I've lived there, opens the car door for me. "Good evening, Ms. Braden," he says as I step out.

"Hi, Ivan. Thank you." I'm not ready to go upstairs and face the luxury apartment where Harvey and I lived, so I head down the sidewalk to finish my call in private. "Sorry, Seth." I pick up where we left off, speaking quietly. "Not only did I jump into bed with the first man who offered, I did it with *Wells Silver*." I whisper his name, as if that somehow makes it better. "I don't know what I was thinking. He's not much older than *Noah*." Our youngest brother is barely thirty.

"At thirty-seven, I guess that makes you a cougar," he says with amusement.

"*Seth!* That's not helpful."

"Sorry," he says. "But I'd like to point out that we both know Wells is not the first man to offer."

"I'm in turmoil, and *that's* what you focus on?" I pace the sidewalk.

"No. I just want to be clear that you've had plenty of offers over the years from some very prominent men, and you turned them all down. I'm not saying that has to mean anything, but it might."

And there it is, his brilliant analytical side, which I admire when it's convenient and find annoying when it's not. This is the latter. "It *doesn't*, so let's move on."

"Okay. I spent some time with Wells at the wedding. He's a good guy."

"Seriously? He's a total player, and he dated Leni, which makes me a horrible friend. I broke the girl code. Everyone knows you don't sleep with your friend's ex."

"Leni is marrying an A-list actor this summer. I highly doubt she gives a shit who Wells sleeps with, but—"

"Maybe calling you was a mistake. You are *not* helping."

"And you are not letting me finish my sentences." He pauses, and I know he's making a point, so I bite my tongue. "I think it's great that you finally cut loose and had a good time. You've lived your life in a box for *five* years."

"I have not." I definitely have, but I don't like the way he makes it sound wrong. I like my alone time, but if I don't keep myself busy and distracted, my thoughts return to the awful night Harvey died.

"No? You go to the gym, then you go to work, and then you either order dinner to take home or you eat out, and you never go home before seven o'clock. Except on Friday nights, when you go to your and Harvey's favorite restaurant, where you've had a standing reservation for five years."

"I like the tavern." It's the truth, and it's the least I can do for the man I love.

"Nobody likes a restaurant enough to go every week for years on end by themselves. I get it. Especially after what happened the night Harvey died."

"*Don't,*" I warn. Seth is the only one who knows the truth about that night, and I can't go there right now.

"I'm not. I'm just saying that I get it, but you are living in a box, sis. I know it's not easy to move on, but I have to ask, if Leni weren't in the picture, would you be interested in Wells?"

"God *no,*" I snap, but I don't know if that's the guilt talking or the truth, and I don't have the bandwidth to think about it.

"Why? Did he suck in bed?"

"No, he was amazing, but he's not my type."

"Because you prefer guys who suck in bed?" he teases.

"What is wrong with you? Are *you* drunk?" I laugh, but my humor doesn't last. "Do I have to spell it out for you? In addition to everything I've already said, Wells and I are completely different people in very different places in our lives. He has no *real* life experience. He grew up with a silver spoon in his mouth on an island as big as my fist. I doubt he's ever dealt with a hardship of any kind." I stop pacing and huff out a breath. "Why am I even explaining this? We had a one-night stand. That's all it was to both of us, and I'm not interested in more."

"Good, because I don't think he's right for you. But if it was just a fling, then why did you call me? What's the issue?"

"I'm *drowning in guilt!* I feel like I cheated on my husband, and the worst part is that I was excited to do it." I lower my voice to almost a whisper. "I thought about Harvey tonight, and I pushed those thoughts away just so I could feel good."

"That's okay, Vic," he says reassuringly. "It doesn't mean you love Harvey any less."

"Then why does it feel like the worst kind of betrayal? Like I gave away the one piece of myself that was *his.*"

Seth is quiet for a beat. "Because I guess in a way, you did," he says carefully, and it cuts like a knife. "But that's how you move forward after losing someone."

"Well, moving forward sucks. I don't know why I let myself do it tonight, but it was a mistake."

"I get why you feel that way, but for what it's worth, I don't think Harvey would want you to cut yourself off like you have. He loved you too much to have you miss out on a damn thing. There's a whole world out there, Vic, and you used to love exploring it. Harvey would want that for you. He'd want you to live your life without constraints."

"Then he shouldn't have died," I snap, and immediately regret it. It's not like he could have saved himself. "Sorry. I don't mean that. I'm just tired."

"I know. Do you want me to come over? We can hang out and watch a movie or do some shots until you feel better."

I look up at the gorgeous skyscraper where Harvey and I lived and consider asking Seth if I can spend the night at his place to avoid going home. I remember the first time Harvey took me here. His apartment was so elegant, I wasn't sure it could ever feel like home. Now I can't imagine living anywhere else. The thought of walking into the home we shared after what I did kills me, but spending the night at Seth's would only delay the inevitable, so I pull up my big-girl panties and say, "No, thanks, but thank you for listening to me gripe about my fall from grace."

"Anytime. Listen, Vic. I know it was hard to rip off the bandage, but I'm proud of you for taking that step. As with everything hard in life, I'm sure the more you do it, the easier it'll get."

"I wonder what Mom and Dad would think about you cheering me on to have meaningless sex with people who are practically strangers."

He laughs. "G'night, sis. Love you."

"You too." I end the call, emotionally exhausted, and head inside.

When I get to my apartment, guilt clings to me like a second skin as my gaze moves over the high-end furniture in the expansive living room and dining room, to the lights of the city through the nearly floor-to-ceiling glass along the far wall. I haven't changed a thing since Harvey died. I can still see him making drinks at the bar, eating at the dining room table, reading a book, or sitting on his favorite side of the couch by the windows working on his laptop, his feet resting on the coffee table, his ankles crossed. I can still see his smile, which appeared when I walked into a room.

I've always taken solace in the quiet. It allows me to hear Harvey's familiar footsteps down the hall, his voice whispering to me in every room, and the sound of him pulling books from the bookshelf as he chose his nightly read. I used to wonder how he ever finished a book, because he'd alternate reading two or three at the same time. I don't know why my heart allows me to spend time *with* him like that without overthinking the night I lost him, but I'm thankful it does.

Pushing past those painful memories, I make my way into the master bathroom, guilt following me like a shadow as I step into the shower. It's still there when I climb into bed, and for the first time since Harvey died, I can't bring myself to lie on his side of the bed.

My phone chimes on the nightstand. Annoyed with myself for forgetting to silence it, I snag it and see another text from Wells, adding another heap of guilt for not texting when I got home like he'd asked.

Wells: *Ghosting me already? Or did you pick up another lucky bastard on the way home?*

A devil emoji pops up.

I stare at the phone, trying to decide how to answer. It's sweet that he wants to make sure I got home safe. He's sexy and charming, but all the things I said to Seth hold true, and nothing is worth the guilt I feel.

Not even a night of the best sex of my life with a man who makes me smile and remember what it feels like to let go of my guilt for a little while and just be me.

I silence my phone, turn it face down on my nightstand, and scoot over to Harvey's side of the bed.

Chapter Four

Wells

I see two unimpressive properties Friday morning before heading over to meet Seth for lunch at one of his restaurants. I never heard back from Victory last night, and that bugs the shit out of me. I was tempted to text her this morning, but I don't want to be *that* guy. I've replayed our evening together a hundred times, and I'm either really good at convincing myself of shit, or there was definitely a bigger connection than just incredible sex. We clicked in conversation, sense of humor, and snark. Even those few blissful moments of cuddling felt different.

The fact that I'm still stewing over her as the cab pulls up in front of The Grill tells me it's not in my head, but I push that thought away, because as I told Fitz, this is a business meeting, and *that* was pure pleasure.

I'm ten minutes early. As I climb out of the cab, I see Seth walking down the street. He's an interesting guy. I wasn't sure what to make of him at first. It's not often you meet a self-made billionaire who's as laid-back as a surfer and always looks a little disheveled.

As he approaches, I notice his flowered blue shirt is buttoned wrong, hanging askew. His salmon shorts have yellow boats on them, and his red leather boat shoes have got to be hot as hell in the summer heat. But to each his own.

"Hi, Seth. Thanks for meeting me." I shake his hand.

"It's good to see you again, Wells."

"I would've been happy to come to your office."

"I don't really have an office. Too confining." He pulls open the door to the restaurant, and we head inside.

The Grill is classy but not stuffy, with dark hardwood floors, elegant candle-style chandeliers, and brick walls with circle-head windows along one side. The hostess lights up when she sees Seth. "Hi, Mr. Braden. Your table is ready in the back. Melanie should be right up to seat you."

"Gretchen, what have I told you about calling me that?" Seth asks.

She blushes. "That every time I say it, you think your father followed you in."

I chuckle.

"That's right. Please don't age me before my time," he says kindly. "We'll seat ourselves."

I follow Seth through the dining room and beneath one of three brick archways into a massive bar area with tables and private, curtained booths. "This is a beautiful place," I say as we sit at a table by a window.

"Thanks. There are two private dining rooms back here." He motions to doors on either side of the bar across the room.

A waiter comes over with water and menus, and we take a minute to order drinks and sandwiches. When the waiter walks away, Seth says, "So, a new restaurant. That's exciting. Have you seen anything you like since you got into town?"

Just your sister. I take a drink to distract myself from that thought. "I've seen a few properties that would probably be fine, but nothing has wowed me yet. I'm looking for a certain vibe."

"And what vibe would that be? Something that draws people in for a hell of a good time, and then you never see them again? Or are you going for more of a long-term scenario?"

Victory must be really screwing with my head, because I wonder if we're still talking about restaurants, which is ridiculous. "I definitely want people to enjoy themselves, whether they visit for a night or return every week, but my goal is to build long-term relationships that stand the test of time. And I want to say that I appreciate you offering to fill me in on the differences you've encountered while running restaurants in touristy areas and bigger cities, but I don't want you to think I'm here to get your trade secrets. I don't believe our brands are in competition."

"They're not, and I wouldn't have suggested we meet if I thought you were that kind of guy."

"I appreciate that." *I wonder if he'd be so forthcoming if he knew I spent last night with his sister.*

"There are plenty of challenges that come with running a business on an island, some of which you'll encounter here. But running a restaurant in this particular city has its own unique set of challenges…"

Seth shares his wealth of knowledge, covering everything from real estate, business infrastructure, and logistics, to the fierce competition in the city, costs and struggles with staffing, and the difficulties of managing the sourcing of high-quality ingredients, supply-chain delays, and even transportation delays that commonly occur in the city and can screw up the best-laid plans for deliveries. We discuss keeping up with food and marketing trends, and I'm proud to be able to hold my own in the conversation.

We talk well past when we're done eating lunch, and then Seth sits back and says, "You've got a good sense of things."

"Thanks. I've been looking at expanding for a while. I've spent the last year researching this area."

"It shows. Can you paint me a picture of what you envision for your restaurant?"

"Sure." *What is it about Bradens and painting pictures?* "Ideally, it will be on the water, which I know is nearly impossible. But a water view would be nice, or some other element that would make it a truly unique experience. I prefer to offer indoor and outdoor seating, like I have at Rock Bottom. I'm hoping this will be the first step in carrying my brand forward to other locations."

"I've got my pulse on the market, and I know of nothing that's got a water view."

"That's why I'm looking at other options. That said, while water view or waterfront locations are limited, if I can find it, with the right marketing and experience, it should draw people like flies. I built my reputation at Rock Bottom by getting to know my customers by name and expecting my staff to do the same. I realize city clientele will be different, but personal attention goes a long way. Everyone likes to be recognized, and I know it means slower service, but that extra few minutes per table has proven to be worth it with my current location. My customers come back year after year, and I'm confident that in combination with excellent food and service, I can make that happen here."

"I like that idea, but it might be even harder than you think to pull off in this area."

"Maybe so, but we see roughly one hundred and fifty thousand tourists on the island each year. Many come from this area and other big cities. My methods haven't failed me yet. That's not to say they won't fail, but if I have it my way, the people of New York will see Rock Bottom as the comfortable, happy place they think of first when they're going out with friends or family to enjoy a great meal and a good time. But the experience goes further than that. I'd love to have space for live music and dancing, but I also want families with children to feel comfortable in the dining room. I'll keep it rustic and beachy, which I know is very different from city life, but my goal is to bring a slice of paradise to the city. When customers leave, I want them to feel like they've been on a mini vacation."

"That's a fresh idea, and a lofty goal."

"What other kind of goals are there?"

Seth grins. "You're asking the wrong guy. Everything I do is over the top in one way or another." He takes a drink. "I've had my eye on a few properties that might interest you. They're not waterfront, but they're unique."

"I don't want to steal anything out from under you."

"I'm considering them as investments, but I haven't made any decisions about what I might do with them yet. Maybe we can work something out. I've looked into your business, and your annual growth is impressive. Have you ever considered partnering with another company? I know you have plenty of capital, but my business partner, Jared Stone, and I have restaurants down to a science. He's a world-renowned chef and an excellent businessman. Partnering could accelerate your ability to expand to different areas, and we've got connections with local architects and contractors to do the build-out."

The question takes me by surprise. I've looked into Seth's

businesses, and everything he and Jared touch turns to gold. I'm hit with several thoughts at once, but two speak louder than all the rest. *I'd be a fool not to explore this opportunity* and *Victory.* I'm not done with her, even if she thinks she's done with me.

Seth is looking at me expectantly. This could be the chance of a lifetime, so I take the biggest risk I've taken since buying the restaurant, knowing full well it might stop this conversation in its tracks.

"I haven't considered partnering in the past. A number of aspects are important to me, including maintaining creative control. That said, I'd be interested in talking about it, but before we have that conversation, I want to be completely transparent with you about something."

Seth lifts his chin. "What's that?"

"I'm interested in your sister." I hold my hands up in surrender. "I might be barking up the wrong tree. You saw her rebuff my advances at the holiday dance at the Silver House and at Flynn and Sutton's wedding."

He arches a brow. "I'm pretty sure everyone saw that."

"Yeah, which probably makes me a fool. But I can't shake the feeling that there's something between us, and if I can convince her to give me a shot, I'd like to explore it. If that's a deal-breaker for you, I understand."

Seth studies me for a moment. "You're willing to walk away from this opportunity on the off chance that Victory will go out with you?"

"Yes. I know she's fiercely independent, which I admire, and she might kick me to the curb again, but that's a chance I'm willing to take."

"Might?" He chuckles. "I love my sister, but she's built some pretty thick walls around that heart of hers. She hasn't dated

since she lost Harvey, and she doesn't like to talk about him. Especially with people outside the family. If she lets you get close to her, it'll be a miracle."

Then miracles do happen, and I've got one foot in the door. Physically at least. That's a start. "I hear you loud and clear. I'm going into this with my eyes open."

"In that case, I appreciate your transparency. It says a lot about the type of person you are, but what my sister does with her personal life is none of my business. If you feel that strongly about her, go for it. Whether she gives you a chance or tells you to get lost won't affect our working relationship."

Relief washes over me. "I'm glad to hear that."

"I will give you one piece of advice. Whatever you do, don't ask anyone to put in a good word for you with Victory."

"I can do my own bidding, but now I'm curious why you'd say that."

"Because if anyone tells Victory to run right, she's not only going to run left, she'll fucking zigzag just to piss you off."

Victory

I couldn't have picked a worse night to hook up with Wells. As if functioning on little sleep isn't hard enough, add in an ongoing battle of deliciously dirty memories making me hot and bothered and the guilt those feelings stir, and it's impossible to focus at my monthly management meeting. I thought a lunchtime workout would clear my head, but then the songs Wells and I danced to last night came on my playlist and blew that plan out of the water.

It's late afternoon, the management meeting is in full swing, and I still feel like I'm going to climb out of my skin. Blank Space recently purchased M&O, a smaller talent agency, and I put Padma Desai, our director of operations, in charge of overseeing their transition and integration into the company. As she brings us all up to date, my mind tiptoes back to Harvey.

Padma had worked for Harvey for several years before I was hired, and in the years since he's been gone, we've gotten closer. She's become the person I rely on most to fill in when I'm traveling or unavailable. I look around the room at the faces of our other most trusted executives, each of them listening intently to Padma, nodding and taking notes. Harvey would be proud of our team.

Most of these men and women are working their asses off to achieve their dreams, but I think the few who knew Harvey still carry his dreams in their hearts, too. Harvey had that kind of lasting effect on people. I hope I make him proud.

My attention catches on my cell, silenced and face down, lighting up with a message or call. My thoughts go straight to Wells, and my pulse quickens. I hate that, but I can no sooner control it than I can stop feeling bad for not texting him back last night. But the intensity of our chemistry is dangerous. It's best to cut myself off cold turkey and let it fizzle out.

I lower my cell to my lap to check it so I don't distract the others. I'm hit with a pang of disappointment when I see my assistant Yvette's name on the screen, and I hate that I feel that, too. I tap the message bubble.

Yvette: *FYI. Ms. McVay can meet with you Thursday morning. I confirmed and moved your return flight to 2.*

I'm glad Ms. McVay is able to work around my busy schedule. I'm heading to Los Angeles tomorrow for a week of meetings, and to support a client who is recording their first album. It's a big moment for them, and I want to be there to cheer them on.

I thumb out a thank-you and send it off, quickly scanning my other unanswered texts. At the bottom of them, Wells's name stares back at me. Like an idiot, I open the thread.

Hit me up the next time you're down for some fun.

Ghosting me already? Or did you pick up another lucky bastard on the way home?

The devil emoji at the bottom has me thinking about last night. His husky voice tramples through my mind. *Lean up on your elbows, sexy girl. I want those beautiful eyes on me when I make you come.* The image of my legs over his shoulders, his piercing dark eyes watching me as his mouth worked its magic, has my heart racing. *You taste too fucking good. I could eat you all—*

"Victory?" Padma asks from the front of the room.

I startle and turn my phone over. *Shit.* All eyes are on me. "Yes? Sorry, I was handling an issue." I wave my phone as if to validate my excuse.

"I'm sorry to interrupt," Padma says. "I was just wondering if you have any questions."

"No. Thank you. That was an excellent presentation. Unless anyone else has questions for you, I believe we're done for the day."

There's a flurry of activity as everyone gathers their things, and I silently chide myself for getting lost in Wells *again.*

As I push to my feet, Padma picks up her laptop and comes around the table. At forty-nine, she's as striking as she is sharp, with light brown skin, straight raven hair cut just above her shoulders, and keen eyes that never miss a thing. She stands with her back to the others and lowers her voice. "Are you okay? You seem a little distracted today."

"I'm fine. Thanks. Just sidetracked by a few things I need to take care of." *Like erasing my memory.*

"Anything I can help with?"

"I wish," I say lightly, although I don't wish she could help me with Wells. For some strange reason, the idea of him with another woman bothers me, which is ludicrous. The man has probably slept with half the women on Silver Island.

"Okay. I'll send you my report and my notes on the other presentations in case you missed anything."

"You're a lifesaver. Thank you." We walk out together, and Mark Savnor, the creative director, falls into step with us.

"Vic, sorry to do this on short notice, but I'm about to send you mock-ups for the strategy meeting tomorrow. Do you have time to review them?"

"Sure, I can do it tonight and get it back to you first thing in the morning."

"Sounds good. Thanks." He heads down one hall, and Padma and I head in the other direction toward our offices.

As we walk past Yvette's desk, our bright-eyed assistant looks up from her computer and smiles, her blond hair covering her shoulders in gentle waves. "Padma, Corbin called. He can't make dinner tonight. He said he'll call you later."

"He needn't bother," Padma says. "Cancel once, it's bad timing. Twice, and it's iffy. But three times in one month? He's done."

"Good for you. You've got to know your worth," Yvette encourages. "Victory, the two messages on your desk need to be returned right away, and the car will pick you up at seven tonight for Cage's birthday party."

"*Shoot.* I forgot about the party." Cage Rekyrts is an MMA fighter. He and his brother, Boone, a musician, along with a few of Boone's friends, were special clients of Harvey's. I took over managing them after Harvey died.

"Do you want me to tell them you can't make it?" Yvette asks. "I canceled your dinner reservation at the tavern, but I'm sure they'll still find a way to fit you in."

"They better. She's their best customer," Padma says.

"No, it's okay." I would never let Harvey down by blowing off any of his favorite clients. "I need to make an appearance at the party. Pad, since Corbin canceled, would you mind taking a look at the mocks for Mark?"

"Not at all. It'll probably be more exciting than Corbin would've been anyway."

"Great. I'll forward them to you."

As Padma heads into her office, Yvette says, "Do you have an outfit for tonight? Or do you need me to have one sent over?"

"I've got something I can wear, but I could use a blowout, if you wouldn't mind making an appointment." I usually tame my thick mane myself for work, but the party is at a rooftop bar, and the humidity will wreak havoc with it.

"Consider it done."

I head into my office and return those important calls. When I'm done with the calls, I move on to returning emails and reviewing reports. I'm elbow-deep in a document when Yvette rings through on the intercom.

"Excuse me, Victory?" she calls.

"Yes?"

"There's a Wells Silver here to see you."

I freeze, and my chest goes hot. What is he doing here? *Shitshitshit.*

Yvette clears her throat, indicating I'm taking too long.

"You can send him in, thanks."

I push to my feet as he walks through the door, looking like sex on legs in jeans and a navy T-shirt, both of which hug him in all the right places. He closes the door behind him, flashing the slow grin that did me in last night. Butterflies swarm in my chest, and my legs are rooted to the floor behind my desk. "Wells, what are you doing here?"

"I was out looking at properties and thought I'd pop in to say hello." He comes around my desk, closing the distance between us, and leans in to kiss my cheek. His masculine scent infiltrates my senses, awakening my entire body. "I haven't heard from you," he says gently, like he's stating a fact, not accusing.

"I—"

"No need to explain. I get it." He brushes the back of his fingers along my cheek, sending shivers of heat down my body. "It's been a long time since you've allowed yourself to take what you wanted. You're probably having all sorts of thoughts about me, and I bet they make you a little nervous."

What are you, a mind reader? "Didn't we talk about you not showing up in my *kitchen?*"

"I got hungry," he says with a seductive glimmer in his eyes.

As hot and exciting as his flirting is, I need to shut it down because I know where it will lead, and the aftermath is too hard to deal with. "I thought we were on the same page about last night."

"We were. I had a great time, and I think you did, too."

"I did," I admit, because he deserves to hear the truth.

"Then let me take you to dinner tonight. It doesn't have to be anything more than that. I just want to spend time with you, have a few laughs, and get to know you better."

"As tempting as that sounds, I can't. I have to attend a birthday party for a client tonight."

"Need a plus-one?" He motions to his chest. "I look sharp in a suit."

I laugh softly. "I remember from the wedding, but no thank you."

"Afraid I'll put your client to shame? That *is* a concern. Especially if he's insecure."

"He's an MMA fighter. He doesn't have an insecure bone in his body."

"No, I guess he wouldn't. Then there's only one explanation for why you wouldn't want to show up on my arm." His gaze turns serious, and he takes my hand. "I get that whatever this is between us scares you—"

"I'm not *scared*." I tug my hand free, because even that simple touch makes me want more.

"Maybe I used the wrong word. What do you think is holding you back?"

My mind reels through excuses. I like him more than I thought I would, and the sex was phenomenal, but that doesn't change any of the facts. He's still a player, we're in vastly different places in our lives, and he should be with a woman whose heart isn't trapped in the past. But I don't want to discuss any of those things, so I go with, "I'm just not that into you."

He grins. "Nice try, but those blue eyes don't lie, sweet thing. Come on. I'm not asking for a relationship. Can't we just be friends and have fun?"

"Like that's going to work?" *We practically set the bar on fire last night.*

"Why wouldn't it? Unless you're saying you want to be friends with benefits? I mean, if that's what you want, we can negotiate."

"You're relentless," I say with a laugh.

"And you love it, which is why we've clicked from day one. Think about it. Even on the island when you were turning me down, we bantered all night at the holiday dance *and* the wedding. Face it, sweet thing. We're drawn to each other."

He's not wrong, and that makes him hazardous to my hormones. "Okay, you know what, charmer? This has been fun, but I don't need a boy toy tonight, and I have work to do. You need to leave." I give him a playful shove toward the door.

"I'm going, but I'm not buying any of this." He looks back at me as he reaches for the doorknob. "See you soon, *friend.*" He tosses me a wink and walks out, closing the door behind him.

Chapter Five

Wells

It wasn't hard to figure out whose birthday party Victory was attending. One social media search about an MMA fighter's birthday party gave me all the information I needed. I got lucky when I discovered that Leni Steele is Cage's PR rep. Convincing her to get me on the list of attendees was nothing short of a miracle. I'm sure I'll owe her forever, but if I have it my way, it'll be worth it.

The party is hopping when I get to the upscale rooftop lounge. The views of the city are spectacular, and the place is decked out with twinkling lights, blazing fires in massive rectangular firepits, and HAPPY BIRTHDAY on a banner above the bar. Photographers are snapping pictures of celebrities decked out in designer clothes, and a band is playing at the far side of the lounge. As I weave through the crowd looking for Victory, I wonder for the tenth time since she turned me down whether she already had a date lined up for tonight.

I hear the sweet, melodic laughter that tugged at me last night and turn toward it, scanning the crowd. A couple heads for the dance floor, and as I step aside to let them pass, I spot my sexy temptress. She's wearing a killer silver halter dress that shows off those lean shoulders I cannot wait to kiss and her long, gorgeous legs, which will hopefully be wrapped around me again tonight. She's talking with a petite, attractive woman with mahogany hair, and they're leaning in close, like they're good friends.

Victory hasn't noticed me, so I take a moment to admire her in that sexy dress and assess the situation. She and her friend aren't holding drinks. I look around, but I don't see anyone bringing her one or keeping an eye on her.

If she is here with someone, it's their loss.

I snag two champagne flutes from a waiter and head for Victory. Her friend sees me before she does and nudges her with her elbow. Victory looks over, and our eyes connect, igniting the space between us, but shock douses the flames in her eyes as I blaze a path to her.

"Hello, *friend*. It's nice to see you again." I lean in and kiss her cheek. "This is a great party, huh?" I hand her a champagne flute.

"It is," Victory says with a curious expression as I offer the other flute to her friend.

"Thank you," her friend says, her gaze moving appreciatively over me. "Victory, aren't you going to introduce us?"

"Yes, of course," she says a little tightly. "Jillian Braden Bad, this is my friend, Wells Silver."

"It's nice to meet you, Jillian."

"You as well. How do you know Victory? Are you an industry friend or a personal friend?"

Victory scowls at Jillian, who arches a brow with a mischievous grin, clearly taunting her, which I fucking love, so I play along. "I'm whatever kind of friend she wants me to be." I toss

Victory a wink, and her eyes narrow. "How about you, Jillian? How do you know Victory?"

"I'm her cousin."

"You're family? Really? I bet you know *all* her secrets."

"Apparently not *all* of them," Jillian says with another nudge.

"Wells, Jillian is an elite clothing designer," Victory says, abruptly changing the subject.

"How exciting." I motion to Jillian's little black dress with colorful designs running through it and triangular cutouts at her waist. "Is that gorgeous dress you're wearing one of your designs?"

"It *is*, thank you," Jillian says proudly. "It's one of my hubby's favorites. You should meet him. He's around here somewhere." She looks around.

"Jillian is married to Johnny Bad."

Floored, I say, "As in, the hottest rock star on the planet? The lead guitarist and singer of Bad Intentions? How cool is *that?*"

"I'm a lucky girl, for sure," Jillian says.

"He's just as lucky to have you, Jilly," Victory says. "Wells, I wasn't expecting to see you here. How did you get on the list?"

I bet you weren't. "I have connections."

Jillian's gaze moves curiously between us, and she says, "It's very hard to get into an exclusive party like this. You must've really wanted to be here."

"I did, and seeing Victory is the highlight of my night."

Victory's eyes narrow. "Surely you didn't come only to see me."

"Let's just say there are important people here that I wanted to network with and leave it at that."

Jillian nudges Victory again. "You've got to admire a man who will stop at nothing to get what he wants."

Victory ignores Jillian's comment and says, "Networking? How's that going for you?" She smirks and sips her champagne.

"I think it's going fairly well. A group of women just tried to coerce me into being a professional cuddler. I didn't even know there was such a thing." I roll my shoulders back. "But with these arms, I guess it's to be expected."

"Why don't you take off that jacket and let us be the judge of those arms?" Jillian suggests.

"*Jillian*," Victory chides. "I think I hear Johnny calling you."

"She wants to be alone with me," I say, earning a glower. "You know, to network."

"You really do need to meet Johnny. You two will hit it off." Jillian looks at Victory and says, "When you're done *networking*, you and Wells should come find us."

"Mm-hm," Victory says, and as soon as Jillian is out of earshot, she turns a serious stare on me. "What do you think you're doing?"

"Enjoying a party with the most beautiful woman here. You look radiant, by the way."

"Thank you, but these are my business associates."

"And relatives, apparently, but I know you're happy to see me."

She shakes her head, a smile curving her lips.

"Come on," I coax. "I saw the look on your face when you first spotted me. Your heart beat a little faster, didn't it? I bet you couldn't help conjuring images of us between the sheets, could you?"

A challenge rises in her eyes. "It was the champagne I was

lusting over, and I'm going to need a lot more of it if you're staying." She drains her glass.

"Oh, I'm staying, sweet thing. I want to see you in action. Fully dressed, professional action, of course."

A warning hovers in her eyes. "If you're going to stay, you need to behave."

"Don't worry. I can be as professional as the next guy. Nobody will know I'm your boy toy." I lean in and whisper, "Even if I'll be picturing you naked every minute we're together."

Her eyes flame, but her tone is sharp. "I mean it, Wells. Everyone who knows me knows I'm a widow, and I can't tell you how many of them have either tried to set me up with someone or are uncomfortable around me at events where there are couples. No offense, but I don't need people asking if we're dating or assuming we are. You're a great guy, but those are not questions or rumors I want to deal with."

"I understand, and I'm sorry I was too playful with your cousin. I will not make that mistake again. The last thing I want is to make your life harder."

"I hope you're being sincere," she says carefully.

"I am. I like spending time with you. I want to be the friend who makes you smile when you think about me. The one you have to share a joke with because you know I'll get it, and the one you can lean on when you need to vent. If that means being a bit more buttoned-up, I can do that for you."

"Thank you."

And there it is, the genuine smile I can't stop thinking about. "Sure thing. Now fill me in, so I appear to know more about you than the fact that you feel like heaven wrapped around my cock."

"*Wells.*" She swats my arms, and we both laugh.

"Sorry, but it's fun to rile you up. I had to get one last ribbing in."

"I'll rile that fine ass of yours right out the door," she threatens.

"Don't make promises you don't intend to keep."

She doesn't respond, but her eyes narrow slightly. She's so fucking cute, trying to be stern, but those gorgeous eyes give her away every time. "I'm sorry. I'll stop messing around. Let's go over there so we can talk." I guide her out of the crowd, toward the railing that surrounds the rooftop, and snag two more flutes of champagne along the way. "Friends should know a little something about each other, and I don't want to embarrass you, which means I need a little info. You're here for Cage, right? How does that work? Are you his agent? How long have you repped him? Did he come to you for representation?"

"You sure you want to bother with all of this? I don't think anyone will ask about that."

"*Yes*. I like teasing you, but I meant what I said. I want to be the friend you can rely on in whatever situation arises, and I want to know what makes you, *you*. You're here, and you came alone, which means Cage must be important to you. That makes your relationship with him important to me. As a friend, of course."

"Okay." She sips her champagne. "Now that I'm running the company, I don't represent as many clients as I used to, for obvious reasons, but I still have a few, and I took over managing the clients that were most important to Harvey."

"What made Cage so important to him?"

She looks a little surprised by the question. "It's kind of a long story."

"Can you give me the condensed version?"

"I can try. This all happened years before I met Harvey and before he opened Blank Space. Harvey was one of the biggest entertainment agents around. He loved scouting what he called underdog talent, or people who don't have the resources or direction to make it on their own, and helping them make it in the industry."

"Why underdogs?"

"Because Harvey knew what it was like to have big dreams and little support. He was raised by a single father who had substance abuse issues, and he was in and out of the system until he was fifteen, when his father got clean and was finally able to take care of him. And it was important to him to build relationships with them, like family." She pauses, and her tone turns wistful. "That ended up being something we had in common. It's how I got started in this business before I met him. But that's a story for another time."

Treating people like family is something we have in common, too. "I look forward to hearing it. Do you still scout underdogs?"

"I wish I had time. I'd do it every night if I could, but I'm too busy running the business. Anyway, Harvey saw this video on YouTube of Charlie Evers, who now manages Bailey Bray and a handful of other top musicians, but twenty years ago, Charlie was just a guy who played music. In the video, Charlie and his buddy were talking about what song they were going to play, and there was a teenage boy playing guitar in the background. Harvey said he knew right then that teen would be a star, and he tracked him down. That was Cage's brother, who goes by Boone Stryker—"

"The lead singer of Strykeforce? Holy shit. That band is amazing."

"Yeah. It turned out their mother was on the janitorial staff at the Epson School of the Arts. She was raising Cage and Boone, and their brother and sister, Lucky and Maggie, on her own. She couldn't afford daycare, so they'd been going to work with her from the time they were little. Boone fell in love with music, and they got to know students and teachers, who showed them a thing or two. Eventually, Boone ran into Charlie, who taught him more. In the end, Harvey paid for Boone, and a few of his equally talented friends, to attend the Epson School of the Arts. But as you know, Cage was a different beast than Boone, and his forte was fighting, so Harvey hired a trainer for him. Blank Space was born not long after that."

"That's incredible. Harvey sounds like he was a great guy."

"Greater than most people know."

"I hope you'll share that with me, too, sometime." As I say it, her gaze warms. "You really do rub elbows with some very cool people."

"Does that surprise you?" She smiles. "I mean, I rub elbows with *you*, right?"

I lift my glass in a silent toast, loving the compliment, and I can't resist leaning in and saying, "You have no idea how much I want to kiss you right now."

She holds my gaze. "Who ever said flattery will get you nowhere?"

"When *you're* the one doing the flattering, it'll get you everywhere." I tap her glass with mine, and she gulps hers down.

She looks out at the crowd and draws her shoulders back. "Come on, troublemaker. I need to make an appearance with some important people. I might as well introduce you to a few rock stars while I'm at it. Think you can behave?"

"I didn't kiss you, did I?"

"You get a gold star," she says as a waiter takes our empty champagne flutes.

"I'd rather have the kiss."

She gives me a look that I swear says she'd rather have it, too.

Or maybe that's wishful thinking.

As we make our way around the lounge, Victory is the epitome of grace and professionalism. She introduces me to her colleagues and business associates and Cage's brothers and sister, not as her friend but as a restaurateur—*Wells owns the hottest restaurant on Silver Island, and he's in the process of expanding to the city*. It's easy to see how well respected she is, as celebrities and other elite guests light up when they see her. She's clever and sexy, and she gives each person her full attention, doling out heartfelt compliments and graciously accepting just as many. I listen intently as she discusses the entertainment industry, gleaning what I can about Victory and the glamorous world she lives in.

I should probably be starstruck by some of the guests, but they don't hold a candle to Victory. The way she goes from one conversation to the next without so much as a sigh is impressive. As a guy who takes personal service to the next level with my customers, I know how exhausting it is to be *on* for hours at a time. I love that part of my job, and I can tell Victory enjoys doing it, too, but as the night wears on, I grow protective of her and try to make sure she has what she needs.

She hasn't stopped smiling all night, but I've learned the difference between her practiced smiles and her genuine ones. I dig them all, but it's the secret smile she gives only me when couples joke about relationships or fawn over each other that twists me up inside. Like the one she's giving me now as we stand by a firepit with Jillian and Johnny Bad and Boone Stryker and his wife, actress Trish Ryder, listening to them talk about their kids. It takes everything I have to stick to my word and fight the urge to slip my arm around Victory and draw her into a kiss.

Victory

As Trish talks about motherhood, Wells leans closer to me and whispers, "Do you think they can tell I'm silently fan*man*ning about talking with two of the world's biggest rock stars and the rest of the *in* crowd?"

I smile. "I think you mean fan*boy*ing."

His brows slant, and he whispers, "Do I need to take you home and remind you there is nothing *boyish* about me?"

Yes, please.

Wells has been amazing tonight. I had forgotten what it was like to go to events with someone who wanted to be there with *me*. He's been sweetly attentive, asking if I need a breather or a drink, and seamlessly fitting into conversations, asking interesting questions and injecting *appropriate* humor. At least for others to hear. He's proven to be an even better seducer than I ever imagined, whispering enticingly naughty things in my ear, keeping my body humming with desire, as he did last night.

He's surprised me in other ways, too. He's protective, reading cues I didn't realize I was giving. He whisked me away from people I wasn't enjoying talking with, and when a guy who had obviously had too much to drink got handsy, Wells stepped in, handling it swiftly without making a scene. I'm having such a good time tonight, it's kind of scary.

"Wells, do you have any children?" Trish asks, drawing me from my thoughts.

"Not that I know of," he says, earning a chuckle from the guys. "But I like kids. My oldest brother, Grant, and his wife, Jules, just had a baby a couple of weeks ago. They named him Stephen—Stevie—Alexander after Jules's father and ours, and he's the cutest little guy."

Harvey used to get that same warm expression when he talked about our friends' kids. I'll never forgive myself for putting off having children to focus on my career, robbing him of that experience.

Swallowing hard, I push those thoughts away and say, "Leni showed me pictures of him. He really is precious." Jules is Leni's younger sister.

"All babies are precious," Jillian says. "Do you want kids, Wells?"

"I haven't really thought about it, but I've got two brothers and two sisters, and I can't imagine my life without them. So, yeah, I guess I'd like to have a family one day."

I don't want to know that, or to like that he wants kids, but there must be some truth to the biological clock, because I've felt pulled in that direction lately.

"Dude, kids will change your life," Boone says. "We only have two, and I swear we're outnumbered."

"Try having twins and a teenager who thinks she's twenty-one," Johnny says.

"It's exhausting in the best way possible," Jillian says. "Lyric and Lennon are a year old, and I swear they stay up all night scheming ways to drive us batty."

"They run everywhere, and it's always in opposite directions," Johnny adds, and we all laugh.

"There are benefits. How do you think I got my body back so fast?" Jillian jokes. "Chasing those little monkeys."

"Just wait until they're a little older and see what new things they get into," Trish says. "You have to see this video of Paisley and JR. It's the cutest thing ever. Boone, can I have my phone?"

As Boone pulls her phone from his pocket, he says, "I'm just going to preface this by saying, what you're about to see is Trish's fault, not mine."

"He's right. It is totally my fault." Trish navigates to the video. "Paisley is two, and JR is four and a half. I was videoing them playing on the patio when this happened."

She holds out the phone, and we all gather around as the video starts. Their adorable little boy is wearing overalls and no shirt or shoes, and his brown hair curls around his ears. He's making motor sounds, pushing a toy truck across a table. Paisley, also barefoot and dressed in overalls, is playing with toy dinosaurs in the grass a few feet away. Her light brown pigtails stick straight out, and she has the sweetest little face.

JR pushes the truck hard, sending it flying off the table and crashing to the patio. "Uh-oh!"

"I get it!" Paisley toddles over and picks it up. Her tiny brows knit as she discovers a crack in the toy. She shakes her head, carrying it to JR, and says, *"Ohdamnit. Ohdamnit. Ohfuckingdamnit."*

We all crack up.

"Are they really your kids?" Wells asks. "Because that little girl is all over social media."

"Yes, that's our dainty little Paisley, showing the world how good of a mother I am," Trish says. "I never thought it would go viral."

"You are the *best* mother," Boone says, hugging her against him.

"Good moms curse," Jillian says. "It's part of life. We just have to teach our kids not to repeat us at inappropriate times."

"That must be the part I forgot," Trish jokes.

"Speaking of our little rascals, when can we get out of here?" Boone asks. "I'm whipped."

"Me too," Johnny says.

"Boone, it's your brother's birthday," Trish exclaims. "We can't just leave."

"Like hell we can't. Maggie and Lucky took off half an hour ago," Boone says. "We showed up. Cage knows we care." He scans the crowd. "Look at him. He won't even notice we're gone."

We follow his gaze across the rooftop and see a tall blonde feeding Cage a cupcake.

Wells leans closer to me and whispers, "I'd like to lick frosting off your cupcake. Let's snag one of those on the way out."

My body ignites. I know if I go home with him, I'll be swimming in a sea of guilt afterward, but as we say goodbye to the others, I'm not ready for my night with Wells to end.

With his hot hand on my back and those piercing eyes urging me on, I decide to allow myself one last night of pleasure. Then he'll go home to the island and I'll go to LA and resume my normal, comfortably scripted life.

"Next time I'll have cupcakes waiting," Wells promises as we climb into the cab. In our haste to be alone, we forgot to grab one on our way out.

The car barely pulls away from the curb before I tug him into a kiss. He makes that growling sound that lights me up like a firework and deepens the kiss. Time blurs in a gust of want and need. By the time we reach his hotel, I have no idea how my legs carry me inside, because I'm so turned on, I'm ready to combust.

"It was hell keeping my hands off you tonight," he grits out as we step into the elevator.

Knowing he's as desperate for me as I am for him is the best kind of aphrodisiac. I reach for him as the elevator doors close, and he pins me against the wall, devouring my mouth as he pushes his hand into my thong. Those talented fingers and thumb work their magic, stealing my breath and sending the world spinning away in record time.

My body screams for more as we stumble into his hotel room in a flurry of urgent kisses and greedy gropes. He kicks the door closed and savagely reclaims my mouth. Our tongues tangle, our bodies grind, and my back hits the wall. He tugs my dress up to my waist, gritting out, "*Jesus*. You make me crazy."

He yanks down my thong, and as I step out of it, he pulls his wallet from his pocket and withdraws a condom, holding it in his teeth as he shoves his pants to his knees, freeing that glorious cock.

"*Hurry*," I plead as he sheathes his length.

His eyes are volcanic as he lifts me into his arms. My legs circle his waist as I sink down and he thrusts, burying himself to the hilt, sending pleasure radiating through me. We both cry out. "Kiss me," he demands, and I do, with everything I have, as he pounds into me.

Every thrust sends an explosion searing through me like thunder and lightning. I fist my hands in his hair, kissing him harder, wanting to feel his roughness, his power. His thick cock fills me deliciously with every forceful stroke of his hips, I can barely breathe for the pleasure consuming me. His muscles constrict, and I know he's as close as I am.

My head falls back as I chase that high, clinging to his shoulders, feverishly riding him. He thrusts faster, harder, gritting out curses to my every moan. "*Wells*" falls desperately from my lips. His next thrust sends me reeling into ecstasy, and he's right there with me as he finds his release. "Vic…*Fuck…Vic*—"

We ride that high until we collapse against each other, panting for air. "Give me that mouth," he growls, and then he kisses the ever-loving hell out of me.

I feel him toeing off his shoes and stepping out of his pants, and I smile against his lips. "You can put me down, you know."

"And take a chance of you walking out that door? No fucking way." He carries me toward the bedroom. "I'm not nearly done with you."

"Funny, I was thinking the same thing."

Chapter Six

Wells

Not reaching out to a woman has never been an issue for me, but as I grab my phone from my kitchen counter, trying *not* to think about being blown off by Victory again, reaching out to her is all I want to do.

It's Sunday morning, and I'm back on Silver Island. A breeze comes through the window, and I look out at the ocean, wondering how I could have been so wrong about us. We had a great time at the party Friday night and an even better time at our private after-party in my hotel room. We laughed a lot, and the way we clicked was as phenomenal as the sex. But she got up to leave right afterward again, and when I asked her to stay the night, she said she was flying to LA in the morning. That wouldn't have bothered me if she hadn't followed it up with, *Wells, you're a nice guy, and this was fun, but I think I'm over my need for a boy toy.*

A fucking boy toy.

I clench my teeth against the term I've come to hate and pocket my phone. I must be a glutton for punishment, because I texted her yesterday afternoon to see if she got to LA safely. I don't know why I thought she'd be thinking about me as much as I'm thinking about her, but I was wrong. She blew me off again. *I'm here safe and sound, but I'm going to be really busy. Thanks for asking.*

I'm usually the one who walks away without wanting more.

This fucking sucks.

I head out to my Land Rover. I'm meeting my family at my mother's house for breakfast. On the way, I stop to pick up flowers, and when I get to my old stomping grounds, it brings mixed feelings. My father moved out when I was young, but my parents never divorced. Not long after, they were best friends and ridiculously in love again, but to this day, they still live in separate houses. Needless to say, my childhood was confusing, but we did a good job of acting like nothing had changed and everything was fine. As Silvers, that was expected of us. Things are great now, but there's no pretending it didn't fuck up my view of relationships.

It's no wonder I misread things with Victory. It's not like I have a lot of practice with relationships. Hell, I've run from them for so long, I can barely spell the word.

So why can't I run from whatever this is with her?

I'm still mulling that over when I pull up to my mother's seven-bedroom waterfront captain's home overlooking Silver Harbor. I park in the driveway behind Fitz's and my sister Keira's cars. As I throw my door open, I hear honking and see my youngest sister, Bellamy, a lifestyle influencer, coming down the road. I grab the bouquet I bought for my mother as Bellamy parks by the curb.

"Hey, Wells! Wait for me!" She jumps out of the car and runs over, her brown hair bouncing around her shoulders. She looks cute in a yellow plaid tube top and white linen pants.

That is, until she shoves her phone in my face and demands, "What is *this*?" Her big brown eyes are as accusatory as her tone. "How did you end up there?"

"Get your phone out of my face and maybe I can see what you're talking about."

She pulls it back a few inches, bringing the picture on the screen into focus. It was taken at the party Friday night. I'm with Victory, Boone, Trish, Johnny, and Jillian, standing by the firepit. Before I can say a word, Bellamy says, "I'll tell you what this is." She points to each person as she speaks. "Rock star, actress, rock star, mega designer, entertainment mogul, and *you*. Do you know who's *not* there? *Me*. What the hell, brother dearest? You couldn't invite me?"

Bellamy is as petite as she is fierce, and she is determined to make herself a household name. I have no doubt she'll get there. She doesn't need a stage to shine, and despite her vehemence, she's the sweetest of my siblings.

"Sorry, Bell, but you weren't in the city."

"I could have been," she says as we head up the walkway. "What were you doing at that party, anyway? I thought you were looking for property."

"I was, but I got invited, so I went."

She sighs. "I need to hang out with you next time you go to the city."

"I don't think so."

"Why not? You might get invited to another party, and I want to be there. Do you know what pictures like that would do for my following?"

"You have almost two million followers."

She rolls her eyes. "I can never have enough. Besides, a party like that could help me get on *InstaLove*."

InstaLove is a reality dating show like *The Bachelor*. "This again? You're too smart for that reality-show crap."

As we step inside, Keira runs out of the kitchen into the hall, and her smile fades. "It's not the baby. It's just Wells and Bellamy." A dead ringer for Rachel Bilson, with light brown hair cascading over the shoulders of her red sundress, Keira is a spitfire. She has never sugarcoated anything other than the pastries in her coffee shop, the Sweet Barista.

"Where is the love in this family?" Bellamy complains.

"Hey, Kei, you look cute. Got a date?"

"*She* looks cute?" Bellamy says incredulously. "What about me?"

"You always look cute. It's your job," I say as we head into the kitchen.

"*Hey*," Keira snaps. "What are you implying?"

Fitz, the sandy-haired golden boy of the family and the brother I'm closest to, glances over his shoulder as he sets plates around the table, which is loaded with platters of toast, steaming eggs, bacon, sausage, cut-up fruit, and an array of fresh pastries that I'm sure Keira brought with her. "Dude, think before you answer that."

Always the mediator, Fitz doesn't like to ruffle feathers. I, on the other hand, have done my best to make up for his failure in that area.

"That's never been Wells's strong suit," my father jokes, his baritone voice ringing out. At six three, with thick dark hair that's silver at his temples, he has a commanding presence, but his teasing smile softens his hard edges.

"Alexander." My mother shakes her head, but she's smiling, too, as she draws me into a hug. "Don't listen to him, honey." She still wears her dirty-blond hair in the same smart style she has since I was a kid, cut just below her ears with a fringe of bangs that gives her a youthful appearance, and she looks classically elegant in cream slacks and a silk top.

"I rarely do," I tease.

My father slings an arm over my shoulder, giving me a side hug. "That's my boy, always looking to stir up trouble."

We hear the front door open, signaling the arrival of Grant and Jules, one of Bellamy's besties. Bellamy squeals and runs into the hall with Keira on her heels, the two of them arguing over who gets to hold the baby first.

Grant comes into the kitchen looking exhausted. His usual almost imperceptible limp from his prosthetic leg is more pronounced, and his collar-length hair is still damp from a shower. He's changed a lot over the last few years, but this new-daddy-tired version of him takes nothing away from the tough warrior I know him to be.

Grant is made of pure grit. He often went head-to-head with our father when we were growing up, but I always knew he'd lay down his life for any of us. After his tours with the Special Forces, he worked at Darkbird, a civilian organization that carried out top-secret military missions. He lost his leg during one of those missions, and when he returned to the island, he did *not* want to be here. He pushed everyone away, but he was no match for Jules, a cancer survivor who spreads joy everywhere she goes. She was determined to help him through his losses, and she brought our brother back from the brink of hell, which was nothing short of a miracle.

Grant drops the baby bag on the counter and pushes a hand through his hair. "Where were they at three this morning when Stevie refused to go back to sleep?"

"Don't let him fool you into thinking it's Stevie's cries keeping him up at night," Jules says as she breezes into the kitchen wearing a loose-fitting nursing top and shorts, the ponytail on top of her head spilling like a fountain over the rest of her golden-brown hair. "He's been sleeping with one eye open since we brought Stevie home from the hospital."

"Now, *that* sounds like my brother," I say.

Jules wraps her arms around Grant's waist, smiling up at him. "And that's just one of the many things I love about our great protector."

Grant looks at her with a softness I never knew existed until he and Jules came together and says, "Love you, too, Pix." Pix, or Pixie, is his nickname for Jules, because she flits about like a pixie spreading happy dust. I never would have put Jules and Grant together. Happy-go-lucky Jules, a self-professed music aficionado who can never remember the correct lyrics to songs but sings like she's onstage anyway, and the brother who seemed to live under a dark cloud for too many years to count. But she's the yin to his yang. Grant is an incredible artist, and he's not only painting again, but he founded and runs the Silver Lining Foundation, which provides resources for amputees.

My father claps a hand on Grant's shoulder. "I've said it before, and I'll say it again, son. Get used to it. You're going to be perpetually tired for the next twenty years."

I don't know what went down between Grant and my parents, but things have gotten better since he and Jules got together.

"Stop being a baby hog," Keira says as she and Bellamy join us in the kitchen.

Bellamy is holding Stevie, tickling his belly. "You don't want to go to Auntie Keira, do you? I know you love your Auntie Bellamy best."

"Ohmygod," Keira says exasperatedly. "You're such a brat."

Bellamy flashes a cheesy grin.

I'd like to hold the little guy, but I'm not about to step into that spider's web.

"Careful, Bell," Fitz says. "I hear babies are contagious."

"That might be possible if there were a man in my life, which there isn't," she quips. "And that's another reason *I* should hold him and not Keira. *She* had a date last night. I wouldn't want her catching baby fever."

That surprises me, since Keira claimed to have sworn off dating a while ago. "Who'd you go out with?"

Keira rolls her eyes.

I glance at Fitz.

He shrugs and says, "It's not my day to keep tabs on her. Are you still hosting poker tomorrow night? Jamison is in town, so he's coming with Brant, and Jock and Levi are busy, but Archer will be there." Jamison and Brant Remington and Jules's brothers, Jock, Levi, and Archer, are some of the guys we grew up with. Brant and Jules's brothers live on the island, but Jamison and Brant's other brother, Rowan, moved away years ago.

"Yup," I say. "It'll be good to see Jamison. Grant, are you coming?"

"We'll see," Grant says.

"He'll be there," Jules says. "He's not missing another game just because he's a daddy."

"Does Jamison even know how to play poker?" Bellamy asks. "He's a science nerd."

"A *hot* science nerd," Keira says.

"He's an astrophysicist," my father interjects. "I doubt there's anything he doesn't know how to do."

"Except women," Keira says. She and Jamison dated in high school, and it did not end well.

"You'd know," Bellamy says.

"Shut up and give me the baby," Keira snaps.

"See, Grant?" Jules exclaims. "*This* is why we shouldn't wait too long to have another baby."

Grant looks at her like she's lost her mind, and I laugh.

"She'll just hog that baby, too," Keira complains.

"All right, enough of the baby war." My mother holds her hands out, wiggling her fingers. "May I please have my grandson?"

As Bellamy hands Stevie to my mother, Keira says, "Are you freaking kidding me? Am I invisible over here? Do you not hear my voice?"

"Oh, honey, why do you think I asked for him?" My mother nuzzles Stevie as she walks over to Keira and then hands her the baby.

"At least now we know who Mom's favorite is." Bellamy rolls her eyes.

Keira flashes her own cheesy smile.

And so begins our typical family get-together.

Breakfast is delicious, and as usual, there's never a lull in conversation. "Jules, honey, how are you feeling?" my mother asks, as if she and Jules's mom haven't been by their house every other day to see the baby.

"Like I just pushed a watermelon out of my body, but it is totally worth it." Jules gazes lovingly at Stevie, nestled in the crook of Grant's arm.

"Fitz, is there a problem at the resort?" my father asks.

"No," Fitz says, focusing on his phone.

"Then how about putting your phone down and joining

us?" my father suggests.

"Sorry." Fitz pockets his phone. "I was just checking out the hotel for that conference you're sending me to."

"There's plenty of time for that later," my father says.

"Fitz, you're going *away*?" Keira asks. "As in, leaving the island?"

We all look at him with surprise.

"Yeah. I'm taking Mom and Dad's place at the resort own-ers' conference in December," Fitz says.

"Try not to sound so excited about it," I tease.

Fitz gives me a look that says he's not going to fake excite-ment for my benefit.

"I know you love the island, Fitz, but you need to get used to going to things like that," my mother says. "This place is going to be yours one day."

"It's about time you got out of here and saw the world," Grant says.

"A conference sounds exciting," Jules says. "Where are you going?"

"Costa Rica," Fitz says.

"I'll go with you!" Bellamy offers. "We'll have so much fun, and it'll be great for my social pages. Think of all the women you'll get with that kind of exposure."

"As if Fitz needs your help?" Keira says. "He has to fend women off every time he goes out."

"Think of all the new female resort customers he'll get if he's featured on my social pages," Bellamy says.

Fitz picks up his coffee cup and shakes his head. "Sorry, Bellamy, but this is a solo excursion."

Bellamy rolls her eyes. "You're no fun. What if I promise to stay out of your hair?"

Fitz looks amused. "You think I'd let you run around Costa Rica alone? Not a chance."

"Whatever," Bellamy says. "Hey, Kei, you and I should book a trip. Have you thought any more about selling your goodies online?"

"What *goodies* are those?" Grant asks sternly.

"Her tasty treats, you weirdo," Bellamy says.

"Don't worry, Grant, I'd never sell my body *or* my baked goods online. I don't like working for other people," Keira says.

"You work for other people now," Fitz points out.

"I work for myself," Keira insists. "Customers buy the things *I* choose to make."

As they dispute the subject, my father speaks over them. "Wells, how did things go in New York?"

"Yes, honey. Tell us all about your trip," my mother adds.

"He had a great time hobnobbing with the stars," Bellamy chimes in.

"I heard about that from the Bra Brigade," my mother says. "They said your picture was all over social media." Jules's grandmother Lenore is the ringleader of the Bra Brigade, a group of women who seek out private areas on the island and sunbathe in their bras. She started the group decades ago when she was a teenager. She and her friends have continued the tradition, and over the years, they've recruited their daughters, granddaughters, and friends.

"It was. I saw the pictures," Keira confirms.

"How'd you get invited to that party anyway?" Bellamy asks. "Did you go with Victory Braden?"

"You were with Victory?" my mother asks with far too much excitement. "As I recall, you showed quite an interest in her at Sutton's wedding, and it's no wonder. She's as sharp as a tack, and beautiful."

"She blew him off at the wedding," Keira throws in casually. "I don't think she's into guys like Wells."

You'd be surprised at just how into me she was.

Until she blew me off.

"What do you mean a guy like Wells?" Grant challenges.

"He's not exactly boyfriend material," Keira says.

"Neither was I," Grant says. "But things change."

"Thanks, Grant, but it doesn't matter. I didn't go with Victory."

Fitz raises a brow in a silent question.

I kept my word to Victory about our tryst staying between us and didn't tell him we hooked up Friday night. I'm not about to give him any indication of it now. "I wanted to network for the restaurant, so I asked Leni to get me on the list."

"Does that mean you saw an acceptable property in the city?" my father asks.

"Not yet, but I met with Seth Braden while I was there, and he's interested in partnering." As I say it, my thoughts return to Victory. If she really wants to forget we ever hooked up, is it fair to partner with her brother? But even that thought feels wrong. I can't shake the feeling that whatever this is between us isn't over.

"Are you sure you want to be in New York City?" my mother asks, drawing me from my contemplation. "Did you get the listing of available properties in Chaffee from Charmaine?" Chaffee is one of the other small towns on the island.

"I did, Mom, and I appreciate the time you took speaking with Charmaine, but as I said before, I want to branch out."

"I thought you didn't want a partner," Fitz says.

"I wasn't looking for one, but partnering with Seth might make sense. He and Jared Stone own a number of highly successful restaurants. Partnering could save me from making mistakes. It would also allow me to expand faster."

"Those are good points, son," my father says. "But be careful expanding too fast. You don't want to spread yourself too thin. I assume you'll talk to your attorney about this before doing anything?"

"Of course," I say.

"Are you planning on moving to the city?" Bellamy asks.

"Not permanently, right, honey?" my mother asks.

"If you're in New York, who's going to run *this* Rock Bottom?" Keira asks.

I've been wrestling with all of those questions, but now I can't think beyond Victory.

My family is waiting for an answer, so I go for a change in subject. "There are a number of things to consider before I make any decisions, like whether I should try Keira's blueberry pastry this morning instead of a scone."

"Scone," Fitz says, and snags the last blueberry pastry.

"Dude!" I complain, reaching for it.

Fitz licks the top of the pastry, which makes all of us laugh.

"You're a jackass," I say.

As I reach for the scone, Grant steals it from the platter and eats half of it in one bite, flashing a gloating grin and making us all laugh harder. I fucking love my crazy-ass family.

After breakfast, Keira is holding Stevie when he starts fussing. "Better give him to Uncle Wells," I suggest. "Your grumpiness is scaring him."

"*My* grumpiness?" she says as I take him from her. "Have you met his father?"

"Your daddy isn't very grumpy anymore, is he?" I say to Stevie. He's a sweet little guy, with soft brown peach fuzz and the cutest button nose. When Jillian asked me if I wanted to have children, I answered off the cuff. But there's no denying that every time I hold Stevie, I feel *something*. A tug, an urge. I don't know what it is, but it's definitely there. I smile down at my nephew, and he stops whimpering. "See, Auntie Kei? We understand each other."

She scoffs. "Makes sense. Your intellectual age is closer to his than mine."

I nuzzle against the baby's cheek. "Hear that, Stevie? It's called jealousy. Get used to it. Good-looking guys like us get it from every angle."

After helping our parents clean up, Keira and I say our goodbyes to the others and walk out together. "Hey, you never told me if you have a date today."

"Only with some cupcakes," she says.

Great. Now I'm thinking about Victory again. *Fucking cupcakes.* As if the idea of eating frosting off her luscious body hasn't messed with my head enough already. I really need to get her off my mind, and there's only one surefire way to do that.

"What about you? What's on your agenda today?" Keira asks.

"I'm going to catch a few waves, and then I'll head over to the restaurant."

"Have fun." She opens her car door and says, "I hear the water is colder than usual this weekend."

"Perfect." *Maybe I can freeze Victory out of my head.*

Chapter Seven

Wells

A long day at work during tourist season is usually the best distraction from anything I don't want to think about, but just like surfing followed by hours of work yesterday, work did nothing to keep my mind off Victory today. I swear the fucking universe is paying me back for a lifetime of messing around. Poker with the guys should be just what I need to take my mind off Victory. We've got an endless supply of cold beer, and the guys are in great moods. That's a recipe for a perfect night, but I'm so frigging frustrated, I can barely sit still.

"Wells, are you going to pick up those cards, or are you waiting for them to saunter into your hand?" Archer asks gruffly. With his short dark hair and neck tattoo, the barrel-chested vintner looks more like he belongs in the military than working at his family's winery.

Shit. "Sorry." I pick up the cards, but I don't give a damn about the game. I try to focus on the guys heckling each other and the music we're listening to, but for fuck's sake, nothing is helping.

"What's going on with you, Wells?" Grant asks. "You've

been out of it all night."

"Nothing. It was just a long day."

"I hear ya," Brant says. As a boatbuilder, he's always worked his ass off. "Have another beer. It's not like you're driving home."

"Want to talk about it?" Jamison offers, taking off his glasses and wiping them with the hem of his shirt.

While Brant is the charmer in their family, as my sisters pointed out, Jamison has a serious demeanor, and with his wavy brown hair and chiseled features, he's got plenty of women vying for his attention, though he seems oblivious to them.

All these guys are like brothers to me. We've gotten into trouble together, played heinous pranks on each other, and have been there to pick up whoever needs it when they fall. I trust them with my life, but I'm too frustrated to talk about what's going on with Victory. "Nah. I'm good. Thanks, man."

"You won't be good after this hand," Fitz says. "I'm going to wipe the floor with all of you."

"Dream on, little brother," Grant says.

"Put your money where your mouth is." Fitz places forty bucks in the center of the table.

That gets my attention, and I look at my cards again. I've got three jacks and two useless cards. "I'll see your forty and raise you ten." I put fifty bucks in the middle.

"Game *on*." Fitz throws in another ten.

"You're both going to wish you kept your money in your pockets." Grant tosses his money onto the pile.

"I'm out," Archer says.

"Too rich for my blood." Brant tosses down his cards.

"Fifty it is," Jamison says as he puts his cash in the middle.

"Jamison's in? It'll be my pleasure to take your money,

Remington," Fitz says with a smirk.

Jamison takes a pull on his beer without reacting. The guy has mastered his poker face.

We discard our unwanted cards, and after picking up the replacements, we do a second round of bidding, but we all hold at fifty.

"Full house," Fitz says as he lays down his cards.

"Bastard." Grant lays down three queens.

"Shit. You got me, too." I lay down my cards, and we all look at Jamison.

"You know, Fitz, when you said it would be your pleasure to take my money, I thought your bar for pleasure was pretty low. But you're right." Jamison lays down four twos and an ace. "It feels pretty damn good taking your money."

"Damn, done in by deuces," Brant says, and we all laugh.

"It was a pity hand," Fitz says. "I know Jamison needs to get pleasure any way he can, since he's not getting laid."

Jamison chuckles, but he's too cool to respond.

"Are you going to let him put you down like that, Remington?" Archer asks.

Jamison eyes Fitz. "I don't get involved in playground games."

"He's too busy building a new dating app with his buddies," Brant announces.

"Really?" Fitz lifts his chin. "Is it different from what's out there now?"

"Yes, sir," Jamison says. "In addition to the typical data used to match people, like location, age, gender, and interests, among other things, ours will use astrological data to find potential matches."

"You mean like zodiac signs?" Fitz asks.

"Sure, among other things," Jamison says. "Like the user's birth chart, their moon sign and rising sign compatibility, and more complex astrological calculations that analyze aspects of different planetary positions in your natal chart, for example—"

"Whoa, dude." Fitz waves his hands. "That's more than I need to know or can understand. But you can use me and Wells as your test subjects, right, Wells?"

"Fuck no" comes out before I can stop it, and I push to my feet too aggressively, sending my chair skidding back.

Jamison catches it before it hits the floor, and as he sets it upright, he looks at me with concern.

"What the hell, Wells?" Archer barks.

"Sorry. I'm just in a shitty mood. Count me out." I head into the kitchen with my empty beer bottle to grab another.

"What do you mean count you out?" Fitz asks as he and the others head my way.

"Yeah, when do you ever give up a chance to meet women?" Brant asks.

I shrug and scratch my knuckles. I notice Grant watching me like a fucking hawk. *Damn it.* He knows all my tells, and scratching my knuckles has been a nervous habit since I was a kid. I grab a beer from the fridge and turn my back to him as I open it.

The bastard walks around me so I have no choice but to look at him. He's wearing that all-knowing expression he's had for as long as I can remember. The one that says he's not going to let up until I spill my guts. He used it on me when our father moved out and got me to break down like the fucking sad, confused kid I was.

"*What?*" I bark.

"Whatever it is, you don't have to carry it alone," Grant says like a true military dude.

"Yeah, man. We're your friends," Brant adds. "Let us help."

They're all looking at me, like an immovable brute wall. "A'right. *Fine.* I met someone in New York, and after we hooked up, she blew me off."

Archer laughs.

I glower at him.

"Sorry, man," Archer says. "It's just that you're the king of blowing women off, and now the tables are turned. It's fucking funny."

"It fucking *sucks*," I correct him.

Grant puts a hand up, silencing Archer. "What's the big deal?"

"I fucking like her. That's what the big deal is. We got together two nights in a row and had an amazing time, but both times she left like a bat out of hell afterward. I don't think she takes me seriously."

"Do you blame her?" Brant asks. "You don't exactly have a history of long-term relationships."

"No shit." *Jesus.*

Fitz lifts his chin and says, "Is this…that woman you met at the bar Friday night?"

I'm grateful he didn't call me out with Victory, but I can't lie to him. "Yeah."

"So what happened that makes you think she doesn't take you seriously?" Jamison asks.

"Jamison, you haven't seen our boy Wells in action in a while," Archer says. "This guy can't talk to a woman without coming on to her."

"Bullshit." I level Archer with a dark stare. "Do you know how many people I talk to at the restaurant every fucking day without coming on to them?"

"Families, sure, but single women?" Archer shakes his head. "We've all seen it, Wells. Shit, you joke about it."

Jamison's brows knit, and he says, "If that's the case, it sounds like he can't hide it. She probably knew what she was getting into when she slept with him, right?"

"She did," I say sharply. "And I did, too. I thought it was just going to be one night of fun. But then we hooked up again, and now I can't get her out of my head."

"So let her know," Jamison says.

"I *did*, but she's a few years older than me, and her life is a little complicated, which I totally get." I grind my back teeth and admit the worst part. "But she called me a fucking boy toy."

The guys crack up.

"Thanks a lot, assholes." I take a pull on my beer. "Remind me never to bend your ears again."

Jamison stops laughing and studies me. "You really like this woman?"

"Yes, I do."

"Then fix it," Jamison suggests.

"How do you propose I do that?"

"If you want a different outcome, you've got to change your approach," Jamison says. "If you come across as a guy who's only good for sex, then she's right to think that's who you are. Have you tried getting to know her?"

"Yeah, Wells. That's what I did with Indi," Archer says about his wife.

"What are you talking about?" I snap. "You and Indi were fuck buddies for months before you got serious."

Archer smirks. "I was getting to know what she likes in bed.

That's important."

The guys laugh.

"All I can say is, if you're that into her, don't give up," Brant says. "I had to co-parent a puppy with Cait for her to see me for who I am."

"I don't want a fucking puppy," I grit out. "And I *know* she's interested in me. We've got a great connection. It's just that she thinks I'm—"

"A fuck boy," Fitz supplies unhelpfully.

I glower at him.

"Let's work on your approach, Wells," Jamison says. "Pretend I'm her. What's her name?"

There's no way I'm giving them her real name. "We'll call her Cupcake."

They crack up again.

"Is she a porn star?" Brant asks.

"*No.* She's a businesswoman."

"No woman wants to be called Cupcake," Jamison says.

"It's just for *now*," I argue. "I don't really call her that."

"Fine." Jamison thrusts out his chest and lifts his chin. "Pretend I'm a woman. You see me at a bar. What do you say to me?"

I walk over to him, trying to put Victory's face on him, and say, "Hey, sweet thing—" I throw my hands up. "I can't do it. You're a dude."

"Use your imagination," Jamison says.

I shake my head and huff with frustration.

"I know what the problem is. Jamison makes an ugly woman." Archer strides over. "I'll be the chick." He leans one hand on the kitchen counter, pretends to flip long hair over his shoulder, and sticks his chest out. "Okay. My boobs look fantastic in a tight black dress, and I've got a great ass and long legs." He clears his throat and speaks in a higher voice. "Hi, handsome. I'm Cherry."

"Hey, sweet…" I shake my head. "I can't do it. You give off way too much dick energy to be a woman."

Now we're all cracking up.

"A'right, you idiots, that's enough." Grant shoves Archer out of the way. "Get your fantastic boobs out of here." He crosses his arms, staring me down. "Jamison is right. You've got to change your approach. Both times, you said 'sweet thing.' That says you want to sleep with her."

"I do want to sleep with her," I say.

"I *know*," Grant says exasperatedly. "But you need to put that aside and get to know what makes this woman tick. What she's interested in and what she likes."

"Outside the bedroom," Jamison clarifies.

"I already know what she likes. Work, music, whiskey, family, anything challenging, my sense of humor, dancing, dirty sex—"

"I said *outside* the bedroom," Jamison says.

"Yeah, and?" I laugh.

"You're hopeless," Jamison says.

I hold my hands palm up. "I can't help it if she likes having dirty sex with me outside the bedroom. What am I supposed to do with this information anyway?"

"Use it to get to know her," Jamison says. "To find some common ground other than sex."

"You say that like good sex is a bad thing," Archer says.

"No, I don't," Jamison insists. "I say it like there's more to a woman than what she has to offer sexually."

"No shit. That's *why* I'm interested in her. For all the other things about her. She's smart, and strong, and snarky, but she won't give me the time of day to show her as much. *Shit*. Never mind. This is useless. Let's just get back to the game." I head over to the table.

"You sure?" Grant says. "I'm sure we can figure it out if we try."

"Thanks, but I'm good." I feel Grant watching me as we take our seats.

"Women are complicated creatures, but you're a great guy, Wells. She'll come around." Brant claps a hand on my shoulder. "And if she doesn't, a puppy works wonders."

Chapter Eight

Victory

I've been in the studio in Los Angeles for most of the afternoon listening to the Tuck Wilder Band record their first album. They sound incredible, just as I knew they would. Tuck and two of his bandmates gained a following when the band they previously played with, Surge, opened for Johnny Bad's final concert tour. That was a favor for Jillian. Surge was fantastic, and I tried to sign them, but the lead singer had only done the tour so her bandmates could gain exposure. She and the keyboardist, who's married with small children, wanted nothing to do with stardom. I don't blame them. Celebrity life isn't for everyone, and once you're in it, it's very hard to reclaim your privacy. But signing Tuck and his bandmates was a no-brainer for me. They were a small-town band without the means to go farther, and I have loved every second of helping them soar.

These guys are young and attractive, and they know how to put on a show. Tuck, the lead guitarist and singer, is a soulful twentysomething with rich light brown skin, longish dark hair, and an air of mystery that fans can't get enough of. They're going to blow this album out of the water. If only I could concentrate on *that*, instead of the lyrics he's singing.

As he sings about a woman who tastes like tequila living rent-free in his head and being unable to forget the feel of her skin and the sound of her voice, all I can think about is Wells. I don't want to think about him. I don't want to remember how he tastes or the way he seduced me with little more than words, much less the way he made me laugh and feel more than I've felt in years. But the lyrics don't lie.

I close my eyes
Push you away
But you keep showing up
Like a song on replay

My phone vibrates in my skirt pocket, startling me. I pull it out and see Leni's calling. I've been avoiding her calls for two days, which isn't fair. It's not like she knows I hooked up with Wells, but I still feel funny for sleeping with a guy she went out with—even though it was a lifetime ago.

I leave the studio and answer the call as I walk down the hall, heading for the exit. "Hi, Leni. Sorry I haven't gotten back to you. I'm in LA, and it's been a little chaotic."

"That's okay. You told me you'd be traveling when we had drinks last Thursday."

"Oh, right." *Why does it feel like that was a month ago?*

"Has the band started recording yet?"

"Yes, and they're amazing. With the marketing and PR Shea has lined up, these guys are going to shoot straight to the top."

"Let's hope so. How are *you* doing?"

The way she asked, like she knows I have a secret, makes me a little nervous, and I walk farther away from the building.

"Fine. Good. You know, busy. How about you?"

"I'm doing well, thanks, but I'm curious about a call I got on Friday."

"From who?"

"Wells Silver."

Shitshitshit.

"He asked me to get him into Cage's party," Leni says. "He said he wanted to network, and I didn't think much of it at the time, since he's looking at opening a restaurant in the city, and the restaurant is the one thing he takes seriously. But then I saw pictures of you guys together at the party, and it got me thinking. Wells has *never* asked me for that kind of favor before, and I remember the way he hit on you when you were on the island. I don't know if he knew you were going to be at the party or not, so I could be way off base, but...Actually, now that I'm saying it out loud, it sounds really far-fetched. He couldn't have known you'd be there. Never mind."

My stomach clenches. I could just let it go, but one of the things that drew me into a friendship with Leni was her no-bullshit approach to work and life. I value honesty above all else, and when it comes to the people I let in my inner circle, that's nonnegotiable. It would be hypocritical of me to expect it and not give it in return. Hoping it won't interfere with our working relationship, I say, "It's not as far-fetched as you might think."

"Really? Go on," she urges.

"Wells knew I was going to be there. Last week, after you and Shea left the bar, he walked in, and we got to talking. I don't know what kind of spell he put me under, Leni, but he was funny and charming, and we were drinking whiskey, and dancing, and..."

"*Victory.* Did you hook up with Wells?" She sounds as

shocked as she does excited.

"Yes, but please keep that between us. Everyone kept telling me to *get out there*, and *rip off the Band-Aid.*"

"You go, girl. There's no shame in that. Shea and I have been telling you to rip that particular Band-Aid off for a long time. I know it wasn't easy for you to take that step, and I'm really proud of you for putting yourself out there."

I'm so relieved she understands. "It wasn't easy, but I swear that man could charm the panties off a nun."

"That's our Wells." Leni laughs. "Did you have fun?"

"*Yes*, but that's all it was." Or rather, all it was supposed to be. I shouldn't still be thinking about him three days later.

"Wells is the perfect guy for a no-strings-attached fling. He's always up for a good time, and he doesn't do long-term relationships."

I cling to that red flag like a lifeline and use it to shore up my resolve to stop thinking about him.

"But, Vic, if you wanted him to go to the party, you could've just taken him with you."

I almost forget that was why she called. "I didn't *want* him there. He showed up at my office Friday and asked me to dinner. I told him I had a party to go to, and I told him I wasn't that into him." *Which still feels like a lie.* "We agreed to be friends, and the next thing I knew, he was at the party, acting just as charming and fun as he was the night before." *Only this time, he was also protective and attentive in a different way, and interested in hearing what I had to say.*

"Wow. That's new. Wells doesn't chase women. Did you set him straight?"

I tell myself not to overthink the fact that what she said doesn't fit the man who showed up at my office *and* at the party. "Of course." Then, softer, "After we hooked up again."

"*Victory.*" Leni laughs.

"I *know.* But it's been a long time since I've done that, and you know how Wells is. He's charming and persistent and funny." *And way too good in bed, which led to another guilt-ridden night.* "But it's over. I severed those ties, and I haven't heard from him since." I'm not about to tell her that I kind of miss our banter or that being with him wasn't just fun. It was invigorating. He made me feel sexy and alive, instead of like a widow stuck in the past.

I swallow hard against the fresh wave of guilt that brings.

"Maybe he got the message."

"I hope so," I say, wondering if she can tell the words feel like double-edged swords.

It's after six when I finally get back to my hotel room. I take a hot shower to decompress, put on comfortable shorts and a T-shirt, and snag the room-service menu on my way out to the patio.

My unconventional childhood left me with a longing to be near nature, which is why I spoil myself when I come to LA by staying in a suite at the Hotel Bel-Air, with a private garden patio surrounded by lush greenery. It isn't exactly nature's paradise, but I've gotten good at pretending. The trouble is, lately I feel like my whole existence is pretend.

As I try to escape those thoughts, I realize pretending not to have them is in and of itself part of the problem. I add *that* to the stacks of other unwanted thoughts hiding in the recesses of my mind.

Annoyed with myself, I toss the room-service menu on the table beside the lounge chair and begin flipping through playlists on my phone, looking for one that doesn't have songs that will remind me of Wells. When I find one, I hit play, silently chiding myself, because now Wells, and my conversation with Leni, are at the forefront of my mind.

I still can't reconcile that Leni has known Wells all her life and she thinks he doesn't chase women. It just doesn't make sense. I set my phone on the table, tuck my feet beside me on the lounge chair, and close my eyes, letting the music wash over me.

When my phone vibrates a little while later, I snag it and see an invitation to play WordLink, an online Scrabble-type app, from WellsSpells. A smile stretches across my face. My heart beats faster as I click the link and download the app. After a quick skim of the directions, I join the game with the username Victorious.

A message pops up in the chat feature.

WellsSpells: *Hey, friend! Thanks for accepting the challenge. If you're busy, we can play later.*

Me: *We can play. I'm at my hotel for the night.*

WellsSpells: *Where are you staying? The Waldorf Astoria?*

Me: *No. I like the Hotel Bel-Air better. It's less concrete jungleish.*

WellsSpells: *Jungleish? I see you won't be living up to your username.*

I send a laughing emoji.

Me: *Watch me take you down.*

WellsSpells: *I'd like to watch you all night long.*

A thrill skitters through me.

Me: *Do you send dirty messages to all your friends?*

WellsSpells: *??*

WellsSpells: *I was talking about watching you play the game.*

An angel emoji pops up.

WellsSpells: *What were you talking about?*

I send a deadpan emoji.

WellsSpells: *You can go first. Like I said, I like to watch.*

A heart-eyed emoji appears.

As I ponder my tiles, I can't stop smiling or thinking about those sexy dark eyes watching me come, as they had several times the night of the party. My body flames, and I try my best not to think about it as I play the word SHIFTY.

WellsSpells: *Nice.*

Me: *I was thinking of you.*

WellsSpells: *That's funny, because I'm thinking of you, too.*

He plays the word TEMPTING and sends a winking emoji.

I laugh and play SECRET. He plays HIDE.

Me: *I think you need to read more to build your vocabulary.*

I play EAT, and he plays EGGPLANT.

Me: *Seriously? Tempting, hide, eggplant? Did you rig this game?*

WellsSpells: *I don't know what you're talking about.*

Another angel emoji pops up.

I shake my head, that silly smile still plastered on my face.

We're about half an hour into our game when there's a knock at my door. I carry my phone with me and look through the peephole. I see a male hotel staff member and open the door. He's standing by a cart that has four silver serving dishes, a bottle of wine, and a wineglass on it. "Hi, can I help you?"

"Good evening. I have your room service."

"I think you have the wrong suite. I didn't order any food."

He consults the receipt. "It was ordered by Wellington Silver. Is this not his room?"

My heart skips. "It's not, but you have the right room after all. Thank you." I step aside, and he rolls the cart in. I grab cash from my purse, thank him, and tip him on his way out.

I hurry back to the cart. The wine is Riesling, and as I uncover three dishes, I find a variety of sashimi, sushi, and rolls. *Sushi and Scrabble?* He must have listened to every little thing I said when we were together. I lift the cover off the last dish, and there in the middle of the plate is a delicious-looking pink-frosted cupcake.

Wells doesn't chase women, huh?

Chapter Nine

Victory

Early Wednesday morning I'm pushing myself hard on the elliptical machine in the hotel gym as I thumb out the word PIQUED on WordLink.

I can hardly believe I have been spending all my free time playing this silly game with Wells, but it's as fun and addicting as he is. We played Monday night until I could no longer keep my eyes open, and I woke up yesterday morning to another game invitation. The thing that shocks me the most is that I'm not only playing during my free time, but I've been fitting in turns between meetings, and my usual hyperfocused-on-work brain has become sidetracked, anxiously looking forward to each notification.

We played late again last night, and I woke up this morning excited for another game, which I know has less to do with the actual game than the man on the other end of the airwaves. I look forward to our banter as much as I do the challenge of the games.

Me: *You're going down!*

WellsSpells: *Is that an invitation?*

It's a struggle not to type *yes*. We've fallen into some sort of flirty friendship that feels safer and less guilt inducing than when we're in the same physical space and can act on those impulses. Or at least that's what I'm telling myself because I don't want to stop playing or chatting with him. Although, when he texted me a picture of himself standing on the beach this morning, one arm around a surfboard, his hair wet, his wet suit stripped down to his waist, and his bare chest glistening in the sun, my thoughts were anything but safe.

Me: *You wish.*

A devil emoji pops up.

WellsSpells: *Still on the elliptical?*

Me: *Yes. Two more minutes.*

I take a selfie and send it to him.

He sends a flame and a heart-eyed emoji.

WellsSpells: *It should be illegal to be that beautiful at 6 in the morning.*

I look at the picture I sent. There's sweat dripping down my face. I forgot to pin my hair up before leaving my hotel room, and it's a mess, with several strands stuck to my cheek and neck, which makes his compliment feel even bigger.

Me: *Always the charmer.*

He plays CLIMAX.

Me: *Now I know you're rigging our games.*

WellsSpells: *Why?*

Me: *Climax?! Really?*

WellsSpells: *You're the one who told me I should read more. The climax is the high point of a story.*

Me: *If I believe that's how you meant it, will you sell me a unicorn, too?*

WellsSpells: *Geez, Braden. What did you think I meant?*

Me: *Don't toy with me, Silver.*

WellsSpells: *You want to play with a toy with me?*

A drooling emoji pops up.

My mind immediately conjures that scenario, and my cheeks grow hotter. *Ugh.* Wells Silver, what are you doing to me? I climb off the elliptical as I respond.

Me: *You're a fool. I have to get ready for work.*

WellsSpells: *Try not to think about me too much in the shower.*

Me: *That's not a problem.*

A voice in my head sings, *Liar, liar, pants on fire.*

WellsSpells: *You're right. You can never think of me too much.*

I head up to my suite for a cold shower, hoping it'll wipe yet another ridiculous grin off my face.

Half of my day is spent at the recording studio and the other half, in meetings, with welcome doses of flirty games in between. The anticipation throughout the day is energizing, and I'm itching to get my toes in the sand before going back to the concrete jungle of the Big Apple tomorrow afternoon, so I pick up a burger and fries after work and drive straight to the beach.

I leave my heels in the rental car and revel in the feel of the warm sand between my toes as I make my way toward the water. There are a lot of people at the beach and in the water. I find a quiet spot and sit in the sand.

With the late-afternoon sun on my face and the salty sea air filling my lungs, my whole body relaxes. I miss the beach, and grass, and not staring at four walls all the time, and I *really* miss relaxing. Letting my mind drift to things other than work or guilt. If I'm honest with myself, I miss living outside my box as much as I like living inside it—or need to, for my own sanity.

As I eat my dinner, I gaze out at the waves crashing along the shore, people watching. A dark-haired guy jogs out of the water toward a woman standing on shore with a dog, and my mind tiptoes back to the picture Wells sent me earlier. I'm pretty sure that gorgeous shirtless image is burned into my brain. We've had so much fun lately, it probably isn't fair to flirt with him when I'm not really looking for more, but I can't seem to stop myself.

Is it leading him on if we've acknowledged it's just a friendship?

My phone rings, stirring the nervous anticipation that has been humming inside me all day. Wells and I finished our last game of WordLink before I left the office, and I was hoping he'd start another. But he's been surprising me so much lately, I wonder if he'd call. *Do I want him to?* I don't give myself time to answer that question and pull my phone from my skirt pocket. I'm hit with an unfamiliar wave of disappointment when I see my brother Clay's name on the screen. That disappointment annoys me. I love my brothers, and I'm always happy to hear from them.

Kicking that disappointment to the curb, I answer the call. "Hi, Clay. Still floating on a cloud of marital bliss?"

Talk about a guy who I never thought would settle down. Clay was the quarterback for the New York Giants before retiring and marrying Pepper Montgomery, a brilliant scientist. The media had long-ago dubbed him "Mr. Perfect." He ate up that attention, using it to his advantage with women for many years, but somewhere along the way that changed, and I've never seen him happier than he is with Pepper.

"You know it," Clay says arrogantly, and I can tell he has me on speakerphone.

"Does that mean you're not driving Pepper crazy yet?"

"I wouldn't go that far. I like showing up at her work, bringing muffins for her staff, and getting a little something *sweet* for myself."

"I do *not* need to know that." I put the trash from my dinner into the bag it came in.

"There are worse things in the world than Clay being madly in love with his wife," Noah hollers in the background.

"You're with Noah?" I ask. "Where are you guys?"

"At the Real DEAL," Clay says. "I'm running the kids' football camp this week, remember?" Noah is a marine biologist. He lives in Colorado, where he and a few of our cousins run the Real DEAL (Discover, Experience, Appreciate, Learn), a total immersion exploratory park for kids.

"I forgot you were doing that. How's it going?"

"The kids love him," Noah says.

"Doesn't everyone?" I say. "Clay, when do you leave for your honeymoon?" They put off their trip until one of Pepper's contracts winds down.

"Not for another two weeks," Clay says.

"How're things with you, Vic?" Noah asks.

I had amazing sex with Wells, and now I can't stop flirting with him and it's really messing with my head. Other than that, I'm great. "Good. Busy as always. I'm in LA until tomorrow."

"You are? Great party town," Noah says. "Are you going to hit up some clubs tonight? Get a little *badaboom badabing*?"

I laugh. "Not everyone comes to LA looking for badaboom badabing."

"You've got to get out there sometime," Noah urges. "It's not like a great guy is going to come knocking at your hotel room door."

"*Noah*," I warn, and hear a phone ringing in the background.

"I need to get that call," Noah says. "I'll talk to you Saturday for Gram's birthday. Love you."

"You too, Noah." We try to get together for birthdays, but our grandfather is a retired archaeologist and paleontologist who doesn't know what the word *retired* means. He and our grandmother are currently on a dig in Alaska, which is why we've scheduled a family video call.

"I took you off speaker," Clay says. "You know he just doesn't want you to be lonely."

"I know."

"There's nothing wrong with getting back out there. *Wait.* Scratch that. I'm a selfish bastard, and if I die, I'll haunt Pepper for life. I don't want another man touching her. So you do you, and if I kick off, don't you dare tell my wife to get back out there."

"There's the competitive guy I know and love. How are things there? How's Noah really doing?"

"Things here are good. The business is booming, and the camp is great. Noah's as wild as ever. You know he'll never change."

I laugh. "How quickly you forget that you were once a wild boy, too."

"I don't miss that time of my life." He pauses, and then his tone turns serious. "As much as I love to joke around, if something happened to me, I wouldn't want Pep to spend the rest of her life alone. I love her too much, and I doubt Harvey would want you to, either. So maybe take Noah's advice and have a little fun."

"I'll take that under consideration. Is there another reason you called, or did you guys just feel like giving me life advice?"

He chuckles. "Yeah, there is a reason. I'm hoping you can hook me up with a few celebs who get migraines."

"Now, that's a request I don't get often. Have you looked in the mirror lately? Few people are a bigger deal than you, and you get migraines."

"I know, but this is to promote the migraine device Pepper is developing. Other celebrity sponsors would go a long way."

"Well, I have no idea which of our clients get migraines, if any, but I'm happy to put out a few feelers and get back to you."

"That would be great."

We talk for a little while longer, and when I end the call, a text from Wells pops up.

Wells: *Busy?*

Me: *Not really. Why? Want to play another game, or…?*

Wells: *That depends what the…consists of.*

I laugh softly.

Me: *Keep it in your pants, boy toy.*

I snap a picture of the water and send it to him.

Wells: *Lucky you. Are you alone? Can you talk?*

My thumbs hover over the screen. I tell myself I should take a breather from him and let this growing affection calm down, but my thumbs don't get the message, and I type, *Sure.*

The phone rings a second later. "Hey, beautiful. How's it going?"

Butterflies swarm in my chest at the sound of his deep voice. "Pretty great. I've got my toes in the sand, and I'm done working for the day. I can't complain."

"And you're talking to me, taking *pretty great* right up to *fantastic*."

And just like that, I'm grinning like a fool again. "So humble."

"Come on. You know you missed hearing my voice."

"Did I?" I tease, running my fingers through the sand.

"Well, I missed hearing yours, and it would suck if I was alone in that."

I did miss hearing it, and I miss him, too, but I can't bring myself to admit it. "Yes, it would."

"It's okay. You don't have to say it. I know where we stand."

"And where's that?"

"I don't want to embarrass you or anything, but I have a feeling you've been doodling my name during your meetings."

God, this guy. "Is that so?"

"That's not all. I think you snuck out to the beach because you can't get that picture of me in my wet suit out of your mind."

"That *is* an unforgettable picture, but I love the beach." I gaze out at the water, unwilling to confess that I wish he were there with me. "What's more relaxing than the sound of the ocean?"

"I can think of a few things we've done that leave us both incredibly relaxed."

"*Wells,*" I warn, but a laugh slips out, betraying it.

"Sorry, did I stumble onto another thing we're not admitting? No worries. So, you love the beach, huh?"

"More than you can imagine."

"Don't be so sure about that, sweet thing. I can imagine *big* beach love. It's one of my favorite places, too. Hold on a sec."

I hear him moving the phone around, and then a text chimes through. I open it and see a picture of his long legs crossed at the ankles, his bare feet resting in the sand, and just beyond, the waves are crashing against the shore. It's dark there, and I realize I haven't thought about the time difference even once when we were playing those games. We stayed up until after midnight my time, which was after three in the morning for him, and he was still up bright and early starting new games and sending me pictures.

I don't know how to process that, so I shelve it for now to pick apart later and say, "You're at the beach, too?"

"Yup. I watched the sunset."

I wouldn't have figured him to be a sunset watcher. In my head he's always out having a good time.

"I knew we were made for each other," he adds casually.

"You and your lines," I say lightly, digging my toes into the sand. "Millions of people love the beach."

"True, but they're not you and me. Can we switch to video chat? I miss your face."

My thoughts stumble, and those butterflies take flight again. "I guess." The video call rings through, and I take a deep breath before accepting it. It's dark there, but his handsome face appears, and the happiness staring back at me makes my traitorous heart leap.

"There you are," he says with the same awe as he did the first night in the hotel, and it warms me all over. "How is it possible that you got even more beautiful over the last few days?"

I roll my eyes and look away shaking my head, unable to stop smiling.

"That only makes you cuter. Are you *trying* to distract me?"

he teases. "Now I can't remember what we were talking about."

I meet his gaze again, and he's looking at me so affectionately, I feel my cheeks heat. "Would you *stop*?"

"If I must. Come on, let's go for a walk." He stands up.

"A walk?" That sounds ridiculously fun.

"Yeah. You know, when you put one foot in front of the other. We'll wander down the beach while we talk. It'll be our Wednesday Walkabout."

"Okay, one sec." I put the trash into my purse and push to my feet.

As we walk down separate beaches, miles apart, with the wind on my face and his eyes on me, it almost feels like he's right here.

"So tell me, my beautiful beach-loving friend, why do you live in the city if you love being by the water?"

"Because my life is in the city."

"But you have an office in LA. Can't you move there?"

"I guess, but I don't love it here. It's too busy, and traffic is a nightmare."

"There are tons of other beaches to choose from. This one is awfully nice." He moves his phone in a sweeping motion, showing me the beach.

"Yes, it is, but as I said, my life is in New York."

"Which begs the question, why did you choose to make your life in New York?"

I gaze out at the water for a second, thinking about it. I look at him and shrug. "It just happened that way."

He shakes his head. "I don't believe life just happens to a woman like you. You're too driven. You said you got your start scouting underdogs. I'd love to hear about that."

"I can't believe you remembered."

"I have a good memory for things that are important or enjoyable, and you are both."

"Uh-huh," I say sarcastically, secretly loving the way he flirts.

His tone turns serious again. "I want to know more about you because I like you, Victory, and that makes you important to me." His eyes spark with heat. "And I could draw you a map of the freckles on your body because you're also incredibly enjoyable."

"You could *not*." He sure knows how to keep me laughing.

"Oh no? There's a smattering of them on your shoulders."

"Tons of people have freckles on their shoulders. That doesn't prove anything."

"You have a few on your right kneecap but none on the left."

I look down at my knees, and I'm floored to see he's right. "Lucky guess?"

"Hardly." He chuckles. "In case you're wondering, my favorites are the freckles that form a heart on your left ass cheek."

My jaw drops in disbelief. I know those freckles exist, because Harvey mentioned them once.

"Shall I go on?"

"*No*. Definitely not. It's a little disturbing to think you've got a catalog of women's bodies swirling around in your head." I'm only half teasing. I have to remember that while I was coming out from a five-year sexual hiatus, he wasn't.

"Who needs a catalog when I have memories of *you*?"

"That would be a sweet line, but I bet you've said it more times than you can count."

"You'd lose that bet."

He sounds so serious, it gives me pause.

"But we can talk about that another time," he says. "Right now I want to hear the rest of your story."

It takes me a second to remember he asked about how I got started in the business, and he looks as interested as he sounds. I walk closer to the water, padding across the cool wet sand. "There's not much to tell. I went to NYU, and during my first year of school, I interned for a talent agency, basically doing grunt work. I figured that was going to be my *in*. I was laying the groundwork."

"You're a planner," he observes.

"I like mapping things out."

"So do I," he says with a devilish glint in his eyes, taking me right back to his line about drawing a map of my freckles.

"Yes, we've established that." I swear he's going to keep me smiling all night long again. "*Anyway*, a guy in my dorm played in a band, and they were having a hard time getting gigs. I couldn't get the agents I was interning for to help them, so I took a stab at it, and it turned out I was good at talking my way into the right places. As time went on, word got around, and soon I was helping other artists find their way, so I quit interning to focus on that and school."

"That's gutsy. You took on more bands?"

"A few musicians, but I helped whoever needed it. One girl had been trying to get into acting, and I helped her get auditions, and that led to other people coming to me for help. And there was a guy who had written a book, but he couldn't get in the door with any publishers, so I came up with a marketing ploy that helped catch their attention."

"Did he get a publishing deal?"

"Not for that story, but they gave him valuable feedback

that eventually led to a contract for another book he wrote a few years later, and I secured that deal for him."

"That's amazing. You became an agent at *what*? Twenty?"

"I was nineteen when I started helping the first band," I admit proudly. It's been a long time since I shared that story, and it feels good. "I wasn't really an agent, but I acted like I was."

"I knew life didn't just happen to you. That's impressive as hell. Now I need you to paint me a picture, so I can envision you doing your thing."

"A picture?"

"What can I say? I'm a visual guy, and you made me paint you pictures. Come on. Don't be shy. Paint me a scenario."

He's so different from any man I've met, I want to paint him a picture. I glance at a couple walking by, thinking about what I was like in college, and when I look at Wells, he's watching me with genuine interest, and that makes me want to share more with him. "It's not a pretty picture."

"That makes it even better."

"This is so embarrassing. I can't believe I'm admitting it to you, but I acted like I was a big deal. I printed out business cards on my little printer, and sitting in my dorm room in my shorts and Keds, I would call the offices of big-shot music producers, heads of major venues, and casting directors, and try to talk my way up the ladder, acting like they were lucky to talk to me."

He barks out a laugh. "I love that. That's not embarrassing. It's empowering."

"It only worked a fraction of time, but with every phone call and meeting I learned what worked and what didn't."

"That's incredible. What about after college? Did you keep

doing your own thing?"

"No. Once I graduated, I needed to earn a living in order to afford rent. I took a job at a small talent agency and absolutely hated it."

He cocks a brow. "Why?"

"Because they wanted me to start at the bottom, doing menial jobs, and they micromanaged me. I felt hamstrung. I stayed with them for almost two years, hoping I'd earn their trust and get promoted. But one day they pushed me to the limit, and I quit without giving notice, which at the time, nearly twenty years ago, was a professional death sentence. Everyone I interviewed with after that called my old boss for a reference, and they were told I was headstrong and insubordinate, which I *was*. But in all fairness, it was because they were running the company wrong."

He laughs. "Of course they were. So, what did you do?"

"I said fuck it and decided to go back to scouting talent myself. But I needed money for rent, and I knew if I took a job outside the industry, I would be miserable and have no time to hustle and make a success of agenting. So I put together a budget and a business plan, outlining how much money I'd need to make ends meet for six months, and presented it to my parents, asking them to basically fund my start-up efforts."

"How'd that go? Your parents seem pretty easygoing."

"They are, and if there's one thing they believe in, it's following our dreams. I'm sure they were a little freaked out that I quit my job so abruptly, but they taught us to stand up for ourselves and not to settle for less than we think we deserve. Most importantly, they believed in me, and that made me want to make them proud. They agreed to help, but they didn't think six months was enough time to get started. They gave me one year to find my footing, and I promised to pay them back every penny. I started networking and searching for talent the next day."

"That's awesome. How did you do it? Stalk social media?"

"No. I watched bands and actors on YouTube, like everyone else, but this was before videos blew up on social media the way they do now, and doing it that way didn't work for me. I needed to feel people's energy if I was going to try to rep them. I went to watch musicians at dive bars and checked out street performers, and I talked to *everyone*. It was really fun." As I say it, I realize how much I miss it. "It was that networking that led to my success. I had buttoned-up professionals referring me to the most outrageous rock bands and other creative types. I was traveling to see bands in underground bars and actors in tiny, little-known theaters, and I was excited by every aspect of it. I was able to support myself after seven months, and a year later I'd paid back every cent I borrowed."

"It sounds like you found what you were born to do."

"I have no doubt about that." The ache of longing for the life I gave up tugs at me. I struggled with that ache often the first few years after Harvey died, and I had to work hard to tamp it down and focus on my new responsibilities. "I really miss that part of the business."

"You should be out there doing it. It's your passion."

"I wish I had the time, but someone has to run the company."

"Can you hire someone else to run it?"

"And risk something happening to Harvey's legacy? No way."

His brows knit. "Would you mind telling me how you ended up with Harvey? Were you working for him, or…?"

I'm surprised he wants to know, and even more surprised that I want to tell him.

Wells

I know I'm walking a fine line, pushing Victory to open up to me about her late husband, but while I see her struggling to decide whether she'll share more, I can feel how much she wants to. I wish I could put my arms around her and tell her it's safe to open up to me. That I won't hurt her or try to *be* Harvey or one-up him. I don't want to undermine what they had. I just want to know more about her and how she came to be this incredible woman.

"I understand if you'd rather not talk about him." *But I really hope you trust me enough to share.* A sea of emotions washes over her face, and I'm sure she's going to take the out I've offered.

"It's okay. I don't mind telling you."

I exhale a breath I hadn't realized I was holding.

"It's not a very exciting story," she says cautiously.

"I'm not looking to be entertained. I want to know more about you, and love stories aren't often exciting. That's a myth. They're complicated. Look at Sutton and Flynn. Didn't he try to get her fired before they got together?"

"*Yes.* But they also survived the Amazon rainforest together, and that's a kind of excitement I can do without."

"Me too, so tell me your impossibly dull story."

That earns another smile. "Fine. I was twenty-six, and I had been working on my own for a few years. I was still working out of my studio apartment, because office space is outrageously expensive in the city, but I had things pretty well figured out by then. I had a solid reputation, and I had found my niche scouting amazing artists who just needed the right help and guidance to shine and get more substantial deals."

"This is probably a stupid question, but what kind of guidance did you give them?"

"That's not a stupid question. But the answer depends on the artist. It runs the gamut from figuring out how to better capture an audience's attention or developing their brand, or getting them professional training to strengthen their weaknesses, to helping them learn how to handle social media or social interactions better."

"You do all of that *and* market them?"

"At the beginning I did. By the time I met Harvey, I farmed out some of that whenever it was financially feasible, because my time was better spent working on deals."

"And that's what you were doing when you met Harvey? Crafting a deal?"

"Actually, no. The night we met, I was in the village scouting a band, and Harvey sat down next to me at the bar. I knew of him, of course. He was one of the biggest names in the industry, and Blank Space was one of the agencies I had submitted a résumé to after I quit that first job. But I never even got in the door for an interview."

"I bet you guys laughed about that after you got together."

Her smile broadens. "We did."

"So, I guess you make a habit of meeting your future lovers at bars in the middle of July?"

"No, I do *not*, and for the record, Harvey and I didn't get together that night." The wind blows a lock of hair into her face, and she tucks it behind her ear. "At least not like that."

"Why not? I googled him. He was a good-looking guy. Older than I imagined, but age is just a number." I was surprised by how much older he looked than her and how distinguished he appeared to be, but he was a handsome, dark-haired guy with serious eyes and a kind smile. He probably had his pick of women. The fact that he chose Victory shows he had good taste, because she's one of a kind. But what I find more interesting is that she chose him, which tells me a lot about the kind of man he must have been.

"You *googled* him?" she asks with surprise. "Why?"

"I wanted to see the man who owns a piece of your heart. I didn't snoop or look for anything about the two of you. I just wanted to see his face. I admit wanting to snoop, but I figured you'd tell me what you wanted me to know, and I don't need to know the rest."

Her brows knit. "That wasn't weird for you?"

"Not at all. It was weird knowing you'd lost someone you loved and not being able to picture him. I'm sorry if I offended you or crossed a line."

"You didn't. I'm just surprised. That's *nice*…I think."

"I promise I wasn't being creepy, and if you don't want to share the rest of your story, I get it. I can put two and two together. You met, you were attracted to each other, and you hit it off."

"It didn't exactly happen that way. He was forty-two when we met, and I admit I was attracted to him, but that alone is not enough to make me want to be with a guy."

"Good to know."

She smiles. "To be honest, I thought he was going to be full of hot air. He had this presence that commanded attention. The type of guy who walks into a room, and everyone stands up a little straighter. Kind of like your father."

"That is *just* like my father, but I can't picture you with a guy like that."

"That's because you didn't know Harvey. He was a brilliant businessman, but he never acted better than anyone. If he saw people reacting to him that way, he'd go shake their hands and sit down to get to know them. The truth is, I made a complete ass out of myself that night."

"I doubt that."

"I *did*. Once we started talking and I realized we were both scouting the band, I got competitive and acted like I was a *way* bigger deal than I really was." She laughs. "I think at one point I told him he should stop wasting his time and just leave because there was no way the band would choose him instead of me."

"You are a trip. What did he say?"

"He egged me on, asking why I thought I'd win them over, and I rattled off everything good about myself that I could think of. We talked for almost two hours and found out we both worked in the same way and had similar values about helping others and giving back. It wasn't about the money for either of us, and that's rare in our industry. It's easy to get jaded."

"It sounds like you hit it off after all."

"We did. But then he told me that if *he* talked to the band, it wouldn't matter how good I was. They'd sign with him because he had the backing, resources, and reputation to take them farther. I said I was up for the challenge, and I'd show him that he was wrong."

"That does *not* surprise me."

"I wasn't about to let him one-up me." She tucks another

wayward strand behind her ear, turning into the breeze. "But then he said he'd walk away and let me have the band if I'd come work for him. He promised he wouldn't micromanage me, and he offered to mentor me, which was a huge deal and the biggest compliment someone in my shoes could ask for. He knew my downfalls, and he was still willing to not only take a chance on me but to teach me everything he knew. He said if I had his resources and connections behind me, I'd be unstoppable."

"Sounds like a smart man. You shine brighter than anyone I've ever met, and he obviously saw that, too." I look out at the water and take a deep breath.

"Am I boring you? Do you want to get off?"

"No. I just love the smell of the ocean." I cock a grin. "I have no interest in ending our call, but I do enjoy *getting off* with you."

She smiles and shakes her head. "I keep forgetting I need to watch what I say to you."

"What fun would that be?" That earns a beautiful, slightly bashful smile as I walk beside the dunes. "So you took the job and started dating your boss?"

"*No.* I took the job and did *not* start dating my boss. I wanted to, but Harvey fought our attraction. He mentored me just like he promised he would, and we worked closely, staying late every night and working weekends. He taught me about business and negotiating and schooled me in the parts of professional etiquette I needed to hone in order to succeed. I was all guts and glory and not enough finesse, working on a shoestring budget and practically living in Keds unless I had to impress someone. He taught me more than I ever imagined possible, and we made an amazing team. We scouted talent together, and I worked my *ass* off. With his guidance, I didn't just soar. I took off like a freaking rocket, and I loved every minute of it."

She takes a deep breath, and her tone softens. "But I fell in love with him during those long nights and weekends, and even though he wasn't flirtatious, I knew he had feelings for me. So I did what any woman in my shoes would do. I *tried* to get him to give in to the heat between us without compromising my professionalism, which was hard, because we had crazy chemistry." She pauses, her gaze moving to the water and back, before she adds, "Like you and I do."

Man, I love hearing her admit that, but I'm also glad to hear that Harvey and I weren't very similar. It's no wonder she struggles with our connection. She says she's not scared, but with the strength of our connection, how can she not be? The last man she gave her all to, the one she thought she'd have forever with, was stolen away too soon.

"He must've had a will of steel," I say.

She smiles. "He did, and it was infuriating."

"Almost as infuriating as trying to get you to dance with me over the holidays? Or at the wedding," I tease.

"I danced with you at the bar last weekend, and look what happened."

"I had one of the best nights of my life." I want to push her to admit she did, too, but I don't want to scare her off, and I'm interested in knowing how she and Harvey ended up together if he was fighting his feelings, so I let that go and return to our previous conversation. "You obviously got through to Harvey eventually."

"Yeah, I did. A few months after we started working together, we hooked up, but he was still fighting it. We'd get together, then he'd back off, then we'd reconnect, and he'd back off again, and all while we were still working side by side."

That sounds familiar. "That must have been torturous for you."

"It was, but I was in love with him, so I just tried harder. It took almost a year for him to fully let down his walls, but once he did, nothing could tear us apart, and we got married shortly after that."

"That's a beautiful story, Vic. I'm glad you had each other. I wonder why he fought his feelings for so long. Was it because you worked for him?"

"Partly. At first it was because he was used to young women going after him for his money and status, and once he realized I wasn't after those things, he said he was protecting me. He knew how important my career was, and he knew people would talk shit about me if we got together, which they did. I was called a trophy wife, a gold digger, told I had daddy issues and that he had a twisted inclination toward younger women."

"People can be judgmental assholes. That must've hurt."

"It stung, but we knew the truth, and that was all that mattered. Or I thought it was. It turned out that Harvey also thought I should be with someone my own age. Someone who was, I don't know, a little wilder or something. He worried that I'd get bored, and if we broke up, it would screw with my career."

"The truth comes out. Were you a wild child?"

"No. I mean, I liked to dance and have fun, but I've never been one to drink myself silly or anything. I've always been too focused and goal oriented to go off the deep end. I'm more of a wild worker bee than anything else. But that's enough about me. I'm sorry for gabbing your ear off."

I take her cue for what it is—an end to talking about Harvey. "My ears are still firmly attached, and I enjoy hearing about your life. Thanks for trusting me enough to tell me."

"I think there must have been truth serum in the burger I ate. Want to see something pretty?"

"I'm already looking at the prettiest thing I've ever seen."

"This is prettier." She shows me the sun setting over the water, casting beautiful ribbons of oranges and yellows against the dimming sky.

"Remind me not to take your word for anything in the future. That's pretty, but it's not more beautiful than you. I wish I were there to watch it with you."

"You are." She turns her back to the water, so I can see both her and the setting sun.

It's not quite what I had in mind, but I'll take it.

After watching the sunset, neither of us wanted to end the call, so I stayed on the line as she drove back to her hotel, and I headed up to my house. That was almost two hours ago. Now we're on our beds, thousands of miles apart, lying on our sides with our phones propped up, and somehow it feels even more intimate than if we were together.

Victory's long sleek waves are frizzier and untamed from the sea air, which I love. We're talking about our favorite things. I've already learned that her favorite color is forest green, her favorite music is rock and roll, and her favorite foods are brownies and lobster. "How about movies?" I ask.

"You're going to think I'm weird."

"I already think you're weird."

"Fine, but if you make fun of me, I'm going to climb through the phone and pummel you."

"In that case, I'm definitely going to make fun of you."

"I *really* need to come up with better threats." She laughs softly. "I have a lot of favorite movies."

"Let's hear 'em."

"Well, there's *The Princess Bride*, because it's a funny love story, and the first *Rambo*, because he's an underdog and Stallone is wicked tough in that movie. I had a huge crush on him when I first saw it."

"You like tough guys, huh? I'll have to pull out my fatigues."

"Sorry, Silver, but you could never be Rambo."

"I can bulk up." I flex my arm.

"It's not that. You're too well spoken. You're not rough around the edges."

"I can fix that." I do my best Rambo imitation. *"Yo, Victory, you're looking hot. You wanna come over here and take off them clothes?"*

She laughs. "I don't remember Stallone saying that in the movie."

"I had to improvise. What else ya got? *The Matrix? The Godfather?*"

"They're good, but they're not my favorites. I love *Silence of the Lambs.*"

"So you're into tough guys and wearing human skin," I tease. "I don't think that makes you weird, but it might make you creepy."

"Shut up. I'm not telling you anything else until you give me something back."

I'm tempted to say, *I'll give you something*, and get dirty with her, but now that we're lying on beds, I don't want her to think that's the only reason I've spent this time with her. "I already told you my favorite color is blue, and my favorite foods are lobster and you."

She rolls her eyes.

"And you made fun of my movie choices, so I'm not telling you any more favorites."

"I didn't make fun of them," she insists. "I merely said it's not often you hear about guys liking *Legally Blonde* and *The Proposal*."

"Hey, Reese and Sandra are badass babes in those movies."

"I agree. It's okay. I don't need to know more of your favorites. I'm more curious about why you went into the restaurant business."

How I got my start in the business is tangled up in family history, and I don't want to weigh her down with that, so I go for an off-the-cuff answer. "It happened the same way I do everything in my life. On a whim."

"As much as you seem like a guy who *could* live life on a whim, I've seen you at the restaurant schmoozing with customers, and I heard the pride in your voice when you reminded me that you own the hottest restaurant on the island. I feel like it had to be purposeful."

"You've got me all figured out. It's all I wanted to do since I was a little kid."

"I love that. But why?"

"Because of my friend Abby's father, Olivier DeMessiéres. Their family owns the Bistro that Abby runs on the island, and her father ran it when I was young."

"I met Abby and her sisters at the wedding. It was one of the small-world moments. I've known her husband, Aiden, for years through the industry. He manages his sister Remi's acting career. He's a great guy."

"Yeah, he's a good egg."

"What was it about Olivier that made you want to own a restaurant?"

"Everything. He was the coolest guy, laid-back and earthy. He came from France with nothing more than a backpack full of money and a dream and made the Bistro a place where everyone felt like family. And he was always happy. You could tell how much he loved what he did."

"Paint me a picture so I can imagine him."

I love that *that's* becoming our thing. "He had long white hair and a scraggly beard, and he spoke with a thick French accent. Every morning he'd drink coffee and read the newspaper on the patio of the restaurant, which is right on the beach not far from the Silver House. Sometimes he'd set up an easel and paint. When I was a kid, I'd ride my bike down there just to be around him."

"I bet he enjoyed that."

"I think he did. When the restaurant was open, he'd take breaks from cooking to walk around and talk with customers. He'd sit right down at their tables and chat with them. It didn't matter if they were tourists or locals. Everyone loved him, and the way he loved his family and the people around him was *everything*. I wanted to *be* him when I grew up. I wanted to create a place where people wanted to bring their friends and family, and I wanted to help make people as happy as he did and connect with them in a memorable way."

"Well, you definitely have a knack for making people feel special and included. I think as far as business goes, we have that in common. I try to make an appearance in every department every week, just to touch base and say good morning. I never want anyone who works for the company to feel like they're just a number."

"That's exactly why I do it. It's that extra connection."

"I get it. But your parents own a resort," she says carefully. "When my family stayed there, we saw your parents at the resort often and they were friendly. Didn't they make people feel welcome back then?"

"Sure, but it was different. My old man was running a whole resort, managing dozens of staff."

"I get it. You liked the intimacy of the restaurant. How did you end up with Rock Bottom?"

"You want all the gritty details?"

She smiles. "Didn't you?"

"Ah, fair's fair. The restaurant was called Topside back then, and it was going under. The service was crappy, the food was subpar, and the owner was kind of a dick, but the location was great. I had access to my trust fund, so I made an offer to the owner, and he accepted it on the spot. He couldn't wait to get off the island, but I pissed off my parents pretty bad."

"Why? Did they want you to work at the resort?"

"No. They knew I'd never work at the resort. It wasn't my thing. They thought I was too young, too unsettled, and it was a bad investment. Their first two concerns were valid. I was right out of college, and I'd enjoyed four wild years."

"So you were a wild child?"

"I guess you could say that. For the first time ever, I wasn't seen as a Silver. I could blend in and be a normal guy, and I took full advantage of that freedom. I was a party boy and gave zero fucks what anyone thought about me. I drank too much, my grades weren't great, and I was everyone's friend. But when I bought the restaurant, I was determined to prove my parents wrong, and I did."

"I'd say so. I'm sure they're very proud of you, and Olivier must be, too."

"Thanks. I'd like to think so. Unfortunately, Olivier passed away when I was young, and he is sorely missed."

"Oh, I'm sorry. I didn't know." She yawns. "Sorry about *that*, too. What do you miss most about him?"

Nobody has ever asked me that question before, and I know she's tired, but I like that she wants to know about Olivier, so I try to keep my answer brief. "I miss being around him. He was the most authentic person I've ever known. He didn't try to live up to anyone else's standards by dressing to impress or making the Bistro glamorous. It was a renovated boathouse, and he kept it rustic. He was all about good food and real relationships. I miss his cooking, too. Especially the tarte tatin. That was my favorite dessert."

"What is that?"

"Caramelized apples with butter and sugar in a pastry dough."

"Yum. That sounds delicious."

"It's heaven on a plate. Abby is a great chef, and I'll never admit to saying this, but I've never had French food as good as Olivier's."

"Maybe because he was from France? Or because you adored him so much. How long ago did he pass away?"

"It's been more than twenty years. I was nine or ten. His wife, Ava, never got over losing him. She lost herself in alcohol."

"That's so sad."

As she says it, I realize talking about Ava losing Olivier

might stir hard feelings for Victory. "Shit. Sorry, Vic. We shouldn't talk about this. I wasn't thinking."

"No, it's okay. People die. It's an unavoidable part of life, and Olivier was special to you. Please, go on. That must have been awful for their girls."

"It was. They basically had to raise themselves after Olivier died, because Ava was like a half-functioning alcoholic. We all tried to help."

"Your family?"

"Mine, and the Remingtons and the Steeles. When Ava went downhill, all of us kids took turns working for free at the Bistro, and we did it for years. I helped on college breaks, too, and our moms helped the girls however they could. After I opened the restaurant, I hired Ava to cater small events that I knew she could handle, and I paid her three times what it cost, to be sure she could make ends meet."

"That's amazing, but didn't she realize you could have catered them yourself?"

"No. I always had an excuse. We all did things like that. Our moms had her cater lunches and birthday parties, and they'd do the same thing, overpay to be sure she could keep food on the table for the girls and the Bistro open."

"Wow. She's lucky to have lived in such a great community."

"That's what I love most about living here. Usually when kids go to school in a city or town, most of their friends are from that school. But on the island, all three K through eight schools feed into *one* central high school, Silver Island High. It doesn't matter whether you grew up on the wealthier part of the island or an old fishing town. The kids you go to school with end up feeling like family, and everyone comes together for those who need it."

"I miss tha—" Her words are lost in another yawn.

I want to ask if she misses a sense of community, or misses living near the families she grew up with, but it's late, and I've kept her up late every night this week. I tuck those questions away with the many others I have and say, "As much as I love talking with you, it's almost midnight there. You need to get some rest. You have a long flight tomorrow."

Her brows knit. "I didn't realize it was that late. It's three hours later where you are. *You* must be exhausted."

"I'm fine. I had fun tonight. I like talking with you."

"Me too. You're a fun friend, Wells, but you're a sucky playboy."

I scoff, more at her use of *friend* than sucky *playboy*, but I'll play along. "You and I both know that's not true."

"You're not supposed to become friends with your conquests."

"I don't. One day you'll realize you're a hell of a lot more than a conquest." Before she can argue, I say, "I'm sure you'll see me in *your* dreams tonight. G'night, sweet thing," and end the call.

Chapter Ten

Victory

It's nice to be back in New York. It felt good to sleep in my own bed last night and to go to the gym in my building this morning. While I was working out, Wells sent me a picture of himself jogging on the beach and an invitation to another game of WordLink. We had fun playing and chatting, but I've been at work for four hours now, and I haven't had time to play a single word since I got here. I'm surprised by how much that annoys me. I've never gotten frustrated over work coming ahead of friends before.

Then again, I've never slept with a friend before.

But I can't get lost in that right now, so I try to push those unwanted thoughts away—which feels like a habit, I've done it so often recently—and focus on the litany of excuses coming from one of my top agents over speakerphone about why his client has missed, or shown up late, to the last several events. I'm *not* in the mood for this.

"I don't want to hear any more excuses, Kevin," I say sharply, and stop pacing behind my desk. "Every time your client misses an event, this company's reputation takes a hit. You've got one week to get Bo under control. If you can't manage that, I'll give him to someone who can." I end the call, and a knock rings out on my office door. "Come in."

The door opens, and Padma peers in, surveying me. Her dark hair is pulled back at the nape of her neck, and she's the picture of professionalism in a black pantsuit. "I was going to ask if you had a minute, but you look like you want to kill someone, and I'd rather it wasn't me."

That makes me smile. "You're safe. Come in. I just hung up with Kevin Mickelson. Bo Jasper missed another engagement, and the company called *me*."

"Bo's a handful."

"I'm aware, but Kevin's an excellent agent. He's been with us for six years, and he's one of the best at reining in clients. There must be something going on with him."

Padma lowers her voice and says, "Don't take this as gold, but I heard through the grapevine that Kevin and his husband are going through a rough patch."

"Damn. Haven't they been married for eight or nine years?"

"Almost nine."

I sigh. "Now I feel bad. I just told him he's got one week to fix this, or I'll give Bo to another agent."

"Business is business. He knows that."

"I know, but I think I'll call him back and see if he has time for lunch early next week. Maybe I can suggest something to help with Bo and offer a softer out if he needs a little time to get things back on track in his personal life."

Padma smiles and shakes her head.

"What?"

"Kevin is worth the extra time and attention, but you're just like Harvey. Hard as nails when you need to be and a soft place to land when your team needs it."

As much as I love hearing that, it brings rise to the undercurrent of guilt I've been pretending hasn't been there all week. "I'm not soft," I say as we sit down.

"Being empathetic is not a bad thing," Padma says. "Seeing past the bottom line when you're the boss is a skill some people don't have. Running this place is a thankless job, and you deserve to be commended for it."

I wave my hand dismissively. "I appreciate that, but I love what I do." Although, talking with Wells about the aspects of my job that I gave up when Harvey died was a harsh reminder of what I'm missing. "And I couldn't do it without you, Padma, so you deserve a pat on the back, too. But I know you didn't come in here to pat me on the back, so what's going on?"

"I wanted to bring you up to speed on what went down with the M&O transition when you were gone. We hit a bump in the road with the software system. The company that was handling the software transition fell behind schedule, and they wanted us to push our deadline back by two months."

"That won't work. I'll call them, and if they can't meet the terms of the contract, I'll get another tech company who can."

"I already took care of it," Padma said. "And don't worry. Before terminating the contract, I checked with legal. The old company was terminated Wednesday, and the new guys were here at seven o'clock yesterday morning. I just wanted to make you aware of what went down."

"Good job, Pad. That explains the message I have from Meckland. What did Jack say about the termination?" John Meckland is the head of the tech company that was terminated, and Jack Ross is the head of our legal department. "Failure to perform?"

"Material breach of contract since we had a time-is-of-the-essence clause."

"Perfect. That leaves no room for negotiation. We're not seeking compensation, are we?"

Padma shakes her head. "No, and it was a seamless transition. That said, Meckland is not happy about this."

My cell vibrates on the desk, and Wells's name appears in a text bubble. I try to hide the stroke of happiness his name brings and turn the phone over as I say, "I'll handle him, and, Padma. I think you've made Harvey proud, too."

"Thank you." She pushes to her feet. "Are you going to the tavern tonight?"

"Yes, ma'am. No client birthday parties this week. What's happening with you? Did you end things with Corbin, or are you giving him another shot?"

"No way. I told you, three strikes are all they get, and even that is generous. But I do have a date tonight with a guy I met when I was picking up dinner the other night."

"Oh yeah? What's he like?"

"Tall, blond, and a little too dreamy."

I laugh. "I've never heard you use *that* word before."

"Dreamy? I use it all the time. You always tell me it's outdated."

"I meant *blond*. I've never heard you talk about a blond guy before."

She lowers her voice like she's sharing a secret. "I'm pretty sure he dyes his hair. At my age, men are either going gray or losing their hair. Fingers crossed he's not a nut." As she heads for the door, she says, "Want me to close it on my way out?"

"Yes, please."

With the door safely closed, I snag my phone to read Wells's message.

Wells: *Hey, beautiful boss lady. Busy day? I miss Victorious.*

I like knowing he misses me, too.

Me: *Sorry. Crazy morning playing catch-up. How's your day?*

Wells: *Better now. I know you said you usually have a solo Friday-night dinner date, but I wonder if you'd be up for something different?*

I can't believe he remembers about my Friday dinners at the tavern. I never miss dinner at the tavern for anything other than a family or work event. The fact that I'm excited to hear what he has to say has the guilt I've been trying to ignore rising to the surface again.

Me: *What do you have in mind?*

Wells: *Keeping in line with our Wednesday Walkabout, I'm wondering if you'd like to join me for a Friday Flitabout.*

I whisper, "*Friday Flitabout?*" and laugh softly.

Wells: *I want to take you on a talent-scouting outing. I found a rock band I think you'll like.*

Excitement prickles my limbs. It's been ages since I've gone to see a rock band. Guilt presses in on me. I think about what Seth said about living in a box. I like my box. But I also like spending time with Wells, and I haven't gone scouting in forever. Scouting is work. That's how this business was built. I cling to that like a lifeline to ease my guilt.

Me: *I'd love to. Where should I meet you?*

Wells: *I can pick you up at your office. Any chance you can get out at 4:30?*

My nerves are vibrating. I need to go home to get clothes to change into. I look at the emails on my computer and the messages on my desk. I could skip out now for half an hour.

There are a dozen reasons I should back out of this. But I

want to go with Wells, so I respond before I can chicken out.

Me: *Sure. I'll meet you in front of my office at 4:30.*

Wells: *Looking forward to it.*

I type, *So am I.* My thumb stills over the send icon, guilt hovering like a villain. We're friends. There's nothing wrong with that. I look at the words I've typed, and they don't sound like just a friend, do they? Am I just overthinking?

I add, *I love rock bands* and a musical note emoji and send it off.

With my heart in my throat, I grab my purse and head out of my office.

Yvette looks up as I approach her desk. "Are you leaving?"

"Yes. I have to run an errand, but I shouldn't be gone long. Can you please cancel my dinner reservation? I've got a line on a new band I want to check out. I'll be leaving the office at 4:30 this afternoon."

"I'll take care of it. I'm excited for you. You haven't done that in a long time."

"Thanks. I'm excited, too." I head out, praying I don't look as guilty as I feel about canceling my dinner reservation and skipping out of work early to have fun with a guy who is the very antithesis of my late husband.

The afternoon moves quickly, and I'm on fire, making it through my to-do list with time to spare. I change into my Bad Intentions T-shirt and jeans and push through the glass doors of my office building at four thirty on the dot. Wells is waiting out front, as promised, looking too damn good in faded jeans and a gray T-shirt that hugs his broad chest.

Our eyes connect, and that familiar zing of electricity sizzles between us as smiles bloom across both our faces. His dark eyes drink me in, and he says, "There you are," in the way that has become as familiar as the butterflies it causes.

"Hi," I say as he leans in and kisses my cheek. God, he smells as good as he looks.

"I'm glad you could make it. Thanks for tabling your solo date. That means a lot to me."

"You had me at *rock band.*"

"And here I thought *Friday Flitabout* would hook you." With a hand on my lower back, he guides me toward the waiting black sedan and opens the back door.

I take my seat and watch him walk around the car and fold his big body into the seat beside me. My nerves prickle again as the driver pulls away from the curb. I can't remember the last time I took off early from work on a whim like this, but surprisingly, I don't feel guilty. I'm excited about seeing a new band with Wells.

"How was your day?" he asks.

"Busy but good. Sorry I couldn't play WordLink much today." I did fit in a few good rounds, but we never finished the game we started this morning.

"No worries. You can't be Victorious all the time. Sometimes you have to be Victory Braden and wear your badass boss hat while you run your empire."

"True, but I'm still going to beat you."

He pats my hand. "It's good to have hope."

I love our banter, and I think I've figured out why it comes so easily with him. This is the type of back-and-forth I grew up with. My brothers and I were always teasing each other or giving each other a hard time about one thing or another. While it's different with Wells, more intimate, it's familiar and fun and puts me at ease.

"How was *your* day? Isn't this tourist season? Don't you have to be at the restaurant?"

"I spent all morning there before coming here."

"I didn't know you were going to be in the city tonight. Did you see more properties this afternoon?"

"No. I had a meeting with Seth."

"My brother? About what?"

"We've been talking about partnering for the opening of the restaurant, and this afternoon we decided to move forward with it. His attorney is putting together a partnership agreement."

It takes a second for me to process that. "You and Seth have been talking about partnering, and neither of you thought to mention it to me?"

"I can't speak for Seth, but I didn't see a reason to mention it until he and I were sure we were moving forward with it."

I guess that makes sense. "When did you guys start talking about this?"

"The morning after you and I got together at the bar. I met with him to pick his brain about opening a business here, and that's when he brought up the idea of partnering. I had to be honest and tell him I was interested in you, but I did *not* tell him we hooked up. I just said I was into you, and I hoped you'd give me the chance to get to know you better, and if that was a problem, then we shouldn't even discuss partnering."

You'd give up a business opportunity on the off chance that I'd want to get to know you better? As that sinks in, I remember that Seth said Wells was all wrong for me. "What did Seth say to that?"

"He said he didn't get involved in your personal life and that whatever did or didn't happen between you and me wouldn't affect our business relationship. I'm sorry if I overstepped, but I couldn't talk about partnering without being honest with him."

"It's okay. You didn't overstep. I'm just surprised neither of you mentioned it to me. But I think I'm the one who overstepped," I say apologetically.

"What do you mean?"

"Seth has always been my confidant, and I was sort of freaking out when I left your hotel that first night and I called him."

Wells's brows slant. "He *knew* we'd gotten together?"

"Yes." I nod, unsure if I should be amused by the situation or irritated at my brother. But if anyone has a right to be annoyed, it's Wells. I demanded he keep this between us, and I spilled the beans. "Sorry."

"It's okay. He's a loyal brother. He never let on that he knew."

"He's good at keeping secrets." *Apparently too good.* "Does he know we got together after the birthday party or that we're going to see a band tonight?"

"He doesn't know about after the party, but he invited me to dinner tonight, and I told him I'd heard about a band that I thought you should see and that we were going to check it out. He seemed happy that you were interested in scouting again."

"Yeah. It's been a while."

I glance out the window, wondering why Seth hasn't called me, given all that he knows. Maybe Seth doesn't think anything of my friendship with Wells, since he believes Wells is all wrong for me. I thought he was, too, but he's been surprising me at every turn, showing up at the party, sending me sushi, talking for hours, watching the sunset, playing games, sending pictures, and now, taking me to do something else I haven't done in years.

As I turn my attention back to Wells, I catch a glimpse out the front of the car and realize we're heading out of the city. "Wells, where are we going to see this band?"

"To a park in Baltimore," he says casually, as if he said Greenwich Village.

"Baltimore, *Maryland*? That's hours away."

"Not for us. Tessa Remington is a pilot. She's meeting us at Teterboro Airport and flying us there. There will be a car waiting to take us to the event when we land."

Shock and elation bubble up inside me. "Who *are* you?"

He cocks a grin. "Just a guy who thinks you shouldn't give up your passions and likes to see you smile."

He is so wrong. He isn't *just* anything.

After everything I've heard about Wells from his friends about being a player who doesn't take anything but his restaurant seriously, it makes me wonder if they really know him at all—and if Seth and I were both wrong, too.

Chapter Eleven

Wells

The Battle of the Bands is everything I hoped it would be for Victory. We grabbed burgers from a food truck and found a spot among the crowd in the grass. Hundreds of people are milling about, singing, dancing, eating, playing air guitars, and beating invisible drums as another band rocks out onstage. Thumping bass and screeching guitar riffs blast through massive speakers, electrifying the air and reverberating in my chest as we dance.

Seeing Victory this happy and relaxed is like watching a butterfly emerge from its cocoon. Gone are her professional demeanor and sleek, styled waves, replaced with a new carefree energy and a wild mane that bounces over her shoulders as she moves to the beat. It's hard to imagine how she reins in all this energy on a daily basis to be the woman she wants the world to see. What's even more curious is *why* she wants to.

As the song comes to an end, the crowd explodes into applause and cheers, and Victory's hands shoot up as she joins in, sending beer sloshing over the side of her plastic cup and drenching the front of my shirt.

She gasps. "Sorry!"

We both crack up as she swipes at my chest. I grab her hand, and her smile lights up the night as I pull her into a kiss. "I'm onto you Braden," I say against those temptingly sweet lips. "If you want me to take my shirt off, all you have to do is ask."

"You're so arrogant." She goes up on her toes and says, "And I *like* it," then presses her lips to mine, shocking the hell out of me. Loving this carefree side of her, I wrap my arm around her and take the kiss deeper.

When our lips finally part, I keep her close and say, "That's good, because I like *you*, too, sweet thing."

"What's not to like?" she teases as the band starts playing another song, and we sway to the music. "This is *so* fun! I feel like I'm back in college."

"I bet you were a blast in college. I wish I knew you then."

"You were probably still in high school when I graduated from college." Her beautiful eyes narrow. "How old are you, anyway?"

"I'll be thirty-two at the end of this year."

"*Ohmygod.* You *were* in high school!"

I grin and sing, "*You know I like my sweet thing a little bit older,*" to the tune of "Your Love" by The Outfield. She laughs, and I tug her into another kiss.

We dance and drink and have an amazing time for the rest of the concert. When the last song comes to an end, everyone in the park is on their feet cheering, clapping, and whistling. Winners are announced, and there's a flurry of commotion as concertgoers gather their things.

"What did you think?" I ask as we toss our empty cups in a trash can. "Are any of the bands worth sticking around and talking to?"

"I thought they were all really good, and the second band has potential."

"You liked the Naked Monkeys?"

"Yes." She laughs. "What a name."

"I like it. You can't help but smile when you hear it, and that's got to be good for marketing, right?"

"It can be. Thanks for offering to stick around and for bringing me here. This was incredible, but I need to do some research on the band and its members before I talk to anyone. What did you think of the bands?"

"I thought they were all great, but I'm just here for the company. What do you say we get out of here and explore?" I take her hand, heading toward the path that winds through the park.

She glances at our joined hands.

"What?"

"Nothing. It's just been a long time since I held anyone's hand."

"Five years?" I ask carefully.

She shakes her head. "More like thirty. Harvey wasn't a hand holder. My dad was. Sometimes he still is."

Once again, I like that what we have is different from what she had with Harvey. I lift our joined hands. "What do you think?"

Her smile reaches her eyes. "It's kind of nice."

"I'll take that." I squeeze her hand, and we walk along the path for a few minutes in comfortable silence. "I'm glad you had fun. Have you always been into music?"

"Pretty much. My dad plays guitar, and when I was young, he'd play classic rock, which is probably why I like it. He taught us all how to play when we were kids."

"I bet that was fun. Do you guys still play?"

"I don't think Clay and Flynn play anymore, but that's not a bad thing. They were never very good."

"Ouch." I laugh.

"They *weren't*. Clay didn't have the patience for it. He always wanted to be running around playing ball, and Flynn wanted to be out exploring."

"How about the rest of you?"

"Noah still plays, and he's gotten better over the years. Not to brag or anything, but Seth and I have always been pretty good at it. We used to do these ridiculous concerts for our parents. I don't know how they watched us without laughing."

"I bet you were adorable, rocking out with pigtails, on a guitar that was bigger than you."

She laughs. "Painting your own pictures now?"

"Absolutely. I want to see you play."

"I don't play much anymore."

"Don't you enjoy it?"

"Yes, very much, but life got busy, I guess," she says as we walk beneath an umbrella of trees.

"Sounds like you've slipped into the trap of living to work instead of working to live." I can't resist stopping right there on the path and drawing her into my arms. Moonlight filters through the branches, glittering in her eyes. "You need to make time to play, and I'd love to be there when you do."

She smiles and shakes her head, like I've said something silly.

"I'm serious. When I was a kid, Olivier said, 'Make a life you don't need a vacation from.' I didn't understand what he meant back then, but as I got older, I realized *that* was why he was so happy all the time. He built a life around the things he enjoyed doing and the people he loved. I know you love your work, and maybe you built a life you didn't need a vacation from with Harvey."

Her expression turns contemplative.

"I also know you're still trying to figure out what life looks like without him, and there's no rush." I caress her cheek, letting her process that. "All I'm saying is that I'm hearing how much you miss some of the things you've given up, and I like exploring them with you. It doesn't have to mean anything big or scary. I told you I want to be that friend you can rely on and share things with, and I meant it. You can call me and say you want to play jacks in the middle of the sidewalk in Manhattan, and I'll show up with a box of them and one of those little rubber balls my sisters used to play with."

She laughs a little.

"If that's not your thing, and you want to fly to the South of France and hit the nude beaches, I'm your guy."

"Nude beaches?" She arches a brow.

"I like hanging out with you, Victory. Doing things you miss, and discovering new things you like makes it even more fun."

She grabs my shirt with both hands and bangs her forehead against my chest. "Why do you do this to me?"

"Do what?"

She tips her face up, confusion riddling her brow. "Make me like you so much when I'm trying not to."

"It's a curse. Just go with it." I press my lips to hers, and she smiles against them. I take her hand again and start walking, hoping to keep her from overthinking. "So you wanted to be a rock star when you were little, and Victorious was your rock-star name, wasn't it?"

"*No*, and I didn't want to be a rock star."

"I think you did," I tease. "Did you go to many concerts as a kid and pretend you were the one onstage?"

"*No*. But my parents did take us all to see Bon Jovi's Crush tour when I was a teenager because I was so in love with them."

"A'right, Mom and Dad. That's awesome. What *did* you want to be when you grew up?"

"I don't think I had any idea of what I wanted to be. I spent most of my time wrangling my younger brothers, trying to keep them in line and organized. I guess I always thought I'd be someone who did something like that."

"A bossy people wrangler?"

"Exactly," she says proudly. "And I'm damn good at it."

As we come out from under the umbrella of trees, I spot a playground. "Check it out." Tugging her with me, I jog in that direction.

"Why are we running?" She laughs, hurrying to keep up.

"You have to run when you see a playground. It's a rule." I grab the chains of one of the swings and hold them. "Your seat, m'lady."

"Seriously?"

"You know you want to. Now get that fine ass of yours on this swing."

"Always the charmer." She sits on it and swings a few inches forward and back as I get comfortable on the one beside her, matching her slow pace. "This is kind of fun. I haven't been on a swing in years."

Everything is fun with you. "Does it bring back memories?"

"Not really. We never had these kinds of swings." Holding one of the chains, she angles herself toward me. Her hair falls over one shoulder, and she drags the bottom of her flat-soled black boot as she swings backward and lifts it so it skims the ground as she swings forward. "Our home base is in Ridgeport, Mass, but we grew up traveling overseas for months at a time for my dad's job. We lived in remote villages in tents and huts and modest homes that were more like shacks. Our swings were mostly vines or homemade contraptions."

"Now I have to know what your father does for a living."

"He and my mom are wildlife biologists, but my mom works as a wildlife photographer. She gave up her job as a biologist after Seth was born to have more time for us, so we could continue traveling with my dad. They weren't about to slow down just because they had kids."

"Sounds like they took Olivier's advice and made a life they didn't need a vacation from."

"You know what?" she says with awe. "I think that's exactly what they did. We traveled all over the world—South America, Asia, Africa—exploring mountains, rainforests, and jungles, learning about nature and other cultures. My grandfather is an archaeologist and paleontologist, and we spent time with him and my grandmother when they were at dig sites, too. That was Flynn's favorite thing to do."

"I remember Flynn saying your family traveled a lot when you were kids, but I didn't realize it was that extensive. That's amazing. Did you enjoy it?"

"Mostly. It was all I knew, and I enjoyed learning about different cultures and being part of their communities and holiday celebrations, like multifamily feasts we'd all help cook. My family didn't have normal holidays with decorated trees and lots of gifts. We made each other gifts, and every year my parents would make a treasure map that my brothers and I had to work together to figure out and to find our presents."

"Treasure maps? That must've been fun."

"It was, and we still do it. When we went to that Bon Jovi concert, we were living in Portugal, and my parents made this elaborate map that included clues that we had to work together to figure out, and the answers led us to the airport. We didn't have any idea where we were going, and we ended up in Germany at the concert."

"That's *wild*. And they still make treasure maps?"

"Yes. It's complicated now that we live in different places, but they still make them, and we still have to work together to find our treasures. That's how we ended up on Silver Island last Christmas."

"That's awesome. I'm formally lodging a request for a treasure map."

She smiles. "Maybe one day you'll get one."

"Yes." I do a fist pump and steal a kiss.

"You're a nut. What are your family holidays like?"

"Very traditional. We all get together for Thanksgiving and Christmas, and we spend an afternoon decorating my mom's tree. The island hosts a flotilla every year, and we all help decorate the boats, and there's a community tree lighting in the park by the monument and the annual holiday dance at the Silver House, but you know what that's like."

"I enjoyed that dance."

"Yeah? Then why didn't you dance with me?"

"Probably because I thought we'd end up naked on the beach."

We both laugh.

I push to my feet and hold out my hand. "There's no chance of you ending up naked on a beach now."

"You want to dance? Here?" As she looks around, a couple walks by on the path.

"Don't act like you don't want to." I take her hand, drawing her into my arms, and sway to the nonexistent music. "You're always safe with me."

"Who are you kidding? That charm of yours is dangerous."

I waggle my brows and twirl her in the moonlight. As I gather her in my arms again, swaying slowly, I say, "What did you like about the holiday dance?"

"Seeing the community come together. I could feel how close everyone was, and now that I know what you and the others did for Olivier's family, it makes it even more special."

"You haven't found community in the city?"

She shakes her head. "No, and I really miss it."

"Then you'll have to come spend some time on the island."

She gives me a look that says I'm overreaching.

"What? You know you'd enjoy it." I twirl her again. "But maybe you should tell me what you didn't like about the places you lived, because there may be some areas we need to avoid on the island."

"I visited quite a few places when I was there with my family. The island is nothing like the jungles or rainforest where we lived."

"I don't know about that. Our wildlife refuge has a lot of creepy-crawlies."

She gives me an amused look. "My parents spent my entire childhood teaching us how to respect nature. I know which creepy-crawlies to stay away from and which ones I can eat."

"Then you're definitely staying in my tent, because I'm *not* a fan of spiders."

"So now we're camping on the island? Am I building us a

shelter in the woods, too?"

"Maybe."

"Well, you *did* fly me out here for this incredible night. I guess the least I can do is protect you from creepy-crawlies."

"I knew I could count on you." I hold her tighter, gazing into her eyes. "One day you'll see you can count on me, too." I lower my lips to hers in a long, slow kiss, aching to be closer. When our lips part, I take her hand and say, "Let's explore the park," hoping a walk might ease that ache. "Tell me, world traveler, what *didn't* you like about traveling?"

"You mean in addition to the obvious, like the lack of flushing toilets and showers in some of the places we lived?"

"That would not be fun. I, too, like my creature comforts. So yes, in addition to those inconveniences."

"We didn't always speak the local languages, which made it hard to make friends. Eventually we'd learn enough to get around and we'd find other ways to communicate, but I never really felt like I fit in with the other kids."

"Because of the language barrier?" I ask as we walk around a tree.

"That was part of it, but it was bigger than that. I think it was just me. I don't know if it's just who I was always meant to be or because of the way we grew up, but as I got older, I didn't want to roam the landscape and build forts or search for animals or plants. I wanted more, and I never really knew what *more* was. I just knew I wanted it."

"I understand that."

"Do you? Because it took me a long time to even figure out what I was feeling."

"I definitely do. I have a great life on an island I love and a successful business, and I still felt like there was something more out there for me. I didn't know what it was, but that's why I started looking to expand my business. I felt like something was missing." What I don't say, because I don't want to scare her off, is that since we've gotten closer, I'm realizing that wasn't the only gap that needed filling. "Sometimes what's missing in our lives isn't easy to decipher."

"You can say that again. I spent a lot of time feeling like I was floundering. We were homeschooled while we traveled, and we didn't have a lot of structure. I finally realized *that* was part of the problem. I like having things mapped out, knowing what's expected, and working toward bigger goals." She glances at a seesaw as we walk past. "My parents are incredible. They built this amazing life for us and tried to do things we'd each enjoy, but as I got older, all I wanted was a normal life with public school and friends I could relate to. Thankfully, by the time I was a teenager, Seth and Clay felt the same way, and we fought to go back to Ridgeport permanently. My parents finally agreed, and we moved back when I was fifteen."

She steps onto a large rock, her hair curtaining her face as she comes down the other side. "Sometimes I feel guilty about making my parents come back."

"I understand why you feel guilty, but you shouldn't." That brings her eyes to mine, and I see tension around them. "Your parents had fifteen years of living out their dream, and I'm sure it wasn't easy to live like that with five kids. Maybe they were ready for some normalcy, too."

That tension eases. "Maybe."

"Were things better after you moved? Did you make friends?"

"Yes, but I never felt like I fit in there, either. I grew up with a gaggle of rambunctious brothers in far-off lands. My life wasn't about hair and makeup or parties and cute boys. I didn't even know who most of the celebrities were that kids were talking about. It was a whole different type of culture shock, which made me feel a step behind. And for a girl who liked to excel, that made it even harder."

"Knowing how into those things my sisters were as teenagers, I can only imagine how uncomfortable that was for you."

"It was, and my parents tried to help, but it's not like my mom is about anything superficial, either, so it was kind of like the blind leading the blind." She laughs softly. "She took me to salons and out shopping. We bought gossip magazines, and I tried to copy other girls' hairstyles and clothing trends. My dad tried to help us, too. He took us to local restaurants and places where kids our age hung out, and I learned how to fit in, but I always felt like an impostor."

I'm all too familiar with impostor syndrome, and I hate that she experienced it, too. I reach over and take her hand, wanting to heal all her bruised parts. "I'm sorry you felt that way. I hope you don't feel like an impostor with me."

She looks at me for a long moment before responding. "I don't feel like that with you, and that's a really nice feeling."

"Good." I lean in and kiss her. "Because I think you're as real as it gets."

Chapter Twelve

Victory

I can't believe I confessed so much to Wells. I always thought my parents were a little selfish for the way they raised us, but I never admitted that to a soul. Not even to Seth, for fear he'd think I was ungrateful or selfish. I hope Wells doesn't see me that way. "I must sound like an entitled brat complaining about living places most kids can only dream of."

"I don't think you sound like that at all. I know all about impostor syndrome, and it sucks. Try growing up as a Silver and wishing you were a Steele or a Remington."

That surprises me, but something in the way he said it tells me it's true. "Why did you feel that way?"

"Because being a Silver comes with certain expectations, and like you, I craved normalcy. I love my parents, but they did some stuff when we were kids that messed me up."

My chest constricts. "What do you mean? They seem lovely."

"They are, but if they were having problems, you'd never know it. They fought a lot when we were young, but never in public, and we knew better than to talk about it. It's not like they ever told us not to—it's just part of being a Silver. We learned early on how to put on our *happy family* faces, and my parents were the king and queen of it."

"*Oh, Wells,*" I say softly, holding his hand a little tighter. "That must've been stressful."

"It wasn't fun, that's for sure." He motions across the grass to more playground equipment. "Let's check that out."

He leads me toward an enormous climbing area with steps and slides and a bridge between landings, and I can tell he's uncomfortable. "We don't have to talk about this."

"I don't mind talking about it." He stops in front of a colorful rock wall that leads up to a landing and guides me in front of him, then pats my butt. "Go on up."

"There are steps over there." I point to the other side of the equipment.

"I thought you grew up in the jungle, but if you can't handle it," he teases, and moves to the side, clearing a path for me to walk around to the steps.

"*Please.* I'll beat you up it." We race up the rock wall laughing, and when we get to the landing, he boxes me in against the railing and kisses the hell out of me. "That's one way to distract me from the conversation."

"There's not much to distract from. My father moved out when I was six and they said nothing would change, but of course everything did." He takes my hand, talking as we walk from one landing to another, and I get the sense he needs to keep moving as he shares this with me. "Grant was angry all the time, and Fitz got really quiet. I think that's when he started trying not to cause trouble, and my sisters were so little, they cried a lot, wanting to know when our dad was coming home."

"That's really sad." I look up at him as we start crossing the bridge. I want to wrap my arms around him, but he doesn't meet my eyes, so I let him lead us to the next landing. "What about you? How did you handle it?"

"I remember doing whatever it took to keep my sisters happy. Keira was about four, I think, and she loved pretending to be a baker. We'd have tea parties with Play-Doh cupcakes, and since Bellamy was into frilly princess dresses, I'd dress up in my suit and be her prince."

"That is the cutest thing I've ever heard. What a great brother." I hook my finger into the waist of his jeans. "But that was for them. What about you? Your world was turned upside down."

He shrugs. "I'm told I acted out, which I'm sure is true. I was worried about my mom. She tried to hide her sadness, but we knew how hard it was. I used to pick her favorite flowers and put them on her pillow with notes telling her I loved her."

"I bet you made her day every time you did it." He does such a good job of hiding his big, loving heart behind his cocky bravado, it's easy to see why it's overlooked by so many people. Including myself initially. I have the strange thought that maybe Harvey had a hand in us getting together on the anniversary of the night Harvey and I met. But that thought is too big to wrestle with right now. I tuck it away and say, "Your poor mom. It must have been so hard taking care of five kids, and trying to keep her emotions in check in front of all of you, when she was heartbroken, too."

"As an adult I can look back and see it must've been excruciating for both of my parents, but as a kid I just wanted to make it better. It was all very confusing. I mean, they fought, so I knew something wasn't right. But after some time apart, they started acting like they were happy and in love again. Sometimes my dad even spent the night at our house, but we never spent the night at his, which was also confusing. Needless to say, I cried myself to sleep a lot. But again, when we were in public, we pretended things were normal, even though everyone in town knew our parents weren't living together."

"So, while your family was falling apart, you'd go to school, or out to play, and act like you weren't sad?" Imagining him as a confused, scared little boy breaks my heart. "You weren't kidding about understanding impostor syndrome. No wonder you wanted to be a Remington or a Steele."

"They had issues, too, but at least with them, what you saw is what you got. If they were upset, they didn't hide it. They talked it out and made up and were smiling again. I know *now* that my parents kept up appearances because of the Silver House, and I get it, but because of that, it was hard to know what was real in my family. That's probably why I spent a lot of time at Leni's house. Her mom would make snacks and tell us funny stories. All three of our families were together a lot, and all of us guys were always pranking everyone and having fun."

"I've heard about those pranks. Leni said her brothers used to scare the crap out of her and Jules when they were little, and didn't Sutton's dad prank Archer by saying Flynn was a porn star and dating their grandmother?"

Wells laughs. "Yeah. Miles Long, but those pranks are nothing compared to others they pulled. One year Jock and Archer shaved a penis into the back of Levi's hair, and he went to school like that without knowing it." Levi is Leni's twin brother.

I laugh, then quickly cover my mouth. "That's horrible."

"Yeah, but it was funny. Our fathers went to college together, and they were the original pranksters, so we had to carry on the tradition."

"What kind of sons would you be if you didn't?" I tease, earning a smile.

"Exactly." He takes my hand and heads to the top of a curly slide. As he sits down, he says, "Our pranks have escalated over the years, and no one is safe from them."

"I'll keep that in mind next time I'm there."

He pats his legs. "Climb on, sweets."

I'm loving this jaunt into youthful times as I climb onto his lap. "I can't imagine your father as a prankster. He seems buttoned-up. Your parents can't be all that bad if your dad was involved in pranks."

"Like I said, I love my parents. They just did some confusing shit when I was young, which I guess all parents do on some level."

"Maybe it's a rite of passage to give your kids something hard to deal with."

He pushes off the edge of the slide, and we whip down it, both of us laughing, and we stumble to our feet at the bottom. He pulls me into his arms and kisses me. "Back to the swings?"

"Sure. Do you have good childhood memories other than the pranks?"

"Absolutely. Some of my best memories are from when all of our families would get together. We'd turn on music and barbecue and play games in the yard, or my father would take everyone out fishing on his yacht. Even though my parents weren't living together, things seemed more normal when we were all together like that."

"You could disappear into the fantasy and pretend."

"For a little while. But then we had our family dinners a few times each week at the Silver House, which is where abnormal came in. We'd have to get dressed up and act the part of the perfect family, because it was the Silver House and we had a reputation to uphold for the guests, none of whom knew my parents had separated."

"That had to be awkward."

"Sometimes it felt painfully fake, but other times, what started as pretending ended up feeling real. I guess you were right about the fantasy. There were lots of times when I hoped my father would come home with us for good, but of course he never did, and that made me angry and sad all over again."

"And here I thought that as Silver Island royalty, you had no idea what hardships even were."

He scoffed. "You're probably not alone in thinking that."

"But your parents act like they're madly in love. How can that be fake?"

"Their love isn't fake. That's one thing I learned as time went on. Other than that period of fighting, which was probably only a couple of months, they've always been happy, like best friends who are in love."

"When did they move back in together?"

"They never did. They still don't live together."

"Are you serious?"

"Yes. I know it's weird, but it works for them." He holds the swing out for me as he did before, and as I sit down, he says, "A couple of years ago they got us all together and apologized. I think something happened between them and Grant that brought it on." He lowers himself to the swing. "They told us they were so young when they had us, the pressures of family life and some personal things they didn't divulge got the better of them, and they didn't want to confuse us by having us spend nights at my dad's house. They thought they were doing the right thing."

"I can see that. It makes sense."

"Yeah. They did the best they could. We found out all sorts of things we didn't know that night. We found out my dad was a painter, which explains where Grant got his talent from, but none of us knew that until then. We didn't know my father didn't want to take over the family business, or that he and my mom had plans to go to Paris after college so my dad could make a name for himself as an artist. My father wasn't given access to his trust fund until he was older. He was literally going to make his way as a starving artist, and my mom was all in."

"That's so romantic."

"I know. I can't imagine my parents like that. But then they found out my mom was pregnant with Grant, and they did the responsible thing and went home to make their life on the island. I think that's why they made sure we got access to our trust funds when we turned twenty-one, so as adults we wouldn't be stuck choosing between the life we wanted and the one we needed."

"Wow. My parents forced us to live out their dreams, and yours gave up their dreams for your family. It's amazing how life is so different for everyone."

"It really is. We also learned that they spent every night together but that they like living apart because it's exciting, and they don't get on each other's nerves that way. The exciting part was a little TMI for me."

"I bet." I laugh. "I can't imagine not wanting to be in the same space as the person I love, but most families probably can't imagine living the way my family did, either. Did growing up like that make it harder to have relationships?"

"Yes, but I never realized how it messed me up until high school."

"What happened in high school?"

"Leni didn't tell you?" he asks with disbelief.

"She just said you went out for a while and had to keep it secret because she was afraid her brothers would get mad."

"That's true, but I fell hard for her. She was my first love. The one who got away."

Holy shit. A pang of jealousy shoots through me. "She never told me that."

"Probably because she wasn't in love with me *and* we were just kids." He presses both hands to his thighs. "Or maybe because I cheated on her with Abby and hurt her so badly, she carried a chip on her shoulder toward me for years."

The pit of my stomach sinks, and I can't hide the shock widening my eyes. "You cheated on her?" *I can't believe she didn't tell me that when I told her I'd been with you.*

"I'm not proud of it, but yes," he says remorsefully. "I was terrified of my feelings for her. I thought if my parents couldn't make their relationship work, there was no way I could, and in my stupid teenage brain, cheating was the only way I could end it for good."

"That's an awful thing to do to someone. Why didn't you just break up with her?"

"I loved her too much. I knew I wouldn't follow through with it. But after she found out and we broke up, I realized how stupid I'd been. We were both devastated. I tried many times to explain why I did it, but she couldn't even look at me, and I don't blame her. It was a dick move, and I have *never* cheated on anyone since. Not once, and I never will."

"Because you hurt her so badly?"

"I wish I could tell you that was the only reason, but the hurt I caused her was only about half as bad as the pain and guilt I caused myself. Remember, she didn't love me. I was the one who was madly infatuated. It took me a year to get over her, and we remained friends, but it wasn't the same."

"She's never said anything to lead me to believe she thinks badly of you."

"Maybe that's because a couple of years ago, when she and Raz got together, she finally let me explain. I think that helped both of us."

I stare absently out at the trees in the distance, swinging a little, thinking about the things he shared and our complicated childhoods and lives. It's no wonder he went the player route after having his heart broken when he was young. We're not so different after all. He took the left fork in the road, and I took the middle one after Harvey died, cutting off men altogether. I wonder if there is a right fork. Maybe that's what we're on now. A path of deep friendship, attraction, and understanding.

"Second-guessing being with me?" he asks.

I meet his worried gaze. "No. You were a teenager. Lots of kids make that mistake, and for worse reasons. I was just thinking about how our parents' decisions and life affected us."

"This is going to sound bad, but at first when they told us they'd always been madly in love and when we were kids my dad would sneak into the house to spend the night and leave before we got up so they wouldn't confuse us, I thought it was selfish."

"I'm relieved to hear you say that."

"Why?"

"Because I felt that way about my parents, too, but I've never told anyone because I was afraid they'd think I was being ungrateful or selfish."

He squeezes my hand. "I don't know if that makes us selfish

or not. Maybe everyone needs to be a little selfish. Otherwise would we ever really succeed at anything?"

"Good point. I don't hold my childhood against my parents or anything, but if I ever have kids, I'll think twice about what I put them through." I walk my feet back and swing slowly. "Life would've been a lot easier for me if I were more like you. A laid-back partier who's everyone's friend." That's actually one of the things I like most about him. He's comfortable in his own skin, easy to be around, and gets along with everyone.

"I'm not a party boy anymore."

"Just a playboy," I tease, putting my feet down to stop the swing.

He shakes his head. "You keep saying that, but I'm really not. I like to flirt, and I enjoy a fling now and then, but it's not like I'm sleeping with a different woman every night."

I hold up my hand. "I don't want to know."

"Yes, you do." He grabs the chains to my swing, turning me toward his wolfish grin. "You're the only woman I want to be sleeping with, and I don't see that changing anytime soon."

I can't stop smiling even as I say, "I didn't ask."

"But you wanted to know." He slides one hand beneath my hair, palming the back of my head and drawing my lips to his in a delicious kiss. "Want to have some fun?"

"That's a loaded question."

He flashes a playful grin and lets go of my chain. "Let's see how high these things go." He starts swinging.

I laugh.

"Afraid you can't beat me?" He swings higher. "Where's that adventurous girl who danced with me at the concert?"

"She's about to kick your butt." I grab the chains of my swing, push back until my legs are straight, and swing forward as hard as I can.

"Is that all you got?" he taunts.

We egg each other on, pumping our feet, swinging so high we bounce at the top. The sounds of the chains creaking and our teasing and laughter fills the air.

"Let's see who can jump farther!" he shouts.

My heart races. "Are you crazy? I'm not jumping!"

"You definitely won't be victorious with *that* attitude. Are you afraid?"

I haven't jumped off a swing since I was a kid, so yeah, maybe I am a little afraid, but I'm not about to admit it. "No!"

"Yeah, you are!"

"Shut up. I am *not*!"

"Okay, then! On the count of three," he shouts.

"You're nuts!"

He laughs. "Be nuts with me, sweet thing! *One!*"

I try to remember how I gripped the chains when I was a kid. As I move one hand so it's upside down gripping the chain, my elbow pointed out, I see he's doing the same thing. My competitive nature drives me to pump my legs harder as I grip the other chain.

"Two!" he hollers.

We pump our feet, and as we swing forward, we both yell, "*Three!*" and jump. We fly through the air. My arms flail, and for a split second, as the world sails by, our eyes meet, and I feel young and free and not at all afraid. Our feet hit the ground, and we tumble into a tangled heap in the grass, cracking up.

"I can't believe you got me to jump!" I say through my laughter and roll off his chest onto my back.

He leans over me. "I can't believe you doubted I could." He presses his lips to mine, and we both laugh again. "Let's stay here tonight and explore the Inner Harbor tomorrow."

My heart nearly stops out of sheer nervous excitement. "What about Tessa? Isn't she waiting for us?"

"I *might* have told her that there was a chance we'd stay. I wasn't sure if you'd want to go bar hopping or take advantage of me. I know how you are."

"*Might* have, huh?"

"Believe me, I wanted to assume we'd stay and plan a whole night, but I feel lucky that you gave up your regular Friday-night dinner to come with me, and I didn't want to push it."

I'm having such a good time, I haven't even felt guilty about not going to the tavern. "You're serious? You really want to stay?"

"Absolutely. When's the last time you explored someplace new?"

"I don't know. I usually work on the weekends."

"I got that impression when you said you buried yourself in work. Do you have anything lined up that can't wait until Sunday?"

"No," I say honestly, but even if I did have plans, I'd cancel them to stay with him.

He starts to get up and takes my hand, tugging me up with him, and then he wraps his arms around me. His coaxing dark eyes make my heart race. "Then let's do our thing and go on a Saturday Scoutabout. See what trouble we can get into."

I kind of love this. "Since when is this our thing? You're just making up names for every day of the week."

He gives me that devilish grin I can't get enough of. "Gotta start somewhere."

I laugh, and he crushes his lips to mine. "Where are we going to stay?"

"That's part of the adventure. Let's see what's around here."

He pulls out his phone and searches for nearby hotels. As we scroll through them, there are several typical-looking waterfront hotels. When we come to one that's built on a pier, we both say, "*There*," and laugh that we chose the same one.

"You've got good taste, Braden."

"So do you, Silver. It reminds me of your restaurant."

"I'd love to find something like this for my restaurant." He angles the phone toward me. "Look. It says it used to be a shipping warehouse."

"Maybe you can convince them to sell it to you and you can open your restaurant here."

"You can't get rid of me that easy." He drapes an arm around me. "Let's go get a room, sweet thing."

Chapter Thirteen

Victory

I wake up in the same position as I fell asleep, wearing Wells like a second skin. My hips are nestled in the curve of his body, his arm draped around my middle. Last night left me feeling euphoric, from the surprise plane flight and concert to our laughter and deep conversations and the incredible sex that followed. I haven't slept that soundly in years. But waking up in Wells's arms in this incredible hotel?

This is the icing on my euphoria cake.

I close my eyes, reveling in the feel of him. He makes a sleepy sound, his warm breath coasting over my cheek as he holds me tighter. It feels so good, I snuggle deeper into him, bracing myself to be swallowed by guilt.

Minutes tick, stacking up like bombs waiting to explode, but the guilt doesn't come. My pulse quickens as confusion sets in. I open my eyes, trying to figure out why I don't feel guilty. Is it because I didn't wake up in the bed Harvey and I shared or because we're not in the city?

Maybe it's because I really like being with Wells, and I've man-aged to block out the guilt. On the heels of that thought comes,

Could this be the natural course guilt takes? Easing off when I'm not clinging to it like a lifeline?

I should untangle myself to figure that out, but no part of me wants to leave his arms. I close my eyes again, breathing deeply, telling myself it's okay to enjoy it.

"Morning, beautiful," Wells says in a gravelly voice, and nuzzles against my neck. It's as titillating as the feel of his arousal pressing against my ass. He shifts me onto my back and moves over me. His body is enticingly familiar, and he looks as content and happy as I feel, like there's no place else he'd rather be, as he whispers, "There you are."

That gets me every time, making my insides go soft. "Morning."

"Did you sleep okay?"

"Mm-hm. Did you?"

"Better than ever. I'm glad we stayed."

"Me too." I wonder if admitting that will bring guilt, but it doesn't.

"I like waking up with you, Vic." He brushes his nose along my cheek and presses a kiss there. "I could get addicted to this."

I don't want to admit that if I were always guilt free, I could get addicted, too. "You're just addicted to sex," I tease.

"That's not true. Sex is great, but holding you while you fall asleep and waking up with you snuggling in my arms? That's different. It's *better*."

Just as I process that he feels it too, he dips his head to kiss me. I press my lips together, turning my cheek. "I haven't brushed my teeth." We stopped on the way to the hotel last night and bought toiletries.

"I don't care." He lowers his lips to mine in a slow, sensual kiss, flooding my entire being with desire and leaving no room for worries. "You taste so fucking sweet," he whispers. "I want to kiss you all day."

"Then do it."

His eyes flame and his mouth covers mine in another smoldering kiss. I meet every stroke of his tongue, every guttural, appreciative sound, with greedy ones of my own. His heart hammers against mine as we rock and grind. He pushes his hands into my hair, kissing me harder, more possessively, and then he slows us down, kissing me sweetly and seductively, then roughly and devouringly, and then sweetly again. My head spins as I try to keep up, want and need pulsing through me like thunder.

He tears his mouth away with a wicked grin and kisses his way down to my breasts, grazing his teeth over one sensitive peak and then sucking it to the roof of his mouth, the way he knows drives me wild. "*Wells—*" flies from my lips, and my hips shoot up, my nails digging into his shoulders. He does it again as he shifts to the side, moving a hand between my legs, and *good Lord*, he teases, sucks, and taunts, playing my body like his own personal fiddle. It doesn't take long before I'm crying out his name, bucking and writhing, consumed with pleasure so intense, I'm sure it'll steal my last breath.

I ride that high, soaking in every spine-tingling second. When I finally sink to the mattress, a quivering, panting mess, his mouth covers mine, and he breathes air into my lungs. We kiss for so long, our passion takes over, and we're pawing and groping, nipping and moaning.

"Fuck," he grits out. "You're killing me."

"I'm not sorry." I laugh, earning a sexy smile.

"My evil temptress." He gives me a quick kiss, then stretches across the mattress, reaching for his wallet on the nightstand. *"Fuuck."*

I watch him through a fog of desire as his head falls between his shoulders. "What's wrong?"

"We used the last condom. Sorry, sweet thing. I should've stocked up at the store last night."

The apologetic look on his face makes me want him even more, but I can't help teasing him. "You really are a sucky player."

"I told you I'm not the player you think I am, but don't worry, I won't leave you hanging."

He starts to kiss his way down my body, but I stop him. "I'm on birth control, and unless there's a reason to worry, I want this."

The well of emotions in his eyes makes my stomach flip. "There isn't."

"Then get over here."

The head of his cock presses against me, but he doesn't rush. He laces our fingers together and gazes deeply into my eyes. There's something so intimate about the way he's looking at me, I know this is one of those moments I'll never forget. One of those moments that changes things. That should terrify me, but I can't muster fear or worry or anything other than the need to be closer to him.

"Are you sure?" he asks as if he feels the power of it, too.

"Yes," I whisper.

Our mouths connect in a kiss vastly different from all the others. I wonder what kind of magic this bed has in it. It's not urgent, sweet, or seductive. It's the kind of trusting kiss that slithers beneath my skin and takes root deep inside me. As our bodies come together, the feel of him inside me is wholly and completely different, too. The pleasure radiating from my core spreads like hot sun after a storm, until I feel us in every ounce of my body.

He breaks the kiss, gritting out, "*Jesus*, Vic," and our eyes connect with that same scorching intensity. It's all I can do to pull his mouth back to mine. We thrust and rock, finding a rhythm that binds us together. When he unlaces our fingers to slide his hands beneath my ass, lifting and angling, taking me deliciously deeper, it intensifies everything. I cling to him, consumed with pleasure so thick and vast, it's a world unto its own.

"God, Vic," he says against my lips. "Feel that?"

"So good," I pant out.

"Fucking perfect." He quickens his efforts, holding my ass tighter. Pleasure and pain coalesce, and an orgasm crashes over me. I cry out, and he stays with me, thrusting so perfectly, he keeps me at the peak for what feels like an eternity. Just as I start coming down from it, he quickens his efforts, sending us both spiraling into ecstasy, his curses and my moans filling the air. We ride that high all the way to the clouds and back.

When we finally sink to the mattress, sated and sweaty, he buries his face in my neck, gathering me in his arms. I snuggle into him, and we lie tangled together, basking in the sunlight streaming through the open curtains as our breathing calms. But it's our hammering hearts that refuse to ease that have me feeling like we've crossed into some new invisible plane.

When his eyes find mine, there are so many emotions brewing in them, I know he feels it, too, as he whispers, "What are you doing to me, Braden?"

"I don't know, but I sure like it." My honesty takes me by surprise, and I like that, too.

He nips at my lower lip. "Maybe we should try to figure it out in the shower."

And just like that my body floods with desire again.

Chapter Fourteen

Wells

We take our time in the shower, exploring and enjoying each other. While Vic's drying her hair, I sneak a piece of paper from the hotel notepad, write the date and draw a heart around it, and slip the paper into her purse so she'll remember our trip. I wonder if she kept the napkin from the bar that first night.

When we finally force ourselves to leave the hotel, we stop at a café for breakfast, where we share pastries, and I buy us touristy Inner Harbor T-shirts to change into since mine smells like stale beer. Victory looks cute as hell in hers, fresh faced, her hair untamed, and that unstoppable smile that does me in every damn time I see it.

We check out the shops, and I buy matching key chains with little boats on them, and Victory looks at me like I'm being silly. But I can tell she likes it when I say, "Twenty years from now, we'll look back at these and say, 'Remember when we stayed at that amazing hotel and went on our first Saturday Scoutabout?'"

"That assumes we'll still be friends in twenty years," she says as we leave the store.

I take her hand, tugging her into a quick kiss. "We'll be more than friends, and you know it."

"Oh yeah? Are you just going to be my boy toy forever?"

"If that's what it takes."

I keep hold of her hand as we make our way toward the docks to check out the historic ships, trying not to focus on how much I like that she didn't fight me on my response. I glance at her, and she's watching a butterfly fluttering beside us as we walk. "Looks like you made a friend."

"Yeah," she says softly, her eyes still trained on the butterfly.

"What makes butterflies special enough that you wanted one permanently inked on your wrist?"

"I was mystified by them when I was little." She turns a thoughtful gaze on me. "We saw the most gorgeous, vibrant ones in the rainforests and jungles when we were overseas, but when I moved to the city, I never saw them until after I lost Harvey. Then I saw them often enough that I couldn't ignore them. I'd be walking down the sidewalk, and a butterfly would flutter around me, like that one just did. Or I'd see a picture of one in a store, and it was always when I was contemplating something important or having a really hard day. My mom was visiting when we saw one together. She was surprised to see it flying around the busy city sidewalk, and it stayed with us for a whole block. I told her how often I'd seen them, and she reminded me that they represent hope and new beginnings, and in some cultures, they're seen as messengers from the spirit world."

"*Harvey*," I say as understanding hits with warmth, not disbelief, earning a smile.

"Yeah. That's when I started thinking of them as a sign from him, and maybe I needed that crutch, I don't know, but seeing butterflies gave me the courage to make the difficult decisions and push through hard times. That's why I got the tattoo, so Harvey would always be with me."

"It doesn't matter if you needed a crutch or not. I think that's beautiful, and I'm glad you have a little piece of him with you." I lift our joined hands and kiss the butterfly.

She doesn't say a word, but that slightly bashful, relieved smile appears, and as we make our way to the ships, she holds my hand a little tighter.

As we explore one of the ships alongside other tourists, Victory leans in close and says, "What kind of boat do you have?"

"What makes you think I have one?"

She gives me an incredulous look. "You live on Silver Island, you have a restaurant on the water, *and* you said you'd love to find a place like the hotel for your restaurant because it's on the water. It's not that hard to figure out that you're a boat guy."

"I'm going to have to work on being more mysterious. I do have a boat, but it's nothing fancy. Play your cards right, and I'll take you out on it someday."

"What makes you think I'd want to go out on your boat?" she asks sassily.

I slide my arm around her waist and haul her against me. "Something tells me you'd like to lie in the sun as I pilot us out of the harbor and anchor far from shore." I press my cheek to hers and whisper, "Where I'll strip off your bikini with my teeth and make you come so loud, it echoes in the sea."

She eyes the people milling about, her cheeks pinking up. When those gorgeous baby blues land on me, she whispers, "I think I might like that boat ride after all."

I laugh and kiss her. "For the record, I'm usually right."

"And you're always cocky."

"I didn't hear any complaints about my *cockiness* this morning."

Her eyes widen. "You're so…"

"Unbelievable?" I drape an arm over her shoulder and kiss her temple. "Let's stick with that."

She just shakes her head.

After checking out the ships, we have lunch at an outdoor café, where we enjoy fresh crabs, cold drinks, and more fun conversation, before heading to the National Aquarium.

The place is busy. Couples are walking arm in arm, parents are chasing after children, and groups gather around tanks and displays as little ones put their sticky fingers on the glass, *ooh*ing and *aah*ing. Victory is watching the kids with a longing in her eyes that I haven't seen before.

"They're cute, huh?" I pull her closer.

"Mm-hm. Look at the excitement in their eyes. I remember that feeling from when we were young and our parents would show us a monkey or a colorful bird we'd never seen before. They weren't new to my parents, but they were as excited as we were."

"Because they were excited for you."

"I know. Parenting is such a big undertaking. Can you imagine how great it feels every time your kid discovers something new or when they take their first steps or say their first word?"

"I'd imagine it is pretty special. Do you want a family one day?"

She blinks several times, as if she's thinking about it. "Maybe. *Look*." She points to a tank of jellyfish, their translucent bodies shimmering beneath the lights, and drags me over to them, effectively putting an end to *that* conversation.

It's a good thing. She's too easy to get lost in, and if I start imagining her holding our babies, it might just pull me over the edge.

We make our way through the aquarium, reading about the animals and chatting. When we head into Shark Alley, we're surrounded by massive tanks. Sharks lurk in the shadowy depths, making them feel even more ominous as they come into view, their powerful bodies slicing effortlessly through the water as they pass by the viewing windows.

"It's their cold black eyes that freak me out the most," Victory says. "Have you ever seen a shark when you were surfing?"

"Yes, but there's never been a shark attack near the island."

"That's lucky. They terrify me," she says. "My cousin Dane is a shark researcher and tagger. Every time I see him, he offers to take me diving to show me that they're not as dangerous as everyone thinks."

"You should take him up on it. I'll go with you."

"Are you crazy? I'm not willingly going near sharks. Even walking through here makes me nervous."

She's so damn cute. I put my arm around her, pulling her closer. "If these tanks break, I'll save you from the big bad sharks."

"I'm holding you to that, Silver."

Doesn't she know there's nothing I won't do for her?

We stroll through one exhibit after another, admiring sea creatures and exchanging glances filled with unspoken affection. Every look, every touch, every joke we share and every challenge we give, draws me deeper into her. I want to spend time like this with her every day, exploring and discovering things about each other.

As we head to the tropical fish exhibit, she slides her arm around me, and I catch another alluring glance. Everything I never knew I wanted is right here in front of me. I want to jump in with both feet and tell her I'm crazy about her. But even though she's opening up with me, I can tell she's still holding back, and I know I have to be careful. She's been through a lot, and it'll take time to fully earn her trust, so I'll take what she's willing to give and hope that one day she'll trust me enough to give me all of herself.

After seeing the sharks, we head into the tropical fish area. "Look how beautiful they are," she says as we step up to a tank of vibrantly colored fish. "Can you imagine seeing something this beautiful every day?"

Thinking of seeing *her* every day, I say, "That would be a dream come true."

She catches me watching her and arches a brow. "I was talking about the fish."

"I know you were, but they don't compare to you."

"Do you *ever* turn off that charm?"

I pull her closer. "Is it still called charm if I'm being honest?"

"Everything you do is an effort to charm me."

"Is it working?"

Her eyes narrow. "Yes. Annoyingly well."

"In that case, you'd better get used to it, because I am not about to stop." I lower my lips to hers.

Her phone rings, startling us apart. She pulls it out of her back pocket, and her smile fades. "Shoot. I forgot I have a video call with my family for my grandmother's birthday."

"We can head out so you can take it."

"I don't want to leave. I'm having too much fun." She looks

around. "I'll just take it over there."

I follow her to a spot at the far side of the exhibit, and she answers the call.

"Hi, you guys. Happy birthday, Gram."

"Thank you, honey. Where are you? It's so dark."

"Sorry." Victory turns toward the light of the tank. I can see her family on the screen. "Is this better?"

"Oh yes," her grandmother says.

"Are those fish?" Noah asks.

"Hey, is that Wells behind you?" Flynn asks, and Sutton's face appears beside him, looking as curious as the rest of them.

Victory looks over her shoulder at me, wide-eyed, like she's been caught with her hand in the cookie jar.

That stings, but I get it. We're still new, and she's not ready for them to know, so I play it cool and wave to her family. "Hi, guys. Happy birthday, Grandma Braden."

"Thank you, dear," her grandmother says.

Seth is grinning like a Cheshire cat.

"Well, isn't this a nice surprise," her mother says. "What are you two up to today?"

"It looks like they're at an aquarium," Clay says. He's sitting with his arm around Pepper, who waves to us.

"We are," Victory says tensely. "Wells is opening another restaurant, and he's thinking about putting in fish tanks. We're just checking them out. Right, *Seth*?" She levels Seth with a serious look. "I hear you're partnering with Wells. I'm sure *you* know about the fish tank idea."

"I do? Oh, *right*, yes, we are," Seth says. "Fish tanks in the walls. We're tossing around lots of ideas."

"You boys are partnering up for this?" her grandfather asks.

"We are," Seth says.

"That's great," her father chimes in.

"I can't wait to see this new union come together," her mother says.

Something about the way she says it makes me think she's talking about me and Victory, not the restaurant. "Me too," I say. "I'm excited about our new endeavor."

"I love the idea of fish tanks in the restaurant," Pepper says.

"That would be cool at Rock Bottom, too," Sutton adds.

Noah lifts his chin. "Vic, where are you? That doesn't look like the New York aquarium."

"Baltimore," Victory admits tightly. "Wells took me to scout a few bands here last night, and we decided to stay over and check it out."

Clay laughs. "I bet you did."

Pepper nudges him, giving him a chiding look.

"You're scouting talent again?" her father asks. "That's my girl. Get back on that wagon and have some fun."

"I'm sure she's having a lot of fun with the Wells wagon," Noah says, and her brothers laugh.

"Really, Noah?" Victory snaps. "You couldn't just let that go? Wells and I are friends, okay? We like some of the same things, and I think it was really nice of him to find those bands for me to check out."

"I bet you do," Noah says.

"*Noah*," her father says sternly. "That's enough."

Noah holds his hands up in surrender. "I'm just having fun with her."

"Friends are good, honey," her mother says. "And, Wells, you're such a nice young man. I'm glad you two have become friendly."

"Thank you, Mrs. B," I say. "I am, too."

"Pep and I started out as friends," Clay says with a smirk.

"Pepper ran from you every time she saw your ugly mug," Noah reminds him.

"He was just too cute to look at," Pepper says in Clay's defense.

"He's jealous, babe." Clay kisses her.

"So, Gram, how's your birthday so far?" Victory asks. "What have you and Grandpa been up to?"

"You know there's never a dull moment with us," her grandmother says, and goes on to tell everyone about the things they've been doing lately.

They talk for another fifteen minutes or so, and when Victory ends the call, she exhales loudly as she pockets her phone. "Well, that was awkward."

"Nah. They're just giving you a hard time."

She looks at me apologetically. "I'm sorry for how I reacted. I'm just not ready to be the center of all *that*."

"I get it. But it's obvious they love me."

She laughs softly.

I drape an arm over her shoulder, walking to the next exhibit, and say, "If you want my advice, I think you should just get on board with it. We both know you're going to end up there anyway. I'm irresistible."

Victory

Wells makes it easy to move past the hiccup with my family, and the rest of the day is a whirlwind of exploration—of the

Inner Harbor and each other. We hold hands as we meander through museums and gift shops, learning more about each other with every passing minute and losing ourselves in every stolen kiss, of which there are many. Wells found a cute onesie for Stevie that has I'M NOT CRABBY above a picture of a crab and YOU'RE CRABBY beneath it.

I love that he thought of his nephew.

I haven't been this happy or free in years. I don't know if it's because we're not in New York or something else, but everything feels different. I'm noticing things about Wells I haven't noticed before. Like when we walk along sidewalks, he always moves to the side closest to the street. He opens every door for me, and one of my favorite things he does is when we're talking and he tucks my hair behind my ear and says, *There you are*, like he did last night and this morning, as if just seeing my face is special.

When we get back to Teterboro Airport, I feel like I've been gone a month. I'm sad our trip is over but grateful for the time we had. "Thank you for everything," I say as the plane lands. "I had an amazing night, and today was the best day I've had in years."

He lifts our joined hands and kisses the back of mine. "I'm glad. I had a great time, too. I wish we had one more night, but I have to be on the island for a staff meeting early tomorrow morning."

"I know. You mentioned it earlier." *But I love knowing you want more time, too.*

His eyes brighten. "Why don't you come with me to the island? I've got that meeting and a couple hours of work to take care of, but we can have the rest of the day together. You can see my family, hang out with my friends, and be back by Monday morning."

Half my heart screams, *Yes, go!* but the other half holds me back. Somehow going to the island seems like a much bigger statement than when he comes to the city. I know that's not fair. Especially after the great time we've had, but I'm just not ready to go there.

"I wish I could," I say lamely.

"It's okay," he says with tempered disappointment. "I guess the car ride to your place will have to hold me over until next time."

"You don't have to come with me. You can't make Tessa wait."

"She won't mind. I pay her well, and I want to be sure you get home safely."

"That big heart of yours is really something. I appreciate the offer, but I've been getting myself home for a long time. I'll text you when I get there."

He tries to debate me, but I win, and when we get off the plane, he insists on walking me to the car. He gazes warmly at me and slides his hand along my jaw, brushing his thumb over my cheek, and says, "I'm going to miss you."

My heart squeezes, and I lean into his touch, knowing I'm going to miss him, too. I open my mouth to tell him as much, but the words won't come, so I hook my finger into his belt loop, pulling him closer, go up on my toes, and press my lips to his.

He opens the car door for me, and as I get in, he says, "See you Wednesday, sweets."

"What's Wednesday?" I try to remember whether we made plans, but nothing comes to mind.

He cocks a grin. "Our weekly walkabout. See what kind of

trouble we can get into."

A little thrill runs through me. "I guess I'm not working late on Wednesday."

"Now you're catching on." He leans in for one more kiss and closes the car door.

He watches as the car drives away, and I watch him, too, until I can no longer see him.

My heart is pounding from the wonderfulness of the day. I revel in that, and then I tuck it away like a treasure, knowing I'll revisit the memories a hundred more times tonight.

I reach into my purse for my phone to call Seth, and my fingers touch something furry. I peer into my bag, and laughter bubbles out at the sight of a red furry crab with BALTIMORE stitched on its back, sitting among napkins from the places we ate, a piece of paper from a notepad at the hotel where we stayed, and cards from some of the shops we visited. I pick up my keys to see the tiny boat dangling from the chain, and my heart skips.

Feeling like a teenager with her first crush, I take another minute to try to calm that joy so I can be appropriately annoyed at Seth.

He answers on the first ring and says, "I wondered when you'd call."

"When were you planning on telling me that you were partnering with Wells?"

"I figured he'd tell you."

"*You* should've told me." I lower my voice so the driver can't listen to my conversation. "First you tell me he's all wrong for me, and the next morning you're talking to him about partnering? I thought you didn't trust him."

"I never said that. I said he was a good guy."

"You said he was *wrong* for me."

"Yeah, because I could tell how much you liked him, and if I told you he was right for you and I thought you should see him again, you never would have."

"What kind of mixed-up psych bullshit is that?"

"Vic, you always do the opposite of what anyone tells you."

"I do *not*. When have I ever done that?"

He laughs. "How much time do you have?"

"Seth, I'm serious. I should be able to count on you to have my back."

"Hey, I *always* have your back. Didn't I have it today when you asked me about fish?"

I huff out, "*Yes.*"

"Then stop giving me shit. It sounded like you guys were having a great time."

"That's beside the point."

"No, sis. That *is* the point, and we're all happy for you. Like I said, Wells is a good guy."

"I *know* he is, but we're just friends, so don't go making it into anything bigger." The word *friends* leaves a bad taste in my mouth, and I don't know why I'm upset with Seth, which is also frustrating.

"*Friends* who scout bands together and stay overnight in a new city to do fun things the next day," Seth says. "You've needed a *friend* like him for a long time."

"Okay, *fine*. I guess we're more than friends, but don't get carried away."

He scoffs. "When do I ever get carried away? Look, I'm sorry I didn't tell you when Wells and I were negotiating. But honestly, your personal life has nothing to do with our partnership. Wells is a sharp businessman, and I have no doubt he'll be a great business partner. He brought his restaurant back from the dead, and he did it grassroots style, which you know I respect."

"How do you know he did it grassroots style?"

"Because I talked with him about it at the wedding, and then I researched him. He had a vision of how he wanted to build his business, and he wasn't going to let anyone dissuade him. Instead of throwing money at it and buying the expertise he needed to make it work fast, he sought advice from people he trusted in order to learn along the way. That's a guy who cares a hell of a lot about bettering himself and the business."

"He told you that?" Why am I jealous that he knew that before I did?

"Yeah. He didn't want to ask his father for advice, but Alexander Silver is a stellar businessman, so he did. He also asked his father's cousins, three self-made billionaires. He wanted to see how their advice fit into *his* goals, not the other way around. He made mistakes early on and corrected them, and revised his plans to form a better path. Not many people have the wherewithal to do that and succeed at it. So, if you want to know why I told you not to go after him when I knew you'd do the opposite, it's because looking at who he was beneath the surface was just like looking at you."

Seth has only said something like that to me once before, and it was about Harvey. When my family was struggling with our age gap, Seth saw past it, and that unlocks something inside me.

"Vic? You still there?"

"Yeah, sorry. You're right. Wells and I do have a lot in common."

"I figured, since you stayed in Baltimore with him. Does

that mean you skipped dinner at the tavern Friday night?"

It's hard to admit, but I manage, "*Mm-hm.*"

"How about that," he says with awe, and it's not a question. "Does this mean we have to buy fish tanks for our restaurant?"

We both laugh.

We talk almost the whole ride home, and I tell him about our weekend. It feels good to share that happiness with Seth. I'm still reeling when I get up to my apartment.

I set my purse down, and as I walk into the living room, I'm hit with a pang of guilt. It's strange to feel it after days of being free of it. I try to push it away, but as I look around at the lavish room, my eyes fall to Harvey's candy dish full of Hershey's Kisses beside the couch, taking that pang deeper.

The silence presses in on me.

Has it always been this quiet? It's stifling. I feel like I can't breathe.

Is this some new form of guilt? Maybe I'm just tired. A little music and fresh air will probably help. As I head for the terrace doors, I open the app on my phone that controls my home electronics and turn on a playlist. Music streams from the speakers as I step outside and fill my lungs with fresh air.

I lean on the railing, looking out at the lights of the city, thinking about how much fun I had with Wells. My phone chimes, and as if his ears were burning, *Wells* pops up in a message bubble, instantly bringing a smile.

Wells: *I know you're worried about me getting home safely, and you probably miss my face, so here you go.*

A picture of him pops up, and I laugh softly.

Wells: *Send me a pic so I know you weren't kidnapped on the way home.*

I take a selfie and send it to him.

Wells sends a voice message. I tap the play icon. *"There you are. How is it possible that I miss you already?"*

I get goose bumps, his deep voice wrapping around me like an embrace, and a kernel of missing him blooms in my chest. I lower myself to a lounge chair and gaze up at the starry sky, debating sending him a voice message back. It only takes a moment for me to decide to do it.

My pulse quickens as I record "There must be something going around, because I miss you, too." I take another deep breath. My heart races as I send it to him, then quickly thumb out another text.

Me: *Don't let that go to your head or anything.*

Wells: *Too late.*

A smiling emoji surrounded by hearts pops up.

A WordLink invitation appears, and I accept it.

Half an hour later, I'm still sitting on the terrace listening to music and playing our game, when I realize I no longer feel stifled. How can something as simple and silly as an online game make me feel so good?

As Wells plays the word SWEETS, I know my happiness has little to do with the game and everything to do with the man who was currently whipping my butt in it.

Chapter Fifteen

Victory

"I'm not sure we can be friends anymore," I joke after Wells orders a saltless soft pretzel and cheese dip from a sidewalk pushcart vendor.

It's Wednesday evening, and it's been a busy week and a half since we went to Baltimore. We play WordLink every day and talk every night, but nothing compares to spending time together. Last Wednesday's walkabout turned into an overnight at the hotel where Wells was staying, and I was pleasantly surprised that I didn't feel guilty when I woke up the next morning. There is something to be said about not waking up in my own bed after spending the night with him. Last Friday's flitabout led to another steamy night at the hotel and a lazy Saturday morning in bed. I haven't spent a lazy morning in forever, and I loved every second of it with Wells. We spent the rest of the day knocking around the city together until he had to go back to the island, and as I've come to look forward to, when I got home, I found more secret memories tucked into my bag.

Wells hooks his arm around my neck, pulling me against his chest as the vendor fills our order. "You're stuck with me,

Braden."

"At least until tomorrow morning," I say playfully, and he presses his smiling lips to mine.

We collect our pretzels, and as we step away from the cart, I hold up my cinnamon-sugar pretzel and say, "*This* is the bomb."

He scoffs. "What's wrong with keeping it classic?"

"More like *boring*. How can you even pretend to be living your best life if you're missing out on cinnamon and sugar?"

A wolfish grin slides into place on his handsome face. "You're all the sweetness I need," he says, and leans in to kiss me again.

"Well, well, isn't *this* cozy?"

We turn at the sound of Leni's voice and find her and Raz watching us curiously. Leni's eyes glitter with a look that says, *Just friends, huh?*

"*Leni*…Hi. Hey, Raz," I say, futilely hoping I don't sound as *caught* as I feel.

"How's it going, guys?" Wells asks casually. "Raz, I haven't seen you in a while. Everything good?"

"Things are great," Raz says, his gaze moving between us. "Looks like things are going well for you, too."

"No complaints here," Wells says as he settles a hand on my back.

"What are you guys up to tonight, besides kissing?" Leni smirks.

"Really?" I ask sarcastically.

"Come on, Leni. Can you blame her? I mean, look at me." Wells motions to himself.

Leni rolls her eyes.

"He's got a point, babe," Raz says. "He's a good-looking

guy." He and Wells high-five.

"Seriously," Leni says. "What are you guys up to tonight?"

"Just hanging out," I say at the same time Wells says, "We're on a Wednesday Walkabout."

"Hanging out and walking about. Got it," Leni says with amusement.

"Are you getting excited about your wedding?" Wells asks. "It's what? A little more than a month away?"

"Excited and nervous," Leni says. "I wish we could just elope. We'll have security to keep paparazzi off the island, and our moms have been having fun planning everything, but it's a lot."

"My beautiful bride-to-be doesn't like to be the center of attention." Raz slides his arm around her and says, "I cannot wait to see you walk down that aisle in your wedding gown and become mine forever." He kisses her.

My heart squeezes. "I'm really happy for you guys."

"Thanks." Leni looks between us and arches a brow. "Should we seat you two together at the wedding?"

"Definitely. Right, Vic?" Wells asks.

"Yeah." I don't know why that makes my stomach feel funny, when I know damn well I'll want to sit with him at the wedding. It just seems like a big step. Like we're coming out to everyone he knows as a couple, which is silly. Especially if what Leni says is true about gossip spreading faster than colds on the island. If Sutton mentioned the video call with my family to anyone, or if Wells has told friends or family that we've been spending time together, then that grapevine is probably already buzzing.

"You guys want to hang out with us tonight?" Wells offers, and I'm glad he does.

I have no idea why being together on the island seems like a bigger deal than hanging out with Leni and Raz here in the city. Maybe I'm just losing my mind.

"No, thanks," Leni says. "We just picked up dinner."

Raz holds up a to-go bag from the Thai restaurant down the street. "Rain check?"

"That would be great," Wells says.

"Yeah, let's plan something," I suggest.

"Okay. I'll text you," Leni says. "Good to see you guys."

"You, too," we say as they walk away.

Wells turns to me with a playful grin. "You're now officially my date for their wedding."

"Don't count your chickens, Silver. I still haven't decided whether I can hang out with a guy who slathers cheese on his unsalted pretzel."

He cocks a grin as we head down the sidewalk. "Is that so?"

"Yes, sir."

"*Sir?* I like that," he says seductively, and I laugh. "You can't knock the taste of perfection until you try it." He breaks off a piece of pretzel, dips it in the cheese, and tries to feed it to me.

"*Ew.*" I turn my face away.

"Don't be a baby."

"I'm not. I just know it's not going to be as good as mine."

"I'll make you a deal. I'll taste yours if you taste mine." He waggles his brows.

"My pretzel is good. Yours is probably gross."

"Have you ever had a pretzel with cheese?"

"No, but look at it. It doesn't look nearly as yummy as mine with all this sugary goodness."

"Yours does look good," he admits as we cross the street. "I'll tell you what. If you don't like it, you don't have to be my date for the wedding.”

“Even though I don’t want to be the topic of island gossip, I’m *not* giving up my seat next to you.”

“That’s my girl.” He steals a kiss. “Besides, the gossip mill is already churning. Sutton must have said something, because Jules asked Bellamy about us, and my sisters cornered me last week. And then Brant asked about us on Monday.”

I blow out a breath. “Okay. I guess the cat’s out of the bag.”

“Does that freak you out?”

“Only mildly. That’s silly, right?”

“Nothing you feel is ever silly. You told me at Cage’s party that you didn’t want to have to answer questions from your colleagues, but I think you’re safe from that. It’s just island gossip, so how about we don’t think about it today?”

“There you go, making me like you even more,” I tease. “That sounds like a good plan. I’ll even reward you by tasting your pretzel.”

I tear off a piece of my pretzel, and we feed the pieces to each other. His dark eyes never leave mine, as the cheese and pretzel melt together in my mouth. “Well?” he asks.

“*Mm.* That’s not bad,” I say with surprise.

“Stick with me, Braden. I know my stuff.”

“What did you think of my pretzel?”

He leans closer and lowers his voice. “That cinnamon and sugar would taste better sprinkled on you.”

He steals another kiss. After we finish our pretzels, he drags me into a small market and buys cinnamon and sugar.

“You’re a nut,” I say as we walk out.

“And you’re going to be one tasty treat later.”

He kisses me again, and anticipation simmers inside me as we continue meandering down the sidewalk, window-shopping and chatting.

"You should come to the island next weekend. I'll show you around."

My nerves tingle. "I don't know," I say, trying to tamp down that flutter of anxiety.

"How about the weekend after? Give yourself time to get used to the idea."

"I have to go back to LA a week from Sunday."

"Date with your West Coast boyfriend?" His brows slant. "Whose ass do I have to kick?"

I smile. "All of the directors in the LA office. We have our annual meetings on Monday and Tuesday."

"Uh-huh. A likely story," he teases, and we head into a gift shop.

We make our way through the shop, showing each other postcards, magnets, and more touristy gifts.

"This is exactly what I've been looking for," Wells says excitedly, and picks up a small black wooden box with a metal clasp that has NEW YORK IS FOR LOVERS painted in neon pink across the top. "You need this."

"I do? For what?"

"For our memories." He opens the top and shows me the inside. "It's perfect."

"I don't know about you, but my memories live in my head."

"I mean the trinkets I've been putting in your purse." He steps closer, and his eyes turn seductive. "The napkin from the first night we were together, and the other memories I've been sneaking in there."

I was wondering if he was ever going to bring them up. I'm collecting them on my dresser, and every time I see them it makes me happy. But I can't help teasing him. "What makes you think I didn't throw them away?"

"Because I know you. You're a keeper of special things, and I'm buying this for you."

As the evening wears on and the sun sets, our conversations are as breezy as the warm summer night.

He drags me into a music store. "What are we doing here?"

"I figured I'd get myself a guitar. Up my street cred." He heads for a display of guitars and grabs one off the rack.

"You didn't tell me you know how to play."

"I don't. I'm hoping you can show me a thing or two."

A tall, tan guy with longish light brown hair saunters over from the register. "Wells, my man. What are you doing here?"

"*Carey?*" Wells says with surprise. "Hey. It's good to see you." Holding the guitar with one hand, he and Carey share an embrace. "I didn't know you were living in the city."

"It's only temporary. I'm helping out my buddy Drake Savage again. He opened this place a few months ago."

"Awesome." Wells puts a hand on my back again. "Carey Osten, this is Victory Braden. Carey grew up on the island. His father is the mayor, and his sister, Tara, is engaged to Levi."

"Hi, Carey, it's nice to meet you. I met Tara. She's a sweetheart, and her girls are adorable." She and Levi have an adorable baby girl named Toni and a beautiful little girl named Joey.

"Yeah, they sure are," Carey says. "Are you the same Victory Braden who owns Blank Space Entertainment?"

"I am. You keep up with the entertainment industry?"

"Music is my life." He rakes a hand through his hair and lifts his chin toward the guitar Wells is holding. "She sounds beautiful. I didn't know you played."

"I don't, but Vic does. Mind if she shows me a thing or

two?" Wells asks.

"Not at all. There's a bench over there." He points to the other side of the store. "Make yourselves comfortable, and let me know if you need anything."

"Will do. Thanks, man." Wells guides me toward the bench.

"Wells, what are we doing?"

"Having fun." He sits on the bench and holds the guitar across his lap. "Now what?"

I can't stop grinning, which is par for the course with him. "You can't learn to play the guitar in five minutes."

"I just want to see if I like it."

"Okay, well, first you have to hold it right." I move behind him and reach around him to adjust how it rests on his leg.

"I like *this*," he says in a low, sexy voice, and turns to kiss my cheek.

"Mm-hm. I'm starting to understand why you wanted to do this."

"I'm no dummy. What do I do with my hands?"

"I can think of a few things," I whisper. "But they don't require a guitar."

He grins. "I should've thought of this weeks ago. Show me something, sweets. Anything. How to play a single chord."

"Okay. I'll teach you to play an E." Still leaning over his back, I adjust his fingers. "Press on the fretboard like this, but do it firmly when you strum the strings."

He strums a few times. "Like this?"

"Mm-hm. Good." I walk around the bench so I can see him play. God, he looks good holding a guitar.

"What do you think?"

"I think you're infuriatingly hotter holding the damn thing.

How does it feel?"

"Not as good as you do." He motions to the bench. "Sit with me."

I sit beside him, and he stops strumming.

"Will you play something for me?"

"I haven't played in years," I remind him.

"I'm sure it's like riding a bike." He offers the guitar. "Please?"

What is it about him that makes me want to do things I haven't done in forever? I take the guitar, and as I settle it on my lap, the peaceful sensation playing used to bring washes over me, as does that old spark of excitement. I start strumming, and it doesn't take long for it to come back to me and for me to get comfortable. I fall back into playing an old favorite, "I'll Be There for You."

Wells starts singing the lyrics. I swear when we're together it's impossible not to grin like a fool, which I must be, because he gets up, singing into an invisible microphone, and Carey calls out, "Sing it, Wells!"

We both laugh, and I get into it, too, playing louder. Wells struts and sings into that imaginary microphone, and when he gets to the line about swearing things to me, he drops to his knees, places one hand on his chest, his eyes pleading, belting out the song with so much emotion, it's like he means every word.

And I'm surprised by how much I hope he does.

Chapter Sixteen

Wells

August brought humid days and steamy nights, and Victory and I have made those nights even hotter. The last three and a half weeks passed in a blur of busy days at the restaurant interspersed with seeing properties in the city with Seth and tumbling heart first down that magical slope with Victory. We text and play WordLink when we can during the day, and every night we talk until neither of us can stay awake. I love our late-night chats, but I wish she was in my arms. We never miss our Wednesday Walkabouts and overnights at the hotel, but it's getting harder to leave her on Thursday mornings when I return to the island and she goes to work. Even though our Friday Flitabouts bleed into sexy nights and Saturday Scoutabouts, it's never enough.

It's Friday night, and I'm back in the city for what Victory has dubbed *her* Friday Flitabout, and she's not letting me in on her plans. Last Friday we went to a concert in Central Park, and we took a ride in a horse-drawn carriage, which neither of us had ever done before. It was pretty fucking great. She hasn't made it to the island yet and I'm trying to be patient, but I'm glad Leni's wedding is next weekend. I want Victory to be a bigger part of my life and for her to get to know my family and friends better.

"Have you talked to Leni?" I ask, reaching for Victory's hand. She looks beautiful in a breezy blue dress that brings out her eyes as we make our way down the sidewalk. "Is she a nervous wreck about next weekend?"

"I talked to her this morning. She's excited to get married, and she is a little nervous, which isn't like her, but it's a big step."

"From what I hear, jitters are normal, and she's so independent." I squeeze her hand. "Like someone else I know. Are you nervous?"

"Why would I be nervous about Leni's wedding?"

"Not about the wedding. About spending time in my world. I would think being seen on the arm of the hottest guy on the island can be a little nerve-racking."

She leans against my side as we stop at a crosswalk and says, "What do you think?"

"If I were you, I'd be excited to show me off."

She laughs. "Okay, let's go with that, or it'll make me nervous."

"You got it." I lean in and kiss her.

The light changes, and as we make our way across the street, she says, "How did your property search go with Seth and Jared today? Did you see anything promising?"

"It was great seeing them, but none of the properties jumped out at us. I figured it would take time to find the right place, but I'm starting to wonder if we're looking in the wrong city."

"You haven't been looking that long. My mother always says the best things come along when you're not looking for them.”

"Like running into you at the bar that first night."

"Exactly like that," she says, flashing a coy smile.

"Are you ready to tell me where we're going yet?"

"No. It's a surprise, and it's just around the next corner."

I love that she planned an adventure for us, but it never matters what we're doing. We've gone out to dinners at places that were new to both of us, listened to bands and solo artists in dive bars, and we even went to a poetry slam in a park one afternoon. Each of those things was just as fun as the times we've aimlessly knocked around different parts of the city or stayed in my hotel room for half of a Saturday.

After we round the next corner, she says, "Surprise!" and stops in front of a little French café. "I haven't eaten here, but I've done some research. The chef came here from France twelve years ago, and he's worked in this bistro for the past eight years. His food is supposed to be out of this world, *and* he makes tarte tatin. It might not be as good as Olivier's, but I knew we'd still have fun trying it out, so I made a reservation."

My heart thunders. I gaze into the eyes of the woman who's making me all too aware of *that* particular organ, and I gather her in my arms. "You're amazing. I don't care if it's as good as Olivier's or not. It'll be fantastic because you thought of it. Thank you." I press my lips to hers in a tender kiss.

"You make it impossible not to think of you," she says. "I'm convinced that on the nights we spend together, you spend all night whispering 'Think of Wells' in my ear when I'm sleeping, like some kind of hypnosis."

"You caught me," I tease as we head inside.

We're embraced by the savory aroma of French cuisine, stirring memories of visiting Olivier at the Bistro. Soft lighting and faint classical music give the cozy romantic bistro an elegant yet relaxed aura. Simple wooden tables are adorned with dainty glass vases and fresh flowers. On the walls, rustic shelves display an array of wine bottles, antique picture frames, and trinkets.

Victory puts her hand on my stomach, gazing up at me with hopeful eyes as she whispers, "What do you think?"

I think I just fell a little harder for you. "It's almost as perfect as you are."

Every dish is sensational, from the silky foie terrine and Sainte-Maure goat cheese feuilleté, to the duck magret and tarte tatin. But as we share our meals, our hushed voices mingling with the din of the other diners, I'm utterly lost in the radiant beauty before me. How has she kept her loving heart tied down for so many years? I hope she knows how much this means to me.

When we leave the restaurant, she is just as excited as she was when we arrived. "So? Was it as good as Olivier's?"

"I feel a little guilty saying this, but it was just as good as his. And le tarte tatin?" I shake my head, still in awe of how delicious it was. "It threw me right back to my childhood."

"That makes me *so* happy." She goes up on her toes and kisses me.

I wrap her in my arms, keeping her close. "You're amazing. You can't imagine how much it means to me. Thank you for a perfect evening."

"It's not over yet. I just need one second to check on our car." She steps out of my arms and pulls out her phone. "It should be here any minute."

"When did you order a car?"

"When I used the ladies' room." She tucks her phone into her purse. "Someone has to take us to your next surprise."

"There's more? What are you up to, Braden?"

"You're going to have to wait and see."

Her knee bounces anxiously on the drive to wherever she's taking me. When we arrive, I smell salty sea air as I climb out of the car before I turn around and see the water. "Where are we?"

"There's Seth."

"Seth?" I follow her gaze to Seth, talking on the phone across the parking lot. He spots us and heads in our direction. "Want to clue me in on what we're doing here, sweet thing?"

"In a minute," she says as Seth approaches, pocketing his phone.

"Hi," Seth says. "What's going on?"

"You don't know, either?" Wells asks.

He shakes his head. "No idea. Vic sent me a treasure map that led here."

"You got a treasure map?" I turn my best forlorn expression on Victory. "Why didn't I get a treasure map?"

Seth laughs.

"Because you got a guided tour," she says.

"What's going on, Vic?" Seth asks. "Why are we here?"

Her eyes dance with mischief. "Early Christmas present. Follow me."

She walks purposefully toward the water. Seth and I exchange confused glances as we follow her down to a dock with an old, weathered building. It has several massive metal garage-style doors along each side and a few broken windows.

She turns around before we reach the entrance to the building, and she's absolutely glowing. "Wells, when we stayed in that hotel in Baltimore, you said you'd love to find a place like it for the restaurant. And, Seth, the other day when we had lunch, I mentioned that idea, and you said you thought it would be ideal, but you'd never find one."

As we walk along the side of the building, she says, "This is an old shipping warehouse. I'm not an architect, and I know nothing about restaurant design, but imagine if you take out those metal garage doors and put in the kind of accordion glass walls that Flynn has in his house." She turns to me. "They fold open like an accordion, so you'd have natural light in the winter and open-air seating that extends outdoors in warmer months."

"I have those in my house on the oceanside," I say.

"Then you know how great they are. There's enough space for a band, and you might even be able to offer rooftop seating with amazing sunset views. Wells, you have dockside service for boats on the island. I don't know if you'll be allowed to do that here, but maybe? I know it doesn't look like much now, but I drew up some ideas." She reaches into her purse and hands us each copies of drawings.

I'm at a loss for words as I look them over. They show a beautiful building with glass doors along the sides, dining tables, a bar, plants, and lights strung over the dock on the outside. I'm blown away. "Vic, this is exactly what I've been imagining."

"Really?" she exclaims.

"It's like you took these drawings right out of my head."

Seth is looking over the drawings with a skeptical expression.

"Seth, what do you think?" I ask. "I know it would be a huge undertaking, but the location is great, and it's a blank slate. We could get creative with the build-out, or go minimalistic to save on capital."

"I have no doubt it would be worth the effort and expense to make it everything we talked about, but there's one problem." He looks at Victory and says, "I could've saved you a lot of time, sis. This place isn't for sale. I tried to buy it a few years ago. It's owned by Bad Enterprises, and Kane Bad said he had plans for it."

"It's true Kane *had* plans for it, but a lot has changed in his life since then." She turns to me and says, "Kane is Johnny Bad's older brother. He bought this place right before Johnny's life imploded a couple of years ago. When that happened, he put his plans for this site and others on hold to focus on temporarily managing Johnny's band. He's since gotten married to our sister-in-law Pepper's twin, Sable, and he's been cutting back on new endeavors."

She unlocks the door and throws it open, smiling victoriously. "I've had three meetings with Kane over the last couple of weeks. If you're interested, he's willing to sell and won't take it to the open market."

My heart feels like it's going to claw its way out of my chest to get to her as we head inside the musty building. "Babe, that's amazing. Assuming the price makes sense, of course."

"I just kicked open the door and negotiated the exclusive opportunity," she says. "It's up to you guys to march in there and make your deal."

"Damn, sis," Seth says. "You really have gotten your mojo back."

"What are you talking about? I never lost it," Victory insists.

Seth gives her a look that tells of their deep friendship. "You know what I mean. That hunger to reach outside the box is back with a vengeance."

"Yeah, well, someone might've sparked that in me." She

flashes that secret smile my way, and I swear I feel it square in the center of my chest.

We walk around the building inside and out, taking pictures and talking about the possibilities. After Victory locks up, we stand on the dock taking it all in. I can see the restaurant in my mind, bustling with customers. Lights and glass and colorful umbrellas over outdoor tables. My heart is so full, I reach for Victory's hand, and the loving look she gives me bowls me over.

I wonder how I've gone my whole life without ever feeling like *this*. It's all I can do to pull her close and whisper, "Thank you," when I really want to say, *I love you*.

"This calls for a celebration," Seth says, as he comes up behind us. "Are you guys up for drinks?"

I glance at Victory. "What do you think, sweets?"

"Considering it took a woman to do what two men couldn't, it's only appropriate that you guys buy me drinks."

Chapter Seventeen

Victory

Music and the din of conversation swirl around us as we wait for our drinks by the bar. Seth is busy texting, and Wells is sending pictures of the warehouse to his family. I can't take my eyes off him. I'm high on his happiness. That has been happening a lot lately. Just seeing his smiling eyes, hearing his voice, or getting a text brings a rush of lightness to my often heavy days.

Wells pockets his phone and leans closer. "I'm going to have to properly thank you for this later."

I thought after nearly two months, the thrill of being together might lessen, but it's only gotten stronger. "I'm counting on it."

He presses those warm lips to mine, and I sink into them. I can't wait to get back to his hotel suite. Our lives have woven together these last few weeks in ways I never imagined, and it happened so seamlessly, it's hard to remember when we didn't spend Wednesday and Friday nights in each other's arms. I love our Wednesday nights and even our rushed Thursday mornings. But Friday nights have become my favorite, because there's no rush to leave the next morning.

Before Wells, I'd never seen the allure of a lazy Saturday. Now I look forward to lying in his arms as the sun comes up, making love or talking, and getting dirty all over again in the shower. We never leave the suite before ten or eleven. We'd probably stay all day if we didn't have just as much fun getting lost in the city.

"Sorry about that," Seth says, drawing me from my thoughts. "I was just filling in Jared and T about the property." Taylor aka T is Seth's virtual assistant.

"What'd Jared think?" Wells asks.

"He loves the idea and wants to see the property. Vic, do you think we can get in tomorrow?"

"You can get in anytime this weekend. I told Kane you might want to go back a few times before making a decision." I hand Seth the key to the warehouse. "Just return the key to him by Monday afternoon."

"Will do." Seth pockets the key. "Wells, Taylor's going to have our legal team get started on due diligence, which will take a few days. Then he'll schedule a time for us and Jared to meet with Kane. What's your schedule like the week after next?"

"I'll definitely be in town Wednesday and Friday evenings." Wells glances knowingly at me. "But I'll make myself available anytime. Just give me a day's notice to get coverage at Rock Bottom, and I'll be there."

The bartender serves our drinks, and Wells and Seth reach for their wallets. Wells is quicker. "I've got this one."

Seth nods. "Thanks. Next round is on me."

"Thanks, Wells." I lift my glass in a toast. "To new endeavors. I hope you negotiate a great deal, and the restaurant turns out even better than your highest expectations."

We all tap glasses and drink.

"Here's to you, sis," Seth says, lifting his glass. "I'm kind of pissed at myself for not thinking of going back to Kane about that property."

Wells slides an arm around my waist and says, "Not everyone can be as on top of their game as my girl is."

"I'll drink to that." I tap his glass, catching a warm, approving look from Seth. While Noah and Clay have taken great pleasure in teasing me about jumping on the *Wells wagon*, Seth and Flynn sought me out separately to talk about it on a more serious level. Now that they know I'm in a good place, they also enjoy their fair share of teasing. I'm glad they're all happy for me. I'm happy for me, too.

Wells pulls his phone out of his pocket to read a text and scoffs.

"Something wrong?" I ask.

"My family. Check out Fitz and my sisters' back-and-forth about the pictures I sent." He turns the phone so we can see the text thread.

Mom: *How lovely! I'm sure you, Seth, and Jared will make it beautiful.*

Fitz: *A bomb might be in order.*

Bellamy: *I'm not stepping foot in that place unless you disinfect it.*

Keira: *Are you at a murder site?*

Dad: *It'll be great, son. They have no vision.*

Bellamy: *Dad needs glasses.*

Fitz: *Wells really has hit rock bottom.*

Several laughing emojis pop up, and Wells puts his phone in his pocket.

"Gotta love family," Seth says.

"Have you guys thought up a name for the restaurant yet?"

"We're thinking about using Rock Bottom, to help build the brand so we can take it national," Seth says.

"That's great," I exclaim. "Then Wells can throw it in Fitz's face when *hitting Rock Bottom* becomes the go-to outing in the city, which we all know it will."

"Damn right it will," Wells says.

Seth lifts his glass again. "To Rock Bottom."

"To Rock Bottom," Wells and I say in unison, and then we laugh, kiss, and drink.

"To you two," Seth says, lifting his glass.

Wells and I share an affectionate glance and say, "To us."

As the evening moves on, Wells and I dance while women flirt with my brother. Then we hang out with Seth, chatting about everything from the restaurant to my work and even our Saturday outings around the city.

"I need to find a friend," Seth says.

Wells lifts his chin in the direction of two women who were flirting with Seth earlier. "Those women seemed interested."

"I don't think I'll find what I'm looking for in a bar," Seth says.

"When did you turn into a negative Nelly?" I tease him. "You know what Mom says."

Seth looks at me questioningly.

"The best things come along when you're not looking for them," I remind him.

Wells lifts his glass. "I can attest to that."

"Me too," I say, and we toast.

When we finally leave the bar, Seth says, "Thanks again for everything, Vic. You really are the best sister I have."

"Ha ha." I hug him. "I'm glad you liked the space, and I

hope it works out."

"Me too." He turns to Wells and says, "Wells, I'll be in touch about the meeting."

"Sounds good."

As Seth climbs into a car, Wells drapes an arm over my shoulders, pulling me in close, and says, "You done good, Braden."

"Thank you. It was incredibly hard keeping it a secret from you. I wanted to tell you so many times. I'm glad you both loved it."

"It's perfect, but you owe me a treasure map."

I tap his chest. "Play your cards right, and maybe I'll make you one someday."

"That's good enough for me." He takes me in a slow, sensual kiss, then brushes his lips over mine and says, "You know I'm picturing you all bossy and demanding with Kane, and I'm a little jealous. That's hot."

"Oh yeah? I don't think he considered it hot when I was shooting down his thoughts on pricing."

"I thought you said you didn't negotiate a price."

"I didn't negotiate *a* price, but I did knock down his suggestions and tell him I wouldn't waste your time with the numbers he tossed out during our first meeting."

Wells grins. "I knew you were too fierce to just kick the door open. Maybe bossy Victory would like to come out to play tonight."

Heat streaks through me at the thought. As much as I love it when he takes charge, it's wicked fun to turn the tables. "She might need a little coaxing. Maybe you can convince her on the way to your hotel."

"I was hoping we could stay at your place tonight."

Apprehension slams into me, sudden, sharp, and as unyielding as it is unexpected at the thought of bringing him into the home Harvey and I shared.

The joy fades from his eyes, and I realize I'm shaking my head. My chest constricts at the hurt and confusion staring back at me. I open my mouth to try to explain, but no words come. Panic flares inside me.

"You're not ready," he says flatly, taking a step back.

I can't breathe. *Say something. Tell him he's wrong.* I want to explain, but my voice is strangled by fear.

"I thought we were on the same page. All this time, all these nights, I've been falling for you, thinking we were building something more." He scrubs a hand down his face. "I should've known. You've never taken me up on spending time on the island, and I've waited weeks for you to invite me over to your place. You don't even let me come up to your office. We always meet out front. All the signs were right there in front of me, but I had blinders on."

A stabbing pain shoots through my chest. *"Wells—"*

"No, it's okay." He holds his hand up, silencing me. "I pushed too hard, too fast. It's not your fault. You were honest from the start. You said you weren't looking to replace your husband, and I got carried away."

"I'm sorry" comes out shaky and weak, but I can't refute the things he's said. "Can't we just go to your hotel?"

"No," he says softly. "I think it's better if we don't. I need time and space to get my head on straight. What's that old saying? Right person, wrong time?" He steps into the street and hails a cab. Then he reaches for my hand.

My heart is breaking, my thoughts spinning, and my throat thickens painfully. I feel like an automaton as he guides me toward the cab. He opens the door, gazing down at me with the dark eyes I've come to adore, but they're not piercing or hungry or playful.

They're as hurt as the sadness permeating the space between us as he caresses my cheek and says, "You really are an incredible woman."

He kisses my forehead, and it's all I can do to duck into the car before my shattering heart takes me to my knees. I startle when he closes the door and watch him through the blur of tears as the car pulls into traffic.

Chapter Eighteen

Wells

Rock Bottom is usually the one place where I can lose myself in work and customers and overcome even the worst of moods, but the noise outside my office door Sunday evening irritates the hell out of me. I've been trying to review a vendor report for an hour, but all I see is the fear in Victory's eyes when I suggested we stay at her place. I've been trying to give that look another name, but nothing else fits, and I just don't get it.

Fuck. That's not true.

I do get it. She lived there with Harvey. I can see how having me there might make her uncomfortable, but it shouldn't *frighten* her. The idea that it does makes me wonder what's really going on. I eye my phone and consider reaching out to her for the millionth time this weekend. But knowing I caused that fear hurts like a bitch, and if I misread everything about us so far, I'm not about to put either of us in that position again.

I flip the phone over on my desk and turn back to my computer, trying to focus on the report. But it's Victory's face I see, her energy I feel shifting and icing over as it had Friday night. I wish I could stop thinking about her, but I worry about her. Is she upset, or did she just bury herself in work again? Or is she thinking about me, too? Wishing she'd asked me to stay?

Don't be a fucking fool. If she regretted it, she would have reached out.

My chest constricts with the thought I've been trying to shove down deep. Has she just been using me as a distraction? *A fucking boy toy?* I can't reconcile that idea with how close we've gotten, but the devil on my shoulder says that's exactly what I was to her, and that makes me want to strangle the imaginary fucker.

But what if that little fucker is right?

What the hell do I know about love?

Maybe Victory saw *that* in me, and that's where the fear came from. It's one thing to knock around the city together, but really letting me into her life? Into her private sanctuary? That might scare the hell out of her because she doesn't think I'm capable of more.

The thought cuts like a hatchet.

I push to my feet and turn to look out the window behind my desk, hoping the view of the ocean will take the edge off my shitty mood. My office overlooks the outside seating and the dockside area, where the waitstaff is hustling between boats and the restaurant and, just beyond, the vast blue sea kisses the horizon. How many times have I imagined showing Victory around the island, taking her out on my boat, hanging out at bonfires with our friends? I can't pinpoint when that desire started any clearer than I can pinpoint exactly when I began feeling like something in my life was missing.

I thought it was my internal drive to succeed, to prove I could do more than what I had already accomplished. But I'm on the cusp of doing just that, and I know that'll be a huge accomplishment and satisfy my urge to do more, but there's still a gnawing inside me. An emptiness I know will not be eased by success alone. This new and different ache is ten times more oppressive than anything I've ever felt. It's soul-deep, not driven by the fear of my family falling apart or misguided teenage love.

Holy shit. Is this history repeating itself? Am I destined to fall for women who aren't going to love me back? *No.* I refuse to believe that. There's no way the affection Victory showed me wasn't real. I felt it in her touch, heard it in her voice. I saw it in the way she looked at me. There's no way I could have imagined all of that.

A knock sounds at my door, jerking me from my thoughts.

"*What?*" I bark, turning as the door opens and Meghan steps in. *Fuck.* Meghan is one of my mother's friends from college. She has raised four children and ran a restaurant in Boston for a decade before getting divorced and coming here to start over. The last thing she needs is the brunt of my bad mood. "Sorry, Meghan."

"You should be." She closes the door and stalks over to my desk. Her dark, shoulder-length hair is side parted, her makeup minimal, and the narrow-eyed look she's giving me is slightly maternal. "You're allowed to have a few crappy days, so I'll let it slide this time." She taps her fingernail on the desk, then points at me. "But straighten up, because next time I might not be as forgiving."

"I knew there was a reason I hired you."

She crosses her arms. "To keep you in line?"

"No, because if you won't take shit from me, you won't take it from anyone else."

She feigns a dramatic sigh. "And here I thought it was for my pleasant demeanor and good looks." She doesn't skip a beat, snapping right back into work mode. "Have you finished looking over the vendor report yet?"

"Not yet. Is there something specific you need me to review?"

"I negotiated higher discounts with our two newest vendors, but they're based on paying within ten days of receiving the invoices. I gave you the figures for our last few orders and the estimated savings over a twelve-month period."

"Good job. I don't need to review it. We can do that during the busy season, and with the right planning, it shouldn't be a problem in our off-season. You're on top of the budgets, so I trust your judgment."

"Thank you. I appreciate your vote of confidence." Her gaze softens. "You're usually three steps ahead of me. Whatever's got you tangled up in knots must be heavy. Anything I can do to help?"

"Just keep holding down the fort."

"That's not a problem." She taps my desk again. "Know what you need?"

Yes. The feisty beauty who slithered into my heart one phone call, one silly game, and one fucking kiss at a time. Gritting my teeth against the heartache that brings, I lift my chin in question.

"You need to get out there on the floor and work your magic with the customers. You can't hold on to a bad mood when you do that."

"That's an excellent idea. I'll do that, and then I think I'll head out for the night."

"Sounds good. I hope your mood improves," she says on her way out.

I snag my phone and shove it in my pocket. As I walk

around the desk, my gaze lands on a photo hanging on the wall. It was taken at a beach bonfire in front of the Bistro the summer before Olivier died, and it's one of my favorites. I'm roasting marshmallows with some of the other kids. Olivier is sitting on a blanket with us, his long white ponytail hanging down his back and Abby tucked under his arm. The older boys are tossing a football farther down the beach, and some of the girls are playing at the edge of the water with our mothers. My father is standing by the fire with his arms crossed, flanked by Roddy Remington and Steve Steele. They're an unlikely and unbreakable trio. My father, in his dress pants and collared shirt, his serious eyes trained on us. Roddy with his windblown collar-length hair and beard, sporting cargo shorts and one of his many flowered shirts unbuttoned too far, is laughing, his head tipped back. Then there's Steve, one hand casually tucked in the pocket of his jeans, wearing a polo shirt, his attention locked on his wife and girls, down by the water.

Those four men taught me too many life lessons to count. I can still hear my father telling me to learn from my mistakes and try to do better today than I did yesterday and Roddy saying not to sweat the small stuff. How many times did Steve remind me that everyone makes mistakes and forgiveness is the greatest gift of all? I don't even have to try to hear Olivier's kind voice telling me to trust my heart. They instilled so much wisdom, but none of it prepared me for surviving a broken heart.

Jesus. I can only imagine the shit the guys would give me if they heard me say that.

I shove those thoughts down deep and head out of my office.

Music filters into the restaurant from the bar, injecting an upbeat, summery vibe. As I make my way around the room greeting customers and making small talk, the pit of my stomach burns. This is the first time in as long as I can remember that my smiles aren't genuine, and I fucking hate it. It reminds me of when I was a kid putting on my happy face, and it's something I swore I'd never do as an adult. But in this situation, I don't have a choice.

I spot Roddy and his wife, Gail, having dinner with Steve and Shelley Steele, and Shelley's mother, Lenore. I head over to them.

"A table full of my favorite people," I say as I sidle up to them. "I hope you're enjoying your evening."

"Wells, we've missed you lately," Shelley exclaims, and the big beautiful auburn-haired woman with a heart of gold gets up to hug me.

"I've missed seeing you all as well," I say, soaking in her embrace.

As she sits down, I put a hand on Lenore's and Gail's shoulders. "You ladies look lovely tonight."

"I have missed your charm, young man," Lenore says. She has a blond pixie cut and a flair for fashion, as proven by her black silk top, gold scarf, and dangling pearl earrings.

"I'll have to rectify that and spend more time here." My gut twists, but I don't let my smile falter. "Nice to see you, Mr. S," I say as I shake Leni's father's hand.

"You too, Wells."

I offer my hand to Roddy. "How's it going?"

Roddy bats my hand away and stands to embrace me, clapping a hand on my back as he says, "You doing okay, son?"

The way he studies my face makes me feel like he can see right through my fake smile. "Yes, sir. How are you tonight?"

"My family's healthy, and we've got good boating weather. All is well on the Remington front."

"I'm glad to hear it." I turn my attention back to the Steeles. "You must be getting excited about Leni's wedding."

"We are beyond thrilled," Shelley says. "Although Leni is with Indi and the rest of the girls right now. You know how she hates people fussing over her. I hope they don't drive her so batty, she cancels the wedding."

I can see Leni throwing her hands up and calling it off to elope, but I don't dare say it.

Steve reaches for his wife's hand. "That's not going to happen. She loves Raz, and she knows how much planning has gone into this wedding."

"Wells, you've been awfully busy running back and forth to the city lately," Gail says. "Have you found a spot for a restaurant yet?"

The high of seeing the property on the dock with Victory comes rushing back, but the ache in my chest overshadows it. I have no idea how I'm going to navigate that, much less going back to the city when everything about it reminds me of her. "We're getting close."

"That's wonderful news," Shelley exclaims.

"Yes, we're all excited about your new business endeavor," Lenore says. "But I'd rather hear the scoop on you and your new lady friend. We hear you're getting *hotsy totsy* with Flynn's sister, Victory."

Shelley gives her a chiding look. "Mom, don't embarrass him."

Roddy laughs. "You can't embarrass this guy. He can have any woman he wants."

No, I can't. Not when the only woman I want doesn't want

me. I grit my teeth to keep those words from coming out.

"Raz mentioned that he and Leni caught you two in a lip-lock right in the middle of the busy city sidewalk," Lenore says.

"Gotta love Raz," Roddy says.

"We're happy for you, honey," Shelley says. "We adore Victory, and her family is lovely."

"We liked her, too," Gail said. "Will we be seeing her at the wedding?"

Fuck. I don't even want to think about navigating the wedding. I need to get the hell out of here. "I'm sure you'll see her there." Before they can ask any more questions, I say, "I'd better get going. It was great to see all of you. Enjoy your evening."

I escape into the bar and weave through the lively crowd, stopping to introduce myself to new customers and catching up with Sunday-night regulars. I chat with a few friends from around town, and when I notice a blonde and brunette eyeing me near the dance floor, I make my way up to the bar to avoid them.

"Hey, Wells," Fitz calls out as he and Grant break through the crowd.

"Hey. I didn't know you guys were here. How's it going?"

"Not bad," Grant says. "We haven't seen much of you lately. We thought we'd swing by and catch up."

"Sorry. I've been pretty busy." I walk behind the bar. "Can I get you a beer?"

"Sounds good," Fitz says, and Grant says, "Sure."

I fill three glasses and then join them on the other side of the bar.

Grant lifts his mug. "To your new restaurant, little bro."

"The property isn't ours yet. The lawyers have to jump through some legal hoops first to make sure it's doable." I take a drink, not wanting to talk about *that*, either.

"You know I was kidding with all that shit talk, right?" Fitz says.

"Yeah, whatever. It's all good." I take another pull of my beer, feeling antsy as fuck.

"It's cool that Victory found it for you," Fitz says.

"That reminds me, why did I have to hear about your new girl from my wife?" Grant asks. "Is that who you were frustrated about when we played poker last month?"

I try to sound casual. "Yeah."

"Guess that means things are going well," Fitz says.

Not really. I take a drink instead of responding.

"What can I say? I give great advice," Grant says.

"What are you, the love guru? Jamison gave him great advice." Fitz lifts his chin at me and says, "How crazy is it that the guys who have dated the least are the ones who helped you win her over?"

Lot of good it did. "Pretty crazy." I guzzle my beer, then set my empty glass on the bar, catching a glance I can't read between my brothers. That's my cue to get the hell out of Dodge. "You guys enjoy yourselves. I've got things to do. I'm heading out." I make a beeline for the exit.

They catch up to me as I step outside. One on either side, like fucking bookends.

"A'right, Wells, what's going on?" Grant asks.

"Nothing. I just have things to do." I continue walking along the stone path that cuts through the lawn to the crest of the hill overlooking the marina.

"Come on, bro," Fitz urges. "We know you better than that."

Grant steps in front of me at the top of the hill, blocking

my way, and crosses his arms. "You wear your emotions on your sleeve. Always have. You can't fake smiles worth shit, and you're usually the first to joke around, so fess up. What's going on?"

"Whatever it is, you can trust us," Fitz says.

Yeah, I can fucking trust them. They've helped me through the hardest times in my life, and as much as even thinking about admitting the truth hurts, I can't stop it from barreling out. "You want to know what's wrong? I'm the fucking good-time guy. That's what's wrong. But ever since Victory and I got together, she's *all* I want. She's all I fucking think about. It's never been like this with anyone, and it's not because she's hot or any of that bullshit," I seethe, as if they've accused me of being shallow.

I pace, unable to tamp down my frustration or my heartache. "When I look at her, I see a woman who is good and honest and so fucking strong. But she's also so damn fragile, and you'd never know it, would you? But *I* know it." I bang my fist against my chest. "I see it and I feel it, and I want to be the guy she trusts with that side of herself. I *thought* I was doing all the right things. That we had something special. I thought I could do this." I stop pacing and realize they're just staring at me. "But by the looks on your faces, you know I can't." *Just like Victory.*

"What're you talking about?" Grant snaps. "What *look*?"

"The one that says you think I'm too selfish or incapable of having a long-term relationship. It makes sense. I've never had one other than Leni, and I cheated on her—"

"You were a kid," Fitz says sharply.

"So what?" I fume. "I knew right from wrong, and I still hurt my best friend. Love scared the shit out of me. I thought I learned from all that crap, but maybe I'm just fooling myself, and Victory somehow knows I'll screw up down the road."

"*Wait*," Grant snaps. "What the fuck happened between you two?"

"I don't fucking know. We always spend the night in my hotel room when I'm there, so Friday night I suggested we spend the night at her place, and she freaked out. She looked scared, or appalled. I don't know how she looked. But it makes sense. I told her what happened with Leni, and she knows how we grew up. Pretending shit was normal. I'm sure to Victory I'm one big fucking red flag. I guess our childhood fucked me up for good after all."

"What kid doesn't have baggage from their childhood?" Fitz asks.

"It fucked me up for a long time, too," Grant admits solemnly. "I've worked through it, and Dad and I are cool now, but, Wells, I don't think you're selfish or incapable of having a relationship. You dropped everything to set up a special night for Jules when I asked you to. You called in favors and gave the woman I love the night of her life, when I'm the last person you should have done anything for."

Thinking about that day, I remember how good it felt to see him come back to life. I would've done anything to help him stay on that path, and I was happy to turn the private rooftop dining room at Rock Bottom into a romantic wonderland for the woman who was helping bring him back to us. "You're my brother. I'd do anything for you."

"That's what makes you a great guy," Grant says. "I was a complete dick to you and everyone else, and you didn't hold it against me."

"Like I said," I grit out. "You're family."

"Dude, you're always the first to help anyone, whether

they're family or not," Fitz says. "When Abby's mom died, you offered to buy the Bistro so she wouldn't have to move back to the island, and we all know you didn't want to own another restaurant on the island."

"You would've done the same thing."

Fitz and Grant exchange dismissing glances and shake their heads.

"No, we wouldn't, and we didn't," Grant says.

"You're a different breed, Wells," Fitz says. "Remember when Goldie Gallow's kitchen at the B and B flooded a few years ago and she had a full house and was hosting a community breakfast that weekend? The second you got wind of it, you handled it. You catered breakfasts for her guests and gave them free dinners at Rock Bottom, and you catered breakfast for the whole Seaport community. A selfish person wouldn't have done *any* of those things."

Goldie Gallow is in her eighties. She owns a bed and breakfast in Seaport and has hosted monthly breakfasts for the entire community since before I was born. We went as a family, and I still enjoy going to them.

"He's right. You've never been selfish, Wells," Grant says. "Not even as a little kid. After Dad moved out, you did whatever the girls wanted just to keep them happy. I could hold them when they cried, but I couldn't do that pretend-prince shit you did. And you used to pick Mom's favorite flowers and leave them on her pillow. They'd wilt by the time she found them, but they made her happy."

I didn't think anyone knew about that. "How do you know about the flowers?"

"I found her crying one night and saw dirt on her pillow," Grant says. "I thought one of you had ruined her sheets or something, but she said they were happy tears and showed me the note you left. It said you were sorry Dad moved out and that you would be the man of the house for her."

Fitz laughs. "Always taking top billing. Even as a kid."

I smile, appreciating the levity. "She was so sad. I just wanted to help."

"She showed me where she kept them," Grant says. "On a bookshelf in her bedroom, pressed between the pages of a gardening book."

My throat thickens. "I assumed she threw them out."

"I bet they're still there," Grant says. "If Stevie ever does anything like that, there's no way Jules or I would throw them out. Mom said you left her flowers all the time, and that you had Dad's heart, which pissed me off, because I was furious at him after he left. I thought he didn't love us."

"I felt that way for a little while at first," I admit.

"I never did," Fitz says. "That must've sucked."

"It did. Why didn't *you* feel that way?" Grant asked.

"I don't know." Fitz's brows knit. "Dad and I have always had a different relationship than you guys have. You and Dad fought all the time, and even as a kid, Wells was the family jokester. Dad used to do things just to get him to make a joke, but I was Dad's serious sidekick. He sat me down before he left and told me how much he loved us and said things would work out. I believed him. And yeah, everything changed after he moved out, and that sucked, but I never doubted that he loved us."

"You always were a kiss ass," Grant said.

Fitz looks at him like he's lost his mind. "You think I liked being tagged as the good one? That's a fucking noose around my neck. I was jealous of you guys when we were younger." He lifts his chin at Grant. "You never took shit from anyone, and, Wells, you broke the rules every damn day and everyone still adored you."

"What are you saying? You wanted to be a bad boy?" Grant snarls.

"Fuck yeah," Fitz says. "You made it look cool, and Wells made it look fun."

"There's nothing cool about how angry I was at Dad," Grant says firmly.

"And I never tried to break the rules. Not back then, anyway," I say. "It's just who I am, and *that's* a noose around my neck. Look at my current situation. Victory sees me as a fucking boy toy."

"If she thinks that, it's *her* loss. You're a great guy," Fitz says.

"I don't know about that," I admit. "Look at my dating history. Everyone knows me as the good-time fling guy."

"Not the people who really know you," Fitz says.

"Who gives a damn about your dating history, anyway?" Grant says sharply. "Your value as a partner isn't derived from the length of your past relationships. It's about who you are and how you treat others. You're as trustworthy as they come."

"Haven't you been showing up to see her in the city a couple of times each week?" Fitz asks. "Or were all those trips just for the restaurant?"

"Both, but mostly her."

"If you ask me, that makes you a fucking knight in shining armor," Grant says.

I scoff. "Hardly."

"Listen, without a crystal ball, you can't know what's going through her head," Fitz says.

"Actually, I think I do," I admit. "She told me she wasn't looking for a relationship, but like a fool, I fell for her. When I saw the fear or whatever it was in her eyes, I gave her an out. I said it was too much too fast, and she took it."

"Well, *shit*. Maybe she'll come around," Grant says.

"Part of me wants to force her to open her fucking eyes and see us like I see us, but the other part of me doesn't want to make things harder for her."

"See? Not selfish," Fitz says. "If you did wrong by her, I'd say grovel your heart out, but it doesn't sound like you did. Maybe she's as confused about it as you are. Some time and space might help. What do you say we head over to my place and play some pool? Help you forget her for a while."

There is no forgetting Victoria Braden, but sitting at home picking this shit apart for another night would be torture.

As we head to the parking lot, Grant claps a hand on my shoulder and says, "Nobody said love was easy, but when it's with the right woman, it's worth it."

"That's great, Grant," Fitz says sarcastically. "Rub your happiness in his face."

Grant glowers at him. "That's *not* what I'm doing."

"It's okay, Fitz," I say. "Pixie's penchant for sprinkling happy dust must be rubbing off on him."

Fitz and I laugh.

"Fuck off. I'm as broody as ever," Grant says, which only makes it more fun to heckle him.

"As broody as a giddy girl who just got asked to prom," I taunt, and Grant's eyes narrow, which makes me laugh harder.

"I'm going to worry if he starts singing 'Girls Just Want to Have Fun,'" Fitz says.

We both start singing and howling with laughter.

Grant looks like he's got smoke coming out of his ears. "Shut the fuck up before I take you both down," he warns, which sends us further into hysterics.

"Uh-oh," I choke out between laughs. "I see pixie wings sprouting from his shoulders."

"I'll give you pixie wings." Grant charges at us, knocking us both to the ground.

We wrestle, cracking up and calling each other names, and it *almost* drowns out the ache of missing Victory.

Chapter Nineteen

Victory

I pedal the spin bike faster, pushing myself harder for the last two minutes of my forty-minute ride. It's Wednesday morning, and I've been at the gym since five thirty. Working out is the only thing that loosens the painful barbs in my chest, my constant companions since Friday evening. I haven't heard from Wells. I also haven't slept and have barely eaten, and in an effort to outrun the heartache, I dove back into the familiar and buried myself in work. Apparently I'm a glutton for punishment, because I've also spent far too much time looking at the memories we've collected in that cheap little treasure box with the neon print on top.

Sweat drips down my face as I climb off the bike. I grab my towel and wipe it away. My phone chimes with a message, sending my heart into a torrent of hope, guilt, and worry. Hope that it's a text or a WordLink invitation from Wells, guilt for the selfish thought, and worry because Leni's wedding is this weekend, and I fear Wells will text to clarify that I'm no longer his date. I wouldn't blame him, but I don't know if I can take seeing it written out like that. I don't know how I'll face him at the wedding without falling apart. And to top it all off, I've been avoiding Seth, which further breaks my heart. But I can't think about him without thinking about Wells.

I snag my phone from the holder on the bike, and the barbs in my chest tighten at the sight of another email from my London office. Of course there isn't anything from Wells.

Why would there be? I hurt him too badly. I hurt both of us.

I've wanted to call him a hundred times, but how can I? What am I going to say? *You're right? I'm not ready for us?* I don't want to say that. It's not what I feel. I'm crazy about him. But maybe I'm also a little crazy in general, because when he suggested we stay at my place, I couldn't fathom the idea of bringing him into Harvey's home. But that doesn't mean I don't want to, or I don't want him.

Ugh. I do sound crazy.

Someone taps my shoulder, drawing me from my unhappy stupor. I pull out my earbuds and turn around.

"Are you done with the bike?" a younger, bright-eyed blonde asks.

"Yes, sorry. Just give me one sec." I wipe down the bike, and I can't help thinking that Wells should be with someone like her. Someone younger, who doesn't have a late husband living in her heart…or her home. "It's all yours."

Saying those words shouldn't hurt, but in my messed-up head, I imagine saying *He's all yours*, and that pain is too much to bear. I put my earbuds in and scroll to "Zombie" on my playlist, turning it up loud as I head to the treadmill, hoping a run will make it easier to breathe.

My day is packed with meetings, phone calls, and putting out fires. It doesn't help that my thoughts churn like the agitator of a washing machine, whipping and shifting as I struggle to focus. Just when I think my head is clear enough to get through whatever meeting I'm in or task I'm working on, my thoughts drag me back to Wells.

In dire need of caffeine, I head to the break room. As I fix myself a cup of coffee, memories of breakfasts with Wells play in my mind like a montage. Images of him stealing a piece of fruit off my plate, flashing that coy smile, and that spark of heat in his eyes tug at my heartstrings.

"There you are," Padma says as she walks into the room.

Those words whisper through my mind in Wells's deep voice, bringing back the heart-melting way he looks at me when he says it.

"Time to recharge." Padma grabs a mug from the cabinet and looks at me curiously. "You okay?"

No. I hate feeling like this.

I manage a smile. "Yeah." Grasping for something to take my mind off Wells, I say, "I'm hearing great things about our new staff from M&O. How did the department meeting go this morning?"

"It went well." She pours herself a cup of coffee. "The managers are up to date, and the reports look good. It was a smart move bringing them in-house."

"We never make dumb moves."

"Cheers to that." She takes a sip of coffee, and we walk out of the break room together. "I wanted to talk with you about—

" Her cell phone rings. "Sorry. I'm waiting for a call from Marco." Marco is the director of accounting, and he's out of town this week. She glances at the screen, and her brows pinch.

"If you need to take it, we can catch up later," I say as we pass another employee and exchange smiles.

"No, it's fine." She sends the call to voicemail. "It's just Corbin."

"I thought you got rid of him weeks ago."

"I did. But I ran into him last weekend and I didn't want to be rude, so we talked over a drink. Now he's like a cat who refuses to find a new home. Story of my life, right?"

"You just haven't met the right person yet." The blond she went out with a few weeks ago ended up being a dolt.

"That's what I keep telling myself, but I'm not getting any younger. You were so lucky to have Harvey. They don't make guys like him anymore. He knew how to treat a woman."

"Yes, he did."

"There should be a test men have to pass before they're allowed to date," Padma says. "I swear men these days are clueless about chivalry or even reading a room, for that matter."

My mind skips back to Wells. He has chivalry down pat, putting himself between me and the street on our walks, opening doors, asking if I need anything, and he is a master at reading any room. *Especially the bedroom.* A wave of longing moves through me, dragging me deeper into the ache of it. I miss waking up with him as much as I miss our talks, playing that silly game, and exploring the city together.

"You and Harvey were so well suited for each other," Padma says. "That's what I hope to find. A once-in-a-lifetime love."

"You will," I say absently, my thoughts turning to Harvey. He was a once-in-a-lifetime love. But can there be more than one kind of love in a person's lifetime? My thoughts stumble. *Love? Am I really asking myself that?* My pulse quickens. *How did we get here so fast?*

"My mother says I lost my chance at love when I chose work over Nevin," Padma says, bringing me back to the moment. Nevin was a man she dated when she was in her twenties. He proposed and she turned him down to focus on her career. "Maybe I should just stop looking. Men are more trouble than they're worth. It's not like I want to have kids."

That maternal pang that has been hitting me harder lately, the one that felt like it swallowed me whole in Baltimore around all those children at the aquarium, rushes in.

"I don't need a man in my life, right?" Padma says.

"I don't think any woman *needs* a man in their life, but there's nothing wrong with wanting one," I say as much for myself as for her as we walk into my office, and find Yvette putting something on my desk.

"There you are," Yvette says.

My chest constricts. I wonder if it would raise eyebrows if I ban that phrase from the office.

"I was just leaving these for you." Yvette picks up papers from my desk. "I know tonight is your scouting night, and I realize you might already have artists on your schedule, but my friend turned me onto this guy who's a musician and a performance artist, and he's playing tonight at the…"

As Yvette goes on about the artist, my heart sinks. *Scouting night.* I was so worried about what everyone here who knew Harvey might think of me if they found out I was seeing Wells, I let them believe I was scouting talent on Wednesdays and Fridays. Not that there's anything wrong with seeing Wells, but this was Harvey's company, his legacy, and I didn't want to do anything that might tarnish it, like giving people a reason to start talking about me behind my back.

That stops me cold, and reality steals my breath.

In an effort to protect the reputation of Harvey's legacy and maybe my own ego, I've become a liar—*even to myself*—and I hurt the best man I know when he's done nothing but be patient and kind and wonderful.

Shitshitshit.

"I emailed you a list of his social accounts and links to some of his videos." Yvette holds the papers out to me. "I also printed out these articles about him."

My thoughts are reeling, and I'm fighting the urge to run as far and as fast as I can, the same way I struggled after Harvey's death—which makes no sense, since it feels like there's an elephant sitting on my chest making it hard to breathe. I take the papers. "Thanks."

"He sounds great," Padma says as Yvette leaves my office.

I didn't catch half the things Yvette said about the artist, and I couldn't focus right now if my life depended on it. But then I remember Padma was there for a reason. "You had something you wanted to talk to me about? Was it important?"

"I just wanted to ask how your breakfast with Mary Denson went yesterday." Mary was one of our newer agents.

"It was great. She's jumped in with two feet and already has meetings lined up for the rest of the month."

"She reminds me of you when you first came on board," Padma says. "Nothing could stop you. I remember warning Harvey that you were going to ruffle feathers."

That gets my attention. "You never told me that. Did you think he shouldn't have hired me?"

"No. I wish he could've cloned you." Padma laughs. "Once

you set your sights on what you wanted, you never backed down, and you didn't give a hoot about what anyone thought along the way."

We've never talked about how my relationship with Harvey came to be, and I have to ask, "Are you talking about Harvey or clients?"

"Both, I guess. You were a force to be reckoned with for your clients, and that lit a fire beneath the butts of some agents who were getting too comfortable. As for you and Harvey, your relationship was inevitable. Being around you two was like waiting for fireworks to go off. I was happy he found someone who cared about people as much as he did and who truly loved him for who he was. But he was such a composed, in-control person, I think you scared him a little."

"I don't know if that's good or bad," I say carefully. "I know some people thought I was a gold digger."

"I never thought that, and my guess is, the people who did, didn't think it for long. I'd never seen Harvey happier than when he was with you, and you always were a dynamo, but you shined even brighter around him. I wish he'd opened his heart to you sooner so you could've had more time together."

A pang of sadness hits. How many tears have I shed over that lost time? How many hours have I spent wishing I'd pushed him harder that first year after we met? And for what? All that heartache and regret couldn't give us that time back. That time is gone. Harvey is gone.

My throat thickens.

"I missed seeing that spark in you after Harvey died," Padma says. "But it's come back now that you're scouting talent again. It's a different kind of spark but every bit as bright."

That's not from scouting. That's from Wells. Guilt slices

through me, and that urge to run returns. "I have to go." I hurry over to the closet and grab my purse.

"Is everything okay? Did I say something wrong?"

"No, Pad. Everything you said was spot-on."

Chapter Twenty

Wells

"You know what, Wells? I like Victory," Keira says, studying me as I refill her wineglass. "She and I are a lot alike. She's smart, accomplished, and confident. I respect that in a person."

"And she's a total smoke show like you, Kei," Bellamy chimes in.

"Thanks, Bell. Right back at you," Keira says, and they clink glasses like they've just solved the world's problems.

My sisters showed up at Rock Bottom half an hour ago claiming to be on a mission to cheer me up. "How is this supposed to cheer me up?"

"I'm getting there." Keira sips her wine. "You said you thought she wasn't ready for a relationship, but you guys were seeing a *lot* of each other, which indicates that you were already in a relationship, so maybe what she's not ready for is your drama."

"What drama? I don't bring any drama."

A pair of brunettes at the other end of the bar flag me down for the third time since I came behind the bar to help out. Ignoring Keira's smug expression, I glance at the other bartend-

241

er, but he's busy with customers. "I'll be right back." I head to the other end of the bar. "Ready for another round?"

The taller of the two women smiles flirtatiously and says, "Only if you'll join us."

I'm not in the mood for this shit. The last few days have been torture. "Sorry, ladies. But I don't drink on the job."

"We figured you might say that," her friend says.

"I'm here through the weekend," the taller woman says. "Maybe we can grab a drink another time." She slides a piece of paper across the bar.

I pick it up and see *Sherry* and a phone number on it. There was a time when I might jump on that offer, or more likely, I'd have been the one offering. But now the thought of being with anyone other than Victory turns my stomach.

"That's really nice of you, Sherry, but I'm afraid I'm spoken for." I motion to the bartender coming back from his break. "When you're ready, Chuck will ring you up." As I head back to my sisters, I crumple the paper and drop it into the trash can.

"See?" Keira says accusingly. "You bring drama."

I grit my teeth. "I didn't instigate that, and I turned her down."

"But Victory has seen you in action," Keira says.

"What are you talking about?"

"You hit on her at Sutton's wedding," she reminds me.

"And at the holiday dance," Bellamy adds.

Fuck. They're right. She did see me in that light at first, but I have to believe Victory knows me better than that now. She knows the real me. The one I didn't even know existed before her.

"There's Kei!" Six-year-old Ritchie Lacroux shouts as he bursts through the crowd followed by his uncle and legal guardian Ryan. Ryan stepped in to raise Ritchie for his brother, who has a substance use disorder. Ritchie stops abruptly a few feet from Keira and starts jumping with both feet toward the bar. He has a thing for kangaroos.

Behind him, Ryan smiles, shaking his head.

Ritchie hops between Bellamy and Keira, flashing a toothy grin, and says, "Hi, Bellamy! Hi, Wells!" Then he pats Keira's legs excitedly, beaming up at her. "I didn't know you were here!"

"Hey, Ritchie Roo." Keira ruffles his sandy hair. "How is my favorite customer?"

"I'm good, thanks for asking," Ryan says, his eyes locked on Keira.

"Uncle *Ryan, I'm* her favorite!" Ritchie insists.

"Yeah, Uncle Ryan," Keira teases, and we all chuckle. "There's no competing with this cutie. What is that on your cheek, Roo? Icing?" She brushes something off Ritchie's cheek with her thumb.

"Uh-huh! Me and Uncle Ryan shared red velvet cake!"

"You guys are cheating on my baked goods, huh?" Keira glances coyly at Ryan. "I see how you are."

Ryan leans in and lowers his voice. "Don't tell your brother, but it wasn't as good as yours."

I scoff.

"Sounds like Wells needs to up his dessert game," Bellamy says.

"I'll get right on that," I say.

"You should use Keira's bakery," Bellamy suggests. "I can negotiate a good deal for you."

"*No,*" Keira and I say in unison, earning an eye roll from Bellamy.

"Where are you off to, Roo?" Keira asks.

"Home," Ritchie says sadly.

"We've got a fun night of bath time and stories ahead of us," Ryan says. "Say goodbye, buddy."

"I wanna stay with Kei," Ritchie pleads.

Ryan puts his hand on Ritchie's shoulder and says, "We can't stay, but if you get up a little early, we can stop and see Keira at the bakery before school."

"We can? *Yes!*" Ritchie pats Keira's leg again. "Bye, Kei!" He turns to us and waves. "Bye."

"Bye, buddy," I say.

"See you, cutie." Bellamy sets a serious stare on Keira and crosses her arms. "Did you see the way Ryan was looking at you? You can't tell me he's not into you."

Keira rolls her eyes. "We're friends, Bellamy. That's *it*. You know what I see when I look at them?"

"The most lusted-after cop on the entire island?" Bellamy asks. "A tall drink of champagne with a body made for giving pleasure?"

"Bellamy." I glower at her.

"What?" Bellamy picks up her wineglass. "You know darn well why he's always in her shop."

"He might be hot, but he is drama waiting to happen," Keira says. "All men are. Look at Wells. He doesn't even have to do anything but exist, and drama finds him. It's woven into the fabric of their beings."

"Bullshit," I say.

"Leave him alone, Kei. You're making him feel bad." Bellamy eyes me. "I've got your back, Wells, and I'm about to make you very happy. I came up with an idea for a new reality show that will make us both stars."

For Christ's sake. "This shit again?"

Bellamy waves her hand dismissively. "Hush up, and hear me out. *Love Match, Sibling Edition.* We go on the show together and choose each other's matches. Every week I'll eliminate one for you, and you eliminate one for me."

"*No*," I say flatly.

"Come *on*. It's a great idea," she pleads. "I'm going to pitch it to Flynn this weekend."

"Flynn doesn't produce dating shows," I remind her. "And please leave me out of it."

"You'd get good ratings and probably find a slew of hot babes," Bellamy urges.

"You do have a face for drama," Keira adds, then finishes her wine and holds up her empty glass, her eyes glittering with the same teasing look she used to give me when we were kids and she thought she was being clever.

"Sorry, guys, but the only woman I want is in New York City." I turn to grab the wine bottle.

"Actually, she's on Silver Island, if you still want her."

My fucking heart leaps into my throat at the sound of Victory's voice. I turn around as my sisters greet her, and our eyes connect with a thunderous beat, drowning out everything else. I set the bottle on the bar, disbelief swamping me. "Vic…?"

Victory steps closer to the bar, her hopeful, apologetic eyes tugging at something deep inside me. "I'm sorry to show up unannounced, but I screwed up, Wells, and I had to see you. You weren't wrong about what you said, but you weren't totally right either. You did push me, but that's who you are, and I *like* that about you." Her words fly so fast, she barely takes a breath. "You just caught me off guard. I know I'm messed up when it comes to Harvey, but I don't want to be. I hate that I hurt you, and I don't blame you if you're done with us and want to be with someone who doesn't have my baggage. But before you make that decision, you need to know that I'm *not* messed up about my feelings for you. I want this, too. We just happened so fast, and my feelings are so strong, it scares the hell out of me. But what scares me more is how empty I feel without you."

She takes a breath, and my heart is so full of her, beating so fast, it takes a minute for me to realize the entire bar has gone silent, and all eyes are on us. She must feel it, because her cheeks pink up, but my strong girl draws her shoulders back and lifts her chin. *There you are.*

Her eyes never leave mine as she says, "If you haven't kicked me to the curb yet, I'm hoping we can go on our Wednesday Walkabout and talk."

It takes everything I have to say, "I don't think I can do that."

There's a collective gasp as I come around the bar, drinking her in. She's wearing a sleek sleeveless cream blouse and black slacks. When I meet her toe-to-toe, her teary eyes crush my heart. "I'm sorry, Vic, but I'd like to keep our walkabouts upbeat. How about tonight we call it a Wednesday *Workitout*?"

Nervous laughter tumbles from her lips. "I'd like that very much."

Someone yells, *"Yes!"* The bar erupts into cheers as I take Victory in my arms, kissing the ever-loving hell out of her, and Bellamy says, "There goes my reality show."

I'll take my reality with the incredible woman in my arms over a show any day.

Chapter Twenty-One

Victory

I'm more nervous than ever as we leave the bar, despite my overwhelming relief that I didn't ruin things with Wells after all. I steal a glance at him, still a little in shock about my outburst, his reaction, and that he's right here by my side. "I'm sorry for making a scene. I wasn't thinking clearly."

His expression turns serious. "Are you saying you didn't mean the things you said? Because I'm hoping you were thinking very clearly."

"I meant all of it, but I didn't plan on pouring out my heart in front of an audience. I left work early and went straight to the ferry. I was so focused on getting here and apologizing, when I saw you standing behind the bar, it just came out. I guess I'm the one who had blinders on this time."

His jaw relaxes into a tender smile. "I'm glad you meant it, because the rumor mill is definitely churning now."

"Sorry. The last thing I wanted was to embarrass you. Especially at work."

"There's no need to be sorry." He nods toward the beach and puts a hand on my back as we follow a path in that direction. "Nothing you do could ever embarrass me. Besides, you just secured our place in Silver Island history. We'll be the couple they're still talking about in twenty years. Our story will twist and change and morph into an epic legend."

More relief washes over me. "I've missed your sense of humor."

"I've missed everything about you." He takes my hand, drawing me closer as we make our way down to the path.

We leave our shoes by the dune grass and head down to the beach. The sun hangs low on the horizon as we walk hand in hand across the cool sand. The sounds of waves kissing the shore mingle with voices carrying in the breeze from a family packing up to leave and others along the beach. My nerves kick up again as I try to figure out where to start with Wells, and I know I just have to dive in with both feet.

"I owe you an explanation about Friday night—"

"No, you don't." He stops walking, his expression serious. "You don't *owe* me anything. I want to be in your life, Vic, and I want to understand what happened the other night, but only if you *want* to share it with me."

How could I have ever thought he was just a playboy? I almost missed out on this incredibly patient man who sets my world, and my heart, on fire. "I want to. It's just not going to be easy."

"There's no rush."

"Yes, there is. I want us to work out, and we can't unless I'm completely honest with you."

"I appreciate that." He squeezes my hand. "I'm just happy you're here."

"I'm glad you didn't tell me to bug off."

"You know better than anyone that when you know someone is the one for you, you don't kick them to the curb just because they're scared." He kisses me tenderly, loosening the painful barbs in my chest.

When we reach the beach, he takes my hand again, and as we walk along the shore, I take a deep breath and lay my heart bare.

"Before we talk about Friday, you need to understand what happened when Harvey died." My nerves flame, and he must sense it, because he holds my hand tighter. "The night he died, we were working late at the office. Everyone else had already gone home. We'd had a really stressful day dealing with issues with two of our biggest clients. We were both on edge, and we got into an argument about how to handle a situation."

I swallow hard, that awful night coming back too vividly. "Harvey and I almost never yelled at each other. If we argued and things got heated, we'd give each other space and discuss it later. But that night, we both snapped. We were yelling at each other, and we weren't making any sense or any headway, and I stormed out. I was so angry, and I don't even remember how things got out of hand."

My eyes well up, and I try to blink the tears away. "I went home thinking he'd show up after he cooled off. When he didn't come home two hours later, I called his cell, and it rang a few times and then went to voicemail. That wasn't normal for us. Even if we were fighting, he *always* picked up. We both did. So I went back to the office, and that's when I found him." My voice cracks. "He was lying on the floor between his desk and the door, and he…he wasn't breathing. I tried to…I couldn't bring him back." Tears spill down my cheeks.

"Jesus, baby." Wells pulls me into his arms, holding me tight. "You must've been terrified."

"I never should've let it get so bad," I choke out, my chest aching. "He had high blood pressure, and his father died young from a heart attack when Harvey was in college. I should've stopped yelling. I never should've left. If I'd been there, I could've…"

He holds me tighter. "I'm sorry, baby, but Harvey's death *isn't* your fault."

"I know I didn't kill him, but the fight didn't help, and I was selfish in our marriage, only I didn't know I was being selfish." I push out of his arms, swiping at my tears. "I didn't take Harvey's last name when we got married because I wanted to be respected in the industry, and there were so many people who thought I was a gold digger. I didn't want anyone to dismiss me by name alone."

"That doesn't make you selfish. Plenty of women don't take their husband's name."

"That's not *all*. He wanted kids, but I wasn't ready." I swipe at my tears. "He never knew his mother, and he had no other relatives, so when he died, his family name did, too—" Sobs steal my voice, and Wells wraps me in his arms again. "That's *my* fault. The company is his only legacy. And to make it worse, as time passed, I started feeling like I might want kids one day, and I've been burying those feelings. But then I met you, and…I just feel so guilty."

"It's okay. Let it out." He kisses my head and rubs my back. When I burrow into him, he holds me tighter. "I've got you."

Sharing the weight of those long-held secrets draws more tears. I don't know how long we stand there on the beach, my tears wetting his shirt, his strong arms holding me up, but it feels like forever. But he doesn't rush me. He holds me until my breathing calms and my tears stop.

He cradles my face in his hands and wipes my tears with his thumbs. "I understand why you feel guilty, but not taking his name and not having babies doesn't make you selfish. You were a young woman with career aspirations, and I'm sure Harvey knew *exactly* who you were every step of the way."

"He did," I say softly. "But that doesn't take away the sadness of knowing everything about him except his business and the memories people hold is gone. And that's not all. Can we sit down?"

"Of course." He touches his shirt. "Do you want me to put my shirt down so you don't get your slacks dirty?"

Chivalry at its best, even when things are emotionally charged. "No, it's okay."

We sit in the sand, and I take a moment to let the sea breeze wash over my face. Wells puts his arm around me and kisses my temple.

"I'm sorry," I say. "I didn't mean to unload on you."

"You're not unloading. You're letting me in. I wondered why you never talked about when Harvey died or how you felt afterward. Now I understand."

"I've never told anyone about that fight except Seth. I was too ashamed."

"You've held it in for all these years? No wonder you've been so conflicted." He hugs me against his side. "You have nothing to be ashamed of. Couples fight. As special as it is that you and Harvey managed not to raise your voices most of the time, that doesn't make raising them a malicious act."

"I know. I just hate that it happened."

"I hate it for you." He kisses my temple. "I've never lost someone that close to me, but after just four days of missing you, I can't imagine losing the man you built a life with."

I rest my head on his shoulder, feeling like a huge burden had been lifted. "I could barely get out of bed for the first couple of weeks. I tried to push everyone away, and then I buried myself in work. But my family wasn't having any of it. My parents called all the time, trying to get me to talk to a therapist or come stay with them. Clay was busy with his football career, but he'd come by every time he had a break, and he texted all the time. Noah did the same, but Seth checked on me every day, and Flynn basically parked his ass at my place until I found my footing. I was so irritated with them. All I wanted was to grieve *my* way."

"By disappearing from everyone who loves you? A self-imposed penance?"

"Pretty much. Then one day Seth asked me what Harvey would think if he could see me, and that changed everything. I knew Harvey would be disappointed, and I felt like I owed it to him to make him proud, so I went to therapy, and after a few months I thought I had it all figured out."

I turn so I can see his face. "Then I met you, and you awakened parts of me that I had stowed away before I even met Harvey. I'm not the same person with you as I was with him. I never realized how much of myself I'd set aside in order to work on my career and then my marriage and to fit into those roles. But with you, I never think about how or *if* I fit in. I'm just myself, and I don't think I've ever had a chance to just be me before."

"I like everything about you, Vic."

"I'm glad, because I like everything about you, too, but you might change your mind after you hear what I'm about to say."

"I doubt that. But you can give it your best shot."

I smile, thankful he's not running scared yet, but I know

this might do it. "I went through therapy, as I said, and I'm not living in some fantasyland thinking Harvey's coming back. I've dealt with losing him, and thanks to Seth and Flynn, I've had a closet full of boxes and packing supplies for years just waiting to be used, but I never got rid of Harvey's things. I kept putting it off, and I guess I got used to seeing them. His stuff is everywhere, and when you suggested we stay there, I couldn't figure out how to do it. I *wanted* to, but I panicked. I mean, how do I tell a guy who I'm crazy about that my late husband's clothes are still in the closet, his candy dish is by the couch, and his favorite books are on the shelves?"

Compassion brims in his eyes. "The way you just did. If you'd told me that Friday night, I probably would've gone back to my hotel with you, and maybe we could have talked about it. But I'm at fault, too. I couldn't see past my own pain that night. When I saw the fear in your eyes, I thought I'd misread everything, and I was just a fun distraction for you."

"You *weren't*, and I hate that I made you feel that way."

"I know that now, but we all have insecurities, and what do I know about relationships?"

"You know more than I do. You do *all* the right things. You're the only person who has ever made me want to step outside my weird, insular world and *really* try to move forward." I take his hand. "But today I realized how unfair I've been to you. I've spent my life trying to prove myself to everyone else and myself. At first with grades and fitting in, then building my agenting career, and eventually proving I wasn't a gold digger. And after Harvey died, I had to prove I deserved to run the business."

I soften my tone with my next confession. "I was afraid of what the people who knew Harvey would think of me if they knew we were dating. That's why I kept our relationship to myself and let them believe the happiness they saw in me was caused by my scouting talent again. That was wrong of me, and I'm really sorry. I love who you are, and I'm proud to be with you. I just didn't know how to handle it, but I will. I promise."

"I appreciate you telling me, and I understand why you did it. Once you're seen as a good-time guy, it's not easy to keep it up or live it down."

Another pang of heartache hits me. "You shouldn't have had to live it down with me."

"Yes, I should have. You knew me as that guy before you got to know the real me. Hell, before I got to know the real me."

"You did come on pretty strong," I say teasingly, glad the heartache is lifting.

"I know a good thing when I see it." He lifts my hand and kisses the back of it.

"I'm glad you didn't give up on me, but the truth is, you showed me who you were the first night we were together. I was just too scared to admit it to myself. But I don't want to hide anything anymore. I know better than anyone that there's no promise of tomorrow, and I don't want to go another day wishing things were different. I want to let you into every part of my life, and I *will* if you still want to be there. But it's scary. I've held on to Harvey's things all this time because I love him, but more so because, as you said, it's like penance. The thing is, it's been so long, I'm not sure who I'll be without it, and I know that sounds crazy."

"No, it doesn't. It sounds honest, and I'd like nothing more than to be the guy you try to figure that out with."

Relief swamps me, and I lean in to kiss him. As our mouths

come together, so do all the shattered pieces of my heart.

We sit with our feet in the sand as the sun goes down. I remember with a start that Wells left work to talk to me. "Do you need to get back to work?"

"No. Do you have to get back to the city tonight, or do I get you all to myself?"

"Actually, I don't have to be back at work until Monday. I asked my director of operations, Padma, to cover for me. I figured I was either going to go home brokenhearted and hole up with eight gallons of ice cream until Leni's wedding on Saturday, or we'd make up and I wouldn't want to leave."

He flashes a seductive grin that spurs those butterflies to life. "Good. Then you're mine for the weekend."

"You have no idea how perfect that sounds, but I came from work, remember? I left *everything* at home. I don't even have my toothbrush or any extra clothes."

"Lucky for you, there are stores that sell toothbrushes here, and once we get to my place, you won't need any clothes at all."

Chapter Twenty-Two

Wells

I've wanted to bring Victory into my world for so long, helping her out of my Land Rover in front of my two-story cedar-sided home feels surreal. Her gaze sweeps over my house, which is nestled among dune grass and wild flowering bushes, to the bluff and the vast ocean views beyond.

"This is beautiful. You have a crow's nest," she says with surprise.

"Yeah. It's really cool to watch lightning storms from up there."

"I bet. This is your own not-so-little slice of paradise."

"I'm glad I finally get to share it with you." I take her hand, drawing her into a kiss. "I'm really happy you're here."

"I am, too." As we walk up the slate path to the porch, she says, "This reminds me of my parents' house in Ridgeport."

"It's on the water?"

"Mm-hm. I loved living there and waking up to the smell of the ocean."

"I knew you belonged in my bedroom. I always sleep with the windows open." I kiss her smiling lips, and then I open the door and wave her in. "After you, sweet thing."

She steps inside, and her eyes light up as she takes in the view from the foyer straight through the living room to the accordion-style glass doors across the back of the house. "*Wow*," she says as we head into the living room. Those baby blues sweep over the open floor plan. Her gaze lingers on the bookshelves flanking the stone fireplace, where pictures of family and friends decorate the mantel.

I set the bag of toiletries on the couch as she glances at the kitchen and dining room, which boast more views of the water. My taste is classic, substantial furniture, decorated in earth tones and beachy blues. I wonder what her home looks like. "It's probably a far cry from what you're used to."

"It's better than what I'm used to." She runs her finger along the back of the couch, looking a little tentative. "Can I let you in on another secret?"

"I'm hoping you'll let me in on all your secrets."

She smiles, lowering her eyes for a beat, those long lashes fluttering as she takes a deep breath. When she lifts those gorgeous eyes to me, her fingers stop moving along the back of the couch, like she needs the stability of it. "When I first saw the apartment, I couldn't imagine it ever feeling like home. It was so different from everything I knew. Not just physically, but in here." She touches her head. "And in here." She puts her hand over her heart. "I told you how I grew up. We had family money, but you'd never know it. We each had one suitcase or backpack that fit all of our belongings, and we didn't miss or need more materialistic things."

"Other than a flushing toilet?" I say to lighten her confession.

"I definitely would have liked that. Eventually the apartment felt like home because Harvey was there. But this?" She motions around us. "This is warm and inviting, like you. It already feels like *home*." Her eyes widen. "That sounded presumptuous. Sorry, I didn't mean—"

I silence her with a kiss. "Be presumptuous, baby. Be scared or silly or happy. I want you to be *you*, whoever that is at any given moment. Okay?"

"I think it's harder *not* to be me around you." She laughs softly. "I'm going to start calling you my truth serum."

"You can call me anything you want, as long as you call me yours." I take her in a slow, sensual kiss. I ache to be close to her, and it takes everything I have to temper that desire and pull back. "God, I've missed kissing you." I can't resist going back for more and taking the kiss deeper. *Fuck.* I don't want to rush her. "Sorry, baby. Are you hungry? I can whip something up, or we can go out and grab some dinner."

She hooks her finger into the waistband of my jeans, gazing up with desire brimming in her eyes. "I really just want to be close to you. Unless you're hungry?"

"Only for you, sweet thing." I lower my lips to hers in a soul-searing kiss that breaks the dam, unleashing days of pent-up emotions. Our kisses turn deep and devouring, and it doesn't take long before we're all over each other. I tear my mouth away, gritting out, "I've fantasized about taking you on every surface in my house, and I intend to, but I've waited weeks to have you naked in my bed." I crush my mouth to hers and lift her into my arms, carrying her into my bedroom.

She breaks the kiss and says, "I love when you go all caveman on me."

"I'll give you *caveman*." I toss her onto the bed, and she laughs as I take off her heels and my shoes and socks. I take off my shirt, and as I come down over her, she puts her hands up, keeping me at bay.

"How about if I give you *cavewoman* first?" She pushes me onto my back and straddles me. Her hair tumbles around her face as she unbuttons and unzips my jeans.

I reach down to help her, and she swats my hand away.

"I've got this." She grabs my jeans and boxer briefs at the hips.

"Oh yeah? Are you a professional cavewoman?"

"I did paleo once. I learned a few things." She shimmies lower as she tugs my jeans and briefs down to my thighs and stops. "Your monster thighs don't make this easy."

I laugh as she slips from the bed and tugs my clothes the rest of the way off. When she starts to climb onto the mattress, I say, "Uh-uh. I want you naked. If you get to play, so do I."

"You're so needy," she teases, and takes off her blouse.

I fist my cock, giving it a stroke as her bra falls to the floor. "*Mm*. Look at those gorgeous tits. Why do I want to come all over them?"

Her eyes flame as she takes off her slacks. "Because you're a Neanderthal, and you want to mark me as yours."

"Damn right I do." I give my cock another stroke as she hooks her fingers into the hips of her pretty black panties. "Take them off slowly, baby. I want to sear this movie into my brain."

She smirks, swaying her hips seductively as she slides her panties lower and turns around, showing me her gorgeous ass as she bends at the waist to take them off.

"Careful, sweet thing, or I'll come on that ass, too."

She struts toward the bed. "Only if I let you."

"You'll not only let me. You'll beg me to." She's owned her

sexuality since the first time we were together when she said, *Lay your handsome ass down and let me ride that cock*. But tonight feels different. Like my victorious tigress is uncaged for the first time in years.

"That's big talk," she says. "But I'm in control now."

She crawls over me and stops when her mouth is above my cock. I am about to let go of it when she wraps her hand around mine and squeezes. Her hungry eyes are trained on mine as she drags her tongue along the broad head. What a sexy sight she is. My cock jerks in my hand. "Fuck."

"Eventually," she promises. "Now stroke your cock with me like a good boy."

Jesus, that's hot. I stroke it as she teases the head with her tongue, then follows our hands down my cock, licking my shaft, getting me wetter with each stroke. "*Fuck* that feels good." She lowers her mouth over my dick, following our fists down. "*That's it,*" I growl. "Look how beautiful you are sucking my cock." She slows, grinning as she slides her tongue around the broad head again, our hands still stroking.

She dips lower and licks my balls. "*Fuuck*, baby." She sucks them into her mouth, and my hips shoot up. "*Jesus…Feels good.*" She does it again and peels my hand off my cock, fisting it herself as she takes it in her hot, eager mouth. Seeing my sweet, powerful girl, my secret vixen, enjoying every second of pleasuring me magnifies *my* pleasure. She strokes faster, tighter. "That's it. So fucking perfect, baby." I need to taste her. I grab her hair, tugging her face up. "Get up here and straddle my face."

Her eyes narrow. "I'm not done with you."

God, this woman. "I'm not asking you to stop for good. I want to make you come while you suck my cock."

"Oh." Wickedness shimmers in her eyes. "In that case, forget I objected."

Before she can move into position, I pull her into a savagely intense kiss. "I fucking love your mouth," I grit against her lips, and then reclaim them for another devouring. She hungrily returns my efforts, and we both come away panting. "I'm a greedy bastard for you. Don't stop sucking my cock while you come. Think you can do that?"

"I guess we'll see. I've never done it like that before." She lowers her voice to a whisper. "But I want to."

I really am greedy, because that makes me feel like a fucking king.

"That is, *if* you can continue pleasuring me while *you* come," she challenges.

I fucking love this domineering side of her. "That is *not* a problem."

As I guide her pussy down to my mouth, she wraps her hand around my cock and takes it in deep. We both moan, and she strokes me faster. I hold her tight against my mouth, fucking and licking as she sucks me off with mind-numbing intensity. Her hand is tight, her mouth is hot, and her pussy is as sweet as fucking heaven.

I grab her ass as I devour and tease. The tighter I squeeze her ass, the more sinful sounds she makes, and I don't miss those cues as we take and taunt each other right up to the brink. She whimpers with every slick of my tongue, grinding against my mouth. When I bring my teeth into play, her lustful sounds vibrate along my dick. I clench my teeth, trying to stave off my release in order to bring her even more pleasure. I intensify my efforts, using my fingers on her clit, until she's trembling, her needy, pleasure-drenched sounds vibrating through me as she works my cock so perfectly, I can barely hold back. I quicken my efforts. Her thighs flex, her hips buck, and her hand tightens like a death grip on my cock as she comes, hurling me into ecstasy with her. We thrust and moan, riding out our unrelenting pleasure until we have nothing left to give.

I'm bowled over as I gather her shaking body against me. Her eyes are so full of emotion, I feel it in my bones. We lie nose to nose, and as I kiss her forehead, her cheek, and finally her lips, she melts into me, like I'm her safe haven, and damn do I want to be.

"That was…" I am at a loss for words, but it turns out I don't need them, because she whispers, "*I know.*"

We kiss, basking in the aftermath of our lovemaking, and I whisper, "I think I'm going to have to get my secret dominatrix leather lingerie."

She laughs. "I don't know where all that came from. I've never been like that."

"I like bringing out your wild side. It turns out there are some pretty great benefits to being your *good boy.*"

"Ohmygod." She buries her face in my chest, laughing. "I can't believe I said that."

"I wonder what other benefits I can eke out of this."

She tips her face up. "Shut up and kiss me."

"There's my bossy babe." I kiss her lovingly, wanting her to feel my affection, not just my lust. But as happens so often with us, our passion takes over. I can't get enough of her, and I know in my heart, I never will. That should scare the living hell out of me, but it doesn't. I want more of us. I press my hand to her lower back, holding her tight against me.

"*Mm,*" she murmurs against my lips, gyrating her hips against my revived erection. "There are definite benefits to falling for a younger guy."

I sweep her beneath me, and her hair falls away from her face. "There you are," I whisper.

"You're like an emotional ninja, slaying me with your charm."

"I'd rather love you with my body than slay you at all."

As I lower my mouth to hers, she whispers, "There you go again."

I kiss her slowly and sensually. I slide my hand down her hip and lift her leg at the knee as our bodies come together. I feel her need in the catch of her breath, hear her emotion in the contented sigh as I bury myself to the hilt.

I brush my lips over hers, whispering, "I can't get close enough. I want to be so close, you carry me with you wherever you go. *Here*." I kiss her forehead. "And here." I kiss the silky skin just above her heart.

A sweet smile appears, and she touches my face. "You did that weeks ago without even trying."

Emotions billow inside me like an all-consuming wind as our mouths come together, and we find our rhythm, and the rest of the world fails to exist.

Victory

"I think I found my new favorite place," I say, burrowing closer to Wells. I had wondered if being intimate would be awkward after everything I revealed to him, but we feel even more connected. Like everything I've gone through, worried about, and fought against has been leading me to trusting him with all my flaws and fears—leading me to this moment—all along.

"In my bed?" he asks.

"In your bed, your house, your arms." I tilt my face up, and as he kisses me, my stomach growls.

"Sounds like I need to feed my girl."

My girl. I love that. "I've been pretty stressed. I haven't eaten today."

"Then I'll whip something up for us."

We peel ourselves out of bed, and as I put on my underwear, he snags his T-shirt and carries it over to me buck naked. "Wear this." He helps me put it on, and it tumbles to the tops of my thighs. "Perfect." He leans in for a kiss.

I like wearing his shirt. It smells like him.

He's pulling on his boxer briefs when his phone chimes. "I hope that's not work." He snags it from his jeans and reads the text. His jaw ticks as he thumbs out a response.

"Everything okay?"

"Yeah. It's Fitz. He knew you kicked me to the curb and heard about what happened at the bar. He's just checking on me."

I wince. "What did he say?"

He reads the text aloud. "'I hear Vic showed up. Now you can finally stop crying into your pillow. Try not to blow it this time.'" His phone chimes in quick succession, and his brows knit. "*Shit.* It's the group chat."

"Why do you look like that?" I ask carefully.

"You sure you want to know?"

"Kind of," I say, moving closer.

He shows me the phone.

Grant: *I hope you let her grovel a little.*

"He's not wrong," I say, and Wells rubs my back as we read more of the texts.

Bellamy: *Who are you kidding? Wells was practically on his knees begging her to take him back.*

Fitz: *Way to play hard to get, bro.*

Keira sends a GIF of a guy on his knees.

I laugh. "They're so much like my family."

"They're fools." Wells types, *Okay, enough*, and sends it.

Bellamy: *Don't get your briefs in a bunch. We're having a bonfire at Grant's tomorrow at 8. You better bring her.*

"A bonfire sounds fun," I say. "I'd like to get to know everyone better."

Wells slides his arm around my waist, pulling me against him. "What makes you think I'm going to let you out of my bedroom this weekend?"

"As much as I love the idea of never leaving this room, it might be nice to have clean clothes, and I need to get a dress to wear to Leni's wedding at some point. I still can't believe I left everything behind."

"I'm worth it." He kisses me. "But don't worry. I planned on showing you the island tomorrow. We'll pick up whatever you need."

More messages chime as they roll in.

Bellamy: *Tell me you're coming.*

Keira: *Ew! Don't!*

Laughing emojis pop up from Grant and Fitz.

Bellamy: *To the bonfire!*

"They are *just* like my brothers," I say. "We should definitely go to the bonfire. It sounds like it'll be fun."

"Fine. I'll share you for a little while," he concedes, and thumbs out, *I'm taking Vic out on the boat tomorrow to show her the island. We'll stop by after we're back. Now stop texting.*

Excitement bubbles up inside me. "We're going out on your boat tomorrow?"

"I was thinking we'd take it around the island and maybe spend the night on it if you want."

"*If* I want?" I wind my arms around his neck. "You promised me an ocean tryst, Silver."

"I will always keep my promises to you." We kiss, and my stomach growls again. "Come on, sweets. Let's eat before the alien in your stomach gets angry."

Moonlight spills through the windows as we make our way from the living room to the kitchen, which is spacious, with a large center island and expansive windows. Wells touches my hand and says, "How do you feel about crepes?"

"Like I could eat a hundred of them. *Wait.* You know how to make crepes?"

"You're not the only one with secret skills." He kisses my cheek as he walks past me and gets a mixing bowl from a cabinet and a whisk from a drawer. "I take it you don't cook much?"

"When we were overseas, I loved cooking with everyone for the community feasts. But I've never been big on cooking for myself, and I'm not one of those people who inherently *knows* how to cook. But I am big on eating."

"Yes, you are," he says wickedly. "And I'm very appreciative."

I laugh and glance out the window. Moonlight sprays a path over the inky water, like a secret revealed in the darkness. "It's really beautiful here."

"It's almost as pretty as you. Would you mind grabbing plates?" He motions to a cabinet.

As I reach up to get them, he swats my ass. I half laugh and half squeal, then spin around to swat his butt, but he catches my wrist and pulls me into another kiss.

"You look awfully cute in my T-shirt."

"Thanks, but it's mine now."

He grabs my butt with both hands. "Is that so?"

"Mm-hm. If we're an official couple on this island where gossip never sleeps, your clothes are fair game."

"Baby, you can have anything of mine you want."

"I'm glad you agree, because I'm hoping you have a comfy hoodie I can wear to the bonfire tomorrow night."

"I think I can hook you up." He gives me a quick kiss, and then he loads up the counter with strawberries, blueberries, Nutella, eggs, and milk.

"Yum." I open the Nutella, dip in a strawberry, and give it to him as he mixes ingredients. Then I make one for myself. "*Mm.* Who needs crepes when we have this deliciousness?" I dip another strawberry and hold it out for him.

"Now you're just trying to seduce me." He eats the strawberry out of my fingers.

"Nutella and strawberries? I think *you* are the seducer in this scenario, Mr. Silver. All that's missing is whipped cream."

He flashes a wolfish grin. "I'm saving that for later."

Chapter Twenty-Three

Wells

"What do you think?" Victory asks as she comes out of the dressing room at Oceanside Boutique on Main Street, looking like a million laid-back bucks in cutoffs and a light blue tank top that brings out her eyes and has I CHILLED ON SILVER ISLAND printed above a silhouette of a lighthouse, waves, and two birds flying over the water. This is the second outfit she tried on. The first was just as gorgeous, though dressier.

"You look dangerously sexy." Her hair is loose, untamed waves spilling over her shoulders, just the way I love them, and the smile she's been sporting all morning is another new one. She not only looks happier and more relaxed than ever, but she also has a bounce in her step that wasn't there before. Seeing her come out from under the weight of her secrets is like watching her bloom to life again, and it's the most beautiful thing I've ever seen.

I draw her into my arms and lower my voice. "Keep looking at me like that and you're going to land right back in my bed."

She taps my chest. "That is not a threat, my friend."

We slept in and spent the morning loving on each other

before heading into town.

"Good." As I press my lips to hers, her hand flattens on my chest, and I wonder if I've embarrassed her and she's going to put distance between us. But her fingers curl into my T-shirt, keeping me close.

When our lips part, she says, "If they're going to talk about us, we might as well give them something to talk about."

"Who?"

"Anyone and everyone," she says cheekily.

"I like the way you think." As I lean in to kiss her again, I spot the owner of the boutique headed our way.

"Wells Silver, I thought that was you." Mrs. Smythe, a short, stout brunette, says. She gives Victory an appreciative once-over. "I see you brought a friend, and she found one of my favorite tanks."

"Mrs. Smythe, this is my girlfriend, Victory." *Girlfriend* rolls out full of pride, and I fucking love the way it feels to claim her. As I put my hand on her back, her smile tells me she's into it, too. "Mrs. Smythe owns this boutique."

"Hi," Victory says. "I love your shop."

"Thank you. It obviously loves you, too," she says kindly. "You were made for that outfit. You look beautiful."

"Thanks."

"I was in Trista's café this morning getting coffee, and the air was buzzing about our Wells being hit by Cupid's arrow," Mrs. Smythe says. "I'm happy to see it's true. They don't make 'em any sweeter than this young man." She touches my arm.

"I agree," Victory says. "I'm a lucky lady."

"Don't let her fool you. I'm the lucky one." I go for a change of subject before things get awkward. "How is your granddaughter?"

"Missy is a hoot," Mrs. Smythe says. "And your nephew, little Stevie?" She puts her hand over her heart. "What a doll baby he is. Maybe one day you two will give him a cousin."

Jesus. "How about we make it through the weekend first?"

Amusement rises in Victory's eyes.

"Of course. I didn't mean to push," she says. "It just comes naturally when I talk about grandbabies. I'd like to have a house full of them. But enough about me and my nana needs. Is there anything I can help you find, Victory?"

"I was about to take a look at your footwear," she says.

"And a bathing suit," I add. "Something skimpy."

"*No*," Victory says with a playful lilt in her voice. "Something *not* too skimpy, please, or knowing this guy, we'll never leave the boat."

"That's a good problem to have, honey," Mrs. Smythe says. "Let's start with footwear. Are we dressing the outfit up with wedges or strappy sandals or keeping it casual?"

"I'm here for the weekend and looking at other outfits, too, so maybe a cute sandal and something comfortable for knocking around town."

"I think we've got just the thing. Come this way." As we follow her to the footwear, she says, "We got a shipment of the cutest Keds slingbacks yesterday, and we have an array of strappy sandals."

Victory's eyes shimmer with delight. "You had me at Keds."

When we leave the shop, Victory is wearing new lingerie, which I can't wait to strip off her, the outfit she tried on, and white slingback Keds with navy polka dots. We bought two more shorts outfits, more lingerie, sandals, a sexy pink bikini, and a breezy white skirt.

"I love that woman," Victory says.

"You love that she had Keds," I tease, taking her hand.

"That was a definite bonus, but I like that she knows you so well. It's nice."

"Silver Island, where everyone knows your name and your business."

Main Street is bustling with tourists. OPEN flags wave by the entrances of shops, and window boxes are overflowing with colorful flowers.

"Isn't that Leni's sister, Jules?" Victory asks as we head down the sidewalk.

I look around the family in front of me and see Jules standing next to a stroller, putting sunglasses on one of the two iron giraffes by the entrance to her gift shop, the Happy End. Red balloons dance from strings tethered to the giraffes, matching the red-framed picture windows on the shop.

"Yeah. That's her gift shop."

"I know. I went in with Leni last time I was here. She has the cutest stuff."

Jules looks up as we approach. "Hey, you guys!" Her hair is pinned up in her signature water fountain on top of her head, and she looks cute in shorts and a flowy top. "Bellamy told me your *secret*."

"It's not much of a secret anymore, Jules." I lift our joined hands.

"Good! I'm so happy for you!" Jules hugs me. Then she hugs Victory and lowers her voice like *she's* sharing a secret. "I have been pulling for you two since the holiday party. Sparks were *flying*, and at Sutton's wedding I thought for sure you'd end up together."

"I tried to escape his charm, but he was relentless," Victory says.

"Don't listen to her, Jules. She practically stalked me."

"I did *not*."

"Well, I don't care who did the stalking," Jules says. "I'm just glad you're together and happy."

"Is that Stevie?" Victory peers into the stroller. Stevie is lying on his back in a white-and-blue striped onesie. He yawns, and his tiny fingers curl into fists. "Look, Wells. He's even more precious than his pictures."

"That's Uncle Wells, thank you very much. Jules, is it okay if I pick him up?"

"Always," Jules says cheerily. "He loves his uncles."

"Hey, little buddy," I say as I pick him up and tuck him into the cradle of my arm. I tickle his belly, and he pulls his tiny legs up. "I want you to meet someone special." I glance at Victory, and she's watching me with a dreamy expression, shaking her head. "What?"

She waves a finger at me. "This whole *you*-with-a-baby thing is…" She puts her hand over her heart and sighs.

Damn, that feels good.

Jules giggles. "He looks good with a baby, doesn't he?"

"Ridiculously good. Would you mind if I hold him?"

"It's only fair." Jules eyes me. "Wells, give my sweet little one to your sweetheart and see how fast your heart goes *thumpity thump thump.*"

As I hand Victory the baby, I say, "She already makes my heart go…" My words are lost as Victory nuzzles Stevie's cheek. Her eyes are closed, and she has the most serene expression on her face.

Hell if my heart isn't doing something funky. I think back to the way she looked at the kids when we were at the aquarium, and on the heels of that comes yesterday's grief-stricken confession. *I started feeling like I might want kids one day, and I've been burying those feelings. But then I met you, and...I just feel so guilty.*

"See?" Jules says gleefully.

Victory lifts her face, and something in her eyes tells me we're both tumbling down the same hill, and I ache to reach the bottom first, so I can catch her.

We stop at Rock Bottom on the way to the marina to pick up lunch, and while we're there, I show her around and introduce her to the staff. She's her usual easygoing self, and I can tell she likes meeting everyone.

"There's something to be said about seeing you in your element as a caring and effective boss," she says as we head to my office.

"You might have to visit more often."

"Aren't you worried I'll dole out demands to your chef?"

I can't believe she remembers that. "I wouldn't care if you did." I tug her into a kiss.

"Guess you're not cranky anymore," Meghan says as she comes down the hall.

I texted her this morning to let her know I was taking the weekend off and would be available by phone for emergencies. "Way to call a guy out." I put my hand on Victory's back. "Victory Braden, this is Meghan Young, our ever-efficient manager. Meghan is the reason I'm able to open a second restaurant."

"It's nice to meet you, Meghan."

"You as well." Meghan smiles. "I was hoping I'd get to meet the woman who swept Wells off his feet last night. It's all anyone could talk about."

"Sorry. I didn't mean to cause a scene," Victory says.

"Don't apologize," Meghan reassures her. "If any guy is worth a scene, it's Wells. You guys have fun this weekend, and don't worry about a thing. I've got this place covered. I have to get back to work. It was great meeting you, Victory."

When we get to my office Victory says, "So this is where you put on your boss hat."

"You could say that."

"I like it." She checks out the photographs. "I love this picture of everyone together. That has to be Olivier." She points to him. "He looks as kind as you described him to be."

"He was."

She walks over to the window and looks out at the water. "I bet this view never gets old."

"It sure doesn't," I say, referring to her.

She saunters toward me. "I was talking about the water."

"It doesn't compare to your ass in those shorts."

"You have a one-track mind, Silver." She eyes the desk and the leather couch. "How many women have you had your way with in here?"

"None." I draw her into my arms and kiss her neck. "But I've thought about bending you over my desk many times." Her breath hitches, and I brush my lips over hers. "And watching you ride my cock on that couch too many times to count."

Her eyes flame. "Well, I *am* here all weekend."

"I fucking love"—*you*—"the way you think." I seal my mouth over hers, kissing her until she melts against me. It takes everything I have not to lock my door and take her right here and now, but we have other plans, so I whisper, "Soon."

We drive down to the marina. Victory grabs her shopping bag, and I snag my backpack with our toiletries and my clothes since we're spending the night on the boat. There's a warm breeze coming off the water as we make our way down to the docks.

Roddy is talking with Grant, Fitz, Brant, and Archer outside the harbormaster's office. The Remingtons have owned the marina for several generations, and Roddy runs it.

They glance over as we approach, and Roddy says, "You two look like you're ready for a day on the water."

"We're going to boat around the island," I say. "You all remember Victory."

"We sure do," Roddy says as Grant and Fitz say, "It's nice to see you again."

Archer lifts his chin. "How's it going?"

"It's great to see you again, Victory," Brant says.

"Thanks. It's nice to be here," she says.

"Is something going on down here?" I ask. "I didn't expect to run into everyone."

"Nah," Grant says. "We're just shooting the shit. I'm helping Brant fix a boat today, and Roddy was giving us his two cents."

"Which is worth about half that," Roddy says with a chuckle.

"I came down to talk to Archer and found him giving these guys a hard time," Fitz says.

Archer cocks a grin. "It's the highlight of my day. Wells, are you going to the bonfire tonight? Sutton and Flynn should be in town by then."

"Yeah, I think so," I say.

"I'm looking forward to it, and it'll be nice to see my brother," Victory says. "Are all of you going to be there?"

"Not me. I have a hot date with my missus," Roddy says.

Victory smiles. "Good for you. I look forward to seeing Gail again at Leni's wedding."

"She's looking forward to seeing you, too," Roddy says.

"The rest of us will be there tonight with our better halves," Brant says.

"Except Fitz," Archer says. "He's still learning how to pick up women."

The guys laugh.

Fitz scoffs. "I'm single by design."

I slide my arm around Victory, earning a sweet smile, and say, "I highly suggest you think about changing that. We'll see you later. I want to head out before it gets too late."

"Did you warn her about your boating skills?" Archer asks.

"Archer." I shoot him a warning stare.

Grant winces. "That means he didn't."

Fitz sidles up to Victory and whispers, "Wear your life jacket," and makes an *okay* sign with his fingers.

Victory laughs. "You guys are relentless."

"We'll see if you're still laughing when you get back," Brant says.

"*If* she gets back," Grant says.

"We haven't seen Kitchen Kelly since she pulled that stunt at the restaurant and Wells coaxed her out on his boat," Fitz says.

"*Jesus,*" I grit out.

"Don't forget about Peppermint Patty," Archer says.

"Who's that?" Victory asks.

I grit out, "*Nobody.*"

"She was another clingy girl," Grant says. "But Wells knows how to take care of them. They go out on his boat, and they rarely come back."

Victory looks at me curiously, and I shake my head.

"Don't let this whole gentleman in the streets thing fool you like he fools the police," Fitz says. "He's got a long history of being a freak in the sheets."

She meets my brother's gaze and says, "I happen to like his freakiness."

And I fucking love you. "That's my girl."

"More power to ya, but word on the street is that he keeps trophies from the ones who don't return," Archer says.

Roddy tugs on his earlobe and mouths, *Earrings.*

The guys all nod with cautionary expressions.

"*Jesus*, you guys. We don't have time for this crap. Let's go, sweets." We head for my boat.

"Don't forget the life jacket!" Fitz calls out after us.

I flick him the bird without turning around.

"You kids be safe out there," Roddy hollers.

"Always," I call out, and pull Victory closer. "Especially with precious cargo on board."

"More precious than Kitchen Kelly?"

"She was never on my boat, and before you ask, Peppermint Patty was a girl who had a crush on me in seventh grade. She gave me Peppermint Patties every day at lunch, and her family moved away the following year. The guys just like to give me shit."

"I figured as much. It was fun to see you getting worked up, glaring at your friends, that muscle in your jaw jumping as you grit your teeth."

"I'd prefer to get worked up with you." I tug her into a kiss, and the idiots whistle and cheer.

"I grew up with brothers. I've got this." She turns around and takes a bow, then blows them a kiss, earning more shouts and whistles.

Chapter Twenty-Four

Victory

Wells doesn't have a boat. He has a small yacht, and he looks supremely comfortable piloting it out of the harbor, as if he goes boating every day. His thick hair lifts in the breeze, his sunglasses hiding his eyes. His eyes have become one of my favorite things about him. They say so much more than words ever could. Although he is very good with words. The memory of making love in the shower that morning, along with all the dirty things he said, brings a rush of heat.

I look back at the marina, taking in the boats and wooden buildings, his restaurant anchoring the harbor with its rustic charm and dockside service. It's an impressive establishment, and I loved seeing it through Wells's eyes as he showed me around, and meeting his work family. It was easy to see his kindness was genuine as he joked with the staff and took the time to talk with them. He knew a lot about their lives and made a point to ask about them—family, friends, an outing they'd gone on.

I turn my attention back to the big-hearted man who brought his mother flowers and played prince for his sister, and

I can't imagine him not being genuine in anything he does. Yet I know he had to pretend as a child, and now I understand just how hard that must have been for him.

"You have quite a life here, Mr. Silver." I lean against his side and kiss his shoulder. He's wearing a gray tank top and shorts, and his skin is warm from the sun. "You fully embraced Olivier's advice and built a life you wouldn't need a vacation from. Thank you for taking the time to share it with me." We have the whole weekend ahead of us, and I'm already wishing we had more time.

"I've been wanting to share it with you for weeks."

We chat as the harbor disappears behind us, and Wells tells me about each of the boroughs on the island. Ritzy Silver Haven, where he grew up; artistic Chaffee, which doesn't allow cars; and the old-school New England fishing towns, Rock Harbor, where his restaurant is located, and Seaport, where Wells has been going for community breakfasts since he was a little boy.

"The next community breakfast is in two weeks," he says. "Would you like to come back and go with me?"

"I would love to." Something happened when I shared my secrets with him. It's like every word I said carried some of that bottled-up guilt, depleting me of it. Clearing a path for a new beginning. "What's our plan for today?"

"I thought we'd get some sun while we boat around the island and then stop in Chaffee to find you an outfit for the wedding. We can have dinner there, and after the bonfire, we'll anchor the boat in Lover's Cove for the night."

Lover's Cove. "Sounds like a perfect day to me."

He wraps his arms around me. "How are you feeling about being here? Any guilt or anxiety?"

"No. Getting those secrets out was cathartic. I like being here with you."

"Good. If it creeps up, don't keep it to yourself, okay?"

"I definitely won't." *Not when I know I can talk to you about anything.*

He presses his lips to mine, and as he checks our course, I look back at the island, taking in the colorful cottages decorating the lush landscape and the few houses on the bluff, and a sense of peace overtakes me. "I can see Silver Monument and the flag at the Steeles' winery. I went to see them with my family over the holidays."

"I got my first kiss at the top of that monument."

"Oh yeah? Was it with Peppermint Patty?"

"As a matter of fact, it *was* her, but I wish it was you." He pats my butt. "Why don't you go down to the cabin and put your bathing suit on? You can get some sun on the way to Chaffee for our Thursday Trekabout. My bedroom is at the end of the hall."

I'm still stuck on him wishing his first kiss was with me. I wish he were my first kiss, too. I have a twinge of guilt for never having wished that about Harvey, but it doesn't last. Our relationship was so different from the one Wells and I have. It wasn't threaded with those types of wishes or dreams. We lived in the moment, *for* that moment. It's funny how I hadn't really thought about that until now.

"Okay," I finally say, and kiss his shoulder before grabbing my shopping bag, and heading down to the spacious main level, which has two sundecks and a covered lounge area.

I descend the steps to the cabin, and like Wells's home, it feels comfortable even though it's luxurious, with a kitchen, dining area, and another lounge, all decorated with the same warm, beachy vibe. I pass a bedroom on the way down the hall before I get to the master bedroom. It's gorgeous, with wooden drawers beneath the windows and tall cabinets with mirrored doors along the interior wall, facing a large bed. There's a door beside the tall cabinets, which must be the bathroom. I open it, and something falls at my face. I swat at it and turn away, dropping my bag. My heart is racing as I turn to see what it was.

What the hell?

Lying on the floor is a blow-up sex doll with an open mouth, big boobs, complete with pink nipples and a spreader bar holding its legs apart with leather cuffs around its ankles. My gaze moves south. *Yup.* There's a fuck-me hole. *What the hell is he into?*

I look in the closet I just opened, and there's another blow-up doll, only this one is on its knees, with its arms handcuffed behind its back. On the shelf above it is some sort of rubber vagina that is far too anatomically correct.

I stumble back to sit on the bed, and my foot hits something. I peer down, and I'm relieved to see it's just a belt. I pick it up, but it's tethered to something under the mattress. I flip up the covers and see that it's attached to something securing it under the mattress, and unless Wells has friends with four-inch waists, it's not a freaking belt. It's an open leather cuff.

My mind races as I lift the cover at the head of the bed and find another one. I hurry around the other side. Sure enough, there are restraints there, too. Fitz's voice tramples through my mind. *He's got a long history of being a freak in the sheets.* I thought he was kidding. Not that there's anything wrong with this stuff, but I don't want to be with a guy who gets off on sex dolls and rubber vaginas when he has the real thing right here.

With my heart in my throat, I start opening drawers to see

what else he has. I find dildoes, strap-ons—*is he into being pegged?*—a ball gag, a whip, a box of vibrating panties, butt plugs, and a plethora of other sex toys.

I open the bedside drawer and find nipple clamps, lube, some kind of leather harness, and…*What the…?* Something gold and a small colorful feather are sticking out of a metal box in the back of the drawer. *Nonono. Please no.* I pull out the box with trembling hands and lift the lid. My stomach plummets at the sight of several pairs of earrings. I can't think. I can barely breathe as I put the box back in the drawer, quickly fix the blanket, and shove the sex doll back into the closet. I look at my shaky hands, wanting to wash them, but there's no way I'm opening another door.

Fuckfuckfuck. I've got to get out of here.

I grab my bag and take several deep breaths, mentally re-playing our time together, looking for clues I might have missed about this side of him. He *did* get off on my taking control. The strap-on is starting to make sense. I feel like a fool. I was so honest with him, and he's been hiding this? My chest aches with that reality. Forcing myself to push past the heartache, I draw my shoulders back, give myself a pep talk, and head upstairs.

"Find everything okay?" Wells asks as I join him on the top deck.

Maintaining a brave face while looking at him is a test of strength. "I think this was a mistake. You need to take me home."

"What? Why? Are you getting seasick?"

"No. I think we're just into different things."

"What are you talking about?"

Fuck it. "I found your sex toys, Wells. Not that there's any-thing wrong with toys, but sex *dolls* are not my thing, and I can't believe you kept this whole side of yourself hidden from me."

"What are you talking about?" He reaches for me.

I step back and hold my hands up, too confused to keep the accusations from flying. "Don't try to play me. I found the earrings—"

"Earrings?" he asks with disbelief.

"I thought the guys were just teasing. But I guess the joke's on me, and I'll be damned if I'm going to end up at the bottom of this ocean." *Oh my God. I sound like a crazy person.*

"Okay, *stop* right there. I see what's going on. Do you really think I'm capable of killing someone?"

"*No!* But what do I know? I've seen true crime shows, and it's always the perfect partner who slaughters the unsuspecting one."

"Jesus, Vic. I swear to you, this is bullshit. Those assholes are pranking us." He cuts the engine. "That explains why they were all at the marina. Helping Brant with a boat, my ass."

"What are you doing?"

"Going downstairs to see what the fuck they've done. Are you coming?" His dark eyes bore into me.

"*Yes*, but I swear, if you feed me to the fish, I will haunt you every minute of the day and night."

"You're safe, but I can't say the same for the guys who did this." We head down to the cabin, and when we get to his bedroom, he looks around and throws his hands up. "Where is it?"

I point to the cabinet. "Be careful, one of them jumped out at me."

He opens the cabinet, and the doll tumbles out. He swats it away. "I'm going to kill those fuckers." He surveys the other items in the cabinet, and I can tell it's the first time he's seeing them. "What the hell is…?" He reaches for the rubber vagina. His eyes narrow, and his jaw clenches. "Are you fucking kidding me?"

"There's more." I point to each of the drawers where I found paraphernalia, and as he looks in each one, his jaw clenches tighter. I show him the restraints on the bed, and then he opens the bedside drawer and finds the earrings.

He stares at them like they're the enemy, looking like he's going to blow his top. "*None* of this is mine."

"I know that now. I'm sorry I thought otherwise. I was just on such a high today, and then that doll attacked me and I saw all that stuff, and the earrings, and—"

"Hey." His voice softens. "I don't blame you. If I were in your shoes and I saw a rubber vagina and got attacked by a sex doll, I'd wonder, too."

I laugh, thankful he's not mad at me for being foolish enough to fall for their prank. He draws me into his arms, and I wind mine around him, feeling the tension drain from both of us.

"I've got to give them credit," he says. "The bastards went all in."

"Then so will *we*. We can't let them win."

He cocks a brow. "You want to get revenge?"

"Hell yes. If I learned anything growing up with rabble-rousing brothers, it's never let them get the upper hand."

"I like the way you think, sweet thing, and don't worry, I'll get rid of this stuff."

"Don't be *too* hasty. Now that I know you're not a killer, there are a few things that could be fun, like the vibrating panties and the bed restraints."

Wickedness flares in his eyes. "You at my mercy is a delicious thought."

"I was thinking it would be the other way around," I say with as much innocence as I can muster.

He slides his hand down my back to my ass. "Does my secret dominatrix want to come out to play?"

"I guess you'll find out at some point," I tease. "I'm going to let that idea muddle your mind for a while, because you promised me an island tour." I go up on my toes and kiss him, then head out of the bedroom before I cave and tear his clothes off.

Chapter Twenty-Five

Victory

We have a wonderful afternoon on the water, basking in the sun and eating lunch while we're anchored at sea. I love the funny stories he shared about things he's done with his friends and family, and I enjoy sharing mine with him, too. It feels strange not to constantly check my phone for work messages, I don't want to waste a second of this time with Wells on work. I know Padma will text if there's an issue, so I jumped in with two feet and silenced my email notifications. I'm hoping the strangeness will pass, because I want more days like this with Wells, more time in *his* world, and I want more time with him in mine.

While we head for Chaffee, I sunbathe on the deck just outside the helm, where he's piloting the boat. The sun is beating down on me, the cool breeze coasting over my skin, and even with my eyes closed, I feel the heat of Wells's gaze burning a hole through me.

I glance at him and smile.

"Come here, sexy girl. I want to show you something." He reaches for my hand, drawing me into the covered area as we pass a lighthouse. "That's Fortune's Landing Lighthouse." He slows the boat to a crawl as we near the entrance of a cove, surrounded by rocky cliffs. "This is Fortune's Cove. See the beach by the cliff?" He points to a rocky cliff with a small beach at the base. "That's Fortune's Landing. This island was founded in 1601 by Bartholomew Silver. He crashed his boat, the *Fortune*, right at the base of the cliff."

"That's unfortunate."

He squeezes my hand. "Legend has it that he was drunk and found naked with a harem of inebriated women."

"So you come by your playboy ways naturally?" I tease.

"I'll give you a playboy." He takes me in a toe-curling kiss. "Have you ever piloted a boat?"

"I've sailed my parents' boat, but I'm usually just a passenger on my brothers' power boats."

Surprise rises in his eyes. "You know how to sail?"

"Why do you sound so shocked? I grew up eating bugs and walking through swamps. My brothers and I once built a raft out of tree branches and vines."

"Did it float?"

"*Yes*. Although we spent most of our time pushing each other off of it."

"That's my girl. Queen of the raft. Get in here." He guides me in front of him.

"What are we doing?"

"You're going to pilot us to Chaffee." He runs his hands along my stomach, and then he gathers my hair over one shoulder and kisses my neck. "After I show you how, I'm going to distract you."

A shiver of heat moves through me. "What if I crash your boat?"

"Then you won't get to use those restraints you've been

dangling in front of me."

"I definitely won't crash," I say.

"Good girl," he says huskily.

He takes my hands, putting one on the wheel and the other on the throttle, and covers them with his own. Then he proceeds to teach me how to pilot the boat. When I've got the controls down pat, he doesn't just distract me. With his mouth on my neck, one hand in my bikini top, the other in my bikini bottom, and his hard length against my ass, he takes me right up to the verge of losing it.

I'm having trouble holding it together, riding his fingers, when we come to the mouth of the harbor in Chaffee. "Throttle down," he growls in my ear. "It's a no-wake zone."

"You've got me wide-awake." I can barely think past the need to come, but I manage to throttle down and realize there are boats heading out of the harbor. "Someone will see us."

"We're too far away, and they can't see in the sides. Don't take your eyes off the water."

He moves between me and the wheel and crouches down, taking my bikini bottom with him. *"Wells."* My heart races as his mouth makes contact, sending a bolt of pleasure through my core. *"Fuck"* falls from my lips like a plea. I rock against his mouth as he licks and sucks. "More."

He pushes his fingers inside me and takes my clit between his teeth. I cry out, struggling to keep my eyes open, white-knuckling the wheel and the throttle as a tsunami of sensations engulfs me. He stays with me through the very last pulse of my climax, making the greediest, most appreciative sounds, heightening my arousal.

As I come down from the peak, he slows his efforts and then licks me clean. He kisses my inner thighs, sending more shudders through me as he pulls up my bikini bottom, rising to his full height, and quickly assesses our proximity to the marina. He pulls me into a merciless kiss, leaving me whimpering for more as he takes over piloting the boat, and I try to remember how to walk on rubbery legs.

After he docks the boat, he's still hard, and I'm desperate for him. I run my hand over the front of his shorts, giving his cock a squeeze. "Can I help you with something belowdecks before we go on our trekabout?"

His cock jerks against my palm, his eyes flame, and he takes my hand, practically running down the stairs. The second we're belowdecks, his mouth is on mine, and I'm ripping open his shorts as he yanks off my bikini bottom. He lifts me into his arms, and there's no slowing us down. He plows into me, and I hold nothing back, clinging to his shoulders as I ride his cock. There's no finesse, no sweet words or sensual caresses, just primal passion and desperation. Every thrust of his hips sends an explosion of sparks searing through me. My back hits the wall, and we use it for leverage as we pound out a frantic pace.

"Fuck me harder," I pant out. "Come with me."

A rough and heady growl tears from his lungs as our mouths crash together and his entire body turns to one hard muscle as he gives me what I crave. I try to keep up with his feverish pace, try to continue kissing him, but turbulent waves of titillating sensations slam into me time and time again, like a war between heat and ice. He squeezes my ass *hard* with both hands, sending pain and pleasure crashing over me. My head falls back as his name flies from my lips and my name roars from his. My inner muscles grip his cock so tight with every thrust, new sensations thunder through me. I sink my teeth into his shoulder, earning the most sinful, gruff sound I've ever heard, sending me reeling again.

When we finally collapse against each other, our hearts raging, he runs a hand through my hair and grabs a fistful, tugging my head. His eyes blaze into mine, and he says, "What the fuck was that?"

I look at his shoulder and see my teeth broke the skin. "*Ohmygod*. I'm sorry. I didn't realize I bit you so hard."

A wicked grin curves his lips. "I fucking loved it." He takes me in a fierce, possessive kiss and then murmurs a demand. "Tell me you're *mine*."

My heart swells. There's no denying the twinge of guilt that comes with it, but it doesn't swamp me as I say, "I'm yours," and I know that's because the woman I'm giving Wells, the woman I've become, isn't the same woman I gave Harvey.

"*Mine*," he whispers, like he's been given a gift.

Or maybe I'm projecting, because that's how I feel about him.

He kisses me tenderly, and this time when he draws back, he looks amused. "So much for the restraints."

We both laugh.

"You're not getting out of that." I give him a quick kiss. "Care to join me in a shower before we go into town?"

His answer comes in the form of another ferocious kiss as he carries me down the hall.

Chaffee is bustling with tourists, so different from New York. People smile as we walk past and hold doors for us as we check out the cute shops along the marina. The friendly vibe is as alluring as the sweet man who pulls me close and kisses me every chance he gets. Kissing Wells is bordering on an obsession.

One I have no interest in quelling.

We make our way around the corner, and the town comes into view. It's absolutely breathtaking with cobblestone streets and a lush, hilly landscape dotted with colorful cottages and cedar-sided homes. There is a town square that reminds me of some of the European areas my family visited as a child. The enormous cobblestone courtyard is surrounded by three-story shops and art galleries that look more like townhomes with gorgeous wrought-iron balconies. Large planters overflowing with colorful blooms and vibrant leafy plants are scattered around the square. People are meandering through the square with dogs on leashes and sitting at iron tables and benches, while children run around playing. A statue of a man and a dog stands sentinel in a large fountain on one side of the courtyard, where people are tossing in coins, and a few children peer over the edge, their fingers dangling in the water.

We spend all afternoon checking out the shops, chatting and holding hands, admiring art and clothing and whimsical, eclectic items. We buy a tiny metal mermaid that has a blue tail with a white *C* on it for our memory box.

Our memory box. I love that.

Not for the first time since Wells and I got together, I realize just how much living I've missed out on the last few years. But I know in my heart it wouldn't have been the same without him.

Several people stop to talk to Wells, and he introduces me as his girlfriend. I get butterflies every time he says that, which is silly for a woman my age, but I kind of love that, too. He's personable and kind to all of them, and as we walk away, he always takes a minute to tell me how he knows them, which is mainly through the restaurant, island events, or family and friends.

We find a gorgeous light blue floral dress for the wedding. It has delicate shoulder straps, a ruched neckline, and a side slit that Wells swears makes him want to tear it right off. He buys a matching light blue tie, and when I joke that we're not going to the prom, he says, *It's our prom.* As cheesy as that is, I can't help but swoon. If that's not enough to steal the last bits of my heart, he surprises the heck out of me when he buys a guitar.

"You're going to teach me to play, remember?" he says as we leave the shop.

"I thought you were kidding about that."

"Then you thought wrong." He pulls me into a kiss. "Besides, I want to show off my talented girlfriend at the bonfire tonight."

"You're crazy." I laugh. "I'm not that good."

"Yes, you are, and I love watching you play. That's all that matters." He emphasizes his point with another kiss.

The truth is, if it'll make him happy to hear me play, I'll play all night long.

We have dinner at a quaint Italian restaurant and eat at a table outside by the courtyard, where a crowd has gathered around a pantomime. The food is delicious and the performer is entertaining. When we finish eating, Wells takes my hand and says, "Are you up for a quick walk down to the water? I want to get a picture of us for my office."

"You do?"

"Of course I do. When you're in the city, and I'm out here, I want to see your beautiful face."

I don't want to think about being apart, but I'm glad he is, because I want a picture, too. The enormity of how much I want pictures of us not just in my office, but also in my home, hits deep and feels right. "Only if you'll send it to me, too."

The sun hangs low in the sky as we make our way down to the beach and walk along the shore. The land juts into the ocean like a giant hand cradling the harbor, giving us a romantic view across the way to the lights of houses and shops. Wells sets the guitar case and our bags in the sand, and we head over to a jetty of rocks. He leans his butt against them and guides me between his legs.

His gaze moves adoringly over my face, and he tucks my hair behind my ear, his lips curving up. "There's my girl," he says just above a whisper, and my heart takes notice.

"Hi," I say softly.

"What are you thinking about?"

I don't even try to hold back the truth. "Kissing you."

He laughs softly, and then his lips come slowly, sensually down over mine, and I know that it won't matter how many pictures we take. Every moment we're apart will feel like an eternity.

Chapter Twenty-Six

Wells

"You'd better wipe that grin off your face, or they'll know something's up," Victory says as she hooks her finger in the front of my shorts, tugging me closer. She looks cute as hell in my Rock Bottom hoodie and her new shorts.

We purposefully arrived late for the bonfire at Grant's house in order to get the guys back for their sex-toy prank. We snuck one of the blow-up dolls into Grant's shower and tied the other to the top of Fitz's car. We're still in the driveway, which had been overgrown, the bungalow nothing more than a run-down dune shack when Grant moved in to hide from the world a couple of years ago. With the help of family and friends, as he climbed out of his depression, so did the state of his property. The bungalow became a home, and the yard, a welcoming path of dune grasses, plants, and flowers.

"I can't help it," I say, wrapping my arms around Victory. "After the day we've had, it's hard to be anything but happy." Not only do I feel like we've finally jumped over the hurdles that separated us, but Seth called while we were getting ready for the bonfire. He was happy to hear that Victory was with me, and he let me know that we have a meeting with Kane next week about the property for the restaurant. Life is pretty fucking perfect right now. "But don't worry, sweets. By the time I get over that hill, I'll be a heartbroken, angry bastard. Are *you* ready to do this?"

"*Yes*. We'll teach them not to mess with us."

"Damn right we will." We kiss, and then I step back and scrub a hand down my face, wiping away my smile. But the second she smiles, it draws another one from me.

She gives me a shove toward the yard. "Get out of here. Focus on getting revenge."

I head up the hill, trying to concentrate on the task at hand and not on my beautiful partner in crime. *Fuck*. Even that thought makes me smile. I have to dig deep for the will to appear heartbroken and draw upon the feelings I had when I first returned to the island last weekend. That's not a time I want to revisit, but for the greater good of revenge, it's worth it.

The bungalow sits back from the edge of the dunes, buffered from the harsh winter winds of the sea by dune grasses and indigenous bushes. As I near the backyard, the bonfire comes into view. My brothers and sisters and our friends are sitting around it. It's a familiar and welcome sight, but before the fun must come revenge. Shifting into heartbroken mode, I round my shoulders, duck my head, and make my way over to them.

"There he is," Bellamy calls out.

Everyone turns to look at me, and Scrappy, Brant and Cait's tiny black-and-gold Yorkie scurries over, yapping. I scoop him up, and he licks my cheek.

"We were getting worried you weren't going to show up," Fitz says.

"Where's Vic?" Flynn asks as he grabs a beer from a cooler.

I know I can't pull off angry while holding this furbaby, so I put Scrappy down, and he scampers over to Brant. "She went back to the city." I glower at my brothers, who are stifling grins.

"*Why?*" Keira asks.

"What did you do?" Leni pushes to her feet, looking at me accusingly, her auburn hair falling over her shoulders.

I scoff. "It wasn't *me*. It was these assholes."

Leni glares at Raz, who throws his hands up and says, "Don't look at me."

Indi, a petite blonde, smacks Archer's arm. "What did you do?"

"Why do you assume it was me?" Archer asks, but there's no hiding his shit-eating grin.

"Because you're an instigator," Indi snaps.

I step closer, staring the guys down, and they push to their feet. "Whose brilliant idea was it to make me look like some sort of sex-obsessed serial killer?"

Brant, Archer, Grant, and Fitz point to each other saying, "*His.*"

"*Brant*, you were in on this?" Cait asks. She's a dead ringer for the lead actress in *Blindspot*, tall and thin, with jet-black hair cut just below her ears and heavily inked porcelain skin.

"It was my dad's fault," Brant says.

Cait rolls her eyes.

"Assholes," I mutter. "They stocked my boat with sex dolls and other kinky shit."

"Guess she wasn't into your kind of freakiness after all," Grant says, and the guys laugh.

"Grant Silver, you are in *big* trouble," Jules says.

"Come on, Pix. It was a joke." Grant reaches for her, but she steps back.

"They told Victory I made a habit of taking women out on my boat and getting rid of them, and now she's *gone* for good." I eye the guys. "Way to fuck me over."

"Shit." Flynn scrubs a hand down his face. "My sister finally puts herself out there, and *this* is what she gets?"

"Calm your jets, Miles Long," Archer says. "It was all in fun."

"I'm sure it was," Flynn says. "I've got to call Vic."

Sutton touches his arm. "I'm sorry."

"Seriously, you guys," Bellamy snaps. "Wells *finally* gets a girl, and you have to go and screw it up?"

"Idiots." Keira shakes her head.

"There goes my plan to invite her to the Bra Brigade bachelorette party tomorrow afternoon," Leni snaps.

"You know who to blame," I say, knowing full well Victory is going to jump at the chance to hang out with Leni and the girls tomorrow.

"I'm really sorry, bro," Grant says. "We didn't think she'd take off."

"We were just having fun," Fitz says.

"Want us to call her and explain?" Brant asks.

"Fuck that," Archer says. "If she can't take a joke, she's not right for our boy Wells."

"You're going to have to do better than a few sex toys and a tale of serial killing to get rid of me," Victory says as she comes around the side of the house carrying the box of sex toys that we decided not to keep, wearing a cheeky grin, my new guitar strapped to her back.

"Oh man, they got you guys good!" Bellamy cheers, and everyone laughs, while Scrappy barks, wriggling to get free.

"Son of a bitch," Archer grumbles.

"Dude, you had me going," Grant says.

"Good. You deserve it."

As the guys give me a hard time, Flynn quietly checks in with Victory. I can't hear what they're saying, but she's nodding and smiling, and when he ducks his head closer, she says something that makes him chuckle.

When the commotion calms, I say, "Since you guys were so generous with us, we thought we'd share the wealth."

Victory walks over to Archer and says, "A dick for a dick," and hands him a strap-on, which makes everyone burst into hysterics.

She turns to Grant. "Since we expected that Jules might be upset with you, we're gifting you the magic vagina." She hands him the rubber vagina, earning more laughter. "Brant, Wells was pretty sure you were just along for the ride, but I understand you're a pretty chatty guy, so hopefully this ball gag will make sex with you a little more enjoyable for Cait."

More laughter rings out.

Victory faces Fitz, giving him a once-over, before saying, "You seem like the kind of guy who'll get down on his hands and knees for a woman to remain the golden boy. That's why we're giving you the leather collar and leash."

Laughter and jokes ensue, and in the midst of the commotion, Victory announces, "Ladies, the rest are for you!" and sets the box down on the ground.

"Dibs on a Rabbit or a Rose!" Bellamy says as she runs over. "Those babies are expensive!"

"I can't unhear that," Grant complains.

As the girls dig through the box, gabbing and laughing, picking out shit I don't want to know about, I pull Victory into my arms. "How'd I do?"

"You were amazing. Maybe I should get you some acting gigs."

"Baby, you're the only gig I want to do." As I lower my lips to hers, Fitz hollers my name. "Can't a guy kiss his girl in peace?"

Fitz smirks. "We noticed a few things missing from this box."

Victory and I share a laugh, and then, *finally*, we share a kiss, and the heckling begins anew.

Hours pass with a mix of fun banter and deep conversations, the soft sounds of the ocean and the crackling fire filling the gaps. Victory loves up Scrappy, monopolizing him until the girls coax her into playing the guitar. Jules sings the wrong lyrics, and we all join in. It's a perfect night, but what I love most is that Victory's not holding back with me. I worried she might be a little uncomfortable showing affection in front of everyone, especially her brother, but she's her warm, wonderful self, and being the greedy bastard I am for her, I fucking love it.

Leni invites Victory to join the Bra Brigade tomorrow afternoon, and as I knew Victory would, she jumps at the chance. Then she turns to me and says, "Unless you have plans for us?"

"My plans didn't involve leaving the bedroom."

"Dude, I do not need to know that," Flynn says.

"Me, either," Keira chimes in.

"Then don't listen," Victory says, earning chuckles from the others and a kiss from me.

She and the girls make plans for tomorrow, and as the night rolls on, there's more laughter, stolen kisses, and hushed conversations. While the girls roast marshmallows and talk about the wedding, the guys and I walk over to the edge of the dune, looking out at the water.

Feeling nostalgic, I say, "How many bonfires have we been to over the years when our mothers gathered in one place and our fathers in another?"

"It's funny how times change," Grant says.

"Yeah. It's hard to believe Jock and Levi are home playing daddy." Archer takes a drink of his beer. "It's weird."

"Nah, man. It's good," I say. "They're with their families, and it's not like they never come out anymore."

"That'll be us one day," Brant says.

I hope so.

"It feels pretty awesome to be part of the Silver Island brotherhood," Raz says.

"I'll drink to that." I hold up my beer, and the guys do the same, saying, "Hear, hear," and we all drink.

"I'm glad things worked out for you and Vic," Fitz says.

"Yeah, bro," Grant says. "You guys are good together."

"Thanks."

"I haven't seen Vic this happy in years. You're doing something right," Flynn says.

That means the world to me coming from him. "I hope so, because she's really special, Flynn. I know how big of a deal it is that she let me into her life after everything she's been through, and I intend to stay there."

"If he doesn't fuck it up," Archer says.

"Thanks for the vote of confidence, asshole."

"I'm kidding, Wells. She looks at you like you're all she could ever want," Archer says. "And you look at her like she's your queen, which is how it should be. To Wells and Victory." He holds up his beer, and as we toast again, I know it's another moment I'll never forget.

I steal a glance at Victory. She looks my way as she slides a marshmallow off the skewer. Her cheeks are pink from the warmth of the fire, her hair is wilder than when we arrived, and those gorgeous eyes are indeed looking at me like I'm all she could ever want. And I know without a doubt, my once-bitten, twice-shy girl, who isn't shy at all, is the only one for me.

Chapter Twenty-Seven

Victory

I've only been on the island since Wednesday, but the time here is like a dream. Getting to know everyone better last night and seeing Wells with the friends and family who know him best were wonderful. Even though I'd met them all before, last night was different. I felt like one of them, not just Flynn's sister who was visiting. I haven't felt that type of connection with people other than my family in so long, I'd forgotten how it could breathe new life into time itself.

The same way Wells breathes new life into my soul.

We spent the night on the boat in Lover's Cove, where we had a gorgeous view of the Silver House and the Bistro. I can't imagine a more perfect night, and it was followed by another wonderful morning spent tangled up in each other. We hit Keira's coffee shop, the Sweet Barista, for breakfast, and we ran into Keira in the parking lot. She was leaving to get ready for the Bra Brigade outing. By the time we got back to Wells's house, Leni and her sisters and sisters-in-law were pulling in to pick me up.

We drive to what looks like a deserted backroad and park by

a handful of other cars.

Leni's wearing a bride-to-be sash and a crown, and we walk about a half mile through the woods to get to a hilltop where we meet up with the rest of the Bra Brigaders. I'm thrilled to see Shea and excited to see Keira, Bellamy, Cait, and Tessa again. Cait's sisters, Abby and Deirdra, and Tessa's sister, Randi, are there, too, along with about three dozen other women ranging in age from early twenties to probably early eighties. I was a little nervous about seeing Wells's mom, Margot. I have no idea whether she heard about our falling-out last Friday or not, but she, Gail Remington, Shelley Steele, and even Shea's mom, Faye, and Leni's grandmother, Lenore, welcome me with warm embraces and no interrogations about Wells, which takes the edge off.

The sun warms my shoulders as we follow Lenore and a gaggle of her feisty friends wearing colorful floppy beach hats and sunglasses down a rocky hill toward a hidden stretch of beach. These women have their outings down pat, dressed in shorts, tank tops, cover-ups, and sundresses, carrying beach chairs—I borrowed one from Wells—blankets, towels, umbrellas, coolers, a hibachi, and bags full of what Keira calls *vital beach-babe stuff.*

"Mom, please slow down and let me help you," Shelley pleads for the third time.

Lenore and her friends have rebuffed all offers to help them on our walk, preferring to hold on to each other, giggling up a storm like teenagers. I admire their strength and determination and pray nobody falls and gets hurt.

Lenore waves her off. "I've been scaling this hill since I was Joey's age."

"You tell her, Gram." Leni turns to me and says, "I'm going

to be just like her when I'm older."

"You already are," Indi says.

"That's a good thing," Tara chimes in. Levi's willowy blond fiancée does not look like she had a baby only nine months ago. "I love Leni's confidence."

Tara's mother and grandmother are with us today, too. Her mother seems reserved, and her grandmother is as brazen as Lenore, as is Roddy's mother. I know my mother would enjoy getting together with these women, and I wish she were here with us.

"Why didn't Joey come with us?" I ask.

"She's still a little young, and as much as she loves our girl time, her heart lies in skateboards and biker boots," Tara answers.

"There's nothing wrong with that," I say, remembering that Levi is a member of the Dark Knights motorcycle club.

"The sisterhood got smart and stopped allowing little kids on the outings a few years ago to give moms a break," Keira says.

"Days like today give us a chance to get advice from women of all ages without having to worry about what we say," Tara adds.

"Hadley calls these outings my booby parties," Daphne, Jock's curvy blond wife, says about her adorable, serious-faced little girl. "Hadley is such a daddy's girl, if she were with us, she'd run right home to Jock and repeat every word I say out of context."

"You girls should be thankful you got to learn from our mistakes," Margot calls out to us over her shoulder. She and Gail are holding on to each other as they make their way down the hill. Margot's wide-brimmed sun hat has a blue paisley scarf tied around it that matches her cover-up. "I cannot tell you how many times I had to bribe Bellamy to keep her chatterbox closed."

"News flash, Mom," Bellamy calls out. "I knew you'd buy me ice cream if I said I'd tell Dad what you talked about."

"News flash, my sweet girl." Margot looks lovingly at Bellamy as we come off the hill onto the beach and says, "I knew it all along, and I cherished those ice cream trips."

Bellamy rolls her eyes, but her smile tells me she's as touched by her mother's admission as I am. I treasure the stolen time my mother and I had for walks or moonlight talks after my younger brothers went to bed.

As we set up our chairs and umbrellas, Shelley says, "We've had a lot of fun bringing our girls into our brigade, but the most memorable was the first time Keira, Leni, Randi, and Abby came out with us."

"Our little stripper girls made quite an impression," Margot says as she and Gail work together to get an umbrella pole upright in the sand.

"*Mom*," Keira chides. "Can we *not* relive that?"

"Sorry, honey," Margot says. "But as your moms, it's our job to make sure you never forget our best memories."

"That's right," Gail chimes in.

"Like we could ever forget that?" Leni complains, sharing a *here we go again* look with the other three *stripper girls*.

As Abby puts on sunscreen, she says, "We will never live that down."

"At least you were in good company," Gail says, her brown-and-gray curls framing her mischievous expression.

"What happened?" I ask as I drape my towel over the back of my chair.

"The Bee Gees, Archer, and Jock happened," Randi says.

"The Bee Gees?" I ask.

"That's what we called Brant and Grant when they were younger," Tessa says.

"Of course Brant was in on it." Cait waggles a finger in my direction and says, "I know you think he just went along for the ride yesterday, but don't let him fool you. He has a rascally side."

"Brant has been in on pranks forever," Keira confirms. "When our brothers found out we were going out with the Bra Brigade the first time, they pulled us aside and said there was a secret initiation to get into the group for good. They swore us to secrecy, like they were sharing national secrets, and told us we had to sunbathe nude the first time, or we wouldn't be allowed to come back."

"But they didn't stop there." Randi pulls a towel out of her beach bag and says, "They told us that when Lenore yelled, 'Let's get this party started,' we needed to strip as fast as we could and be the first ones in the water, or the senior Bra Brigaders would never let us come back."

Sutton looks up from where she's fishing around in her beach bag and says, "They could've asked *me* if it was true, and I would've told them it wasn't."

"We didn't ask you because the guys said if we asked you or the Bra Brigaders, you would all deny it because it was a secret initiation," Leni explains. "And, Sutton, you were so secretive about your first time out with the brigade, I thought they were telling us the truth."

"If you'd've asked me, I would've lied and let you carry out the prank," Lenore chimes in, making everyone laugh.

"Leni, I was secretive because it was the only thing I had of my own," Sutton says. "The rest of you guys each have a twin, and Jules was the baby. I was just the middle kid hanging out in the wind. I felt special being the first one in on the Bra Brigade. But *sisters before misters*. I wouldn't have let you strip buck-ass naked."

"*Aw*, sissy." Jules hurries across the sand to Sutton and throws her arms around her. "You're the *best* oldest sister I have."

"Yeah, *old* one," Leni teases. "You were so much more than just a middle kid. I wouldn't have survived our brothers without you."

"Yes, you would have. You're as tough as they are." Sutton turns to me and says, "You should've seen them running naked into the water."

I laugh. "*Sorry*. I don't mean to laugh. That was a cruel joke your brothers played on you."

"You've got to have thick skin to survive any of our boys," Shelley says.

"So I've discovered." I tell them about the sex-toy prank the guys pulled on us. The girls chime in, telling them about our revenge, the box of goodies we shared, and the extra prank we played on Grant and Fitz, who texted everyone last night to give us hell after discovering what we'd done.

The ladies get a good laugh out of it.

When the beach is covered with our belongings, Lenore stands in front of the group wearing a colorful cover-up and navy shorts and says, "Let's get this party started!"

The women whoop and cheer as they take off their shirts, cover-ups, and sundresses, proudly displaying their colorful bras. Keira and some of the other girls swing their shirts over their heads. It's an amazing feeling being surrounded by so much upbeat, female energy, and I have only a fleeting hesitation before reaching for the hem of my tank top and pulling it off, earning hoots and applause from older and younger women alike.

The air buzzes with excitement as women gather in groups or head down to the water. Leni and I tuck our shirts and shorts into our beach bags. She's wearing a red plunge bra and bikini bottom. "What a gorgeous day," she says, and plops into the chair beside mine with a sigh. "Looks like your interrogation is about to begin."

As I sit down, I see Keira and Bellamy heading over. They look determined, Bellamy in a yellow bralette and matching bikini bottom and Keira in a blue demi bra and black bikini bottom.

"Pretty bra, Vic," Bellamy says as she and Keira drag their chairs from beside us, in front of mine, and sit down. "Did you get it at Oceanside Boutique?"

I glance down at my pink lace halter bra. "Wow, you're good. I did get it there. Wells and I went shopping yesterday." He picked it out, but they don't need to know that.

"Speaking of Wells," Keira says. "I know you poured out your heart in front of the whole bar, which was amazing, but what are your intentions with our brother?"

Leni laughs. "Her intentions? Seriously, Kei? You saw them last night. They couldn't keep their hands off each other. Can't you just be happy for them?"

"I *am*," Keira insists. "I was pulling for them before she even came to the island."

That's good to know. "It's okay. I get it, but I'm crazy about your brother."

"Yay," Bellamy exclaims. "He was so bummed before you

showed up at the bar. I was worried about him.”

“No, you weren’t,” Keira says. “*I* was pulling for Wells and Victory, and *you* were trying to get him to go on a reality dating show with you.”

“A dating show?” Leni asks. “I can’t imagine Wells going for that.”

“Neither can I,” I agree.

“He *didn’t*. I just didn’t want him to be sad, and I had this great idea for a sibling dating show.” Bellamy lowers her voice, her eyes lighting up. “But with his adorable face? Can you imagine the ratings?”

“He is handsome, and last night we saw just how good an actor he is,” I admit. “I’m sure there are lots of women who would give anything to be with Wells, but that’s too bad. He’s *mine*, and I might not be into catfights, but I’d fight for him.”

Leni holds up her hand, and I high-five her.

“That’s what I wanted to hear,” Keira says. “I’ve never seen Wells like this with anyone. He’s always been there for me, and I hated seeing him heartbroken, so if you change your mind, please be up front with him. Don’t string him along and see someone else.”

“I would *never* do that,” I reassure her, but something about the way she says it sounds like it’s been done to her. “Did someone do that to you?”

“If they did, they wouldn’t live to talk about it,” Leni says.

“You’ve got that right,” Keira says as her mother, Shelley, and Gail approach.

“Now that we know where you stand, I have a non-brother-related question for you,” Bellamy says. “If I send you some headshots, do you think you can help me to expand my brand? Maybe get me into some of those celebrity parties?”

"Bellamy, are you harassing Victory?" Margot touches my shoulder.

"No. I'm just networking," Bellamy explains.

Margot gently squeezes my shoulder. "How about you and I go for a little walk and get to know each other better?"

"Sure, and, Bellamy, we can talk about it later," I say, a little nervous that maybe Margot has her own inquisition in mind. I get up, and Margot loops her arm through mine, guiding me toward the water.

"I'm sorry about my girls. They can be a bit overzealous."

"It's okay. I know how much Wells means to them. They're just protecting his heart."

"He has a soft one," she says as we walk along the cool wet sand. "For all his gregariousness, he's always been my sweetest boy." She holds my arm a little tighter. "You're not going to take him away for good, are you?"

"Oh my goodness, *no*. Family is important to both of us, and honestly, we haven't talked about any of that. He hasn't even been to my apartment yet, which is my fault, and has nothing to do with him."

"You don't have to explain it to me. I think every woman needs her space. As you know, my husband and I have been living apart for years."

"I know, and I'm sure you have your reasons, but it's not that I *want* space from Wells. I just hadn't crossed that particular bridge with anyone since Harvey died. I thought I'd dealt with all of that, but last week I realized I still had more to overcome."

"Do you still live in the apartment you shared with Harvey?"

"Yes."

"I can see how that would be a difficult line to cross."

I'm thankful she understands. "Difficult, yes, but hopefully not impossible." In case she heard about our falling-out, I say, "Wells asked to stay at my place last week, and it threw me for a loop. It wasn't that I didn't want him there. I just panicked. I was holding on to that baggage for so long, I didn't know how to put it down. That's why we had a falling-out. I'm sure you heard about what happened at Rock Bottom."

"I think most everyone on the island did. You might as well have been riding around town with a megaphone."

"That's so embarrassing."

She tightens her hold on my arm again, smiling. "There's never a reason to be embarrassed about your feelings."

"I wasn't embarrassed about my feelings. I was embarrassed that I blurted them out at his restaurant. It was inappropriate and unprofessional. I don't usually air my dirty laundry in public, but everything has been changing with Wells. He's the only person who has ever made me want to put that baggage down for good, and that's why I'm here."

"I'm glad to hear that. When I saw him pursuing you at Sutton's wedding, there was an unmistakable connection. A sizzling one, if I'm honest."

"Was it that obvious?"

"Let's just say, the way he looked at you reminded me of the way my Alexander has always looked at me. I'd never seen Wells that taken with anyone. You reminded me of myself when I was younger, bright, self-assured, and not frivolous. But the right people bring out a lightness in you. I noticed your family does that for you."

"They do."

"But I also knew you'd lost your husband, and I wasn't sure

if Wells was barking up the wrong tree."

"I thought he was at first," I admit. "But it turns out, Wells brings out that lightness in me, too. I hadn't dated in five years, and I wasn't looking for a date, much less a relationship, when Wells and I got together. Believe it or not, that was on the anniversary of the night I met Harvey, which is so weird, and as silly as it sounds, it's like my heart started beating to a new rhythm that night. I didn't even know I could feel like this again, and that scared me. I tried to push Wells away, but he was *always* there. If not physically, he was on my mind." *Like a song on repeat.* "And nothing has been the same since. But I want you to know that Wells is *not* second best, or a replacement for my late husband. What he and I have is completely different from what I had with Harvey. I'm a different person than I was then, and some of that is because of Wells."

When I finally take a breath, I realize how much I've revealed and wince. "I'm sorry. I didn't mean to blurt all that out. That's exactly what happened at Rock Bottom last week. What is it about this island that turns my emotions into tidal waves?"

"That's the magic of Silver Island," she says with authority. "It brings out the heart in all of us, but don't worry, honey. I have a feeling my son enjoyed it just as much as I did."

I breathe a sigh of relief.

"And from what I've heard," she says conspiratorially, "what happened at the bar was less airing dirty laundry and more groveling."

"*Great,*" I say sarcastically, and we both laugh. I fan my face. "Did it just get hotter out here, or is it just me?"

Margot gives my arm a reassuring squeeze. "Let's cool off." As we wade into the chilly water up to our calves, she says, "I'm going to let you in on a little secret. No relationship is perfect.

Take it from a woman who has done more than a little groveling in her time. When you find the person who makes your heart sing, they're worth it, and to hell with what anyone else thinks."

"You sound like my mom. She has never cared what anyone else thought."

"Well, I hate to admit that I cared too much at one point in my life, and I wish I hadn't. I got to know your mother fairly well at Sutton and Flynn's wedding, and she is extraordinary. She told us all about your family's travels. What an exciting life you've lived."

"It was quite an opportunity. I think she'd really enjoy spending time with the Bra Brigade. This reminds me of some of the communities we lived in overseas, where the elders taught the younger generations their traditions, and families and friends supported one another."

"This is the best sisterhood anyone could ever ask for, and I'm so glad you're a part of it. These ladies have helped me through my most trying times. I have never had to pretend around them. They accept me with all my faults, as I do them, and trust me, we're all riddled with them."

I laugh softly. I love how down to earth she is and how good it feels to connect with her.

"Let's plan a get-together," she says excitedly. "Alexander and I invited your parents to come for a week whenever they can make it, and you know we'd love to see more of you. Your brothers are more than welcome, too. We have quite a few single ladies still looking for their special someone."

"I'm not sure my single brothers are interested in getting tied down." As I say it, I think of the bed restraints Wells and I used last night, but I can't afford to get lost in those delicious memories right now. "I'll talk to them, and to Wells, and see what we can figure out."

"*Perfect.* I look forward to it." She swishes her fingertips along the surface of the water and says, "You've become such a big part of Wells's life, it feels like you're already becoming a part of ours, too."

Having never met Harvey's father, this is a new kind of wonderful for me. "Thank you. I love getting to know everyone better."

"Big families have an energy all their own. I know you're leaving Sunday, and I'm sure my son won't want to give up time alone with you, but we'd love it if you'd join us for a family breakfast before you go. Even if you can only come for a little while."

The thought of leaving saddens me, but I'm not going to let that ruin this amazing day. "I would love to."

"Mom! Vic!" Bellamy hollers as she and Jules run into the water, splashing both of us.

We shriek with laughter. Margot kicks water at them, making them squeal and starting a full-on splash battle. Our laughter is a battle cry, and before we know it, all the women are joining us, splashing and laughing. Water flies at my face, and I lose my footing, stumbling backward. I grab Keira's arm, taking her down with me in a fit of hysterics.

"Sorry!" I say.

"No, you're not," she says, and we burst into laughter seconds before Leni and Shea tug us into deeper water, and we all tumble beneath the surface.

As we break the surface, finding our footing, our laughter filling the air, Lenore and a number of older Bra Brigaders take each other's hands and lift them to the sky, shouting, "To the sisterhood!"

Cheers ring out as Keira and Leni take my hands and throw them up, shouting, "The baddest bitches on the island!" earning more whoops and shouts.

"I can't believe I'm doing this," I say as we each tie a rope that has a hot dog secured to the other end, around our waist. We're playing Swinging Weenies, one of many bachelorette-party games Abby and Jules have lined up for the afternoon.

"Don't act like you've never had a wiener in your mouth," Lenore says, and everyone laughs.

"Okay, listen up," Jules announces. "The goal of the game is to swing your hips and catch the weenie in your mouth. If you touch it with your hands, you're out."

"No stroking the dog?" Keira yells, inciting more laughter.

Leni shouts, "No frank wanking? Boring!"

"My baby girl is getting married tomorrow. If she wants to wank a frank, more power to her!" Shelley hollers, and we double over in laughter.

"We taught these girls well," Lenore says to Tara's grandmother, and they high-five.

"All right, ladies. Listen up. The first one to catch a weenie in her mouth wins a prize," Abby says. "Ready?"

"*Wait!* Hold my hair," I say to Keira, and everyone laughs.

"Do we have to swallow?" Randi asks, and we lose it, tears rolling down our cheeks.

When we finally stop laughing and they start the game, there is more hilarity as we cheer each other on, and the hot dogs smack us in the face and chest.

Someone yells, "Don't use your teeth!" and someone else hollers, "That's what he said."

I swing my hips, and the hot dog hits me in the eye. "Ouch! It nearly put my eye out!"

"I hate it when that happens," Margot says, and we all crack up again.

A motorboat roars behind us, and we all turn to look as it speeds toward shore and fishtails to a stop. Roddy's at the helm, Steve is tossing out the anchor, and Alexander grabs a megaphone and says, "Margot, baby, what are you doing with a weenie when you've got a kielbasa at home?"

Laughter erupts anew, and Bellamy yells, "*Ew*, Dad!" as the men jump off the boat and jog through the water to shore.

Margot plants a hand on her hip and says, "Alexander Silver, I expect this from our boys but not from you!"

He bolts out of the water in shorts and a T-shirt, showing off his athletic physique. He swoops Margot into his arms, says, "Then you don't know me at all, baby!" and kisses the hell out of her.

We all cheer, and Keira yells, "Get a room!"

Roddy and Steve jog over to their wives and pull them into dramatic kisses, earning more cheers and a jealous sigh from me. I gasp as strong arms circle me from behind.

"I've got your weenie right here, sweet thing."

Shivers of heat race through me as laughter and commotion erupt around us, and I see about a dozen guys running into the group as Wells turns me in his arms and says, "There you are," and kisses me.

Something hard presses against my chest. I break the kiss and look between us. Laughter bubbles out. "Why are you wearing a coconut bra?"

"It's the Bra Brigade, isn't it?" We laugh, and I realize all the guys are wearing some kind of bra.

Leni's voice cuts through the air. "Is that a Dora the Explorer backpack?"

"I told you I'd do whatever it took to find you." Raz holds up binoculars and turns to show her the picture of Dora the Explorer on his backpack.

"You guys are nuts," I say.

"Your brother led the charge." Wells motions to Flynn, with his arm around Sutton. He's wearing a black bra and has a compass and binoculars hanging around his neck and a map in his hand.

"Point me to the single ladies!" Fitz hollers, strutting around in a coconut bra and shorts.

"Yoo-hoo, Fitzy!" Lenore calls out, as she and a group of older ladies beckon him over.

Fitz makes a show of untying his coconut bra and tossing it to the sand as he saunters toward them. We all laugh.

Alexander waves as he and Margot head our way. I quickly try to untie the rope around my waist. "I can't believe the first time I'm going to see your dad as your girlfriend I've got a weenie between my legs."

Wells laughs.

"Now, that's a great sight," Alexander says, and claps a hand on Wells's shoulder.

The knot is stuck, so I pull up the rope and say, "The embarrassing weenie dangling between my legs?"

Alexander's laugh is deep and carefree. "I meant my son's smile, but that weenie will make a great story to tell our grandchildren. It's wonderful to see you again, Victory, with or without your weenie."

He wraps his arms around me in a warm embrace, and I can't help but laugh. "It's nice to see you, too. I heard you and your buddies were the masterminds behind the island pranks."

"We haven't always been old fuddy duddies." He drapes an arm around Margot.

"We are *not* fuddy duddies," Margot insists.

"And we never will be." Alexander leans down for a kiss.

"Jesus, you two," Wells says. "It's like watching teenagers. Get a freaking room."

I take Wells's hand and say, "Now I know where you get it from." That earns a wolfish grin.

"You're welcome," Alexander says. "Are you ladies still playing with those weenies, or are we going to fire up the hibachis?"

An hour later the beach is teeming with people of all ages, and laughter and conversation fill the air. Leni's brothers Jock and Levi came with their children, and dozens of other Bra Brigade families did, too. We roast hot dogs, eat coolers full of food, and toast to Leni and Raz's upcoming nuptials, all while Tara, a photographer, stealthily captures the fun on film.

As the afternoon wears on, Wells and I play Frisbee with Fitz, Keira, and a handful of other friends, while kids dart around us. Jock shouts as he tackles Brant in a football game on the other side of the beach, and the people around them cheer.

"Heads up, Vic!" Fitz hollers as the Frisbee leaves his fingertips and flies in my direction.

"I got it!" I sprint to my right and jump up to catch the

Frisbee. It bounces off my fingertips, but I catch it before it hits the ground.

"Yeah!" Wells shouts. "That's my girl!"

I take a bow and throw the Frisbee to Keira, but it flies past her. As she runs for it, I spot Margot and Alexander sitting in the sand. Margot is holding Stevie, talking to him, I assume, as she touches his belly. Alexander has his arm around her, and he's looking at *her* like she's his whole world. I know she's not. I've seen the way he looks at not just his kids, but all their friends, too. What a feeling it must be to go through life with your best friend by your side. I thought I lost my chance at having that.

"Hey, sugarplum," Wells calls out, heading toward me with a devilish look in his eyes.

He wraps me in his arms, those dark eyes holding me captive. I feel like the luckiest girl in the world to have a second chance at love, but even more so, to have it with him. I love his patience, his sense of humor, and the sexy beast he becomes when we're alone. Most of all, I love the way he loves me for who I am, flaws and all.

"Penny for your thoughts," he coaxes.

"It's going to cost more than a penny for today's thoughts."

A butterfly flies between us, hovering there like a beacon over our hearts, its delicate wings fluttering. It flutters in place so long, I can't look away. It rises and lands on Wells's shoulder. A warm, comforting breeze washes over me, lasting longer than a typical breeze. Gently demanding my attention the way a long hug goodbye makes your thoughts slow down and take notice. It feels like a sign. My pulse quickens, a lump forming in my throat.

Wells takes my hand and turns it over, brushing his thumb

over the tiny butterfly tattoo on my wrist, as if he senses it, too. He lifts my wrist and presses a kiss to it. As his lips leave my skin, the warm breeze and the butterfly slip away like secrets.

Wells laces our fingers together, stepping closer, and whispers, "Save those thoughts, sweet girl. I know what's in your heart."

Chapter Twenty-Eight

Wells

As I pull on my slacks for Leni's wedding late Saturday afternoon, I glance into the bathroom at Victory putting on her makeup. She's leaning forward, applying eyeliner. Her face is tipped up, her hand steady, and her lips are parted, like an artist midpainting. She's wearing the new dress we bought in Chaffee, the soft pastels hugging her curves. One strap hangs off her shoulder, the back still unzipped. I don't want to think about her going back to the city tomorrow. I like seeing her entrenched in my world, hugging my mom, joking with my dad, brothers, and friends, stealing glances at me across a fire while she's chatting with the girls. I thought our days apart were hard these last two months, but I know they'll be even harder now. Hell, I missed her like crazy this afternoon when I had to go in to work for a few hours, and she hung out with my sisters and some of the other girls.

Last night, when she and the girls were taking turns holding the babies, my future flashed before me like a movie. I could see it so vividly, when Fitz and the guys called out to me, I didn't even hear them. They gave me hell for that, and we ended up having a pretty deep conversation about relationships. I've never given much thought to how people fall in love. But now I know, at least for me, it didn't happen in a single moment or because of one particular thing. It's texts and games and furtive touches. It's holding hands in a city of millions of people and knowing there's no one else I'd rather be with. It's the way her eyes light up with new ideas and her sweet laughter that I can pick out of countless others'. It's the way she cuddles into me when she's sleeping, and takes over my bathroom like it's her right, and that first-morning smile that says, *Good. You're still here*, like she worried it was all a dream.

She's putting on mascara now, her mouth forming an O. She glances over as I put on my tie. "Are you okay out there?"

"More than okay. You look gorgeous."

"Thank you. Would you mind zipping me up?"

She gathers her hair over her shoulder and I step behind her. Our eyes meet in the mirror, my fingers brushing her skin as I zip her dress. It's such a simple thing, zipping up a dress, but it feels much bigger because I want to do it today, a month from now, next year, when we're old and gray.

"What were you and the guys huddled up about last night right before we left? It looked like you were scheming. Were you cooking up a prank for the wedding?"

I wrap my arms around her from behind and kiss her shoulder. "They asked me if you wanted to get married again."

Her brows knit. "What did you tell them?"

"The truth." I have a fleeting worry about the truth scaring her off, but I don't hold it back, because I want to know if it's *her* truth, too. "That we haven't talked about it, but if you do want to get married again someday, it's going to be to *me*."

"Oh," she says so softly, it's impossible to read the feelings behind it. She turns in my arms and straightens my tie. "That was a confident answer."

"I'm a confident guy." I hold her a little tighter. "You're it for me, sweet thing, but there's no pressure to get married. I don't mind being your boy toy until they bury me six feet under."

"Promises, promises." She grabs my tie and tugs me into a kiss.

The winery grounds have been transformed into a magical evening of twinkling lights and gorgeous flowers. Leni and Raz said their vows just before sunset in a beautiful ceremony that left everyone glassy-eyed. I'm not usually moved by weddings, but seeing my childhood best friend, the woman who taught me perhaps the greatest life lesson of all—how precious a trusting heart is—marry the man of her dreams brings a rush of happiness. Leni is beautiful in a white off-the-shoulder satin gown, and Raz couldn't take his eyes off her as she walked down the aisle and then stood before him while they pledged their love.

Now, beneath a canopy of lights strewn over the patio, surrounded by the people they love, as they dance their first dance as husband and wife, Raz is looking at her like she is the only thing he sees. I know that feeling well, and I glance at the woman who owns my heart and soul so completely, even when we're miles apart, she's still all I see.

Victory is watching them with a dreamy expression. I hold her a little tighter against my side and kiss her temple, *I love you* on the tip of my tongue.

"They look beautiful, don't they?" she says softly.

"They do. I'm happy for them."

The song comes to an end, and we all applaud. "Ladies and gentlemen," the DJ says. "Please join Leni and Raz on the dance floor."

The Backstreet Boys' "Everybody" blares from the speaker, and cheers erupt as people rush to the dance floor. Keira and Bellamy run over and loop their arms through Victory's.

"Come on, Vic!" Bellamy urges as they drag her toward the dance floor.

"That's it, just take my girl away," I tease.

Victory beams over her shoulder, her eyes glittering in the moonlight, and my heart nearly explodes. They join Leni, Shea, and the other girls, and they all dance in a hip-swaying, shoulders-shimmying circle. Leni leans in, saying something that makes the others laugh, and Victory's melodic laughter hits me square in the center of my chest. *This* is how she was meant to be, happy and carefree with a gaggle of other women who adore her as much as I do.

"Guess it's just you and me, bro," Fitz says as he sidles up to me, thumbing out a text.

"And me," Grant says as he appears by my other side.

"Where's Stevie?" I ask.

Grant motions to our mother, cuddling the baby on the other side of the patio. "You've been attached to that phone all evening, Fitz. Is that the mystery woman you left to meet up with last night?"

Fitz pockets his phone. "Yeah."

"Is she coming to hang out with us?" I ask. "You know Leni and Raz won't mind."

"No. No need to add grapes to the gossip vine. She's only here for the weekend."

There's a touch of disappointment in Fitz's voice. He has always kept his personal life private, so much so, he usually refrains from texting women when he's out with all of us, which makes me curious. "You seem into her."

Fitz watches the girls dance, giving me a half-hearted shrug, but the way his lips quirk up betrays that nonchalance and has me and Grant exchanging inquisitive glances.

"Are you meeting up with her when you leave here?" Grant asks.

Fitz glances at us and cocks a brow. "Wouldn't you like to know?"

I chuckle. "Does the mystery woman have a name?"

"Yeah, it's *Jen.*"

"Sounding a little dreamy there, bro," Grant says.

Fitz scoffs.

"As much fun as it is to debate Fitz's love life, what do you say we crash the girls' dance party?"

"Hell yeah," Grant says, and the three of us head over to the dance floor.

Jules squeals, and as she reaches for Grant, Fitz says, "Have no fear, ladies, your dance partners are here," sparking snarky comments from Keira and Bellamy and laughter from the others. My eyes lock with Victory's, electricity thrumming between us as I reach for her. "Hey, hot stuff. Lookin' for a date?"

"Only if he's tall, dark, and already mine."

As the evening gives way to night, my father sweeps Victory onto the dance floor, and I accompany my mother for a slow dance. Victory is all smiles, and I wonder what my father is saying to her.

"You haven't taken your eyes off her all night." My mother gazes thoughtfully up at me.

"Sorry, Mom. I don't mean to be rude."

"You're not, honey. It's a good thing, seeing you this happy. You've always been a little restless, and that's probably your father's and my fault, but with Victory, you seem settled in a way I haven't seen in you since the first couple of years after you bought the restaurant."

"It's not your fault I was restless."

"It's okay, honey. We know we're not perfect parents. We were so young when we had all of you. I love our family, but as you know, being a Silver can be a burden as much as it is a gift. Life got overwhelming for a bit, and I got a little lost when you kids were young. Thankfully, your father loved me and all of you enough to stick around while I got my head on straight."

"I get it, Mom. You already explained all of that to us."

"I know, but now you're journeying into an exciting new chapter in your life, and I want to say I'm sorry to *you*. I'm sorry for the difficult years and for trying to get you to stay on the island instead of supporting your dreams of growing your business elsewhere. Now that Grant is back and we're all together, I treasure our occasional family breakfasts, and seeing you at the restaurant and around town. I guess my mama heart doesn't want to lose more time with any of you, but that's not fair. There's a big world out there, and I want you to do what makes you happy."

"I know you do, but when I open the restaurant, I'm not leaving for good. Even if I do decide to move away at some point, you know I'll always come back to visit."

"Yes, I do, but we all know how busy life can get."

"Never too busy for family."

"I'm glad to hear that, because if we didn't see you and your sweetheart, we'd miss you both. As you can see"—she glances at my father and Victory—"she's already taken root in our hearts."

My father twirls Victory, and her smiling eyes catch mine for only a second before she's in his arms again. "Don't worry, Mom. She hasn't just taken root in mine. She claimed the whole damn thing."

The song ends, and we head over to Victory and my father. "Hey, old man, want to swap chicks?"

My father laughs. As we each reach for the hand of the woman we love, the DJ's voice cuts through the air. "This next song is for a very special couple."

Everyone looks around the crowded dance floor as Bon Jovi's "I'll Be There for You" comes on. Victory's eyes fill with disbelief.

"They're playing our song, sweetheart." I take her hand, drawing her into my arms as "*Aws*" and "*Go, Wells*" ring out around us.

"I can't believe you did this," she says quietly.

"I told you I wanted to be the guy you can count on. The one you smile when you think about. The best way to do that is to give you so many reasons to smile, it's impossible not to when you think of me."

"It's already impossible not to smile when I think of you," she says as other couples join us on the dance floor.

"Then it's time for phase two."

"What's phase two?"

"One last night beneath the stars on my boat, loving you so thoroughly, you never want to leave."

Chapter Twenty-Nine

Victory

As Wells pilots the boat out through the moonlit water, my thoughts drift back to dancing with his father. I asked Alexander if he had any advice about dating his son. He joked at first, telling me to be ready for anything, his love for Wells coming through in every word. But it's his serious response that came afterward that I hear now, with the same gentle authority as when he said it. *Raising my children taught me the value of time. Follow your heart, put the people you love first, and don't let anything stand in your way, because every hour you put something off is an hour you can never get back.*

I know that from losing Harvey, and I've preached it over the years to my brothers, but the advice hits different now. Being on the island and spending time with Wells in the city have reminded me what it's like to *not* be focused on work all the time, to be open to new things instead of keeping myself sequestered in my office or sitting alone in a restaurant giving off leave-me-alone vibes, or going from point A to point B without noticing my surroundings.

Seth was right. I had put myself in a box, but those weren't wasted years. I needed them to heal. I feel bad for avoiding his calls last week and slip my phone out of Wells's suitcoat pocket, which I'm wearing because it's chilly while we're cruising, to send him a text.

Me: *I found a box cutter.*

Seth: *Please tell me you didn't use it on Wells.*

I smile as I type my response.

Me: *Not a chance. Thank you for pushing me.*

Seth: *I just pointed out the obvious. You pushed yourself.*

Seth: *Want to get together this week?*

Me: *Sure. I'll let you know my schedule after I get back to the office and see how much work has piled up.* Thinking better of putting him off, I thumb out, *Actually, let's plan it. Pick a day. I'll make it work.*

Seth: *Are you okay?*

Me: *Yes. I'm just learning to work to live instead of living to work.*

Seth: *Excellent. Breakfast 7 Tuesday? The diner?*

Me: *Perfect. See you then.*

When I look up from my phone, Wells is watching me with that easy smile that stirs butterflies in my chest. I picture the butterfly that landed on his shoulder, and my love-drenched heart wants to believe Harvey really did have a hand in all of this.

"Texting your boyfriend?" Wells asks.

I slip my phone back into the pocket and hook my finger in the waist of his slacks. I ditched my heels the minute we got on the boat, and it feels funny being so much shorter than him again. "I've got to keep myself occupied back in the city."

"Poor bastard is probably celebrating." His arm circles me, pulling me closer. "Little does he know it'll be his last hurrah."

"Oh yeah?" I laugh. "What are you going to do, charm him to death?"

"I'll give you charm." He lowers his lips to mine, turning my laughter into hungry kisses.

A little while later Wells anchors the boat, the lights of the island twinkling in the distance.

"Babe, would you mind grabbing a screwdriver for me from the lounge area belowdecks? It's in the top drawer next to the couch. I need it to turn on the safety lights. If it's not there, it might be in one of the galley drawers."

"Sure."

I head downstairs and check both tables in the lounge and the drawers in the kitchen, but I don't see a screwdriver. I'm looking through the cabinets when Wells hollers down to me, "Actually, I think it's in the nightstand in the second bedroom. Sorry."

"It's okay." I head into that bedroom and search for the screwdriver.

After searching the entire room, and his bedroom, just in case it was in there, I head upstairs empty-handed. "Sorry, Wells, I ca—" The air rushes from my lungs. He's standing on the deck, holding a single red rose. Behind him, pink and red rose petals are scattered over fluffy blankets and pillows. If that's not enough to melt my heart, there are at least a dozen electric or solar candles flickering around the deck and an ice bucket with a bottle of champagne beside two flutes. "*Wells*" falls from my lips, an incredulous, awestruck whisper.

"I can't let some city boy one-up me after you leave."

A laugh tumbles out. "Don't you know you're the only *boy* I want? I was texting Seth."

"A likely story," he says teasingly, and gives me the rose.

I lift it to my nose, inhaling the sweet scent. "It's beautiful. All of this is beyond romantic. How did you get all of this on the boat without me seeing?"

"I can't expose my sources."

He takes my other hand, and as we sit on the pillows and blankets, I realize he's barefoot, too. *You think of everything.* He reaches up and tucks my hair behind my ear, his gaze moving over my face. "There you are."

I sigh, knowing I'll never get sick of hearing that.

The edges of his mouth tip up appreciatively. He runs his finger beneath my chin and brushes his thumb over my lower lip. "I didn't think it was possible to feel this much for someone, but you're everything to me, Victory. If I live to be a hundred or through a thousand lifetimes, I want to spend all the days of every last one of them with you."

My heart takes a perilous leap as our mouths come together in a soul-searing kiss, shattering my ability to think beyond how desperately I want to be closer to him. His fingers tangle in my hair as he deepens the kiss. *Yes.* I fumble with the buttons on his shirt, and he draws back with a wicked glint in his eyes. He grabs his shirt with both hands and tears it open, sending buttons flying. I laugh as he tosses it aside.

He strips his jacket off me and takes me in another scorching kiss. We strip each other bare, and a shock of cold air hits before his big, warm body comes down over me. He pulls a blanket over us and brushes a feathery light kiss to my lips.

"I don't want you to leave," he whispers. "I know you have to, but I have half a mind to strap you to my bed and never let you go."

Emotions clog my throat, but I push past them, needing him to know the truth. "If we live to be a hundred, or through a thousand lifetimes, I want to spend all the days of every last one of them with you, too."

"Careful, baby." A storm of emotions brews in his eyes. "I'm not above holding you to that."

"Please do." I pull his mouth back to mine as our hearts, and our bodies, become one, and our passion takes over.

Chapter Thirty

Wells

Everyone is already at my mother's house when we arrive for breakfast. As we step inside, Bellamy's voice rises above the clatter of pans and music coming from the kitchen. "They're here!"

Keira, Bellamy, and Jules, with Stevie in a baby carrier on her chest, barrel out of the kitchen and exclaim, "*Victory!*" as they rush toward us like they didn't just see her last night.

"You look like you have good knife skills," Bellamy says.

"Should I be worried?" I ask as Bellamy and Jules reach for Victory's hands.

"No," they say, tugging her away. I love this for her. She glances over her shoulder with a soft laugh, gorgeous as can be in navy shorts and a white sleeveless top, and I know she's loving it, too.

"Ooh, *pretty!*" Keira snags the bouquet of lilies out of my hand and smells them.

"Hey, those are for Mom."

"I *know*, suck-up. You bring her flowers every time we have breakfast. Mom and Dad are picking something up at his house, so we're in charge of cooking."

"No wonder the music is so loud," I say as we head for the kitchen.

Jules is whisking something in a bowl at the counter, which is littered with dishes, egg cartons, bread, flour, and other ingredients that are not necessary for our usual breakfasts. Bellamy is peeling apples over a trash can, telling them about clothes she got for a sponsorship deal, and Victory is standing at the island, which is covered with more baking accoutrements. She's slicing the already-peeled apples, her hips swinging to the beat like she does this every morning with them. Grant and Fitz are just outside the open French doors, inspecting a chair that's lying sideways on the deck. They glance inside, lifting their chins in greeting. I do the same in return.

I slide my hand along Victory's back. "You okay?"

"She's *fine*," Bellamy says.

"We're making apple crisp and French toast casserole," Keira says as she fills a vase with water for the flowers.

"I love apple crisp," I say.

"Play your cards right, and maybe I'll learn how to make it for you," Victory taunts. She leans in for a kiss, and my fucking heart eats it up.

I squeeze her waist. "Can I help?"

"*No*," my sisters and Jules exclaim.

I hold my hands up in surrender. "Sorry."

"I love this song," Jules exclaims, and sings, "*I'm not gonna waste another tequila shot on you, you, you. No, I ain't gonna waste another spot or shot on silly old you.*"

"Whiskey," Keira corrects her.

"You sing your song. I'll sing mine." Jules kisses the top of Stevie's head. "Right, sweet pea?"

Grant leans into the kitchen and says, "You tell 'em, Pix."

I step outside with him and Fitz. "What's going on?"

"Just a crack in the chair. It's not a big deal," Grant says. "We'll fix it."

"It wasn't cracked last time we were here. How'd it happen?" I ask.

"You don't want to know," Fitz says.

"Now I do," I say.

Grant's jaw ticks. "Mom and Dad and too much champagne."

"*Jesus.* I kind of feel like I should be cheering Dad on, but that's gross."

"Right?" Fitz says.

"We can only hope we're as randy as they are when we are their age," Grant says.

The girls start singing "Walking on Sunshine" and dancing around the kitchen. They're holding wooden spoons like microphones, singing to each other.

My brothers and I exchange a knowing glance. I arch a brow, and slow smiles slide across their faces. I tell them what song I want to sing, and with a confirmatory nod, we burst into the kitchen, and I belt out the lyrics to "Shut up and Dance" as I stalk toward Victory. The girls crack up as I sing about keeping Victory's eyes trained on me. Grant and Fitz flank her, singing, "*Stop holding back.*"

I take Victory's hand, singing, "Shut that pretty mouth and dance with me."

She laughs as I twirl her. I drop to my knees and hug her legs, singing about how she's my destiny, earning roaring laughter from the others. The guys sing harmony as we continue our dramatic rendition of the song, and my parents dance into the kitchen, joining in on the fun.

I pull Victory into my arms, and as everyone sings about shutting up and dancing with them, I sing, "Shut up and put that mouth on me," and then I kiss her breathless.

Breakfast is the usual banter and heckling, and Victory gives it right back to all of us. We catch up on the latest with my siblings, learning that Grant is thinking about expanding the foundation to help veterans who live overseas, and Bellamy is considering another lucrative sponsorship opportunity. We're all glad to hear she's off the reality-show kick. Fitz says he's looking forward to doing some surfing in Costa Rica, and Keira jokes about setting up a retreat for herself at an exotic location as a write-off, which sparks a slew of ideas from us. Although we all know she won't leave her bakery long enough to enjoy herself.

As we finish cleaning up, my father says, "We have something to show you."

"Please tell me you didn't break more furniture," Fitz says.

My father shakes his head. "We thought it would be fun to show Victory some pictures of Wells when he was little."

The girls all talk at once, excited to reveal all my embarrassing stories, and Victory seems just as thrilled to *get the dirt* on me. My mother brings a stack of photo albums down from her bedroom, and they gather around her in the living room and gush over photo albums full of our childhood photos.

I'm talking with my brothers and father when Jules says, "Look at those cute butts!"

I peer over their shoulders and see a picture of me, Grant, and Fitz standing at the edge of the property with our pants around our ankles, peeing off the bluff. *"Jesus."*

"Oh, honey. You were adorable," my mother says.

"I'll say," Victory says with a sexy smile.

"That was my idea," Grant chimes in.

My father claps a hand on his shoulder. "Yes, it was. But you were eight, and when we asked you not to do it anymore, you stopped. Your brothers were not as easy to convince."

"Are you saying Fitz didn't follow the rules?" Bellamy asks.

"He wasn't always a Goody-Two shoes," Grant says.

My mother looks up and says, "Fitz would have stopped if Wells didn't run outside every time he had to pee and holler, 'Pee time, Fitzy!'"

Everyone cracks up.

"*Wells*," Victory says.

"What can I say? I liked to feel the wind on my willy." I wink, and the blush on her cheeks tells me she's thinking of last night, too. We made love three times on the deck of my boat and woke up with the sun, insatiable for each other again.

"TMI," Bellamy says, and they go through more pictures.

"Is that Wells with purple hair?" Victory asks.

"Yes," Keira says. "Remember that, Wells?"

"How could I forget? It lasted forever."

"You got the best brother award for that one." Keira turns to Victory and says, "When I was in third grade, I wanted to dye my hair purple, but my parents thought the other kids might tease me, so Wells did it to his hair first. He said if anyone got teased, it would be him."

Victory looks at me and says, "That was so sweet of you."

"I'm a good guy."

"He's the same guy who pretended to read from Kei's diary at her slumber party when she was a teenager," Fitz reminds us.

"Oh my gosh. You did *not*," Victory says.

Keira scowls. "Yes, he did. Mr. Charming has an evil side."

"It wasn't evil. I just waved your diary around and said something like, *Dear Diary, I think Jamison is the cutest boy on the island.*"

"I was mortified," Keira says.

"I had no idea you really liked him," I remind her.

"It was a momentary lapse in judgment," Keira says sharply.

"What is it with brothers and their need to embarrass their sisters?" Victory says. "I had a sleepover in high school, and Clay and Flynn eavesdropped on us. They found out who my friends and I had crushes on, and then they had their friend call and say he was one of the boys we liked. He asked us to sneak out at midnight to meet him. As soon as we started sneaking out, my brothers called the police and said they thought somebody was breaking in."

"Oh my goodness," my mother says.

I chuckle, but the girls scowl at me. Quickly schooling my expression, I say, "You want me to make them pay for that?"

"You and what army?" Bellamy says.

I look at Grant and Fitz, and they say, "*No,*" making the others laugh.

"Mom," Keira says. "Show Vic the pictures from when Wells played baseball in high school."

"He was so cute." My mom looks at the photo albums on the coffee table and says, "I must have left it upstairs. Wells, honey, would you mind grabbing the photo albums from the shelves in my room?"

"Sure." I head up to the master suite, and as I reach for the photo albums on the bookshelves, I see my mother's gardening books and remember what Grant said about the flowers I'd given her. I pull out one of the thickest books and leaf through the pages, but I don't find any dried flowers. An unexpected pang of disappointment hits, and I pull another gardening book from the shelf and page through it. There are no flowers in that one, either. I look through three more books, and there's no denying the disappointment I feel.

"Those aren't albums, son," my father says from the doorway.

I had no idea he was standing there. "Yeah, I know. Sorry, I was…" I put the books back on the shelf, not wanting to explain myself.

"No need to be sorry." He walks over and crouches in front of the bookshelves. He pulls a thick book from the bottom shelf. It has several rubber bands wrapped around it. "I think you're looking for this."

He hands it to me. *Better Homes and Gardens New Garden Book.* There are gaps between the pages, which I'm sure are from the flowers.

"It was your grandmother's gardening book," my father says. "Every flower you gave her after I moved out is in there, along with the notes you wrote."

My chest constricts. "How did you know I was looking for this?"

"I didn't when I came in. Your mom asked me to see if you needed help finding the album. When I saw you holding gardening books, I figured it out."

I look at the book, bound by old rubber bands like my mother didn't want to chance losing a single flower or note. I'm not sure why, but I feel like I'm invading my mother's privacy.

"I shouldn't have looked for it. Grant told me she kept the flowers, and I was just curious."

"It's okay to be curious. I'm sorry we put you kids in such a difficult position when you were little."

"It's okay. Life happens."

"Life does happen, and it can throw you for one hell of a loop, but looking back now, we could've handled it better. We were just kids ourselves, fumbling through a life we didn't know how to manage. Something happens when you fall in love, Wells. Your world becomes less about you and more about the other person."

"Yeah. I found that out."

"I know. That's why I'm telling you this. Maybe it'll help you avoid the mistakes we made. When you have kids, that special person moves to second place because babies are vulnerable and they just need us more. In our case, your mother and I moved to sixth place in each other's lives. We were so busy trying to become responsible parents, we didn't see the chasm forming between us until it was too late. I fell in love with your mother when I was nineteen, and by the time I was thirty, we were raising five kids and *loving* every minute of it. But we were doing it while I was learning how to put aside my artistic dreams to become a businessman I had *no* interest in being, and your mother was suddenly no longer *Margot*, but someone's mom, five times over, and a Silver to boot. I was busy creating an identity while she was losing hers."

That hits deep, and possibly for the first time ever, I really see my parents not as Mom and Dad, but as a man and a woman who fell in love when they were teenagers and somehow made it through all the pressures of life and family without losing their love for each other.

"Are you telling me this as a warning not to have kids?"

He smiles. "No, son. Kids are worth every second of the joy, and the hell, they bring. Which strangely enough can be intertwined. I'm telling you this as a cautionary tale, so you never lose sight of the person who made you want to bring children into your life in the first place."

"I can't imagine that ever happening." I put the book back and push to my feet.

"Nobody falls in love thinking those all-consuming feelings can ever be nudged aside." He grabs the photo albums from the top shelf and hands them to me. "If you're lucky, and you work hard at it, your love will weather any storm. Look at me and your mother. We've been together nearly forty years, and we're still breaking furniture."

I wince. *"Dad."*

He laughs as we head down the hall. "Would it be cooler to tell you I'd still burn down the world for her?"

"Yes, *much* cooler."

"But nowhere near as fun."

Chapter Thirty-One

Victory

"Do we really have to say goodbye?" Wells asks, hugging me tighter.

We were having such a good time with his family, we stayed for a while. When we finally left, I would have had to go straight to the ferry. We weren't ready to say goodbye, so I decided to take a later one. We went for a walk on the beach and then had lunch at Trista's, a cute café in town. Now we're on the dock by the ferry, and we've been trying to say goodbye for ten minutes.

I tip my face up, struggling to ignore the ache in my chest. "Let's not—"

"Cool." He takes a step toward the parking lot.

"*Wells.*" Everything he does tempts me to stay, but I've already missed too much work. "I have to go back."

He groans and wraps me in his arms again. "Then I'm sorry."

"For what?"

"Between filling you up with happiness and fucking you senseless, you're going to find it difficult to concentrate on anything but us."

God, I'm going to miss him. "What *ever* will I do?"

"Stay." He kisses me. "I'm kidding. I know you have to go."

"I do, but we don't have to say goodbye. We can say, *until Wednesday* for our walkabout."

"I like that better. I got used to you being here."

"Me too. Thank you for chasing me."

His brows slant. "Is your memory slipping? I might have to rethink this age-gap thing."

"*Hey*," I complain.

"I can only assume you've forgotten that you showed up at my work and poured your beautiful heart out in front of dozens of people. That makes *you* the chaser and *me* the sought-after extremely handsome and, if I may say so myself, insanely charming *chasee*."

"Yes, but that was *after* you chased me, and my thank-you was sincere. If you hadn't chased me, I would never have stepped out of my comfortable little box and chased you."

He threads his fingers into the ends of my hair, tugging gently, and his voice turns seductive. "I'd like to step into your *box*."

We made love every chance we got while I've been here, and *still* a thrill skitters through me. "Then I guess you'll need to come to the city. Now kiss me before I miss my ferry."

He makes no move to kiss me.

"Is something wrong?"

"No. I'm waiting for you to miss your ferry."

I love how much he wants me, and I love how much I want him, but if I don't force myself to leave, it's just going to be harder after spending more time in his arms. "You're making this very hard."

He cocks a grin.

"*Don't*," I warn, knowing he's about to make a dirty joke.

The ferry horn sounds, indicating a last call to board.

"I guess it's time." He cradles my face in his hands, gazing deeply into my eyes in that way that makes my heart sing, and whispers, "I'm going to miss your face," and then he kisses me like he's been waiting all day to do it.

We hold hands, sharing more kisses as we walk to the bottom of the ramp like we've just discovered how great kissing is. He hands me the duffel bag he lent me to bring home the things we bought on the island, and as silly as it is, I like that I'm taking a piece of him home with me.

We don't say another word as I step onto the ramp, and our hands slide along each other's palms to the very tips of our fingers. He catches mine and winks before he lets go.

Why does that make me swoon?

I head up the ramp. The ferry is busy, but not as crowded as it was on my way there. I make my way to the back and stand at the railing, waving to Wells as the ferry pulls away from the dock. I stay there, watching the island fade into the distance, reliving every minute of my time with him.

Shivering against the breeze and the emotions bubbling up inside me, I find a seat at the end of a bench. I cross my arms in an effort to ward off the chill and the emotions.

Suppressing those emotions isn't easy when everything from the scent of the ocean to the boat itself reminds me of Wells. I take a deep breath, telling myself I'll see him in three days, and I'll probably have so much work waiting for me when I get back, I'll be lucky if I can get out on time to see him Wednesday night.

That thought gnaws at the pit of my stomach.

No. I am *not* falling back into that trap. I'm not going to work from sunup until I drop into bed too tired to move. I reach for my purse to grab my phone, so I can get a head start on emails. But my purse isn't beside me. I look at the railing where I was standing, but it's not there. Just as I start to panic, I remember putting it in the duffel bag.

Maybe my memory *is* failing.

Or maybe I am so happy and well fucked my brain can't see past it.

I unzip the duffel, and as I pull out my purse, I see Wells's hoodie. *You sneaky thing.* I pull it out like it's a long-awaited birthday gift, and a piece of paper flutters out with it. The wind picks it up, and I chase it like my life depends on it. I lunge for it as it sails toward a railing, and snag it between my fingertips. The people behind me clap.

I turn around, embarrassed, and an older gentleman says, "Must've been mighty important. I thought we were going to have to dive in after you."

"It's nice to know you would have. Thank you." I sit back down on the bench, clutching the hoodie in my lap, and read the note.

Sweets,

I know you're probably doodling my name on your note-pads and dreaming about me day and night. No need to be embarrassed. I'm a hot commodity. Not as hot as you are, but that's my cross to bear. Wear my hoodie on the nights I'm not there to keep you warm, and remember me strip-ping it off you after the bonfire and loving every inch of your gorgeous body.

Your favorite man toy,
Wells

This man sows romance and nourishes it with everything he says and does. I read the note again, then tuck it into my shorts pocket and press the hoodie to my nose, inhaling his familiar scent and the faint smell of the bonfire. I put the hoodie on and take out my phone, thumbing out a message before I dive into emails.

Me: *Thank you for the hoodie. You're never getting it back.*

Wells: *That's fair. I wasn't planning on giving back your panties, either.*

Me: *You took my panties?*

A devil emoji pops up.

A shiver of heat moves through me. I have no idea how he has that effect on me through text, but I hope it never changes.

I open the email app, and as expected, there are pages of unread emails. *Ugh.* I haven't checked them since Friday afternoon. Scanning the subjects, I choose the one that looks most important and open it. I start reading it, but my heart isn't in it, and that brings a niggle of guilt. I gaze out at the water, knowing I have to start sometime. *Follow your heart, put the people you love first, and don't let anything stand in your way, because every hour you put something off is an hour you can never get back.*

Sometime doesn't have to be right now.

I open the WordLink app and send a game invitation to WellsSpells. My phone chimes when he accepts, and a message pops up.

WellsSpells: *Prepare to lose, Braden.*

And like magic, the pressure of work slips away, and I find myself smiling again.

Chapter Thirty-Two

Victory

It's strange being back in the city where everyone is focused on cell phones and in a hurry. I got used to moving slower, feeling more relaxed, and being greeted with smiles and welcoming conversation everywhere we went. This is like a different world, which isn't necessarily better or worse than the island. It's just an awakening. Like when I first started spending more time with Wells, and I felt like I was coming out from under a cloud—*or from inside a box*—and remembered my love of aimlessly walking around the city discovering new-to-me shops and cafés, listening to live music, and *living*.

As we drive past skyscrapers, street vendors, and people gathered on street corners waiting for lights to change, I know this big, exciting city that helped make me who I am hasn't changed. I have.

My phone chimes with a text.

Seth: *How was your weekend? When are you heading home?*

Me: *It was amazing. I'm on my way home now.*

Me: *Wish I weren't.*

Seth: *Must have been a hell of a weekend. I'm happy for you.*

Seth: *Want to have dinner or are you working?*

My pulse quickens as I type what I've been thinking about doing for the last few hours.

Me: *Actually, I think I'm going to start boxing up Harvey's things.*

Guilt tiptoes in. I take a deep breath, knowing I'm doing the right thing. I want to make room for Wells in my life, and I have to be honest with myself. Seeing Harvey's things around the apartment doesn't bring the same comfort it once did, and it leaves me in a constant struggle of not wanting to betray Harvey, not wanting to neglect myself anymore, and more recently, not wanting to neglect Wells.

Seth: *Want me to come help? I'll bring my friend Whiskey or his buddy Tequila.*

Me: *I love you for offering, but I think I have to do this myself.*

Seth: *Okay. I'm proud of you, sis. Call if you need me.*

Me: *I will.*

My nerves are still pinging when the driver pulls up in front of my building, and Ivan opens the car door. "Good afternoon, Ms. Braden," he says with the same professional kindness as usual as I step out of the car.

"Hi, Ivan." As I head for the entrance, I try to remember when the last time was that I asked him about his family and realize grief has overshadowed this part of my life, too. The thought stops me in my tracks. Ivan used to show me pictures of his grandbabies and share stories about his wife and son, and I loved hearing about them.

It's time to reclaim this piece of myself, too. I turn back to the man who has selflessly opened doors and held umbrellas for me more times than I can count. "How are *you*, Ivan?"

"I'm doing well, thank you for asking. And you? It's been

nice seeing you smiling lately."

The fact that he noticed makes me realize just how far I'd fallen. "I'm sorry it's been so long since I've taken the time to talk." I borrow a phrase from Margot that perfectly suits the last several years of my life. "I got lost for a while after losing Harvey, but it feels good to be smiling again."

"We all miss Mr. Bauer," he says somberly. "He was a good man."

"Yes, he was." Ivan and I haven't talked about Harvey since he shared his condolences shortly after he died. I'm relieved that it no longer hurts to talk about him and to discover it feels good to talk about him without being swamped with guilt. "How are Joan and your grandchildren?"

"Joan is still putting up with me. I'm grateful for that, and the boys are a joy. Kenny just started third grade, and he's exactly like his dad. All about the books. Matty is in first grade, and he is already telling his teacher everything she's doing wrong."

"It's good to keep teachers on their toes."

Beaming with pride, he says, "Would you like to see a picture of them?"

"I'd love to."

He pulls out his phone, and as he scrolls through pictures of two adorable boys flashing overzealous grins at the camera, he tells me about his last visit with them, and then he fills me in on highlights from the last few years with his wife and son. Catching up on his family brings me so much joy, and I can see he loves sharing it with me, too.

I silently promise never to let time slip by like that again. "You are very blessed, Ivan. I look forward to hearing how the boys do in school."

"You know I look forward to telling you," he says warmly, and opens the door to the building for me. "Have a wonderful evening, and keep sharing that smile."

"Yes, sir."

When I get up to my apartment, it feels like I've been gone for weeks. I put the duffel bag on the couch, unsettled by the silence. I swear it's been magnifying for weeks. It's always worse after Wells and I spend time together, but this time it feels as different as I do.

I look around at the luxurious furniture and expensive art-work, everything meticulously in its place. Maybe it's the guilt of what I'm about to do, but I feel like I'm seeing my home through new eyes. When I moved in, Harvey said I could decorate however I wanted, but I didn't want to change a thing. I liked being in his space with his things. Even though it wasn't my style, it all felt right at the time, and it became ours.

After he died, apart from his business, his personal belongings were all I had left of him. I needed to swim in that sea in order to survive, but now it feels like a shrine to what we had. I glance at our wedding picture on the mantel, at Harvey's awards on the shelves, and his candy dish beside the couch. My chest constricts at the thought of boxing those things up, but thankfully, it no longer has the power to pull me under.

These last few weeks have breathed new life into me. It's time to breathe new life into this place, too. Tears threaten, but they remain at bay as I open the door to the terrace and fresh air rolls in. I turn on music and then I head to the storage closet for boxes and packing supplies.

Kneeling on the floor of Harvey's walk-in closet, I tape the third box closed. Evening light spills through the bedroom windows, casting shadows across the hardwood floors outside the closet. For all my confidence about doing the right thing, it took a herculean effort to go through his drawers. I lingered on every item, knowing it would be the last time I'd see them. Memories played out in my mind like favorite movie clips as I carefully wrapped his cologne bottles, the silver tray where he laid his wallet and money clip each night, and his many cuff links and watches. As I folded his soft, worn T-shirts, the sweatpants he hated, and the jeans he loved, each one brought more memories, more smiles, and more tears.

My heart physically hurts. I can't imagine how hard it would have been if I'd tried to do this five years ago. Maybe I should have let Seth come over one of the three times he texted to check on me. But it wouldn't have helped.

I snag another Hershey's Kiss from my newly appointed emotional-support candy dish and catch a glimpse of myself in the mirror. My eyes are puffy and red rimmed, my nose is pink, and the twist I'd clipped my hair into is lopsided with wayward strands sticking out. I look like I feel. Like I'm packing away a little piece of myself with every item.

It's only fitting.

I'm tempted to stop going through his things, but I know it'll just be harder to start again. I drag an empty box over to the sweaters and run my hand along the buttery soft cashmere and lambswool. Harvey's favorite clothing indulgence. I take a well-loved sweater off the shelf and rub it against my cheek. I press the sweater to my face, inhaling the faint, stubborn scent of his cologne, wanting to make it a part of me. Tears burn, and I force myself to fold the sweater and put it in the box.

As I turn back to the shelves, my gaze lingers on Harvey's suits, hanging like lonely ghosts, holding his shape. I touch the sleeves, remembering how I used to tease him about having more suits than I had shoes. His deep voice saunters through my mind. *I've got to look sharp standing next to you.* And just like that I'm crying again.

I pick up the sleeve of his Saturday sport coat, which I lovingly called his old-man jacket, and run my fingers along the worn brown corduroy and over the faded suede elbow pads. Harvey used to say they were there so he could lean his elbow on the table and rest his chin in his palm as he stared at me. I close my eyes against the tears slipping from them, and I rub the suede along my cheek.

When I open my eyes, my gaze lands on the garment bag hanging at the far side of the rack. My pulse quickens as I push the other suits away from it and unzip it, revealing the tuxedo he wore to the Billboard Power 100 award ceremony a few months before he died. He received an award as one of the most influential and powerful people in the music industry. I was so proud of him, and he acted like it was no big deal. But that was Harvey. He thought the awards should go to the musicians, because without them, he'd just be another music lover.

Oh, Harvey. I'm so sorry. Tears spill down my cheeks as I take the tuxedo out of the garment bag and run my hands along the shoulders. I slip the jacket off the hanger and put it on, drawing a rush of tears. I wrap my arms around myself and close my eyes as that night comes rushing back.

Harvey was so handsome and distinguished as he crossed the stage. His acceptance speech was short and gracious, speaking of immense gratitude and teamwork and paying homage to talented musicians and agents. Then he looked right at me for so long, everyone in the room turned to see who had caught the magnificent man's attention. I'll never forget the way his smile broadened and his eyes warmed as he stood on that stage in front of our industry's most influential people, all waiting with bated breath for him to say something. But my husband wasn't loud or flashy, and he didn't need to proclaim anything on my behalf. He knew I could feel his love and appreciation from a million miles away, just as I knew he felt mine.

I close my eyes, and Harvey's face blooms to life behind my closed lids. My heart lifts. I see him as clear as day, his warm smile drawing me in like a tide and his loving dark eyes looking at me just as he had that night, mouthing, *I love you*, breaking the dam. Sobs erupt from my chest in unrelenting waves, and a painful wail sends me to the floor, a sobbing, gasping mess, clutching his jacket around me like a lifeline, hoping he'll forgive me for finally letting go.

I don't know how long I wept or when I started scarfing down Hershey's Kisses by the handful, but at some point my sobs abated to sporadic tears, and my closet floor is now covered in foil wrappers and paper plumes. I dig through them in search of one more piece of chocolate to soothe the ache in my chest and spot one between the boxes. Crawling over to it with the desperation of a substance abuser needing one last hit, I feverishly tear off the wrapper and shove the sweet treat into my mouth.

My doorbell chimes, and I sigh heavily. *Seth.* I know my brother means well, but the only person I want to see right now is on Silver Island, and it wouldn't be fair to put him through this anyway. *Why does that bring more tears?* The doorbell chimes again.

Wiping my eyes, I reluctantly get up. Wrappers crunch under my bare feet as I head out of the closet and trudge to the front door, complaining as I pull it open, "Seth, I told you I was fi—" I stop short, startled out of my weepy fog. My voice shakes with disbelief as I say, "*Wells.* What are you doing here?"

His face is a mask of worry. "I'm sorry. I know you aren't ready for me to be here, but you haven't returned my texts, and I realized after our amazing weekend together that you were coming back to the home that set you off about us in the first place. I couldn't stand the idea of it being too much for you." His gaze sweeps over me, and I can practically feel his heart hurting as he takes in Harvey's tuxedo jacket, my tear-streaked face, and the rest of the mess that is *me*. "And by the looks of you, I was right to worry."

He pulls me into his arms and says, holding me tight, "I'm not letting you make the same mistake again. You're not getting rid of me that easily."

Fresh tears fall as I melt into him. "I'm not upset because of *us*, and I'm not trying to get rid of you. I started packing up Harvey's things so I can finally move forward. It's just *hard*." My voice cracks, and his arms tighten around me.

"*Vic*, why didn't you tell me? I would have been here with you. There's no rush, baby. Leave the candy dish by the sofa. When I take a piece, I'll throw a thank-you up to Harvey."

I smile against his chest at his thoughtfulness.

He cradles my face in his hands, a touch as familiar as his tender tone. "I don't want to erase Harvey from your life or your heart. He helped you become the woman you are, and I love who you are. I love *all* of you, including your desire to preserve what you had with him, because you love with everything you have, and I know you would do the same for us."

My heart is so full, emotions clog my throat, bringing more tears.

"If it's too hard for you to be with me here, we can stay in hotels for as long as you need. I just want to be with you, babe. I don't care where we are, as long as you feel good about being with me."

"And that's why I love you, too," I say. "But it's time. I want to do this. It's holding me back in every aspect of my life, not just with you. With my family, at work, and even how I act around other people. I'm ready to come out from my penance and spread my wings."

"Then how about we do it together?"

Chapter Thirty-Three

Wells

I've been awake for a while as the faint glow of the sun peeks over the horizon, casting slivers of light through the terrace doors. The living room is quiet, save for the peaceful cadence of Victory's breathing. She's asleep with her cheek on my chest, her T-shirt bunched around her ribs, her bare leg resting on mine.

We fell asleep on the couch after packing up Harvey's things. The boxes we packed are lined up against the wall to be donated to charity. Victory kept his awards to display in the lobby of Blank Space, underscoring the incredible legacy he built that she will continue to nurture.

I enjoyed learning more about him through the memories she shared as we packed his clothes, shoes, awards, books, and other personal items. Her voice faltered, bringing tears with certain stories and humor with others. When she showed me their wedding pictures and other photographs, I thought I might feel jealous or competitive, but I didn't. I feel a strange kinship with Harvey, as the two men lucky enough to have earned Victory's love. I'm glad they had each other, and I'm grateful she let me stay last night to support her as she came out from under her grief, one box and one heartfelt goodbye at a time.

She talked more about that fateful night when she lost him. This time the guilt in her voice wasn't as thick. I don't know exactly what changed, but I'm glad something did. After everything I've learned about the man who loved her first, I know he wouldn't want her carrying that burden.

I run my hand through the ends of her hair, and she stretches, making a sweet, sleepy sound. I hold her a little tighter, pressing a kiss to her forehead, hoping she doesn't regret letting me stay. "Morning."

"*Mm.* Morning," she says softly, and kisses my chest.

I run my hand down her back. "Did you sleep okay?"

"Mm-hm. Better than I have in a while." She tips her face up. "How about you?"

"I had you in my arms. How do you think I slept?"

She smiles.

"How do you feel? Any second thoughts? We can unbox anything you want to keep."

Her brows knit, as if she's taking stock of her emotions. "I feel different."

"Like you're used to sleeping on a softer mattress?" I tease.

"Last night's mattress was perfect. I feel lighter. Like it's easier to breathe."

"I'm glad, babe."

"Me too. Donating Harvey's things is what he would want, and I have everything I need in here." She leans back and puts her hand over her heart. "Thank you for helping me last night. I couldn't have done it without you."

"You could have, but I'm glad you let me be here with you.

Do you need to get ready for work?"

"That depends. Are you free for lunch, or do you have to get back to the island?"

"What kind of choice is that? I'll take door number one, please. Where should I meet you?"

She traces circles on my chest with her index finger. "I was thinking you could come to my office and meet some of the people I work with."

My fucking heart feels like it's going to burst out of my chest. "You want to show off your arm candy?"

"Maybe."

"I know how you are. You want to parade me through the halls like I'm your trophy boyfriend."

"Do you have a problem with that?" she taunts.

I sweep her beneath me, and her face brightens. She's so fucking beautiful, and her eyes are clearer. "I don't have a problem with that, but you might when women start flocking around me and you have to get in a catfight to keep them off your man."

"I've got strong claws. I can handle them." She winds her arms around me.

"I know you can. The question is, can you handle me?" I press my hips forward and kiss her. "I take my trophy-boyfriend office-visit responsibilities *very* seriously."

"What responsibilities are those?"

"Ensuring you enjoy *all* the benefits of having a trophy boyfriend in your office."

"This is sounding better by the second. What benefits might those be?"

"There are many. Like helping you polish your desk." I brush my lips over hers, whispering, "While I fuck you from behind." I push her shirt up, baring her breasts, and tease her nipples with my tongue and teeth, earning a sexy gasp.

"That's *quite* a benefit."

I nip at her earlobe. "I aim to please."

"What other benefits might I enjoy?"

"Shining your office chair with my ass as you ride my cock." I grind against her, and she moans. "I'll be a big help to you while you're working at your desk." I kiss the corner of her mouth. "On my knees in front of your chair." I tease her other nipple with my tongue, and she moans. "Sliding your panties off." I rock my rigid cock against her and slide my tongue along her lower lip. "Teasing you with my mouth until you're so wet and needy, you beg me to fuck you."

Her eyes flame. "I think I might need a preview."

I lower my lips to hers in a deep, passionate kiss, and then I give her a preview, the main event, and a grand finale, followed by the best fucking encore she's ever had. *Twice.*

Epilogue

Wells

Winter blustered in with all the glow and glory of a soldier returning home after a life-altering tour. It's my birthday, two weeks before Christmas, a whirlwind four months since Victory and I said the three magic words that unleashed our hearts, untethering hers from the past. Harvey isn't gone by any means. I still thank him when I take a candy from the dish, and every once in a while, I catch Victory with a faraway expression, and I know she's thinking of him. Or we'll do something that strikes a memory, and she'll share it with me. She took me to their favorite tavern, and a month later I surprised her by having the tavern put a drink on the menu called the Harvey Bauer.

We've had our share of ups and downs blending our busy lives and navigating between the island and the city while dealing with my new restaurant renovations—we secured the property on the water in our first meeting with Kane—but the highs have far outweighed the lows. Introducing me to her work colleagues was only the beginning of the changes she had in store for her work life. They loved me, of course, and were thrilled that Victory was with someone who adored her. We had a blast at their holiday party last weekend, when she announced Padma's promotion. Victory delegated much of her oversight, easing her schedule enough to do what she loves most in the new year, scouting talent. It's amazing to see the woman I love so happy and free, and yes, even in the cold winter months, we enjoy our walkabouts, trekabouts, flitabouts, and scoutabouts, and WordLink is still our favorite game when we're apart.

Well, that and sexting. I do enjoy her paybacks.

We're meeting for dinner after work to celebrate my birthday. I'm at the restaurant checking out the latest renovations with Seth and Jared. It's just after four, and beyond the accordion-style glass doors, the sun is already starting to fade, casting shadows across the dock. Victory was spot-on with her vision of those glass doors on either side of the building. We've maximized the natural light and water views. Vaulted ceilings with rough-hewn beams and unique elongated arabesque-shaped distressed Italian tile floors in earth tones, blues, and yellows give the rustic feel we were hoping for. The rooms are framed, and the kitchen is coming along nicely. The addition of a rooftop dining area will make an ideal spot for private parties and office gatherings.

Jared comes out of the kitchen, heading our way. He's a hell of a smart guy and an incredible chef, but the tattooed Adam Levine lookalike must have caffeine running through his veins. If his legs aren't moving, the muscles in his jaw are. "The kitchen looks great. The whole place does." He starts pacing. "The live-edge bar and sea-glass tiling are going to look sharp."

"Absolutely," I say. "I heard back from Roddy a few days ago. He's got a line on ships' wheels for chandeliers. The shipment should come in right after the holidays. I put his supplier in touch with Rich." Rich is our project manager.

"I talked to Rich this morning. They've already been in touch. We should be good to go with the grand opening in March," Seth says. "Shea is rolling out the marketing and PR after the holidays."

"Awesome," Jared says.

My phone chimes with a text.

Fitz: *Just got to the resort. Check this out.*

A picture pops up of a crystal-clear infinity pool looking out over stone patios and a lush landscape with colorful plants and palm trees, and just beyond, a stretch of beach and turquoise-blue water.

Me: *Awesome. Make sure it's not all work and no play.*

Fitz has been stuck on the girl he had a fling with this summer, but for all their texting, she always has an excuse when he wants to see her.

Fitz: *Seminars daily. Evening events. Not much free time, but I'm hoping to catch some waves.*

Me: *Make it happen. You deserve it.*

As I pocket my phone, Seth lifts his chin. "Was that Vic?"

"No, it's Fitz. He just got to Costa Rica for a conference."

Jared saunters over. "Lucky bastard."

"Is he staying through the holidays, or will we see him when we come to the island?" Seth asks.

Victory and I spent Thanksgiving with her family in Ridgeport, and my family joined us there. We're heading back to the island for Christmas with my family next week, and Seth and the rest of their family are going to celebrate with us. I'm looking forward to it.

"He'll be back by then. I told him he should stay until after New Year's, but he hates being away from the island. Jared, do you have plans for the holiday?"

He stops pacing and rakes a hand through his dark hair. "I'm going to Jace's in Maryland to see my nephew, Maximus. He's the cutest little fucker." He heads for the glass doors.

Seth laughs and shakes his head. "I'm pretty sure Jace and Dixie wouldn't want you calling him that. Are you seeing Izzy while you're there?"

"Depends if she's talking to me or not." Jared paces again.

"Is that the girl who came to see you in October?" I ask.

"Yeah," Jared says. "I was on her shit list then, too."

The entrance door opens, and a young guy steps inside. "Excuse me. I'm from Expediate Couriers. I'm looking for Wells Silver."

"That's me." I head over to him.

"Great. This is for you." He hands me a scroll of aged paper with a piece of twine tied around it.

"Thanks. Who is this from?"

"I don't know, man. I'm just the delivery guy and driver. I'll wait for you out front. Take your time." He heads out the door.

Wait for me? I untie the twine and open the scroll, taking in the burnt edges of a hand-drawn treasure map. My heart soars. *Start here* is written next to a drawing of a car and waves, indicating water. A dotted line snakes and curves around pictures of a tree and buildings, leading to a cocktail glass. More sharp turns and arrows lead to flowers in a vase. The dotted line whips and curls, landing on a cupcake, which leads to some kind of cart. The next line leads to a musical note, and after more jags and turns, the treasure map ends with a heart.

I glance at Seth. "Did you know about this?"

He shrugs, shaking his head.

"Bullshit." Jared hikes a thumb at Seth. "That's his lie face."

"I don't have a lie face," Seth insists.

"My ass you don't…"

As they argue, I say, "Are we good here? Can I take off?"

"Yeah, man, g—"

I'm out the door before Jared finishes his sentence, racing up to the parking lot where the delivery guy is leaning against the car, his arms crossed. "Hi. I'm supposed to go with you?"

"That's right."

"Where are we going?" I ask.

"You tell me." He opens the back door and points to an envelope on the seat. Then he climbs behind the wheel.

I get in and open the envelope. Inside is a sliver of paper with *Go to the place where you took my widow cherry.* I chuckle and give the driver the name of the hotel where Victory and I first got together. I can't believe she did this.

When we get to the hotel, I take out my wallet to pay, and the driver says, "It's already paid for. Don't take this wrong, man, but I'm supposed to tell you, *Good boy. Now go to the place where I first flirted with trouble.* That's from *her*, not me."

"Yeah, I got it. Thanks."

Adrenaline rushes through my veins as I climb out of the car and head around the corner, passing a tree on the sidewalk that I hadn't remembered was there. When I get to the bar where I first saw her through the window, I glance through the glass, expecting to see Victory sitting there. She's not.

I head inside to look for her. As I walk by the bar, the bartender calls out, "Hey! Are you Wells?"

"Yes." How the hell did he know?

"I got something for you." He grabs a bottle of whiskey with a red ribbon around it and holds it up so I can see it before putting it in a bag. As he hands it to me, he says, "I have a message for you. Go to the place that reminds you of Olivier.

Au revoir."

"Thanks." I head out of the bar, and suddenly the flowers in a vase make sense. They were on the table at the French café. I grab a cab and head there.

I'm too excited to slow down as I burst through the café door, quickly scanning every table, but Victory isn't there, either.

"I take it you're Wells?" the hostess asks.

"Yes, I am."

"Give me just a moment." She heads into the kitchen and comes out with a large bag. As she hands it to me, she says, "Your next stop is where you rubbed elbows with celebrities."

"Thanks!" My mind skips through memories as I put the bag with the whiskey bottle in the larger bag where several to-go containers are giving off savory aromas.

I rush out and grab another cab, heading to the rooftop bar where I crashed Cage's birthday party. When I get up to the roof, I search for Victory again, but she's nowhere to be found. I head over to the bar, and a young brunette calls after me. "Are you Wells?"

"Yes. How did you know?"

"The person who told me to look for you sent a picture. Sorry, I was supposed to meet you at the door, but I had to take care of something in the kitchen. Come with me."

I follow her back to the entrance, and she hands me a bakery box. "Good luck unscrambling your next clue."

"Thanks." I wait for her to give me the clue, and when she doesn't, I say, "Do you have a message from Victory for me?"

"No, sorry. The woman who called said to just give you the box, but her name was Victorious, not Victory."

That's my girl. "Thanks." I head out perplexed, and when I get in the elevator, I open the box. There are two pink-frosted cupcakes, and on the inside of the box top, she's drawn Scrabble tiles with the letters *Z, P, E, E, L, T, R, S* on them. *You sweet, sneaky thing.*

I spend the next fifteen minutes standing on the sidewalk trying to reconfigure the letters into a word. It's hard to think when I'm anxious to see her. When I finally figure it out, I shout, "Pretzels!" The people walking by look at me like I've lost my mind.

Little do they know I've just found it.

Another car takes me to the pretzel vendor where Leni and Raz caught us kissing. As I approach the portly vendor, he grins like he has a secret, and I realize Victory probably showed all of her helpers a picture of me. "Hi. I'm guessing you know who I am."

"Yes, sir. You're one lucky guy, if you ask me." He reaches behind the cart and opens a shopping bag, showing me a Scrabble game.

I laugh to myself, because we were sitting by the fireplace in her apartment two nights ago, and we both said, *We should get a Scrabble game* at the exact same time. "Please tell me I don't have to unscramble all the letters in that game."

"She didn't say anything about unscrambling. But she did say she liked the idea of kicking your butt in the game." He hands me the bag and says, "Go to the place where you first promised to be there for her and swore by those five words."

I thank him and repeat what he said as I walk away, trying to puzzle it out. *Promise to be there for her. Swear by those five words. Promise to be…*I grin as understanding dawns on me and hurry down the street to the music store. When I head inside, Carey hollers from behind the register, "Dude!" and comes around the counter to greet me. "I'm not going to ask how things are going, because you are one lucky son of a bitch."

"I'm not going to dispute that. I thought this place was temporary for you."

"It is. I went out West for a while, and when I got back, the guy Drake hired to run the place flaked, so I offered to pitch in. But I'm heading home for the holidays. Then I'll figure out what's next."

"Cool. Vic and I will be there for the holidays. Let's get together."

"Absofuckinglutely. She told me she's been teaching you guitar. She says you're getting the hang of it." He looks at my bags and the bakery box. "She's been sending you all over, huh?"

"It's been a great trip down memory lane."

"Well, what I've got for you is *really* special." He takes out his phone and thumbs something out. "You have earbuds with you?"

"Yeah. Why?" My phone chimes with a text.

"I sent you a file. Listen to it when you leave here."

"Okay. Is there any other message?" I put the box on the counter and set the bags on the floor to check my phone and pull out my earbud case.

"No, man, that's it."

"Thanks, Carey. I'll see you on the island." I put in my earbuds, turn on the recording, pocket my phone, and head out the door carrying the bags and box with Victory's sweet voice in my ears.

"Hi, Silver. If you've made it this far, you're on the homestretch. I know you're wondering where to go next. Our hearts will lead the way."

Standing out of the path of passersby, I look around, trying to figure out what I'm missing. Guitar music plays in my ears, and I recognize the tune of "Your Love." Victory's beautifully shocked face flashes before me as I recall the night she learned I was still in high school when she graduated from college.

My heart thunders against my ribs, and I step out into the foot traffic looking for clues about which way to go. *Our hearts will lead the way.* I look across the street, past the busy sidewalk, scanning store signs and windows for something that'll spark a memory. I have plenty of memories from walking around here with her, but nothing leading me anywhere.

As Victory sings about the things she wants to say and liking her *boys* a little bit older, I look to my left, seeing more of the same. There's a growing ache inside me with every line she sings, a desperation to get to her. I spin around, looking the other way, and as the crowd shifts, I see it! Two red hearts hanging from a tree. I rush through the crowd, my arms full, and when I reach the hearts, I see she's written *keep going* on them. I hurry down the sidewalk, toward two more hearts on a sign stuck in a small patch of dirt by a tree.

As Victory sings about wanting to use my love and not wanting to lose it, I race to the corner—*cupcakes be damned*—where two more hearts with right-pointing arrows on them are taped to the side of a building. The cold air stings my cheeks as I follow hearts drawn on the sidewalk and hanging from railings, Victory's voice leading me down streets and around corners. When her voice softens, the guitar music fades, and the loss deepens that ache inside me. I sprint around the next bend as if I can catch up to her. As though she feels my need, her voice rings out in my ears, singing about fire and ice and how she's still falling for me.

Grinning like the lovesick man I am, I race down the street searching for hearts. Several come into view, hanging from bare tree branches, and there's a big red bow tied around the tree trunk with arrows hanging from it that point to a brownstone. I stop to catch my breath. I've been so focused on seeking out hearts, I hadn't paid any attention to where I was. The neighborhood is hauntingly familiar, like a friend in a Halloween costume, in those tentative pre-knowing seconds of *Is that you?* Only I know this brownstone.

I take out my earbuds as I head up the steps, but I still hear Victory singing. The door is ajar. I push it open, and as I step inside, her voice grows louder, the guitar chords ringing out. The tune is the same, but the words are different. I follow her voice.

"You're the air I breathe, the goodness I feel. You're it for me."

I step into the living room we'd both fallen in love with two months ago, when we'd been on a scoutabout and had randomly followed signs for an open house. While we were there, we were informed that the sellers had decided not to sell. But the house had sparked my hopes for *one day*, and there she is. Everything I've ever wanted, sitting in the middle of the empty room on the floor playing her guitar beside a picnic blanket set for two.

She smiles up at me with so much love, my emotions soar to new heights, as she sings, *"No one can make me smile or hold me the way you do. Wells Silver, I'll forever be falling for you."* She sets the guitar down and pushes to her feet, gorgeous in black slacks and a royal-blue blouse that makes her eyes look impossibly bluer. "Hi."

"Hey, sweet thing" comes out sounding as stupefied as I feel. She laughs softly, and the sweet sound knocks my brain into gear. I set down the bags and box. "Are we on a new path? Breaking and entering? Because I'm totally down with the whole Bonnie-and-Clyde thing if you're ready to hit the road. But leaving a trail of hearts could lead the cops right to us. We'll have to take care of that on our way out."

She's absolutely glowing. "I was thinking we'd make things a little more permanent."

My heart races at what I think she's saying, but I can't help teasing her. "Like turn ourselves in? Because I don't look good in stripes."

She smiles nervously. "More like this." She picks up a folder and hands it to me. "Happy birthday, Wells."

I open the folder, scan the documents, and look at her with disbelief. "You sold your apartment?"

She nods, her eyes shimmering with excitement. "There's more."

I flip through the documents, and my heart stumbles. "You bought this place? How? I thought they decided not to sell."

"I think it's fate," she whispers. Then her words come fast and impassioned. "I wanted to surprise you. I've been working with a real estate agent, and the day I got the offer on the apartment, this place went back on the market. I put an offer in, and it was accepted. I know it's a lot and I know it's fast, but I know better than anyone how life can change on a dime, and I don't want to wait for some right moment to show itself. Like your dad said, every hour we put something off is an hour we can never get back." She takes a deep breath. "I want to build a life we don't have to take a vacation from, and I want to build it with you. Marry me, Wells. We both want kids, and I'm not getting any younger. Let's bite the bullet and eke out everything this life has to offer together."

The world tilts on its axis as her words burrow into me. The hopeful look in her eyes sears into my memory, and soul-deep joy takes root in my heart. "You want to make an honest man out of me?"

She laughs. "Yes. More than anything."

"Usually a proposal comes with a ring." I cock a brow expectantly.

Her eyes widen in amusement. "Well…yours came with a brownstone."

"I don't know, Vic. No ring?" I shake my head.

"I didn't think you'd want a ring," she says, like she's not sure whether I'm serious.

"You're right about that, but it's a good thing I have one, because my brilliant future fiancée should have a ring that shines as bright as she does."

I reach into my interior coat pocket, withdrawing the jewelry box I picked up earlier in the day with the ring I had my father's cousin Sterling make for her. I open the box, and her jaw drops as she takes in the princess-cut blue diamond surrounded by a halo of lighter-blue diamonds and three white diamonds on either side of the delicate band.

"*Wells…?*" she whispers, full of disbelief.

"You beat me to the punch. I spent my whole life thinking I wasn't built for relationships. That I wasn't enough, or I wouldn't know how to do the right things to make someone happy forever. Then you came along, fighting me every step of the way with your sass and snark, and I realized it wasn't that I wasn't enough or didn't know how. My heart was just waiting for you all along. Yes, Victoria, I will marry you. The question is, are you sure you can handle my charm and good looks for the rest of your life? Because once I put this ring on your finger, that's it. You're stuck with me forever."

She laughs, tears sliding down her cheeks. "There's no one in the world I'd rather be stuck with than you."

"Is that a *yes*? Because I know how you are with wordplay."

"*Wells. Yes!* Now put that ring on my finger and kiss me before I pass out."

"There's my bossy girl." I slip the ring on her finger and say, "The blue diamond represents our love of the ocean."

"There you go again, making me love you more with everything you do." She throws her arms around me, and we seal our promises, and our future, with a kiss.

Ready for More Silver Island Romance?

I hope you loved Wells and Victoria's story. Each of their siblings is getting their own story. Grab *The Trouble with Flings* featuring Fitz Silver below, and then turn the page to read about Victoria's family's series, The Bradens at Ridgeport, and Flynn Braden's story, *Enticing Her Love*, which is part of The Steeles at Silver Island series.

Sometimes you have to break all the rules to find everything you never knew you wanted. Come along for the fun, sexy ride as billionaire Fitz Silver pursues his biggest challenge yet— taming wild child Jennifer Stone.

SHOP.MELISSAFOSTER.COM

Meet the Bradens at Ridgeport

Fall in love with the hot, wealthy, fiercely loyal, and wickedly naughty Bradens at Ridgeport, and join these business-savvy, pleasure-oriented New Englanders as they fall head over heels with their forever loves. Start the series with *Playing Mr. Perfect.*

Cocky quarterback Clay Braden is determined to show serious scientist Pepper Montgomery the benefits of hands-on research.

SHOP.MELISSAFOSTER.COM

Looking for more character connections? Read these series!

The Bradens & Montgomerys

This is the series in which Victoria Braden was first introduced. You'll also meet Clay Braden's heroine, Pepper Montgomery, and get to know her family.

Silver Harbor

This series takes place on Silver Island and features Abby de Messiéres and her sisters, and includes Brant Remington's story. The Silver Harbor series is published by Montlake Romance. The ebook and audiobook are available only from Amazon.

About the Love in Bloom World

Love in Bloom is the overarching romance collection name for several family series whose worlds interconnect. For example, *Lovers at Heart, Reimagined* is the title of the first book in The Bradens. The Bradens are set in the Love in Bloom world, and within The Bradens, you will see characters from other Love in Bloom series, such as the Snow Sisters and The Remingtons, so you never miss an engagement, wedding, or birth.

Where to Start

All Love in Bloom books can be enjoyed as stand-alone novels or as part of the larger series.

If you are an avid reader and enjoy long series, I'd suggest starting with the very first Love in Bloom novel, *Sisters in Love*, and then reading through all the series in the collection in publication order. However, you can start with any book or series without feeling a step behind. I offer free downloadable series checklists, publication schedules, and family trees on my website. A paperback guide for the first thirty-six books in the series is available at most retailers and provides pertinent details for each book as well as places for you to take notes about the characters and stories.

More Books By Melissa Foster

LOVE IN BLOOM BIG-FAMILY ROMANCE COLLECTION

SNOW SISTERS

Sisters in Love
Sisters in Bloom
Sisters in White

THE BRADENS at Weston

Lovers at Heart, Reimagined
Destined for Love
Friendship on Fire
Sea of Love
Bursting with Love
Hearts at Play

THE BRADENS at Trusty

Taken by Love
Fated for Love
Romancing My Love
Flirting with Love
Dreaming of Love
Crashing into Love

THE BRADENS at Peaceful Harbor

Healed by Love
Surrender My Love
River of Love
Crushing on Love
Whisper of Love
Thrill of Love

THE BRADENS & MONTGOMERYS at Pleasant Hill – Oak Falls

Embracing Her Heart
Anything for Love

SEASIDE SUMMERS
Seaside Dreams
Seaside Hearts
Seaside Sunsets
Seaside Secrets
Seaside Nights
Seaside Embrace
Seaside Lovers
Seaside Whispers
Seaside Serenade

BAYSIDE SUMMERS
Bayside Desires
Bayside Passions
Bayside Heat
Bayside Escape
Bayside Romance
Bayside Fantasies

THE STEELES AT SILVER ISLAND
Tempted by Love
My True Love
Caught by Love
Always Her Love
Wild Island Love
Enticing Her Love

THE SILVERS AT SILVER ISLAND
Flirting with Trouble
The Trouble with Flings

THE WHISKEYS: DARK KNIGHTS AT PEACEFUL HARBOR
Tru Blue
Truly, Madly, Whiskey
Driving Whiskey Wild
Wicked Whiskey Love
Mad About Moon

Taming My Whiskey
The Gritty Truth
In for a Penny
Running on Diesel

THE WHISKEYS: DARK KNIGHTS AT REDEMPTION RANCH
The Trouble with Whiskey
Freeing Sully (Prequel to For the Love of Whiskey)
For the Love of Whiskey
A Taste of Whiskey
Love, Lies, and Whiskey
My Whiskey Redemption

THE WICKEDS: DARK KNIGHTS AT BAYSIDE
A Little Bit Wicked
The Wicked Aftermath
Crazy, Wicked Love
The Wicked Truth
His Wicked Ways
Talk Wicked to Me
Irresistibly Wicked

WILD BOYS AFTER DARK
Logan
Heath
Jackson
Cooper

BAD BOYS AFTER DARK
Mick
Dylan
Carson
Brett

SUGAR LAKE
The Real Thing
Only for You

Love Like Ours
Finding My Girl (Graphic Companion Booklet)

HARMONY POINTE
Call Her Mine
This is Love
She Loves Me

SILVER HARBOR
Maybe We Will
Maybe We Should
Maybe We Won't

STANDALONE ROMANTIC COMEDIES
Hot Mess Summer
The Mr. Right Checklist

HARBORSIDE NIGHTS SERIES
Includes characters from the Love in Bloom series
Catching Cassidy
Discovering Delilah (F/F)
Tempting Tristan (M/M)

More Books by Melissa
Chasing Amanda (mystery/suspense)
Come Back to Me (mystery/suspense)
Have No Shame (historical fiction/romance)
Love, Lies & Mystery (3-book bundle)
Megan's Way (literary fiction)
Traces of Kara (psychological thriller)
Where Petals Fall (suspense)

Acknowledgments

I hope you enjoyed Wells and Victoria's story and look forward to reading their siblings' stories. In the meantime, if you haven't read my Steeles at Silver Island series or my Silver Harbor series, Wells appears in both, and they are also set on Silver Island. If you'd like to read the first book Victoria appeared in, pick up *Rocked by Love*, a Bradens & Montgomerys novel, and for more books featuring Silver Island, look for *Searching for Love*, a Bradens & Montgomerys novel featuring Victoria's cousin treasure hunter Zev Braden, and *Bayside Fantasies*, a Bayside Summers novel.

I'm blessed to have the support of many friends and family members and cannot name them all, but I am grateful for each of you. Many thanks to Becca Mysoor and Lisa Filipe for taking the time to plot this book with me, and to my skilled editorial team: Kristen, Penina, Elaini, Juliette, Lynn, and Justinn.

If you'd like to get to know me better and haven't joined my Facebook fan club, I hope you will. We have loads of fun, chat about books and hunky heroes, and members get special sneak peeks of upcoming publications and exclusive giveaways. www.Facebook.com/groups/MelissaFosterFans

Meet Melissa

www.MelissaFoster.com

Melissa Foster is a *New York Times*, *Wall Street Journal*, and *USA Today* bestselling and award-winning author. Her books have been recommended by *USA Today*'s book blog, *Hagerstown* magazine, *The Patriot*, and several other print venues.

Visit Melissa's online bookstore for early releases, exclusive special editions, and discounted bundles in every format (ebook, print, and audiobook). Melissa enjoys discussing her books with book clubs and reader groups and welcomes an invitation to your event. Melissa's books are also available through most online retailers in paperback, digital, and audio formats.

Melissa also writes sweet romance under the pen name Addison Cole.

www.ingramcontent.com/pod-product-compliance
Lightning Source LLC
Chambersburg PA
CBHW030732310726
48969CB00005B/1206